MOONDANCE OF STONEWYLDE

Also by Kit Berry from Gollancz:

Magus of Stonewylde
Moondance of Stonewylde
Solstice at Stonewylde
Shadows at Stonewylde

MOONDANCE
of
STONEWYLDE

The Second Novel of Stonewylde

KIT BERRY

First published in Great Britain in 2011 by Gollancz
An imprint of the Orion Publishing Group
Orion House, 5 Upper St Martin's Lane, London WC2H 9EA
An Hachette UK Company

A CIP catalogue record for this book is available
from the British Library

ISBN 978 0 575 09885 5

3 5 7 9 10 8 6 4 2

Typeset by Input Data Systems Ltd, Bridgwater Somerset

Printed in Great Britain by Clays Ltd, St Ives plc

The Orion Publishing Group's policy is to use papers that
are natural, renewable and recyclable products and
made from wood grown in sustainable forests. The logging
and manufacturing processes are expected to conform to
the environmental regulations of the country of origin.

www.stonewylde.com
www.orionbooks.co.uk

A crone hunched stiffly on the dirty flagstone floor of a tumbledown cottage, crooning her incantation. The circle of salt around her was marked at five points with stubs of candle and symbols of the elements. A large leather-bound book lay open by her side, the spidery writing faded on the parchment. The glossy crow sat in her lap with eyes shut.

With a shrivelled hand Mother Heggy took a pinch of dried essence from a dish and sprinkled it onto the twigs smouldering in the little fire-cauldron. Foul-smelling smoke billowed up into the air and hung in wreathes about her. Her other clawed hand clamped around something soft and malleable, something vaguely human in shape, fashioned from wax, pig fat and a few ginger hairs. In the centre of this mommet lay a strange heart: a crescent of toenail.

Smoke choked the tiny cottage and the crow fidgeted in the crone's lap. Her mumbling invocation gathered in power. She scraped the few remaining desiccated flakes from the dish into the fire. This was all that was left, after her cake-baking, of the concoction she'd prepared one Dark Moon as the boy had sat here, his body battered and his heart seething with dark hatred. The mommet became softer in the warmth from her leathery skin as the energy was transferred.

She uttered the final words, no longer legible in her Book of Shadows but known in her heart. She traced the five-pointed shape of magic in the smoke about her and, with a cry, pitched the tiny figure into the pot-belly of the cauldron. It hit the burning twigs and instantly the pig fat turned to grease and the wax melted to nothing. The gingery hairs shrivelled and the crescent of nail lay in a viscous pool of thick tallow.

1

Mother Heggy raised the crow gently from her lap, kissed its head and flung it into the air. With a frantic flapping it landed on the floor outside the cast circle.

'Fly, my lovely one! Fly to him now!' she croaked.

The crow hopped out, launching itself into the glimmering sky.

1

Magus sprawled across his vast four-poster bed gazing at the bright diamond-paned windows. His sheets lay in a tangled heap, kicked off in the heat of the night as he'd slept fitfully. The sun was well up but he lay spread-eagled, magnificent body dark against the pure white sheets, his eyes glittering with fury. That damned boy!

His thoughts spun around like a vulture circling a carcass. Yesterday, the Summer Solstice, should have been a day of glory. Instead – ruined. For the first time in years the green magic had eluded him. Normally he'd have been teeming with power and energy after receiving the Goddess' gift, but today he felt only a flicker of his accustomed vitality. And it was all Yul's fault for fumbling with the torch and allowing the sacred flame to extinguish. The arteries in his temple pounded as he remembered the look of triumph in the dark-haired brat's eyes.

He recalled how all day yesterday, after that disastrous sunrise ceremony, Yul had excelled at the games held on the Village Green. Despite those two gruelling weeks at the quarry, which should have broken both his body and spirit, the boy had outstripped others in countless competitions. Magus had been furious to see Sylvie watching with shining eyes, cheering the boy on – not that he'd needed it. Magus had a horrible suspicion that not only had the Earth Magic failed to empower him, the rightful guardian of Stonewylde, but it had somehow gone to

Yul instead. What else would explain the boy's brightness and energy?

Magus smiled grimly as he recalled how he'd put an end to his apparently unstoppable success. Yul had stood alone under the shade of a tree on the Village Green, still flushed from the exertion of winning yet another race. Magus recalled with pleasure how the boy's deep grey eyes had clouded with fear at his approach.

'Solstice Blessings, Yul!'

'Solstice Blessings, sir.'

'You're doing remarkably well for someone who's been through such an ordeal so recently.'

'Yes, sir.'

'And for someone who shouldn't even be here today! I don't recall giving you permission to leave the quarry.'

'No, sir.'

Magus noticed how he trembled.

'So why did you leave Quarrycleave and return to the heart of Stonewylde?'

'I ... I was told you had given permission, sir.'

Yul fidgeted, sweat beading his upper lip and beginning to trickle down his flushed face from beneath the heavy mass of dark curls. Magus nodded slowly, looking beyond the boy to where a crowd gathered around the drinks set out on trestle tables. He noticed Sylvie standing slightly apart, covertly watching as he addressed the boy. Anger welled unexpectedly.

'You completely fouled up the Solstice sunrise ceremony this morning,' he spat. 'Never before have I witnessed such fumbling incompetence!'

'I'm sorry, sir,' mumbled Yul, his heart thudding. This was the moment of truth – would Magus send him back to the horror of that white, dusty quarry?

'How dare you not only ruin the whole ritual with your clumsiness, but to then have the effrontery to speak *my* words in the ceremony? Who the hell do you think you are?'

Yul shook his head helplessly. Who was he? Someone special

4

and magical, as Mother Heggy would have him believe, or just a worthless Villager at the mercy of his enraged master?

'I'll tell you then,' hissed Magus, 'as words seem beyond you. You are nothing ... less than nothing. You should never have left the quarry without my express permission and I'm very tempted to send you straight back there, especially in view of your appalling behaviour this morning.'

He enjoyed Yul's start of horror, the way the boy tensed and shuddered.

'However, I think you'll be of more immediate use up at the Hall, where we're so short-staffed. You'll report to Martin in the morning, at first light, and do so for the duration of the Midsummer holidays. I'm sure there are plenty of dirty pots and pans to keep you busy. That will be all, boy.'

Magus watched as Yul loped off back towards his cottage, his earlier vitality and spark now doused. Magus sighed; he wasn't finished with Yul yet, not by a long way, but he must be careful. Justice must always be seen to be done, and he'd sensed the boy's popularity amongst the Villagers today during the races. Whatever happened, his own hands couldn't be dirtied. But there was another option. Magus' dark eyes scanned the hordes of people on the Green, drinking cider and elderflower champagne, laughing and chattering on this, the most special day of the year.

The vertical lines that grooved the skin on either side of his mouth creased further into a grim smile as he spotted the man he sought. Alwyn was quaffing cider outside the Jack in the Green, his bloated face tipped back as he poured the liquid down his throat. Magus noted the tanner's heightened colour and increased girth, his great belly ballooning above his trousers. Alwyn hated the boy with a vengeance and just a few words of encouragement would add fuel to his raging desire to punish. Magus resolved to speak to him later. Alwyn was his instrument and only needed a little fine-tuning.

Magus had then turned his attention to locating Sylvie again. It was her birthday too and he thought of the large white box with its silver ribbon waiting up at the Hall. She was fifteen today and although birthday gifts weren't usually given at Stonewylde, Magus had decided to make an exception. Sylvie was special and needed delicate grooming. She'd never had much, if Miranda's pathetic life story were to be believed. The exquisite dress, nestling in layers of white tissue paper, would be well worth its cost.

He saw Sylvie talking to Dawn and decided against speaking to her yet – the dress could wait till later. He recalled her promise to him the previous night on Solstice Eve to stay away from Yul. He'd be keeping a very close watch over her in future. It seemed that the Village brat had stolen his Earth Magic this Solstice; Magus didn't intend to let him steal Sylvie as well.

As he lay on his vast bed, with the morning sunlight streaming in on him and dancing on the deep crimson walls of his bedroom, Magus' thoughts jumped again, this time to an event a little later in the day. People were wandering off the Green in the warm afternoon, some going home for a nap before the evening's fun began. The Midsummer Dance would start later, with a feast laid out on the Green and music and merry-making in the Great Barn. Magus had noticed Alwyn about to head up the lane to his cottage, and had called him over. The tanner's porcine face had lit up with pleasure at being singled out by the master.

'Midsummer Blessings, sir!'

Magus had looked away from the man's features in distaste. Close up, his ruddiness was a myriad of engorged veins just under the surface of his fleshy skin. Even his piggy eyes were bloodshot. He wheezed from the tiny exertion of walking a few steps along the lane and his massive bulk gave out a hot, sour odour.

'A word with you, Alwyn. I'm sure you can guess the subject.'

The tanner nodded grimly, sweat running down into the folds of his neck.

'Aye, sir, I can that. The brat – he's back now.'

'He is, Alwyn, and already making mischief. Did you see the mess he made of the ceremony this morning?'

Alwyn's face flushed a deeper shade.

'Little bastard!' he spluttered, spittle flying and almost landing on Magus, who took a quick step back.

'I want him held in check this time, Alwyn. You understand me? You've been too lenient with him over the years, which is why he's so out of hand now.'

'But sir, I—'

Magus held up a hand, his face stony.

'No excuses. The boy is out of control and I'm sorry to say the blame must lie at your door. Why else would he be the only one at Stonewylde to constantly defy me and cause such trouble? I'm afraid, Alwyn, that I can only assume you've allowed him too much leeway. But no more! I'm holding you personally responsible for the boy's behaviour. I expect you to be as harsh as is necessary. Is that perfectly clear? As harsh as you think fit.'

'Aye, sir.'

Alwyn's breathing was now so streperous that Magus wondered whether the man was capable of administering any form of beating at all.

'Have you seen Yul yet since his return?'

'No, sir. He's not been home at all. 'Twas a shock to see him at the Solstice sunrise this morning. I didn't know you'd brung him back.'

'Yes . . . the less said about that the better. But he is back. He'll be working up at the Hall for the holiday and I'll make sure Martin works him hard. But when he comes home at night time – then it's up to you. I want that boy crushed and, as his father, it's your duty to do it. I hope you won't disappoint me this time, Alwyn.'

The tanner's eyes, so buried in puffy fat as to be almost hidden, filled with tears and, forgetting protocol, he grasped Magus' hand in a flurry of distress.

'No sir, never. I'm so sorry, sir. I won't let you down again. He'll wish he'd never been born!'

Magus had nodded and disengaged himself from the man's sweaty grip, turning away in disgust.

'Him and me both,' he'd muttered, heading back towards the Green.

But now, as Magus kicked away the twisted sheets and rose

from his bed, white hot fury flooded him yet again. It seemed that Yul had foiled him once more, though he was at a loss to see how. Was the boy responsible? How had it happened? Somehow Yul had evaded the intended punishment, and Alwyn lay now in a wing of this very building looking as if he'd never raise a whip again in this life.

Angrily, Magus padded through into his black marble bathroom and wrenched on the shower. He groaned as the cool water blasted his body, drenching his blond hair and running down his face. He stood for several minutes under the great showerhead until the heat inside him had subsided. He had six months. Six months until the Winter Solstice when Yul would reach adulthood.

Turning off the water, Magus smiled grimly to himself. As he dried his body briskly and reached for his exotic cologne, he met the reflection of his own velvety-black eyes.

'Mirror, mirror on the wall . . .' he muttered and then chuckled to himself. He needed no reassurance, for he knew the answer; he was the strongest of them all. Even without the Earth Magic.

Even earlier that morning, as Magus lay supine in his bed, Yul had arrived at the back of the Hall. Dressed in rough work clothes rather than smart festival ones, Yul had stood in the enormous cobbled yard outside the kitchens waiting for Martin to appear. In the pearly-grey half-light, the sun not yet risen, Yul had shivered and yawned in the slightly chill air whilst all around him the birds sang their divine dawn chorus. Eventually Martin had opened the wide oak door and scowled out, looking quite surprised to find Yul ready and waiting.

Yul had never liked Martin. He was about forty or so, clearly a Hallchild with his thin blond hair, but had never made it to the Hall School and thereby a life of privilege. He was dogged rather than quick-witted, relentless rather than resourceful, and had served at the Hall since he was a lad. He had no humour or warmth and was intensely loyal to Magus.

'Ah, there you are,' he grunted sullenly, as if Yul were late. He came outside into the yard and looked Yul up and down. He knew the boy of course, for everyone at Stonewylde knew everyone else, but he acted as if Yul were a stranger.

'The master has warned me about you, boy,' he muttered. 'Don't mess me about or try to skive off or Magus will hear about it. He specially wants to know if you haven't pulled your weight. Understood?'

'Yes, sir,' said Yul wearily.

'Right then, I've got you for the next five days, which is just as well seeing as we're so short staffed. There's extra Hallfolk here all needing to be served, and served well, mind you. Get in the kitchens and see what Marigold wants doing. And when you've done everything she needs, go down to the stables and report to Tom. Remember boy – no slacking or you'll be very sorry.'

At the old butler's sink in the scullery, Yul scrubbed hard at the baked-on grime in a huge pan. His thoughts turned to the events of yesterday, the Summer Solstice. It had been the most amazing day of his life, starting with Solstice Eve the previous night. He recalled the magical kiss he and Sylvie had shared under the yew tree on the Village Green. Standing with his sleeves rolled up and a scouring pad in his hand, Yul relived that moment of joy and certainty, when he knew without any doubt that they belonged together, the darkness and the brightness, just as Mother Heggy had predicted.

Then there was the incredible experience as the sun rose over the Stone Circle at Solstice sunrise, and the Green Magic pierced his soul. He'd never, as long as he lived, forget the bliss of receiving the Goddess' bounty, nor the look of utter bewilderment on Magus' face. He'd felt the effects of that magic all day as he won race after race. He sparkled with it, and every time he looked up there stood Sylvie, her silvery-grey eyes dancing with joy. The sight of her smiling at him as he competed in the races filled him with happiness, and then she'd beckoned to him. They'd managed to find a quiet corner round the back of the Great Barn, and she'd grasped his hand desperately.

'I've brought the cake for you, Yul!' she'd said hurriedly, gazing up into his eyes. 'The cake Mother Heggy made. I've hidden it just outside your gate in the undergrowth. It's all wrapped up in rhubarb leaves so it's quite camouflaged. She said only Alwyn must eat it and nobody else. That's absolutely vital.'

He nodded slowly, doubt clouding his intent now that the moment had come. Sylvie had seemed to sense this.

'He'll kill you, Yul,' she said quickly. 'Remember the last time? Remember what Mother Heggy warned? Please, don't back down now. You *have* to go through with this.'

Yul nodded again. He kissed her slim hand and then joined the other lads for the next race. Not long afterwards, Magus had taken him to one side and informed him that he was to work every day throughout the holidays. Yul had made his way home, his heart seething with bitterness and the celebrations ruined. As he walked up the lane, a path he'd trodden every day of his life, his resolve stiffened. He deserved better than this. He wouldn't spend the rest of his life at the mercy of two men who for no apparent reason hated him to the point of destruction. He recalled Mother Heggy's words all those months ago and felt a surge of power. Now was the time.

'But Yul, my love, where's it from?'

His mother's deep grey eyes were puzzled as she took the package from him. Yul shrugged, not wanting to lie to her.

'Someone from the Hall just gave it to me,' he said. 'She said it was a special gift for Alwyn and him alone.'

'How strange! Maybe 'tis from Marigold up in the kitchens? I know he's been going up there for meals, though Goddess knows why seeing as I feed him well enough. The man has the appetite of a bull at the moment. Oh well, if 'tis come from the Hall it must be special.'

'And only for Alwyn, Mother. Nobody else must eat it, she said.'

'Aye, I understand. Well, he'll be home soon enough for a nap no doubt, after all that cider he's been putting back. Maybe he'll have a slice of the cake then. And you make yourself scarce, my boy. 'Twill be the first time you've been under the same roof for a while and I don't want trouble today of all days. You go back to the Green, my love, and enjoy yourself. And Yul ... I thought my heart would burst this morning at the ceremony, I was that proud of you.'

Maizie took her eldest son in her arms and hugged him fiercely, the fears and unhappiness of the past months forgotten for a moment. Yul felt her shudder with suppressed emotion and squeezed her tightly. During his exile first in the woods and then up at the quarry he'd missed his family a great deal, especially his mother.

They heard laughter and chatter outside and then the front door was flung open. His six siblings piled into the small sitting room: Rosie, with little Leveret in her arms, Geoffrey and Gregory almost as tall as their older sister now, and Gefrin and Sweyn fighting as usual. The children swarmed around Yul, delighted to see their oldest brother home again. Yul took Leveret from Rosie and laughed into her mop of black curls as he hugged her. There was a special place in his heart for this tiny little girl who adored him so much.

'Rosie, where's your father now?' asked Maizie quickly. 'Is he on his way back, or ... ?'

Too late they heard the tuneless whistling and everyone froze, all eyes turning in horror towards Yul. Alwyn stumbled into a still life; his wife and all seven children transfixed where they stood. In the total silence he stomped across the room and allowed his bulk to fall heavily into his armchair. Nobody moved. Alwyn's heavy breathing filled the room and he peered around at the group of statues until his gaze fell on the one he sought.

Maizie jerked into action.

'A bite to eat, Alwyn my dear?' she gabbled. 'There's a fine cake here, sent up from the Hall special, just for you. I'll cut you a nice big slice, shall I?'

She scurried into the kitchen and Alwyn grunted, his belligerent stare unbroken. Carefully Yul handed Leveret to Rosie and straightened his spine. Very slowly, footstep by footstep, each child shrank backwards away from the armchair and the huge ginger-haired mound of flesh that was their father.

Now Yul stood alone, facing the man who'd almost beaten him to death not so long ago. His heart thudded but he found himself lifted with a strange courage. It thrilled through his veins and he felt strong. He looked Alwyn square in the eye, his cool grey gaze unwavering, his chin raised in defiance. He'd never looked into Alwyn's eyes before. They were buried almost completely in his bloated face, but Yul stared hard into the tiny pools of blue rage and felt a thrill of power. At this unheard of insolence, Alwyn's face suffused with blood. A great vein throbbed at his temple.

'Here you are then, my dear!' Maizie's voice was shrill. 'A lovely bit of cake from the Hall! And a nice bite of cheese. You enjoy that, and ...'

Alwyn glanced at the plate she'd laid on his lap and picked up the slab of moist dark cake. He growled and aimed a kick at his wife, who scuttled out of reach, trying to block Yul from his sight. Everyone remained rooted as Alwyn contemplated the cake in his hand. Gently Yul moved his mother to one side and stood again directly in the tanner's line of vision and almost within his grasp.

'You can fetch the strap off the hook,' grunted Alwyn. 'I'll warm your hide first afore we move on to the snake.' He shifted himself uncomfortably in the chair, a frown on his ruddy face. 'No getting away with it this time round, you little bastard. Upsetting the master like that – 'tis up to me to put a stop to it once and for all.'

He raised the thick slice of cake towards his mouth, but then paused.

'You hear me, boy?' he bellowed. 'I said fetch the strap!'

He bit hugely into the dark cake, his jowls swinging as he masticated and swallowed. He took another bite, and Yul folded his arms and remained where he was.

'You'll never lay a hand on me again,' he said quietly, his voice as shattering as a pebble thrown into a lake. Next to him

Maizie jerked with terror. But then her eyes widened as she watched. Alwyn's skin had turned deep crimson, the veins now bulging in both temples and his neck. His eyes were bloodshot and his mouth was working, trying to speak through the mass of half-chewed cake. He began to splutter and cough.

There was a tapping at the window and Yul flicked a glance towards it. The crow sat on the sill surveying the scene with a round eye. Alwyn's coughing turned into a fit of choking. He struggled to suck in breath, the violent rasp and wheeze in his constricted throat sickening to the ear. His eyes rolled up in his head and he pitched forward, crushing his plate and thrashing his arms. A strange noise came from his mouth, along with the dark mangled-up cake and a great foam of saliva. His body heaved and jerked in violent spasms. Then he threw himself back in the armchair and was still, soft wheezing the only sound in the crowded sitting room.

Everyone looked on in total, appalled silence, hands over mouths and eyes enormous. Nobody breathed, nobody moved. It was unthinkable; too shocking to comprehend. Then, unbelievably, Leveret broke the horrified hush. Her gurgle of laughter split the stillness as she pointed a tiny finger at the mess in her father's lap.

'Quiet, child!' moaned Maizie, shaking her head in bewilderment. She sent all the children back to the Village Green to find the young doctor. Only Yul remained with her and they stood together contemplating the tyrant slumped in the armchair, his eyes lifeless and breathing slow and loud.

'Goddess, I don't believe this,' she sobbed. 'What's happened to the man?'

Yul put a strong arm around his mother and kissed the top of her head.

'Don't you worry, Mother,' he said softly. 'I'll take care of the family.'

But as he stared at the bulky mass sprawled helplessly before him, his eyes hardened and he whispered into his mother's curls.

'Those who stand against me shall fall, one by one.'

The crow launched itself from the window sill and up into the sky, heading back to the tumbledown cottage.

As Yul now scoured the pan in the scullery of the Hall kitchens, he smiled at the tiled wall with pure pleasure. He felt as if a set of heavy shackles had been removed after a lifetime of chafing his skin. He felt as free as a swift on the summer thermals. Alwyn lay somewhere in the Hall right now, tucked away in the hospital wing and unable to move. It appeared he'd had some sort of seizure, possibly a stroke. The new doctor, who'd arrived just before the Solstice, said Alwyn might never recover.

Yul recalled the stab of joy he'd felt on hearing this, and the difference to the whole family's enjoyment of the Midsummer dance that evening. Maizie had hesitated at joining in the celebrations at such a time, with her husband lying up at the Hall and maybe at the gateway to the Otherworld. But Yul and Rosie had persuaded her it would be wrong not to honour the festival in the proper way. Reluctantly, Maizie had agreed to attend, and joined her family in bathing and dressing in their finest festival clothes for the feasting and dancing that night.

As Yul wiped the pan dry with a coarse linen cloth he smiled again. What a good thing they had attended the dance, for otherwise he'd have missed the heart-stopping sight of his beautiful moongazy girl sparkling like the brightest star in the heavens.

2

Sylvie lay on the sand, her fingers idly sifting through the grains as she gazed at the blue sky overhead. The sun was scorching hot on her skin and she sighed deeply. She'd hoped to spend some time with Yul over the week-long Midsummer Holiday, but that seemed unlikely now. She hadn't seen him since last night at the Solstice dance, when they'd managed to snatch some brief moments together.

She smiled as she remembered the evening. For the first time in her life, she'd felt like a fairy-tale princess. When she'd returned to Woodland Cottage later in the afternoon to get ready for the dance, a large white box with a huge silver bow had been waiting on her bed. Miranda had stood in the doorway, a strange expression on her face.

'I don't understand, Mum. You said now we're at Stonewylde we'd follow the customs here and not give birthday presents.'

'It's not from me. It's from Magus – look, there's a note.'

For a beautiful girl on her fifteenth birthday – wear it tonight!

Sylvie looked up and was shocked to see her mother in tears. 'Mum! What's wrong?'

Miranda dabbed her eyes with a hanky and sniffed, shaking her head.

'I'm sorry – I'm just being silly. It's nothing.'

'You don't mind Magus giving me a present, do you? I'll send it back if—'

'No, of course I don't mind,' Miranda said quickly. 'It's stupid, I know. It's just that ... when I think back to my fifteenth birthday, it was all so different. I was so naïve, so sheltered. My parents were very strict and they treated me like a child. And then not long after my sixteenth birthday I fell pregnant with you and that was that – my childhood over and none of the fun of being a teenager.'

'I'm sorry, Mum,' said Sylvie gently. 'I know I'm so lucky compared to you. You had a rotten time of it.'

Miranda shrugged and tried to smile.

'Well, it's all in the past now. And I've never regretted having you, Sylvie. Nor do I begrudge you anything, you know that. I just wish that for once in my life, someone would ... oh never mind, forget me and my silly dreams. Come on, let's see what's in the box. Something to wear tonight – sounds interesting.'

Sylvie untied the silver bow and lifted the lid. Carefully she pulled aside the sheets of white tissue paper to reveal the most beautiful dress she'd ever seen. She found it hard to breathe as she lifted the dress from its soft nest, gasping as the layers of exquisitely fine material fell from their folds. The dress was of gossamer silk, silvery grey with thin silver ribbon straps. The bodice flared out into a cloud of gauzy skirts, which ended in little points all the way round the hem, each point tipped with a tiny silver bead.

Most amazing of all was the embroidery; the diaphanous fabric was shot with silver threads depicting small crescent moons and five-pointed stars. The effect was a glint and shimmer that gave the dress a light of its own. As Sylvie held it to her, it seemed to dance with a subtle silver sparkle which perfectly mirrored the strangeness of her eyes. She couldn't speak, but stroked the magical dress against her body as if it had become her skin. Without a word, Miranda had turned and gone downstairs.

Sylvie raised herself on an elbow and gazed out to sea. Many other Hallfolk youngsters had come to the beach today, walking together along the path by the river that flowed through the Village and down to the sea. Her first sight of the beach had filled Sylvie with excitement as it was a beautiful spot. Swans sailed grandly amongst the reeds where the river widened its mouth into a great freshwater pool, before dispersing over large pebbles and into the waiting salt water. The beach itself was a mixture of smooth shingle and coarse sand, shelving quite sharply into the sea.

But the most unusual aspect of the beach was its shape. It formed an almost perfect lagoon, as if someone had etched out a scoop of the sea shore just to provide the people of Stonewylde with safe bathing. The water within the lagoon was very clear and calm, for a huge low rock at the neck guarded the private bay and kept the rough seas out. The choppy waves could be seen out to sea crashing against the rock, but inside the shelter the water was calm.

About twenty young people were over on the rock, looking like a herd of seals as they basked and played. Sylvie squinted against the brilliant diamonds that danced off the water. Holly and her friends were out there making a great deal of noise. They'd already crowded out the Villagers who'd been on the rock first, much to Sylvie's dismay. She'd hoped Yul might be there.

At the dance he'd told her the bad news about his extra work duties, but nevertheless she'd hoped that he'd manage a little free time. As she lay so indolently on the beach, Sylvie thought sadly of how unfair life was at Stonewylde. Here she was, pampered and spoiled, idling away yet another afternoon in the sun with the other Hallfolk teenagers. Whereas poor Yul was toiling away up at the Hall for no reason other than to keep all those visitors, who'd flocked back for the Solstice, in luxury.

After his ordeal at Quarrycleave, Yul more than anyone deserved a holiday. He was still so thin, his face chiselled into new planes and hollows. She thought back to the obscene defilement of his back that she'd seen a few days ago in the white marble bathroom at the Hall. The sight of those deep wheals and lacerations on his skin had filled her with such pity and anger that she'd never trust Magus again. She understood it was he who'd ordered and overseen the vicious whipping. But at least the actual perpetrator had got his just desserts. Sylvie knew that Alwyn lay in the hospital wing at the Hall hovering somewhere between paralysis and death.

She smiled grimly at the thought, remembering the fuss his collapse had caused yesterday on the Solstice. Hazel had only just taken up residence on the estate and this had been her first medical emergency as doctor at Stonewylde, the day after her arrival. She'd rushed off the Village Green to Yul's cottage after his brothers and sisters had arrived breathless and distraught, gabbling that their father had thrown a fit and she must please come quick.

Sylvie had tried to looked as shocked as everyone else as Hazel dashed into the Barn to collect her doctor's bag. Sylvie guessed that Mother Heggy's cake had worked its dark magic but had composed her features into an expression of concern. She'd had to retain her composure again later on, when Magus had shot her a look like thunder as he'd heard the news. She'd been close by when Hazel returned to the Green much later and sought out Magus to give him an update.

'You're positive it was a stroke?'

'No, not positive. I'll need to do more tests. But I believe so.'

'It couldn't be anything more sinister?'

'In what way? I don't understand.'

'I mean foul play. Deliberate.'

'No, I doubt that very much. He presents all the symptoms of a stroke victim. He's grossly overweight, unfit and he'd been drinking heavily. If anyone's to blame, it's himself.'

Magus mouth had tightened at this and then, looking up, he'd caught Sylvie's eye. His expression changed but she couldn't read his dark eyes other than to recognise his anger. Did he really suspect Yul had had a hand in his father's collapse? Sylvie fervently hoped that whatever Mother Heggy had put in the cake was undetectable.

However Magus was back in fine form by the evening and had

18

been delighted when Sylvie and Miranda arrived at the Barn for the dance. The Village Green was lit with hundreds of tiny lanterns which hung amongst the branches of the trees, strung on lines around the trestles set up for yet more feasting and drinking. Light poured from the Barn and the sound of lively music filled the warm evening air, masking the call of wood-pigeons and the joyous trilling of song-thrushes.

Sylvie felt as if she were floating on a carpet of magic as she walked shyly next to her mother along the cobbled street. Hidden amongst the tissue paper under the dress, she'd discovered a pair of pale grey leather pumps which she now wore. Her long hair hung like a silver veil around her bare shoulders. The dress twinkled as she moved, the silver moons and stars catching the light with every step. She really felt as if stardust from a magic wand had transformed her into a princess.

'Perfect!' breathed Magus, emerging from the vast open entrance into the Barn. 'It fits you just as I'd imagined and I knew you'd do justice to that dress. Sylvie, you really are the most beautiful girl at Stonewylde.'

Sylvie had stood awkwardly whilst her mother remained silent. His gaze was warm and approving and she prickled with embarrassment as his eyes swept her from head to toe, missing nothing. Miranda prodded her sharply.

'Sylvie!' she hissed. 'Where are your manners?'

'Oh! Thank you, Magus, thank you so much. I'm sorry – it's so special I don't know what to say. I feel overwhelmed.'

'A moongazy dress for a moongazy girl,' he murmured, leading them across the grass to get a drink. 'Happy birthday, Sylvie! I shall expect several dances with you tonight. And you too of course, Miranda.'

The dress had proved to be a mixed blessing for it had aroused a good deal of attention. The Villagers gawped openly, their expressions full of admiration for the sparkling girl from the Hall who smiled at them far more sweetly than any other member of the Hallfolk ever did. Several of the younger children had been awestruck enough to forget the Stonewylde code of behaviour, and had actually stroked the shimmering material and Sylvie's silky hair. Many of the Village boys blushed and nodded as she caught their eye, unable to stop staring at her, nudging each other and grinning.

She also felt the approbation of the Hallfolk boys who seemed incapable of taking their eyes off her throughout the evening and pestered her for dances. But Holly and her gaggle of friends were another matter, and Sylvie felt their envy like a hail of arrows. The one person whose approval she sought was nowhere to be seen. Sylvie spent most of the evening surreptitiously trying to locate him. As she endured dance after hot dance with an endless stream of sweaty partners, her eyes constantly scanned the crowds looking for her dark, handsome boy.

Eventually she managed to leave the revelry and escape outside into the comparative coolness of the Midsummer Night air. Even though it was late, the sky still retained daylight on this, the shortest night of the year. The sun seemed to have barely dipped below the horizon and the stars struggled to be noticed in the cerulean sky. The fairy lights all around in the encircling trees gave the Green an atmosphere of magical enchantment. Bats swooped low and an owl called from the trees as Sylvie stood in the darkness, breathing deeply of the fragrant air and wishing with all her heart that she was in Yul's arms, tasting his sweet kiss again.

Her heart jumped as she sensed a movement behind and felt a light touch on her hair. She froze, not looking round. As she caught Yul's unique scent of wood-smoke and herbs, her stomach flipped with excitement. He stood close behind, barely touching her, and all her senses jangled. She felt him stoop and whisper into her hair.

'I've been waiting all evening for you to come outside, Sylvie. And here you are at last, fallen out of the sky, a beautiful flying star landed right at my feet.'

She smiled at his words, her heart thudding. She felt his breath on the back of her neck and shuddered as he gently ran his fingers down the sides of her bare arms.

'You're so lovely, Sylvie. I've never seen anything as beautiful as you are tonight. Your dress . . . it's full of moonlight and magic. You should wear this moongazy dress when you dance at the Moon Fullness.'

She nodded and turned around to face him, gazing into his deep grey eyes, drinking him in. She longed to stroke his face – or better still, to fling her arms around him and bury her face in his chest. But there were far too many people milling around the Green. She read the same longing in his eyes as he lifted a strand of her hair and felt the silkiness between his fingertips.

'Come with me, Sylvie. Come with me under the yew tree where we were last night. We have unfinished business there, you and me. I want to kiss you again . . .'

'You know we can't, Yul,' she said softly. 'Last night I promised Magus that we'd stay apart. We must wait until all the fuss has died down. We can't risk anything that'll make him angry with you again.'

He groaned and looked away.

'I can't stand it, Sylvie. How can we stay apart? I think of you all the time, every second of the day and night. All I want is to be with you. It's unbearable knowing you're nearby but not being able to even talk properly.'

'I know, but maybe—'

She stopped abruptly as the unmistakable silhouette of Magus appeared in the light flooding out from the Barn.

'He's looking for me, I'm sure – checking up that we're not together. I'd better go back inside. Maybe I'll see you at the beach? Everyone seems to go there in the afternoons.'

He shook his head sadly.

'No, he's ordered me to report to the Hall every day for extra work, the bastard! But soon, Sylvie. Next week at the Moon Fullness I'll be waiting for you in the woods and we'll go up to Hare Stone together. You can dance and—'

'I'll be there, I promise.'

She turned away reluctantly and made her way back towards the Barn, where Magus stood washed in light. His eyes narrowed as she drew closer and his hand closed around her wrist, stopping her as she tried to brush past him.

'I thought we had an agreement, Sylvie? Stay away from him and so will I. Surely you haven't forgotten the consequences if you disobey me. Must I remind you? Or him?'

'No, Magus,' she said quickly. 'Not at all.'

'Good. Because you're far too special for a lout like him.'

His fingers released their grip and stroked her arm idly.

'You really are absolutely stunning in that dress, Sylvie. Now come back inside and dance with me again, my beautiful princess. I think we make rather a striking couple together, don't you?'

Sylvie gazed out to sea but Holly and July were making so much noise over on the distant rock that she found it impossible to daydream. With a sigh she stood up.

'Coming for a swim, Dawn?'

They went in together and Sylvie gasped as the icy water lapped around her shins. Dawn laughed at her dismay.

'Freezing, isn't it? And it's warmer here in the lagoon than the open sea. But it's only June, remember. By Lammas in August it's lovely and warm. Come on – plunge in and swim fast. It's the only way to warm up.'

She'd intended to splash around in the shallows, but Dawn headed straight out towards the rock and Sylvie felt obliged to follow. She was a little nervous going out of her depth as she wasn't a strong swimmer, but was determined to be brave and join in. Soon Sylvie's skin was tingling as they swam the short distance across the lagoon. She was reluctant, however, to reach the rock, dreading any confrontation with Holly today. It had been bad enough the night before, trying to avoid her gang and their snide remarks about her fairytale dress. But the girl with the bobbed hair and pretty feline features noticed them and called out.

'Hi there! Come and join us! It's so hot up here.'

Dawn swam towards the smaller rocks where it was possible to climb up onto the long, natural platform. Sylvie followed unwillingly and sat dripping on the warm stone, hair in a wet tangle, hugging her knees shyly and feeling self-conscious in front of so many people. She hadn't worn a swimsuit for years – her eczema had put paid to that – and had had to borrow one today. She hoped that maybe Holly would call a truce and was relieved that Buzz was away on holiday with his mother until Lammas. Holly was having a riotous time, messing about with July, Wren and Fennel and his gang of boys, diving into the sea and ducking each other.

Sylvie kept her eyes averted from their antics and looked instead at Rainbow, who was uncharacteristically quiet today. The younger girl was basking on the rock, her sea-blue eyes faraway. She wore a bikini which shone like silver scales in the bright sunlight, with a turquoise and silver sarong wrapped loosely around her waist. Although only thirteen, she had a lovely figure and her skin was already tanned soft apricot. Her hair was darker blond than most Hallfolk's, the heavy waves glinting with natural highlights. She'd be stunning when she was older, Sylvie thought.

Curled on the rock, her long hair fanned out to dry, Rainbow stared dreamily up at the sky. Her fingers played with a seashell and her toes, their nails painted silver, wriggled amongst the strands of green seaweed clinging to the stone. She was completely unselfconscious and beautiful. Then she glanced across suddenly and caught Sylvie's gaze.

'Why are you staring at me, Sylvie? What is it?'

'Nothing. I was just thinking that you look like a mermaid.'

Rainbow burst out laughing at this.

'Do I really? How nice! I love mermaids.'

Wren overheard the conversation and flung herself wetly next to Rainbow.

'A mermaid? They lure men away from their homes and into the depths of the watery underworld.'

Rainbow laughed again.

'Well I won't be doing any of that today. None of the boys here are worth the effort.'

She stood up in a fluid motion and dived gracefully into the lagoon, her silver scales sparkling in the sunlight. Sylvie shivered, and not only from the drops of water that splashed onto her hot skin. There was something about Rainbow – a kind of sinuous, calculated perfection – that disturbed her more than Holly's blatant antagonism and bullying. She thought again of Yul, imagining him here, brown and lithe, putting all the pale Hallfolk boys in the shade. How he must be rejoicing today, free at last from his father's reign of tyranny.

Whilst Sylvie and the Hallfolk youngsters swam and sunbathed, Yul continued with the seemingly endless chores that Martin had lined up for him. After the pans in the scullery had been dealt with to Marigold's satisfaction, Yul was sent across to the stables. Tom was pleased to see him and smiled his welcome at the tousle-haired boy.

'I were going to clap you on the back, son, but I weren't sure if 'twas still painful.'

Yul looked up at the old ostler sharply, his grin fading.

'So you know what happened to me?'

'Aye,' he muttered, 'I do. I heard every single damn stroke, every crack of that whip. Magus got me to rig up the byre with that electric light afore he came and got you. I was outside while it all happened, battling with myself what to do for the best. I ended up doing nothing. I been wanting to say to you ever since how bad I feel about it.'

'No need for you to feel bad, sir. It wasn't your fault.'

'Well, it was partly, I'm sorry to say. 'Twas me as told Magus about you riding Nightwing that day, when the Hallfolk gentleman was thrown and hurt hisself. Not to get you into trouble, you understand. I thought the master'd reward you. You showed great courage and skill riding that stallion back here to get help so quick. Anyhow, I feel bad that I told Magus, and for not coming to help you in your suffering.'

'But you couldn't have, not without disobeying Magus.'

'Aye, well maybe I should've done. Starving you like that was downright cruelty. 'Tis not something I'd have believed of Magus, treating a Villager so bad. And as for that Alwyn ... I tell you, if that man hadn't been taken sick, I'd have done for him myself. All that bragging and boasting about what he done to you, every night down the pub. And I weren't the only one to feel that way neither.' Tom shook his grizzled head sadly. 'No, I won't forgive myself for not helping you, Yul. I could've got some food to you or something. Truth is, I were scared. And I'm ashamed of that.'

'I never expected any help. Magus can't be disobeyed.'

'Aye, but if you're ever in any trouble, you come to me, Yul. What the master did to you weren't right and I feel I owe you. I won't rest easy till I've made it up to you somehow.'

Yul looked at Tom speculatively and nodded.

'Thank you, sir. I'll remember that.'

'So why are you here now, lad? You should be down the Village enjoying the holiday with all them other young folk, not up here working. What've you done this time?'

Yul shrugged, and Tom remembered the boy doing the same thing back in March, the last time he was sent here as a punishment.

'Like that is it? Right, well you'll have to put your back into it. We're rushed off our feet with all them Hallfolk visitors wanting to ride every day. Half the daft buggers don't know one end of a horse from t'other.'

He tossed Yul a pitchfork and the work began. By sunset Yul was exhausted, although he decided he'd much rather be down here in the stables with the horses than up in the confines of the Hall itself. The place made him uneasy and he hated any contact with the visiting Hallfolk. He resented being treated as a servant. How Harold put up with it he couldn't imagine.

It was late that evening when Martin finally released Yul from his duties, with an admonishment to make sure he was back good and early the next morning. He trudged the distance back to his cottage wearily, ignoring the sounds of fun and merriment that drifted down the lane from the Village Green and Great Barn. The festivities would last all week, but Yul was far too tired to get washed and changed and go down to join in. All the other Villagers who had to work during the holiday were given a rota, so they could at least take part in some of the fun. But Yul knew Magus wanted him kept hard at it all week long until it was time to return to his work in the woods with Old Greenbough.

Yul opened the door to his cottage and looked around. The place was as clean and tidy as ever, and his family nowhere to be seen. They must all be in the Barn, Yul decided. He breathed deeply and realised the dread he usually felt when coming home had completely disappeared. Except for one detail.

His mouth a hard line of bitterness, Yul went over to the door and tugged the hateful leather strap off its hook. Near it, hanging from a new nail in the wall, was the whip. Coiled like a malignant snake, it hung dark against the whitewashed wall. The leather handle was thick and solid, the plaited tail long and viciously thin. Shuddering as he forced himself to touch it, Yul pulled the snake-whip off the wall so violently that the nail was yanked from the plaster. He carried both instruments of punishment outside and laid them on the chopping block.

Taking a deep breath, he raised the axe above his head and swung it down hard. It felt good as the sharp blade sliced through the leather. He raised the axe again and again, overcome by a sudden destructive frenzy as the hated objects of pain and subjugation were chopped into ever smaller pieces. The memories swarmed in his head like angry wasps, the years of pain and humiliation reaching back as far as he could remember to when he'd been only a little boy. The strange light in Alwyn's eye as he went on and on with the punishment; he'd never forget that particular look as long as he lived.

As the leather which had bitten so mercilessly into the soft skin of his back became a jumble of tiny pieces on the block, Yul found himself screaming with fury. He dropped the axe, his body heaving. Tears streamed down his flushed face as the rage overwhelmed him. He sank to the ground. Kneeling in the dust, he cried into his hands. Harsh sobs shook him, dragged out from the dark place where he'd locked them away for so long. All those years of injustice and fear were released. Never again would he have to face Alwyn and his violence. Never again would his father brutalise him. A lifetime of abuse had finally come to an end.

Later, and a little calmer, Yul wandered down the long back garden. He looked at the masses of fruit and vegetables growing in the fertile soil, and peeped in at the dripping combs inside the beehives. Maizie tended their produce well. He thought of how much happier her life would be now, free from Alwyn and his cruel domination of the family. He wasn't the only one who'd benefit from Mother Heggy's magic.

Yul stooped and picked a few luscious strawberries, savouring the explosion of sweetness in his mouth. He thought instantly of Sylvie and felt the familiar tugging at his heart. She'd probably be in the Village along with everyone else at Stonewylde. Every cell in his body longed to go there right now and find her; to take her in his arms and smell her, feel her silky hair and smooth skin, drink her beauty with his eyes. And more than anything else in the world, he wanted to kiss her again. He'd been in a fever for her since their first kiss only two nights ago under the yew tree. But the Village was crawling with Hallfolk and Magus was everywhere. Yul couldn't risk angering him at any cost.

He stormed out of the garden and down the lane, tears welling up again in a hot, angry flow. He loved Sylvie but how would they ever find a chance to be together? Now he must work every day at the Hall, he wouldn't even get a glimpse of her during the holiday that everyone else was enjoying. How could Magus do this? Hadn't he suffered enough?

Darkness had fallen and Yul skirted the Village and headed down to the river. He sat on the grassy bank watching the sparkling water as it flowed to the sea. He should've expected this. Had he really believed he'd get away with leaving the quarry? Or climbing onto the Altar Stone and taking the Earth Magic from Magus? He tried to swallow his disappointment at how the Midsummer Holiday was turning out, but his throat ached with tears and bitterness.

The willows whispered all around him, offering their sympathy and comfort. The waxing moon shone brightly again, fuller than last night. Everything gleamed in the moonlight. Fish came up to the surface by the silver reeds of the river bank, their mouths circles as they gulped at the gnats just above the water. There was a movement upstream. Yul saw the glossy head of an otter, its blunt skull clear against the water as it headed in a V-shaped ripple towards the fish. It dived smoothly, long body sinuous and slick in the moonlit water, and disappeared. Yul stood up and gazed at the stars, the noise and merriment from the Village seeming very distant. He felt, as ever, alone and on the outside. The only one who'd broken through his isolation to touch his soul was forbidden to him. Alwyn might have fallen, but happiness seemed no closer.

A week later, the holiday now over, Miranda had just finished teaching her class when Magus walked into the schoolroom.

'Are you free for a while?'

'Yes!' Miranda said breathlessly, standing up from her desk. He smiled and led her out through the French windows onto the stone terrace. They stood looking over the lawns, watching swallows soar and swoop in the blue skies. She leant against him and he put an arm around her, holding her close. She closed her eyes in bliss, unaware that Magus was surreptitiously looking at his watch on the other wrist. A group of blond children ran onto the lawn breaking the silence.

'Let's go into the formal garden,' he suggested. 'We can be more private there.'

She nodded eagerly, and as they strolled along the raked gravel paths, Magus took her hand.

'Did you enjoy the Midsummer Holiday?'

'Oh yes, it was lovely.'

'And still no sign of your period?'

She looked up at him quickly.

'No. I'm never usually late. I really think I am pregnant.'

'That's wonderful, Miranda. Hazel can do a test, if you like.'

'Yes, I'd like to know for sure. I'm a little worried, and ...'

He stopped and turned her to face him, tilting her chin so she had no choice but to look straight into his dark eyes as he held her shoulders.

'Why? Do you think I won't take care of you? You know how it is at Stonewylde, Miranda. Babies are considered a blessing, something to celebrate.'

She tried to look away.

'What?'

'It's just ... what about us? Our relationship? I don't know where I stand with you. I know you like me and when we're together it's wonderful. But then you don't come near me for days on end, and—'

'Oh Miranda,' he sighed, 'you must understand – I can't have normal relationships like other people.'

'But why not?'

'Because I'm the magus and you know what that means. I have to look after everyone in the community and there are hundreds of people here. I can't commit myself to one person – it wouldn't be fair.'

'But I still don't see why not. Don't you want a partner by your side to help you? I could—'

'If that's a proposal, Miranda, I'm sorry but the answer's no. I won't—'

'No!' she said, cheeks flaming scarlet. 'I didn't mean marriage. I just thought perhaps as partners ...'

She stopped, hating herself for being so desperate, for making herself so vulnerable. Magus let his hands drop and continued walking, so she had to fall in by his side.

'I apologise if I've led you to think I'm free or indeed willing to commit myself to a monogamous relationship. I'm not, and I'm afraid that's how it is and always will be. I could never be tied to one woman. I don't think I ever promised you that, did I?'

'No,' she said in a small voice. 'You never promised me anything.'

'But we can be together sometimes, Miranda, and I do promise that when we are, I'm all yours. This baby will be loved and wanted, and will grow up lacking nothing. Of course, you're free to terminate the pregnancy if . . .'

'Oh no – I want your baby!' she said. 'As long as I know you care for me, I'll just have to accept that I must share you with the community. I suppose I have no other option really. But, Magus, I am special to you, aren't I?'

He hugged her, taking the opportunity to check the time again, and chuckled.

'Of course you are. But, Miranda, don't get possessive with me, will you?'

'No, of course not. Our relationship will be special because of the baby and your feelings for me, but it'll be fun and light-hearted too, if that's what you want.'

'Good! I'm so glad you understand and we've got that sorted out. So, how's Sylvie taking the news that you might be expecting a baby? She obviously realises it's mine?'

'Oh yes. She seems fine about it – not bothered at all. She's quite distracted at the moment.'

They'd come to one of the alcoves in the clipped hedging and Magus took her in to sit on the wooden seat. He put his arm around her, his long fingers brushing her breast idly. She closed her eyes and sighed, every nerve ending jangling at his touch.

'Are you keeping a close watch on her to make sure she doesn't see that boy?'

'Yes I am, and she hasn't.'

'Mmn. I still want her watched. I'm going away in a few days' time and you must ensure they stay apart while I'm gone.'

'How long for? Where are you going?'

'Just business. And for less than a month.'

'A month?' she squeaked.

'I have a company in London to run, remember. But I'll be popping back now and again. You must promise you'll watch Sylvie and keep her well away from Yul.'

'Of course, although I think you're worrying needlessly.'

'Let's hope so. The other thing I need to talk to you about is this full moon business. Tell me, has she always been affected by it?'

Miranda shrugged, wanting to talk about the baby and their relationship, not Sylvie and her moon madness.

'More or less. But it was getting worse as she grew older. I didn't realise it was happening here. I thought it was all part of her illness in London and that she'd got over it. I thought she was fine here.'

'Well she clearly isn't, and we can't have her wandering around Stonewylde in the dark meeting up with unsuitable boys in the woods, like she did last month. Anything could happen, couldn't it? So tonight I'll keep an eye on her myself.'

'Yes, of course, Magus. It's a full moon tonight then?'

'Yes, and I want you to leave her alone. Come up to the Hall for dinner and stay here till after the moon rise so she's on her own in the cottage. I promise I won't let her come to any harm. I just need to see how she behaves, what she does. I might be able to help her, of course, as I did with her other illnesses. I also want to see if she'll try to meet the boy in secret behind our backs, despite her promises.' He stood up briskly. 'I must be off. That's settled then, about tonight? You're not to worry, Miranda. You know I'll look after her.'

'Of course, Magus,' she said trustingly.

'Sylvie will always be safe with me,' he said softly, leading her back up the garden path.

All day the tension rose within her until by early evening Sylvie thought she'd explode with it. She felt the familiar tingling inside; the increasing sense of being trapped indoors and needing to get outside and up somewhere high. She was also excited at the prospect of seeing Yul alone; it was so long since they'd been together. She was relieved when, at six o'clock, Miranda announced she was leaving for the Hall for dinner and wouldn't be around that evening.

'Are you coming too, darling?' Miranda asked innocently.

'No, I'm not hungry. I'll have a sandwich and stay here.'

'Sure you'll be alright?'

'Yes!'

'You know it's the full moon tonight?'

'Do you really think I'd be unaware of that?'

'No need to be rude, Sylvie. And I want to make sure you understand you're not to go out gallivanting with that boy.'

'Yeah, I know.'

'Magus wanted me to remind you that you're forbidden to see each other.'

'That man makes me sick! Who does he think he is – dictating who I can and can't see!'

'Sylvie! Anyway, I'm your mother and *I'm* telling you not to see Yul. You're only just fifteen and he's not suitable company for you – running around the woods and getting up to goodness knows what. It's not just Magus telling you, it's me too and I have every right.'

Sylvie glared sullenly at her mother, hating her at that moment. She was being so unfair, judging Yul only by what Magus had told her. The Miranda from the old days would've made up her own mind – and would've liked Yul very much.

'Actually, I'm quite surprised you're not off gallivanting yourself up at that horrible rock on the cliff with your picnics and incense and tent-pegs.'

'Sylvie! I—'

'You're such a hypocrite, Mum! All *I* want to do is watch the moon rise in the company of a very sweet boy I like. *You're* the one going off having sex with a man you barely know and getting yourself pregnant!'

'How dare you, Sylvie! You make it sound so sordid.'

'Well it is sordid!'

'No it's not! Magus cares for me and he's really pleased there might be a baby. I have a special relationship with him. We were talking about it today, in fact. Anyway, we don't know yet for sure that I'm expecting.'

'So why isn't he seeing you tonight if he cares for you so

32

much? What happened to the moonlight picnics in the tent? The rugs and cushions on the rock? Maybe he doesn't want you so much now he's made you pregnant.'

Miranda picked up her jacket and gave her daughter a cold glance.

'Magus has already explained to me that he has business to attend to this evening, so he won't be free to see me. I'll speak to you tomorrow about your behaviour, when you've calmed down. I won't have you talking like this, Sylvie. You must stop being so hostile and rebellious towards Magus. You liked him when we first came here and I don't see why your opinion has changed so much.'

'Because now I know the truth about him,' Sylvie muttered.

'If I'm to be the mother of his baby, Magus will be a major part of our lives and you'll just have to get used to it. Have a nice evening, Sylvie, and remember to stay away from that boy. Or there'll be serious consequences.'

'Good riddance!' snapped Sylvie as the door closed behind her mother. But she cheered up at the news that Magus was busy for the evening. She could now enjoy Yul's company without fear of being found out. She decided to change into the beautiful moongazy dress as Yul had suggested; she wanted to look lovely for him.

By eight o'clock Sylvie was ready. She felt a sharp thrill of excitement deep inside that was nothing to do with the lunar cycle. Half an hour later she could barely sit down. She paced the room, her feet padding up and down the floorboards, the gauzy grey and silver dress floating out around her in soft webs. It was a warm evening, the sky clear but for a few small clouds melting to gold as the sun began its descent. Sylvie was frantic to get outside and finally could stand it no longer. She opened the front door and stepped into the evening, breathing in the balmy golden air.

I shall dance with the hares and sparkle like quicksilver. Yul is the darkness to my brightness, the earth magic and moon magic joined as one!

She skipped to the gate, her feet hardly touching the ground. Her hair flowed around her bare arms and shoulders like a veil of silvery-white silk. She fumbled with the gate and then she was free, speeding up the path towards the woods. But something loomed ahead blocking her way; a tall shape that grabbed her by the arms, smiling grimly into her face as she tried to wriggle away.

'Going somewhere, Sylvie?' asked Magus.

3

Yul sat under a tree listening to the soft call of wood pigeons, the peace of the golden evening like a mantle around him. He thrilled with anticipation. She'd be here soon, dancing up the path on light feet, hair rippling about her. He smiled to himself and felt a knot of excitement in the pit of his stomach. It seemed ages since they'd been alone together properly; not since the eve of the Summer Solstice under the yew tree. He wondered if their new intimacy would make tonight any different from the other Moon Fullnesses they'd spent together. Maybe afterwards, when she'd danced and sung and the desperation had calmed, they'd be able to talk. He wanted so much to hold her tight and kiss her again. He'd spent the past week dreaming about kissing her. He closed his eyes at the thought of it and sighed deeply. Not long now.

Sylvie tried to free herself from the iron grip, her hair flying about her face as she pulled and wriggled.

'Not so fast, Sylvie! I think you've forgotten our deal, haven't you? You're off to meet up with a certain young man whom you've been forbidden to see, aren't you?'

'Let me go! I must go!'

'Oh no you don't! You're staying with me, young lady.'

'No, no, I can't stay here! I must be up there! You let me go, you let me go—'

Magus lifted her bodily and clamped a hand over her mouth as she struggled and shrieked. He hauled her back to the gate and in through the open front door of the cottage, kicking it shut behind him, and dumped her on the sofa. She sprang up immediately so he pushed her down and sat next to her. He turned to face her, his strong hands clamped around her wrists like manacles.

'Stop it! Stop it, Sylvie and listen to me!'

Still she struggled, trying to stand and escape his grasp.

'Sit down!' he shouted, thinking she'd damage her wrists if she carried on like this. 'Sylvie, can you hear me? If you don't calm down now I'll have to slap you. *SYLVIE!*'

But she didn't seem to hear him, kicking out and shaking her head violently from side to side. She began to shout but the words didn't make sense. She was clearly hysterical. He released one of her wrists and slapped her sharply round the face. Her head snapped to the side, hair flying, and she went limp and pliant. She slumped down into a huddle, crying piteously.

'Sylvie, stop it. There's no need to cry. It didn't hurt that much.'

He put an arm around her and she flopped against him, all the fight knocked out of her. A strange little sobbing noise came from deep within her but after a moment she started again.

'Please, please let me go. She's coming, she's rising! I must be there to greet her, to honour her. Please let me go. I beg you. Please, please ...'

'Alright! We'll go outside and you can show me what you must do. Come on then.'

She leapt up, her eyes wild, and he held on to her hand tightly. They went up the garden path, but at the gate when she tried to turn towards the woods, he pulled her round and bundled her in the other direction.

'The woods, the hilltop, my Yul—'

'Oh no, Sylvie! We're not going anywhere near him. We're going somewhere far better for moongazing.'

In the woods, Yul's excitement had turned to anxiety. The sun had already set and it was almost time for the rising of the moon.

Where was she? She'd promised to be here, so something must have happened. Had they locked her up? He decided to go to the cottage and have a look for himself. The light was fading amongst the trees as he moved silently along the path, eyes scanning and ears pricked, ready to melt into the shadows if Magus or anyone else appeared. But nobody did, and no lights were on in the cottage although dusk was falling. He crept in through the wide open front door, hoping he wasn't walking into a trap. It was soon obvious that the place was empty. Now what should he do? Frowning, he left the cottage, closing the door behind him, and started down the lane away from the woods, unsure where to look next.

Sylvie skipped along, still tethered to Magus' hand but tugging him forward.

She's coming, she's rising! I can feel her. Quick, quick, quick! I must be ready to dance and spread my wings. Quick!

Magus was mystified by the sounds she made, which were almost speech-like but didn't make any sense. She was desperate, rigid with tension and quivering with suppressed energy. She tried to pull him into a run, frantic to reach their destination. As they climbed the path leading to the cliff top Magus held on to her tightly. The drop was treacherous in places and he didn't want her running ahead.

Let me go! She's here! I must dance in her quicksilver magic. She's giving and I'm not there to receive her gift. Let me go!

With a sudden twist she freed her hand from his and flew up the path. Her bare feet skimmed the stony ground, her long gauze skirts brushing the grasses and flowers at the side. He called after her, but in vain. She was so fast, haring ahead until she reached the top of the cliff. He was fit and strong but still couldn't keep up with her. When he reached the top a few minutes later she was already dancing. She spiralled joyfully, springing across the grass with pointed bare feet, arms outstretched to the heavens. Magus stood at the head of the path, out of breath from the rapid climb and now breathless with wonder. The great moon

37

had risen, a glowing orb that hung brightly just above the sea. And Sylvie glowed too with a strange silvery light which laced around her body in shining threads, sparkling on her moongazy dress and glimmering hair.

Yul had reached the Hall. Keeping to the shadows, he skirted the main building trying to see inside without being seen himself. Maybe Magus and her mother had dragged Sylvie up here and shut her in one of the rooms. He saw Hallfolk sitting around on big sofas watching a large coloured screen. The lighting was different here from the candlelight he was used to, for the Hallfolk used electricity from the wind-farm. The harsh light reminded him of the byre, its bright glare making him shudder.

Yul crept around the walls peering through the windows. In other rooms people sat talking and reading. He saw servants working in the kitchen, washing up and preparing more food for the next day. He found Marigold sitting in a small room talking to Martin, and stepped back quickly from the lighted window in case they saw him. But there was no sign of Sylvie or Magus. His hopes soared at one point when he spotted Miranda curled up in a chair with a book on her lap. But Sylvie wasn't there. So where could she be? If Magus had confined her upstairs in the Hall he'd never be able to find her.

Magus walked across the grass to the great stone, the one where he'd celebrated the Moon Fullness with Miranda and the place where he liked to honour the Moon Goddess every month with a different woman. He sat on the disc of rock and watched the incredible sight before him as Sylvie danced, arms upraised like wings. The silvery light coursed around her body and then disappeared down into the earth, shooting from her feet as she leapt and skipped. She sang too, a weird unearthly sound. Her face was turned to the great golden moon as it climbed steadily, turning more silvery the higher it rose.

Magus watched in fascination, trying to understand what the silver threads of light could be. He saw them earthing, like lightning in a storm, and guessed they were some sort of electrical or magnetic energy generated by the moon. Sylvie crackled with the force; even her hair, normally so silky, stood out thick and stiff with strange static. He felt a churning in his stomach as he watched her; a sharp excitement as if on the verge of a special discovery.

Sylvie was oblivious to everything other than her dancing. Magus watched for what seemed like ages; he couldn't tell for how long as, strangely, his watch had stopped. He thought she must surely be exhausted by now and noticed she was beginning to slow down, so he called to her. She appeared to listen and stepped delicately on tip-toe over to him, as he sat on the white stone. Her dress glinted in the bright moonlight, the silver embroidery catching the moonbeams.

'Hello, Sylvie,' he murmured. 'That was an amazing dance. Is this what you usually do with Yul?'

But she ignored him as if he hadn't spoken at all. He could see in the moonlight that her eyes were blank. They were strange under normal circumstances; a pale grey with a darker grey round the edge of the irises. But now they were like full moons themselves; silvery and reflective, seeing nothing but beaming out moonlight. In one graceful leap she sprang onto the great stone.

As she landed she froze, her fingers outspread in shock, and uttered a piercing cry. The silver filigree threads still laced her pale limbs, but now they poured downwards into the rock in a cascade of energy. Magus felt it with a jolt. The feeling was similar to that jolt he'd experienced on the Altar Stone at the recent Solstice sunrise. That surge had been so powerful and unexpected it had made him drop the torch. Now he thrilled as the force of the silver energy pulsed up through the stone into his body, filling him with tingling euphoria.

He looked up at Sylvie in awe. She remained frozen, her face anguished and her song silenced. Her eyes rolled to him and focused. She gazed at him in sorrow as if begging for help. The rock around her feet glowed slightly; Magus leaned over to feel it but couldn't get his hand close enough. The energy field was very powerful, like the repelling power of two identical magnetic poles being forced together. Yet his hand, spread above the glowing rock, was absorbing the energy. Magus felt it coursing into his body, a strange icy sensation that tingled and burned. He felt strong, powerful.

Magus laughed with delight, ignoring Sylvie's beseeching eyes. In some ways this was even better than the energy he received on the Altar Stone during the festivals. That was a brief, albeit powerful, flash of irradiation. But this moon magic went on and on, pouring down through her body and streaming up into him from the white stone. He stretched out flat on the rock as close as he could get to the force field around Sylvie, feeling the energy flow into every part of him. He heard a small sound. Her lips were moving.

'Please! Help me down . . .'

'Oh no, Sylvie! I don't know what's going on here but we're staying put. You wanted to moondance. You keep at it, my moongazy girl.'

He closed his eyes and concentrated on the powerful sensations flooding through him.

It occurred to Yul that Magus might have followed Sylvie up to the Hare Stone. He couldn't understand how, for he'd been in the woods waiting and would've seen them. But he had to check. If she was up there with Magus, who knew what might happen. He hated the thought of Magus seeing her moongazy and defenceless. He ran at full speed from the Hall, into the woods and up the hill through the boulders to Hare Stone. It was immediately clear that they weren't there. The hares raced around the stone and the barn owl sat on top of it. But there was no girl with silver hair dancing like a bright fairy, and no dark-eyed man either.

He flung himself down on the grass in disappointment, chest heaving and lungs burning. He'd run a couple of miles, mostly uphill, and to no avail. Where on earth were they? And then the dreadful thought struck him like a thunderbolt. He cursed himself for not thinking of it earlier. Mooncliffe! That was where Magus always went for the Moon Fullness. He'd imagined Sylvie leading him, but it would of course have been the other way round. Yul didn't think Magus would harm her. She was still a child and he'd always treated her so gently. But nevertheless he started to panic, knowing well the significance of that round disc of stone. It was common knowledge how Magus usually chose to honour the moon rising.

Leaping to his feet, Yul raced back down the hill again, through the dark woods, past the cottage, and onto the long path that led eventually up to Mooncliffe. The moon was now higher and brighter in the sky, a golden coin flecked with tiny grey clouds. If anything bad was going to happen at Mooncliffe, it would've happened by now. But that didn't stop him running as fast as he could to find her.

It was late and Miranda had been waiting at the cottage for some time. She was worried about Sylvie, and also about Magus. She didn't like the thought of them alone together in the moonlit night. She knew it was stupid to be jealous of her own daughter, and she trusted Magus of course, but she had no control over her feelings of resentment. She paced up and down the small cottage in a fret of impatience and growing anxiety. She should've asked to join Magus in keeping an eye on her daughter, not left them alone together like this. Sylvie was her responsibility after all. What on earth could they be doing all this time?

Sylvie stood in exactly the same position on the great stone as if rooted there. The glowing area of rock had spread. Her eyes were now shut, her face still agonised. Her outspread fingers had drooped and her arms hung by her sides. She stood like a closed-eyed carving in the moonlight, a strange statue with silver threads travelling down her body and into the rock at her feet. Magus still lay spread-eagled as close as he could bear. His eyes were shut too, but the expression on his face was one of bliss.

41

'Please, Magus, please let me go,' Sylvie whispered. She was aware of what was happening but she couldn't move at all. She felt exhausted, drained of everything. Her legs trembled and were barely able to support her. Magus ignored her pleas. He'd realised that somehow her body was channelling energy from the full moon into the stone. Just like at the Altar Stone in the Stone Circle, he was able to soak the power up from the rock itself. He wasn't sure if the energy would remain in the stone once she'd got down and was loath to let her go quite yet. Another few minutes should do it.

She crumpled almost in slow motion onto the pale rock, her legs finally giving way. Reluctantly Magus sat up and stretched, glancing at the girl lying next to him. He felt as if he could perform any feat in the world. He jumped to the ground and, leaning over, scooped Sylvie up in his arms, feeling an almost superhuman strength. She was as light as rose petals. Her hair hung over his arm in a long silver swathe, the static now gone, and she felt cool to the touch. Her arms and legs gleamed in the milky moonlight and her beautiful dress shimmered as the embroidered moons and stars reflected real moonbeams. He stood on the cliff top, a tall figure gazing at her silvered face as she lay motionless in his arms, eyes closed and seemingly asleep. A moongazy girl indeed, he thought tenderly.

Yul, his heart pounding with exertion, had arrived just in time to see Sylvie fall. He'd thought at first that she was alone on the great stone, and was surprised to notice the dark figure of Magus lying there too. Was the man unconscious? But he moved and effortlessly lifted Sylvie in his arms, then stood staring at her. Yul's instincts screamed to run over and make sure she was alright. Instead he crouched down in the tall bracken, his legs shaking from the punishing run.

He ducked just in time as Magus turned towards him and the path leading down the cliff. It was a striking sight – the tall, powerful man, blond hair gleaming in the bright moonlight, carrying Sylvie's limp body. She lay like a wounded bird in his arms. They brushed past Yul's hiding place and he steeled himself not to leap up and challenge Magus. He waited until they were well down the path before moving. Magus was obviously taking her home, whatever had happened up here now finished.

When he was sure it was safe Yul went over to the great stone and was shocked to see it glowing a ghostly blue-silver, luminous in the moonlight. He reached over to touch it and received the same jolt that Magus had experienced. Yul's eyes widened in surprise, and then realisation. He climbed onto the great Mooncliffe disc and lay down on the spot where Sylvie had fallen. He too felt the energy soaking into him and closed his eyes. All around him the stars twinkled like bright diamonds in the warm June night, the only sounds the distant hooting of owls and barking of foxes.

Magus tapped the front door of the cottage with his boot. It was opened immediately by Miranda, her face twisted with concern.

'Thank goodness! I've been so worried! Magus, what's happened? Is she alright?'

'She's fine, just a little tired. I'll take her straight up to her bed.'

He climbed the narrow stairs and laid Sylvie down. She opened her eyes drowsily as her head hit the pillow, but was asleep again almost instantly.

'You must get her out of that dress,' Magus said to Miranda, who'd followed him up. 'She'll spoil it if she sleeps in it, and it cost a fortune.'

'I'm sorry, I didn't know she intended to wear it tonight.'

'No matter. She'll probably be very tired tomorrow so let her miss school. Take the day off yourself so you can look after her. She'll need to sleep.'

'But what happened? Did she meet that boy? Why's she so exhausted?'

'She's been cavorting about in the moonlight and no, she didn't meet him but only because I stopped her. She was on her way into the woods to find him, despite all my instructions to the contrary.'

They went downstairs and Magus headed straight for the door. It was the Moon Fullness and he had other things to do before he could eventually get to his bed. At the door he stopped to kiss Miranda and she melted into his arms, desperately hoping to keep him there. Sylvie's words earlier in the day played through her head – maybe he didn't want her any more. She fawned all over him but after a minute he extricated himself from her embrace.

'Listen, Miranda. I think Sylvie has some special sort of ... illness, sensitivity, call it what you will,' he said. 'It's linked to the full moon, that's for sure.'

'But I thought she was getting over her illnesses. I thought she'd been healed at Stonewylde.'

'Yes she has, but this is something different – a lunacy in the true sense of the word. I believe I can help her, but it may take some time to cure and I'll need to keep watch over her. And of course I want to have you close too. So when I come back from my business trip, I suggest you both move up to the Hall.'

Miranda was delighted and kissed him again, hugging him tightly. He was shimmering with energy, almost glowing with it, and she felt such an attraction to him. Magus smiled at her enthusiasm and once more disentangled himself from her arms.

'So we'll be moving in with you?' she said excitedly, still trying to cling to him. 'Oh, that'll be wonderful! Especially with the baby coming.'

He frowned at her.

'No, I didn't mean move in with me – not into my rooms. I'll have a suite made available for you and Sylvie, and the baby when it arrives. I've already told you how our relationship has to be and it doesn't entail us living together in that way. I'm sorry, Miranda, but I thought you understood that.'

She stared down at the floor, her excitement crushed.

'Of course, Magus. I just thought ... I thought maybe you'd changed your mind. When you said you wanted me close.'

'Close, but not that close. I need to keep an eye on Sylvie and this moongaziness. She's not well and she's a danger to herself.'

'Oh, I see. So it's not me you want close, it's Sylvie.'

'Don't be silly – it's both of you I'm thinking of. She needs protection and you can't possibly manage her on your own. I want to help, and as the magus it's my responsibility to take care of her. Now I'm sorry, but I really must go. I have things to do. I'll be back tomorrow to check she's alright. Goodnight, Miranda.'

As he walked back to the Hall, Magus smiled to himself. He now had the key to the future of Stonewylde, all thanks to Sylvie and her moongaziness. She was the channel for the moon magic and he could receive it every month through her, fill himself to the brim with her gift. The lack of Earth Magic at the Summer Solstice no longer mattered – he now had an additional power source.

He strode down the corridor and tapped on a door, entering at once.

'Are you ready?' he asked, his voice deep and inviting. 'I'm all yours now. Sorry it's so much later than I said. There were a few unexpected developments with my earlier engagement but I'm sure you'll feel it was worth waiting for. It's a beautiful night out there ...'

The young doctor smiled and left the room with him, shaking with excitement as they went down the wide stairs to the entrance hall. Magus' eyes gleamed as he led her out through the great front door and into the moonlight. It was indeed a beautiful night.

'What on earth are you doing here?' asked Miranda sharply, glaring at the dark-haired boy standing on her door step in the bright morning sun. He wore the rough spun clothes and heavy leather boots of the Villagers. He looked down guiltily, long curls falling over his face.

'I'm sorry to trouble you, ma'am,' he mumbled. Then he

looked up and she was struck by the beauty of his eyes; a deep, clear grey, long lashed and slightly slanted. He was a very good-looking lad and she could quite understand why Sylvie found him attractive.

'If Magus knows you've been here ...' she said, shaking her head.

'I know – please don't be angry. I was worried about Sylvie and I just wanted to know if she's alright.'

His eyes were beseeching and she steeled herself, remembering Magus had said he was manipulative and cunning.

'I don't see that Sylvie's welfare is any concern of yours,' she snapped. 'In fact, it was thanks to you that she was so ill last month. So if you don't mind ...'

She started to shut the door but he took a step forward to stop her. She frowned at his hand holding her front door. It reminded her of Magus' hands; long fingered and square nailed.

'Let go! I'm warning you, Magus will hear about this.'

'Please, ma'am, just tell me if she's alright. That's all I want to know and then I'll go.'

'Sylvie's fine. She's very tired and still asleep, but she's absolutely fine – not that it's any concern of yours.'

His relief was almost comical. He smiled and his whole face lit up.

'Oh thank you, ma'am! When she wakes up please tell her I asked after her. I won't bother you again and I'm sorry I did, but I had to know. Thank you! Blessings on you.'

He smiled at her again and, despite herself, she warmed to him slightly – he did seem a sweet boy.

'Just don't come here again or I'll have to tell Magus.'

Miranda shut the door firmly and sighed. She hadn't strictly told the truth – Sylvie was totally exhausted, drained of every drop of energy. She was deathly pale with great dark rings under her eyes and had been whimpering in her sleep. Miranda had tried to wake her but she was limp and unresponsive. It wasn't anything like the previous month when she'd had a fever after being out in the rain; this was almost more worrying as there seemed to be no reason for her awful lethargy. She wished that Magus would hurry up and call soon.

Magus had every intention of checking on Sylvie but at that moment was in his office. Situated in a wing at the rear of the Hall, it overlooked a beautiful sunken stone garden full of white flowers, whose scent wafted in through the open windows. The large room was lined with many books and several paintings, and one side was devoted to a humming network of computers. Magus looked out through the French windows, not noticing the bright butterflies dancing in the white garden below. His fingers drummed edgily on the woodwork; he was full of restless energy.

A servant brought in a tray of coffee and pastries and Magus looked impatiently at his watch, which was now functional again. When the heavy oak door finally swung open he spun round and exclaimed loudly at the sight of his brother.

'About time too, Clip! I thought we'd agreed to meet first thing this morning.'

The thinner, wispy-haired brother ambled over to the old leather sofas and sank down in one, stretching out his long legs and laying his head wearily against the backrest.

'You sent me a message to come, Sol. I don't think I actually agreed to be here first thing. You know how I am the day after the Moon Fullness.'

Magus sat down on the other sofa and poured coffee, watching as his older brother gulped it down. Clip had clearly been out all night and still wore his summer cloak, full of burrs and twigs. His blond hair was wild and his grey eyes faraway.

'Good journey? I assume that's what you've been doing all night.'

'Extraordinary. I was at the dolmen up past the heath. Remember it?'

'Oh yes, I remember it,' smiled Magus, recalling boyhood adventures at the strange place. The massive stones made a small chamber, with a roof formed by a huge flat stone. It was in this Neolithic place that Clip often spent the nights of the Moon

Fullness and festivals, travelling on shamanic journeys with the help of an aromatic fire and various herbs and spices.

'You're looking full of yourself today, Sol. In fact, you're quite radiant – what's happened? I take it all went well last night with our little moongazy newcomer? You stopped her meeting up with the Village boy?'

Clip helped himself to a pastry and Magus joined him.

'I'm so damn hungry this morning,' he said. 'Yes, it was amazing – you won't believe what happened! You may have to help me, Clip, as I'm off to London soon and we need to get a few things in place before the next Moon Fullness.'

As the two men wolfed down the plate of pastries and drained the coffee pot, Magus told Clip about his experience at Mooncliffe the night before and Sylvie's incredible ability to channel the full moon energy.

'It sounds as if the stone's acting like a kind of battery, storing the power,' said Clip thoughtfully.

'That's right! I went up there early this morning and the rock's still full of it. Not as strong as last night, of course, but still powerful. You must come up yourself and feel it.'

'And you say that once she was standing there she couldn't get down again?'

'No, it was strange. At first she danced around on the grass like some sort of bizarre bird, but once she'd jumped up on the stone she froze, almost as if she'd petrified. I could see that she wanted to get off, that it was ... uncomfortable, but she was completely unable to move.'

'And you left her up there? You're a sadistic bastard, Sol. Always have been, ever since you were a boy.'

Magus smiled sardonically and raised his eyebrows.

'But I get results, don't I? I tell you, once you've experienced that moon magic you'll want more. I've never felt like this before, not even after the Solstice energy. I've been making plans this morning and I've got some great ideas.'

'Just so long as I don't have to do anything,' yawned Clip.

'I may be a sadistic bastard, but you're a lazy one,' said Magus, an edge to his voice. 'Yes you do have to do something. Because you'll benefit from this too.'

'How? I'm not interested in your empire building. I don't want to be any part of your schemes and dreams, you know that. I've always made it clear that you must leave me out of your grand plans.'

'You're the owner of Stonewylde, Clip. You're a part of it whether you like it or not.'

'It's nothing to do with me, Sol, all this expansion. *I* didn't want to open up the quarry and bring in van loads of illegal immigrants to risk their lives quarrying the stone. *I* don't want to build a new school to cope with this population explosion you've encouraged, or holiday homes for Hallfolk so they'll pay through the nose for the privilege of staying here. I don't want any part of the investments or the stock market scams or the off-shore trusts, or this fortune you're earning from your company's wheeling and dealing.'

'Oh for Goddess' sake, Clip, I—'

'No! This is your lifestyle, not mine! I don't want to be adored by every woman and treated like some sort of god. I don't want any part of the whole empire thing, which is why I let *you* be magus instead of me. So don't try and rope me into any of it, Sol. All I ask is to live at Stonewylde when I want to, and to travel when I need to. And to feel the Earth Magic, honour the Goddess, and take part in the rituals and ceremonies.'

'You're a fool, Clip. This moon magic is part of Stonewylde too, as much a part as the Earth Magic. Look at you this morning – worn out, old and tired. And look at me! Come up to the rock now and you'll see just how good it makes you feel.'

Miranda held a glass of water to Sylvie's lips, her other arm supporting the girl as she lay propped up in bed. She took a few sips, then her head fell back weakly against the headboard.

'Try to drink a bit more, Sylvie. It's nearly lunch time and you've had nothing today. You didn't eat last night either, did you? You know you must look after your health or you'll end up as ill as you were in London. Please, darling.'

'I'm sorry, Mum,' whispered Sylvie through pale lips. 'I just want to sleep.'

Sighing, Miranda gently laid her down, making sure she was warm enough. Where was Magus? She couldn't leave Sylvie to go and find him. She wished now she'd asked Yul to take a message to the Hall when he'd called earlier. Why was there no phone in this place? She thought of her old mobile phone lying useless at the bottom of a cupboard; there was no signal at Stonewylde. Why didn't Magus come?

Clip lay spread out on the huge round stone, the midday sun beating down. Magus towered over him impatiently.

'Well?'

'It's unbelievable, Sol! I've never heard of anything like it, but I can see how it's possible. If a battery works by converting chemical energy stored inside it, why not a stone storing magnetic or maybe gravitational energy from the moon? What a wonderful sensation! I feel completely re-energised.'

'What we need is to find out exactly what this stone is,' said Magus. 'I'll bring up a mallet and we can send a piece of the rock for analysis.'

'You can't just knock chunks off it! It's an ancient stone placed here thousands of years ago by our ancestors. Look, they even made it disc shaped like the full moon, and smoothed it out. They must've been able to channel the energy too.'

'Yes, it does make me wonder whether it's only Sylvie who can do it, or if others could too. Remember our mother? She was moongazy, wasn't she? I don't remember too well, but now I come to think of it I'm sure there were tales about her and this stone.'

Clip frowned, sitting up on the rock.

'Yes, you're right. I've heard she used to dance and sing at the Moon Fullness.'

'That's what Sylvie was doing!'

'And I know Magus – I mean your father, not mine – would bring her up here every month. I followed them once but he saw me and shouted at me to go home. So maybe our mother could channel the energy too. And maybe he used it to power himself up. I wonder if *my* father brought her here too? We'll have to find out – some of the older Villagers might remember.'

'That crone Heggy would know,' said Magus speculatively.

'You can ask her if you're so curious – I'm not going anywhere near her! You know how she hates us and she terrifies me. Maybe Violet could tell us? Ask her next time she bakes the ceremony cakes. It'd be interesting to know if both our fathers brought Raven here and whether she channelled the moon magic for them.'

'I'll speak to Violet soon. Get off now, Clip, or you'll use it all up.'

'Oh come on, Sol – just a few more minutes.'

He lay down again and stretched out. Magus sat next to him and closed his eyes.

'I must have a sample but I'll take it from the underside, so it won't show. When we know what the rock is we can do some geological surveying of the estate and find out if there's any more of it. It's an unusual stone, isn't it? It sparkles, which may mean that there's quartz in it. It's certainly different to the stones at the Stone Circle, and the dolmen stones, and even that single one up on the hill by the woods, the one where the hares run wild. Can you think of any others?'

'Near the dolmen there's another small stone circle but I can't remember what sort of rock they are. And at the quarry – there's that enormous stone at the cliff end looking down over the place. Remember we used to climb on it and you'd threaten to push me over the edge? Goddess, I used to hate it there!'

'Oh yes! I'd forgotten that one – the serpent rock. D'you know, I think it may be the same composition as this! I remember it glittering in the sun in the same way. I'll phone the Gatehouse and leave a message for Jackdaw. He can get one of the men to chisel a piece off and then we'll compare it.'

'But why do you want to find more stone like this? I don't understand. You can get the girl to channel the moon energy here every month and then we'll come and soak it up,' said Clip, still lying sprawled on his back, eyes closed in the sun.

'So you do want to be part of it now?' Magus' voice was cynical. 'Changed your mind about joining me, have you?'

'No, this is different. This is Stonewylde magic, not your scheming, and of course I want some of it. It'll help me on my journeying into other realms, this moon magic.'

'I thought you used Violet's cakes for that?'

'Well yes, but we both knew all along that Sylvie had come here for a purpose and now we know what that purpose is. Clearly it's to channel the moon energy for the two of us. But I don't see why you want to find more stone like this. Surely this is enough.'

'I've been thinking about it all night!' said Magus excitedly. 'This is fine in the summer, but what about in the winter, or when the weather's foul? Sylvie was ill last month after getting wet in the rain and she's not really that strong, despite the healing. So I thought if we had small pieces of the same rock, we could make her channel the energy into those to make a portable power source.'

'That's brilliant, Sol! Absolutely brilliant. But be careful with Sylvie, won't you? I don't want her to suffer – she's a sweet girl and it wouldn't be fair.'

'No, we don't want to kill the goose that lays the golden egg, do we? Now I must go and see how she is today, and Miranda too. You know she's pregnant?'

'Already? You didn't waste any time, did you! So you really have gone for it, then ... what you said about producing more heirs?'

'Seemed like a good time, fresh blood and all that.'

'And has Miranda told you who Sylvie's father is yet?'

'No, there's some dark secret that she's hiding. But I'll put pressure on her and find out, now I've got her where I want her. Sylvie's father must be Hallfolk – there are a lot of them out there.

And what about Sylvie's amazing likeness to our mother? Do you remember when you first saw her, how struck you were by the resemblance?'

'Yes, at the Story Web back in March. She's got to be related to us. You must find out from Miranda.'

'I will. Come with me, Clip, down to the cottage. I need to check on Sylvie – she was a little weak last night after the moon dancing.'

'Of course!' He sprung off the stone and followed his brother towards the path leading down from Mooncliffe. 'D'you know, an hour ago all I wanted was to crawl off to bed and sleep? But now I feel I could run a marathon. That moon magic is powerful stuff.'

Miranda almost wept with relief when Magus arrived at the cottage, although she wasn't so pleased to see Clip standing behind him. The two men were bursting with brightness and energy as they entered the small sitting room.

'She's in a terrible state, Magus,' she said. 'Come and see for yourself. She won't wake up, won't drink anything, and she's been whimpering in her sleep. What on earth happened last night? I've never seen her like this before. And there're awful bruises on her wrists too, and a mark on her cheek.'

'We'll talk in a minute when I've seen her,' he said, brushing past her. 'You stay down here, Miranda. There isn't room for all of us in that tiny bedroom.'

The two men filled the room as they stood one each side of the narrow bed looking down at the sleeping girl. Her skin was translucent and the dark shadows under her eyes were shocking. Her arm lying on the white coverlet looked frail and delicate, the bruising round the wrist stark. Her breathing was quiet. They could almost have been looking at a corpse.

'This is no good at all, Sol! I won't be a part of anything that harms her. Why is she bruised?'

'I had to restrain her when she tried to run off and meet that damn boy again. But she's alright – she's not harmed, just tired.'

Magus sat on the side of the bed and picked up Sylvie's limp hand.

'Sylvie, Sylvie, wake up. Wake up!'

He shook her slightly.

'I know you can hear me. Wake up!'

With a visible effort she opened her eyes and looked straight into Magus'. She flinched slightly as she recognised him, but he leant over and kissed her cheek.

'That's a good girl. How are you feeling?'

'Tired,' she whispered.

'See, Clip's here to visit you too.'

His grey eyes watched her more compassionately than Magus's and she smiled weakly at the brother whom she'd always preferred.

'Do you remember what happened last night, Sylvie?' asked Magus softly.

She nodded slightly.

'Tell me then.'

'I was dancing up at Mooncliffe. And then ...'

'And then what?' he prompted.

'And then I went on the great round stone and I couldn't move.'

'And do you remember anything else?'

She looked into his handsome face, glowing with vitality. It all came back to her.

'You lay on the stone and you made me stay there. You knew it hurt but you wouldn't help me.'

She began to cry. She had no energy to sob, but tears spilled onto her cheeks. Magus frowned down at her.

'For Goddess' sake, man!' said Clip, fishing a piece of cloth from his pocket. 'Show some human kindness.'

He leaned over and awkwardly dabbed at her tears.

'It's alright, Sylvie. It wasn't Magus' fault. He was frozen too, just like you were.'

'No he wasn't,' she whispered. 'I remember – he loved it. It was awful and I'll never go up there again.'

'You'll do as you're told!' said Magus, his eyes glittering. 'You're making a fuss about nothing. Isn't she, Clip?'

'Well . . . she does look tired—'

'Nonsense! Come on, Clip – remember how special that moon magic is? You know this is why she came here – you said so yourself!' He glared at Sylvie, who shrank further into her pillows. 'I'm telling you now, Sylvie, I won't—'

'Ssh, leave this to me,' said Clip. 'I think I can help her with this. There's no need to bully her.' He sat down on the narrow bed. 'Sylvie, what you did last night was amazing. You're such a clever girl and we're so proud of you.'

She closed her eyes, shutting them both out.

'You're a magical girl, Sylvie, but you must share your magic. It's wrong to keep it all for yourself.'

She opened her eyes and gazed at Clip, who was staring at her intently.

'I don't keep it for myself,' she mumbled. 'I give the magic to Stonewylde.'

'And we're Stonewylde,' said Clip gently. 'We need to share the magic too. That's why you must dance at Mooncliffe for us.'

She shook her head slightly and shut them out again. She couldn't bear the pair of them staring down at her, overwhelming her with their intensity and urgency.

'I won't go up there again,' she croaked, her face paler than ever. 'It's horrible and wrong and I won't do it.'

'Sylvie—' began Magus, but his brother waved him to silence.

'Open your eyes, Sylvie,' Clip said softly. 'Just look at me for a minute.'

Reluctantly she gazed at him. His grey eyes shimmered before her, luminous and strange. She felt herself drawn to him, pulled in to his will. She tried to look away but found she couldn't. He took her unresisting hands in his and she sensed his power, a gentle but insistent force that locked her into his command. She felt her free will melt away under his unrelenting eyes.

'You love to dance at Mooncliffe,' he said. 'At the Moon Fullness, you love to dance at Mooncliffe.'

'No,' she moaned. 'I want to be with Yul . . .'

'Sylvie, you know you love to dance at Mooncliffe. Look at me, Sylvie. That's better. We understand each other. You're a special moongazy girl and you want so much to serve Magus. It's why you were brought here and you know this in your heart. You love to dance at Mooncliffe.'

Slowly she nodded, and Clip felt Magus twitch with barely controlled suspense. Ignoring this, he smiled kindly, holding the girl in his thrall.

'You love to dance at Mooncliffe for Magus. You want to give him your magic on the great stone. Isn't that right, Sylvie?'

She nodded again, her face impassive. Clip sighed.

'Good girl. We're very pleased with you. This is the right thing and you know it. You're going to rest now and you'll feel much better when you've had a sleep. There's no problem at all. You're not ill.'

'No, I'm fine,' she whispered. 'Only tired.'

'Before you go back to sleep, Sylvie, tell me something. What do you like to do at the Moon Fullness?'

'I love to dance at Mooncliffe for Magus.'

As they clattered down the stairs, Magus turned to Clip.

'You're a bloody genius, brother.'

Clip grinned ruefully.

'No, Sol, I'm no genius. Just a good shaman.'

56

4

After the full moon, Magus left Stonewylde with a group of older students. They all stayed in his London residence and were treated to visits to the theatre and galleries, as well as social functions and shopping trips. Magus knew that the Hallfolk were vital to Stonewylde's economy, and carefully prepared each generation of high-achievers for life in the Outside World. He knew where their loyalty would lie in the future and considered this time spent with them a worthwhile investment.

Whilst he was gone, June slipped into July and the weather at Stonewylde grew even hotter. The hay harvest continued in earnest and scores of beehives were moved around the estate following the nectar in bean fields, wild flower meadows and grassland clover. The Meadery was inundated with fragrant honey sent in daily.

The Villagers spent every hour of daylight bringing in the crops as they ripened; day by day all the soft fruits and many vegetables were picked and preserved. The older Village children were pulled out of school and trooped around the estate to help with the harvest. Every evening the Village boys went out with snares, cudgels and slingshots to the warrens on the downs. The ripening crops mustn't suffer and it was every boy's duty to cull the rabbits that thrived in their thousands. Nothing was wasted as rabbit meat was a staple for the Villagers, the bones were processed into glue and building materials and the fur made into warm winter covers and linings. Rabbits were an important harvest at Stonewylde, and despite the boys' enthusiastic efforts their numbers seemed to remain undiminished.

This was also the time of year for harvesting the flax, which was grown extensively at Stonewylde and spun and woven into linen. Along with wool and leather, this linen provided most of the Villagers' clothing and bedding and was also used by the resident Hallfolk. By July the flax was over a metre high and the fields of pale-blue flowers were beautiful. It was a labour intensive crop that couldn't be harvested in the usual way by cutting, which would damage the fibres. Instead, wearing strong leather gloves, the workers pulled it from the ground by hand. Every Villager young and fit enough was taken from their normal duties for the back-breaking task of pulling the flax. After the flax harvest and retting, all women and girls in the Village were kept busy at home spinning thread for dyeing and weaving into cloth. Most families had their own loom, and men and women shared the weaving when the autumn nights started to draw in.

The fields given over to cereal were rippling with wheat, corn, barley and oats. The oil seed rape had been harvested and the sunflowers turned their glorious heads to track the blazing sun each day. The hemp had been gathered in and the fibres would be twisted and laid in a rope walk, set up in the Great Barn during the winter months. The smaller, more specialised crops such as woad and madder for dye were all ready for harvest, as were the unusual poppies which contributed to the exotic ingredients in the ceremony cakes. Women gathered in their medicinal herbs too, making tinctures and elixirs in their kitchens.

The harvesting was co-ordinated by a band of trusted Villagers who organised the farming system at Stonewylde. Magus left the smooth running of the estate entirely to these farm managers and at this time of year they worked from dawn to dusk and often beyond. Magus had long since seen the economic sense in abandoning the old horse-drawn methods of farming, and tractors, combine harvesters and any other essential machinery were always used.

Because nothing that could be grown in the fields of Stonewylde was imported, it was vital that farming was productive and efficient. But even with mechanisation and the need for high yields, there was no exploitation of the Earth Mother. There was no bleeding the land dry of all goodness and then pumping it back artificially with infusions of chemicals. Stonewylde used traditional organic methods, and the ultimate testimony to its success was the good health and fitness of all the people who lived there.

Clip had left Stonewylde to stay with an alternative community in Ireland, where he was always in demand as a story-teller. The visitors who'd come for the Midsummer Holiday had now gone, and from being crammed full and bursting at the seams, the Hall was suddenly very quiet. With both Magus and Clip absent and many of the resident Hallfolk away on holiday in the Outside World, the atmosphere at Stonewylde was relaxed, despite the extra work in the fields.

Yul felt free with Magus away. He worked harder than ever before, spending hours every evening pulling flax after a long day in the woods, and ate Maizie out of house and home. Rosie was working all hours at the dairy as milk production was at its peak. Much of the excess milk was made into great wheels of cheese which were part of the feasts at both Lammas and the Autumn Equinox festivals. Stonewylde cheese was particularly tasty, and the dairy produced several different types. Geoffrey and Gregory, although still at school, were busy rabbiting and helping with the flax harvest. Maizie was up to her elbows in preserves and wine-making, and trying to keep the two younger boys, Gefrin and Sweyn, under control. Without their father's subduing presence they were running wild and constantly into mischief. Their favourite occupation was tormenting their little sister Leveret, and Maizie had to be extra vigilant and make sure her youngest child was safe from their spiteful pranks.

Alwyn still languished in the hospital wing with no power of speech or movement. Unable to eat solid food, he'd lost much of his bulk and taken on a wasted look. Maizie went to see him weekly but it was a duty visit and she spent less and less time there. She always returned very quiet, feeling guilty for enjoying her life so much more with her husband out of the way.

Yul visited the hospital wing just once, and spent only a little time with the man who'd abused him for as long as he could remember. He went one evening before starting work in the fields, and approached the Hall with trepidation despite knowing that Magus was away. He went round to the kitchen wing where he'd worked so hard during the Midsummer festival. He knew Marigold would welcome him, although she'd barely had time to speak to him when the visitors had been around.

'Come and have a little bite to eat first, Yul my love,' she said warmly, sitting him down at the over-sized scrubbed table where the servants ate.

'I've already eaten,' he protested, smiling at her insistent kindness. She cut him a generous slice of gooseberry pie and smothered it with cream.

'Aye, well you're not greedy like that father o' yours, but a working lad like you needs to keep his strength up.'

'It's him I've come to see,' he explained. 'I won't be a regular visitor but I wanted to see him just once.'

She shook her head and folded her arms.

'That bully being taken ill was the best thing for your poor family,' she said. 'I should think your mother's glad to see the back of him, nasty brute.'

Yul was surprised at this. Maizie had told him how Alwyn had been a constant visitor to these kitchens during his son's time at the quarry, piling on the fat as he was overfed daily by Marigold's generosity. She laughed at the look on his face.

'Aye, I know what you're thinking. We all knew what he'd done to you, Yul, and what he'd been doing to you for years. I saw him that week Magus had you locked up by the stables. Starving you was a terrible thing to do, and making you watch your father eat when you were so hungry ... Magus should never've done it. 'Twas downright cruelty. And that Alwyn! Nasty piece o' work, greedy as a pig after weaning. I said to myself – if that man wants food, I'll give him food. I'll feed him till he bursts! He'd sit in my kitchen like a great porker at the trough. But I reckoned if I stuffed him up enough he'd get heavier and slower and maybe find it harder to beat you. Looks like it worked, eh? They don't come much slower than Alwyn is now!'

Yul laughed at this, pleased to know he had another ally. Marigold's plump face dimpled with mirth, but then her smile faded.

'There's one thing I want to ask you, boy. I heard some gossip the other day, something one of the men up at the Gatehouse let slip in the pub. Now 'tis all round the Village, though he's denying he ever said it of course. Rabbit-scared he is! But you'll know the answer, Yul, seeing as you was up there yourself. Is it true that Jackdaw's back, working up at Quarrycleave?'

She stared at him intently and Yul swallowed. Magus had been insistent that Yul was to tell no one about Jackdaw's return to Stonewylde. He understood why Marigold was so concerned; Jackdaw had been married to her daughter. It was only his immediate banishment that had stopped Marigold organising a lynch-mob after he murdered his young wife. Marigold nodded slowly, her face darkening.

'No need to answer, Yul. 'Tis plain you been told to keep quiet and Goddess knows you've enough reason not to anger the master again. I understand, my boy.' She brushed imaginary crumbs from the table briskly, her eyes welling with tears. 'Well, if that Jackdaw ever steps foot in the Village he won't last long. What is Magus thinking of, bringing him back here? I never thought I'd see this day! My poor girl Lily – what she suffered at the hands of that man don't bear thinking about. Death was a release for her, I can tell you. And their little boy, Jay. Why didn't Magus let me take care of him afterwards? I'll never forgive him for that. My own daughter's son, my grandson. I should've been given the care of him, poor little mite. But oh no, Magus sends him to his other grandmother, that sow Vetchling. No more fit to bring up a child than hatch an egg! I'll never understand the reason for that as long as I live. I ...'

Yul was spared any more of her diatribe by the arrival of

Harold. The young servant grinned at Yul and rolled his eyes. He was pleased to see Yul again as they'd always got on well and Yul had certainly made his life easier during the Midsummer Holiday.

'Could Harold take me to the hospital wing?' asked Yul, for the flax was still waiting to be pulled. 'I'll never find my way alone.'

'Aye, you do that, young Harold. And come and see me again soon, Yul,' said Marigold, taking his empty bowl and ruffling his hair. She smiled as he stood up, towering over her.

'Sacred Mother, but you've grown lately! Send my blessings to Maizie and tell her next time she's up visiting Alwyn to pop in to the kitchens for a chat. Always did like your mother.'

Harold led Yul out of the kitchens and both boys burst out laughing.

'Goddess, she can talk, that one!' said Harold.

'She's kind though,' said Yul.

'Not always, believe me! She can flick a cloth so it catches you so hard on the arse it leaves a mark through your trousers! So how's life treating you now?'

'Life's good. Busy, of course, but it's that time of year. I haven't seen you pulling the flax yet, Harold. Field work too hard for you now you've gone all soft up at the Hall?'

The boy shook his head.

'Come on, Yul, you know what it were like here over the holiday. I was worked to the bone. I think I deserve a break. Anyway, with all the Hallfolk away again I've been doing something ... special. Something Magus wouldn't like if he found out.'

He glanced furtively around as they climbed a short flight of back stairs and went along a corridor. Yul looked at him in surprise. He'd always imagined the servants at the Hall to be, like Martin, intensely loyal and obedient.

'What have you been doing?' he asked, intrigued by Harold's secrecy. The boy was bubbling with excitement.

'It's amazing! I can't believe I'm doing it. I been dying to tell someone! You know all them computers they have here? Maybe you don't. They're these machines, like televisions but different.

And there's this thing called the Internet and I been doing it!'

Yul looked unimpressed.

'Why? Doing what exactly?'

'Oh Yul, you don't understand! I play games and visit websites and 'tis a whole different world! And I'm learning to read! I've got some books from their school and I been visiting this old dear in the Village who remembers how to read. I can type things now and read some o' the stuff on the websites. I practise every day. I use a computer in one of the Hallfolk's bedrooms while he's away. I'm up there every night!'

Yul eyed him suspiciously.

'You're not turning into Hallfolk, are you Harold?'

'Don't be daft – why would I want to be one of them? But 'tis a new world, I can tell you. I could show you the computers sometime. They're the best thing in Stonewylde. You should learn to read too, Yul. I'll teach you if you like!'

They'd reached the entrance to the hospital wing and stopped by the door. Yul frowned, remembering Sylvie offering the same thing. Maybe they were right. He was amazed at Harold learning to read and write. It was unheard of at Stonewylde, except amongst the very oldest Villagers, and most of them had long forgotten the basics. At the Village School Yul had always known that Harold was bright and should have passed the tests and come to the Hall School. But he had no Hallfolk blood and Yul reckoned they'd failed him deliberately. He nodded.

'I'll think about it, Harold. Thanks for bringing me up here.'

He opened the door to the hospital wing and was struck by the different smell. A nurse took him into a small room where something sat in a great wheelchair facing the window.

'I'll leave you alone with your father,' she said gently, her blond head cocked in sympathy. 'You won't get anything out of him, I'm afraid.'

'Will he get better?' asked Yul, his voice trembling slightly at the thought of Alwyn sitting only a couple of metres away. The nurse shook her head, her face concerned.

'You'll have to speak to the doctor,' she said. 'But it seems very unlikely. They've done tests and sent him for a scan at a private hospital in the Outside World. There's nothing much going on in his head and all we can do now is keep him comfortable. But he's losing weight rapidly and his muscles are starting to atrophy. You could always ask the Goddess for a miracle.'

I already have, thought Yul. *And this is it.*

The nurse left the room and quietly shut the door. Yul went round the high wheelchair and gaped at the sight before him. So this now was the hated man. The one who'd frightened Yul all his life, making sure any happiness he ever felt was soon crushed out of him. The one who'd have killed him if he'd been allowed to continue his cruelty. How long did it take to whip a person to death? Yul pondered this as he stared at the shrunken, sallow effigy before him. He shuddered, recalling the awful violence in the byre. Maybe not the whip; it could've been blows that killed him. Alwyn had been just as fond of that form of punishment. Punches and kicks to the kidneys, the head and spleen; maybe that would've been his end.

Yul found to his horror that his eyes had filled with hot tears. He blinked them away angrily, glaring at the pathetic huddle that gazed sightlessly out of the window. Alwyn smelt strange, his gingery hair had thinned to wisps and his skin hung loosely in empty folds. He was disgusting, almost less than human in his rapid decay. The vindictive speech of revenge, the glory and taunting that Yul had thought to enjoy as he finally faced his helpless tormentor all faded to nothing. He stood looking through a mist of tears at the man propped lifelessly in the chair, the evening sunlight on his sunken face.

In his pocket Yul's fingers closed round the pieces of leather he'd brought to toss contemptuously at his father – the remains of the snake-whip and the strap he'd so frenziedly destroyed. He thought of the words he'd dreamt of saying at this moment. But instead of revelling in triumph and gloating at his father's fate, he cried. Standing in the small room, Yul bowed his head and sobbed silently. He cried not for the man next to him, who must have hated him so much, but for his lost and trampled childhood, now gone forever.

Hazel gave Miranda a pregnancy test and confirmed that she was indeed expecting a child. The doctor remembered the Miranda of the Outside World as pale and worn-out, over-worked and worried sick about her daughter. The transformation was amazing. The woman before her glowed with good health, her skin and hair sleek, her green eyes shining. Her figure was now curvy and soft and her movements graceful and calm.

Hazel felt a twinge of jealousy knowing that Miranda was carrying Magus' child. Not that she begrudged Miranda this pregnancy; she was delighted for her. She just prayed to the Moon Goddess as Mother that she too would conceive, even though there were now two women at Stonewylde already expecting his babies. Hazel knew that Magus was normally very careful not to father children, but in the last few months he seemed to have reconsidered. Hazel was currently in favour with him and remained hopeful; maybe she too would be permitted to conceive if he was embarking on a new heir-producing venture.

Miranda was ecstatic on learning she was definitely carrying Magus' baby, seeing it as a way of binding him to her. Hadn't he said he'd love and care for the child? It could only strengthen their relationship. She visited the store in the Village where the baby equipment was kept. Marvelling at the lovely wicker cribs and prams that the women shared and borrowed, she chose some pretty linen to make new covers for hers. Luckily Sylvie felt no resentment towards this new life that was claiming her mother's attention. She was just pleased to be left alone.

Sylvie had gradually recovered from her experience up at Mooncliffe and was nearly back to normal. She'd spent a couple of days in bed, totally exhausted, but then Magus had called before leaving for London and told her to get up and stop malingering. He'd been quite sharp about it, which had upset her. He glowed with energy and she'd wondered if he'd offer to heal her again, but that seemed to be the last thing on his mind. He'd sent Miranda downstairs to make coffee and shut the bedroom door. Sylvie had felt confused when he'd sat down on her bed smiling, having just reprimanded her for being there at all. Her first reaction had been to shrink from him. But there'd been something else pulling against this instinct; a compulsion that she didn't understand.

'Remember the last Moon Fullness, Sylvie?' he'd asked softly, aware of Miranda moving about downstairs. He'd stroked the black bruises circling her wrists with a gentle finger. Sylvie had met his dark gaze and felt a strange sensation inside. She recalled the white disc of stone up on the cliffs. She knew that she must share her magic with Magus; it was why she'd been brought here. She nodded, her eyes luminous and intent as she returned his gaze. Despite himself, Magus had shivered at her strangeness.

'I do,' she said. 'I stood on the rock at Mooncliffe.'

'That's right. You were a good girl. And what about the next Moon Fullness, Sylvie? What'll you do then? Go running off with Yul?'

She swallowed. Of course she wanted to be with Yul up at Hare Stone. She knew it in her heart. But she found herself speaking differently.

'I want to dance at Mooncliffe for you,' she whispered.

Magus had smiled at this. She felt the full blast of his charm and vitality as he leant across the bed to kiss her forehead, his exotic scent filling her nostrils.

'I'm very pleased with you, Sylvie. I shall come back specially and you can dance for me again. Don't forget now. Remember what Clip told you.'

She nodded, her throat aching with unshed tears. She knew this was wrong. She knew how ill she'd felt since the full moon. She wanted to be with Yul. And yet . . .

'You must share your magic with me,' he said, squeezing her hand. 'But don't talk about it to anyone, will you? It's just between us.'

He then went downstairs and made Miranda's day by hugging her and telling her how beautiful she looked with his baby growing inside her. He kissed her deeply before leaving, teasing her for becoming so weak and submissive at his touch. He promised to spend time with her when he returned and reminded her of the imminent move up to the Hall. His final words, though, were about Sylvie.

'I expect to come back and find her completely well again. I will not be pleased if I return and find she's still moping about. I'm counting on you, Miranda, so don't let me down. I want Sylvie strong and healthy.'

A few days after Magus left, Sylvie and Yul came across each other in the woods where they both walked regularly in the hope of such a meeting. They were a little shy and both wished they could get back to their previous easiness with each other. Both also remembered their magical kiss on Sylvie's birthday under the yew tree, which made them slightly nervous about being alone together now. They climbed up the hill to the Hare Stone and Sylvie ran over and rested her cheek against its rough warmth. She breathed deeply.

'I love this stone. It makes me feel safe.'

Yul flung himself down on the short grass carpeted with white clover and sky-blue speedwell. He looked out towards the sea, hazy in the July sun. His deep grey eyes were startlingly clear in his tanned face as he narrowed them against the glare of the sun.

'So tell me what happened at the last Moon Fullness, Sylvie. I was really worried about you.'

'Oh yes, of course,' she said brightly, sitting down on the grass next to him. He wore a thin, sleeveless jerkin; she noticed how brown he was and how well defined the muscles in his arms had become. 'I went to Mooncliffe with Magus and I danced on the moon stone there.'

'What? You danced?'

'I went to Mooncliffe with Magus and I danced—'

'Yes, I heard you. But why there, Sylvie? Did he force you to go with him? What happened?'

She frowned, feeling confused.

'Yes, he was waiting for me, I think. I don't . . . I don't remember that bit too well. He took me up to Mooncliffe and . . . I'm not sure. I danced on the cliff-top for a while I think, and then I went on the white disc of rock.'

'I thought he must've been lying in wait for you. The bastard! I waited for ages in the woods, and then I wasted time looking all over the place trying to find you. I should've realised straight away he'd taken you up there. Was it awful for you?'

'Yes, it – no, it was fine. I don't know. I'm going there next month. I love dancing at Mooncliffe.'

'*What*? I thought you liked coming here with me and dancing with the hares.'

She wrinkled up her face, looking puzzled.

'Yes, I want to be with you, Yul. But . . . I love dancing at Mooncliffe for Magus.'

He stared at her in consternation. She didn't sound like herself at all.

'Sylvie you didn't dance on the stone. Don't you remember? You were standing very still and then you collapsed.'

'No, I think . . . I don't know. I can't remember. I love it there. I know that for sure. I think you're wrong, Yul. I was fine. I want to go there again.'

Yul shrugged, swallowing his hurt. He'd thought that moon-gazing up at Hare Stone with him was special to her. But if she preferred to be with Magus at Mooncliffe, he wouldn't make a fuss.

Her strangeness made their time together awkward and Yul couldn't shake off his disappointment. They watched the young leverets playing below them on the hill for some time, and lay on their backs amongst a patch of pale-blue harebells that grew in the grass, following the swallows arcing in the sky overhead. They could smell the delicious, sweet fragrance of honeysuckle wafting up from the hedgerow bordering the woods. It should have been idyllic; a rare chance to enjoy each other's company without being disturbed or overlooked. After their passion in the moonlight under the yew tree, they should have fallen into each other's arms.

But despite being acutely aware of their proximity, they were careful to avoid any contact. There was an uncomfortable constraint between them which neither knew how to banish.

Sylvie could see how much Yul had changed since Alwyn's departure. He'd lost the hunted look; he no longer jumped if taken by surprise, or constantly looked over his shoulder at every noise and movement. At one point his tunic had ridden up his back a little and she could see where the terrible lashes still marked him, the skin now mended. He'd carry the scars for the rest of his life, she was sure, but it was good to see he'd healed. He looked so well and she imagined his mother must be spoiling him at home. Sylvie could only guess at how the woman must've felt over the years, watching her husband crush her son so brutally at every opportunity. Yul's eyes and skin were clear and glowing and he'd had his hair cut so it no longer flowed onto his shoulders. The dark curls sprang round his face, glossy and soft. Sylvie wanted very much to run her fingers through them.

He could see a change in her too, but it wasn't for the better. She'd lost weight and looked more delicate than ever. Her face was sharper and her eyes different. He couldn't quite pinpoint what was wrong but knew she wasn't herself. She seemed brittle and nervous, as if she might crack at any moment.

He didn't know that Sylvie suffered from nightmares every night and awoke drenched in sweat with her heart pounding. In her dreams she'd frozen into stone and couldn't move, whilst she slowly died inside, her life force draining away. And Magus was in the dreams too. Sometimes he stood there laughing. Other times he lay at her feet groaning with pleasure. And the worst dream of all – once he stood very close, touching her, and she couldn't move away to stop him doing it. She'd told nobody about the nightmares. In the daylight she tried to forget them but the evidence of their damage was plain to see.

After a while they wandered further along the Dragon's Back ridgeway, both remembering the last time they were here escaping from Quarrycleave, and the time before that when Yul had ridden Nightwing. Recalling how happy they'd been together made them both feel sad now, for something had changed. Sylvie reached across and took his hand in hers, too shy to look at his face. He smiled and linked his fingers with hers, careful not to crush her bones. He longed to scoop her up and kiss away her strangeness until there was no awkwardness, only passion and that glorious feeling of being part of the same whole. Yul sighed and contented himself with the warmth of holding hands.

A little later on they were surprised to see a horse and cart approaching. As it drew nearer they recognised Tom at the reins. He pulled the cart to a halt.

'Blessings!' he called. ''Tis good to see you again, boy. And you, miss.'

'Blessings to you too, sir,' said Yul, automatically stroking the old cart-horse's long nose.

'Should you two be out together? I heard that's what all the fuss was about afore.'

'Yes, but Magus and Clip are both away. You won't tell on us, will you?' said Yul.

The old man chuckled.

'Not me. Anyway, I'd best be getting this lot back to the Village.'

'What have you got in there?' asked Sylvie, peering into the cart. She saw a pile of small rocks and shuddered. 'Have you been to Quarrycleave?'

'Aye, that's the one, and I seen Jackdaw there too. You won't know him, miss, but I reckon you do, Yul.'

'Oh yes.'

'Thought he'd been banished from Stonewylde. There's been talk in the Village but I didn't believe it till today. Never thought Magus'd bring Jackdaw back, not after what he done. Turns out he's up there working with a bunch of Outsiders who don't even speak our tongue. You must've known that Yul, but I expect you weren't to tell us. Whatever is Magus thinking of? I don't know … I don't like it.'

'What are these rocks for?' asked Sylvie. 'They're rather pretty, sparkling in the sun. Oh!'

She'd reached in to touch one but drew her hand back sharply.

'What's wrong? Did you cut yourself?' Yul took her hand but there was no mark on it.

'No,' she said, frowning. 'No, nothing like that. It just gave me a funny feeling.'

'Don't know what this lot's for,' said Tom. 'Magus just said to go to the quarry where they'd have it ready to collect. I've to take it to the stone-carvers in the Village. One of his new schemes I suppose. You still do stone-carving in the evening, Yul?'

'No, not since I worked at Quarrycleave,' Yul's tone was terse. 'It put me off stone.'

'Reckon it would, after what you went through. Anyway, 'tis good to see you looking so fit and healthy now, lad. Drop by the stables some time if you're up that way. I know old Nightwing would be pleased to see you.'

As soon as he'd moved on, Yul turned to Sylvie abruptly. He pulled back the sleeves of her blouse and stared at her wrists. The fading purple bruises still clearly encircled them. Yul looked her in the eye and she flinched from the blaze of his sudden fury.

'I noticed these when I thought you'd cut your hand,' he said tightly. 'What happened? Why are you bruised like this?'

She looked away, staring over the downs where the sky met the curve of the land. She shook her head.

'I think it . . . it was when I was struggling, I think. When I was trying to get into the woods to meet you.'

Yul swallowed hard and she felt him shaking. Reluctantly she met his eye again and recoiled from his expression. She'd never seen him so full of rage.

'And you *want* to be with him at the Moon Fullness? You're telling me he isn't making you to go with him against your will? This is proof, Sylvie! Proof that he's forced you into it.'

He almost spat the words at her.

'Please, Yul, stop being so angry. I don't know. I feel so confused. I didn't want to go with him. I fought him, I think, and he held on to me. This isn't as bad as it looks. I bruise very easily. I don't remember him actually hurting me, just holding on to me so I couldn't come to you. Please don't look at me like that. I can't bear it.'

'But *why* do you want to go to Mooncliffe again? I don't understand! Tell me, Sylvie. Explain it to me so I can try to make sense of it.'

But she shook her head and pulled away from him.

'It's just something I must do,' she said quietly. 'I don't understand it either. But I want to go there, Yul. You're upsetting me by going on about it and getting cross. It's between me and Magus and I don't want to talk about it anymore.'

Yul and Sylvie walked for some way that day, but the awkwardness between them remained as impenetrable as the boundary wall. Later when they came to say goodbye, Sylvie felt immensely sad. She still wanted nothing more than to be with Yul, but he was different with her now; angry and cold. She looked up at his sun-tanned face, his deep grey eyes as beautiful as ever, and had a horrible feeling she was losing his affection.

'When can we see each other again?' she asked diffidently. 'We can make the most of Magus and Clip both being off the estate, can't we?'

He shrugged and looked away. He felt uncomfortable with this different Sylvie. How could she prefer to be with Magus than him?

'Whenever you like, Sylvie. You know I'm always here. You know how I feel about you. And I'll still wait for you in the woods at the next Moon Fullness in case you change your mind.'

Her hesitant smile faltered at this.

'But Yul, I've already told you. I go to Mooncliffe now for the Moon Fullness. I love to dance on the moon stone for Magus.'

His eyes clouded with pain.

'If that's what you want, Sylvie, don't let me stop you. See you around.'

He walked off without looking back. Her eyes followed him, her heart like lump of stone. She was going to lose him and she didn't even know why.

5

Sylvie stood at the long sideboard which ran almost the full length of the cavernous Dining Hall. She surveyed the selection of breakfast dishes glumly and finally helped herself to a little scrambled egg and some apple juice. The servants bustled up and down the long tables with fresh toast and pots of tea, and Sylvie stood with her plate and glass looking around for somewhere quiet to sit. She still found it difficult to eat with so many people and so much noise, and normally preferred to have breakfast quietly alone in the cottage. This morning, however, Miranda had been particularly irritating and Sylvie had been desperate to escape.

She spotted a place by one of the long windows, where a group of people had just left, and started to make her way there. But her attention was diverted by Holly's braying voice and she glanced over to the area where a whole gang of Holly's friends sat. In their midst was a funny little man whom Sylvie had first noticed at the Summer Solstice. Unlike the other visitors, he hadn't left a week later and could be seen most days pottering about the Hall or sunning himself on the stone terrace outside. She'd heard his name was Professor Siskin.

'So are they all like you at Oxford?' demanded Holly loudly, biting at a whole sausage speared on her fork. Many of the adults, including the teachers, were away at the moment, and behaviour amongst the teenagers had deteriorated. The elderly man, a little odd-looking in his velvet jacket and bowtie, with long straggly white hair and half-moon glasses hanging on an ornate chain, peered owlishly at her, his faded blue eyes blinking.

'I'm sorry, my dear, I don't—'

'I'd thought of going to Oxford myself, but if all the teachers are like you I don't think I'll bother!'

The noisy group sniggered at this, and Sylvie frowned, still hesitating.

'No, my dear, I'm no longer a don,' twittered the professor, seemingly oblivious to her rudeness. 'I've long since retired, although I keep rooms there as a research fellow.'

'Don? Fellow? What are you on about?'

She rolled her eyes and tapped the side of her head, much to everyone's amusement.

'Titles, my dear, mere titles. What were you thinking of reading?'

'What? I'm not talking about reading! Are we even on the same planet?'

The professor gazed amicably at her as he chewed on his toast.

'Oxford, like many other universities, is a place of jargon. I apologise, my dear girl. One always assumes that everyone is au fait with the terminology. I wondered which subject you were thinking of studying.'

She frowned at him, annoyed that her needling was having no effect.

'I'm only fifteen. I have no idea. But nothing that you teach, I'm sure of that!'

Sylvie could stand it no longer. She took her plate over to the old man and sat next to him at the long table, opposite Holly and her crowd. Her cheeks burned with indignation, giving her the courage to face Holly.

'Excuse me, may I sit here?'

'Ooh look, it's little Miss Sparkle herself, the girl with the fairy dress and the big ambitions.'

'I wonder what Magus would think of your rudeness towards the visitors, Holly?'

'You're not still after Magus are you? You've got another year to wait before he'll even look at you. Running to him telling tales won't change a thing – he won't touch you till you're sixteen.'

'Don't be ridiculous! You're just trying to change the subject. You know I really might tell him how you spoke to the professor just now. I'm sure he'd want to know.'

'Oh yeah? Go on then, I dare you! I've done nothing wrong. I was only trying to make polite conversation with this silly old fool. It's not my fault he's completely gaga!'

'You really remind me of the horrible kids I knew at school in London,' said Sylvie stiffly. 'I thought Hallfolk were above this sort of rude behaviour and treated their elders respectfully.'

'What would you know, you silly cow? You're a newcomer here, an Outsider. What do you know about Hallfolk? You go ahead and tell Magus and we'll all deny it, won't we? Come on, let's leave her to it. She seems to want the old boy's company. I guess she really is interested in older men.'

Holly stood up noisily, leaving her breakfast things littered all over the table. The others followed her like sheep, subdued by the thought of Sylvie telling Magus. She gazed down at her cold scrambled egg and grimaced; this incident wouldn't help her popularity but she felt so ashamed of Holly's bad manners towards the elderly man.

'That was kind of you, my dear,' he murmured, popping a cube of toast laden with marmalade into his mouth. 'She was a little strident.'

'She's a disgrace! I'm sorry she was so cheeky to you. I'm Sylvie, by the way,' she said, 'and I'm quite new here so I'm afraid I don't know anything about you. Do you come every year for the Solstice?'

'Oh yes, without fail!' he beamed. 'Just for the six weeks until Lammas, that's all our present magus will permit. But I'm grateful for that much and I've been doing it for many years now, ever since he took charge. Before that I used to spend the whole summer at Stonewylde, right up until the Autumn Equinox. But I understand that he needs to regulate the amount of Hallfolk living here at any one time. Stonewylde would become another

St Petersburg in the last days of the Tsar if all the aged retainers were permitted to cling on.'

'I see,' said Sylvie, picking at the congealed egg. 'And have you had a nice holiday this year? We've had wonderful weather.'

'Oh I don't come here for a holiday, my dear. No, no. I'm researching, you see, researching the history of Stonewylde. Writing a book in fact. Fascinating subject. Never been done before. Sol has kindly given me access to all the manuscripts and diaries, all the artefacts and letters. Whether or not he'll ever allow me to publish is another matter. In fact I doubt it very much, given the ... er ... the nature of Stonewylde, the insularity of the culture here. But we could probably publish an account for the Hallfolk to read and that would suffice. For me, at least, it's the academic journey that's so pleasurable. Whether or not there's a published book at the end is almost irrelevant.'

He stopped for breath and popped another cube of toast into his mouth, his pale-blue eyes twinkling at her. She smiled, wondering how she could now extricate herself, for there was clearly no stopping him now he was in full flow. But she was also interested. She guessed this was the person Buzz had once mentioned; the one who'd taught some of the students about how Stonewylde had remained intact over the centuries. It would be fascinating to learn about the history of the estate, and she told him so. He patted her hand and beamed at her again.

'You are a lovely girl. New to Stonewylde you say? Indeed, I would've remembered if you'd been before. Even amongst these hordes of youngsters, all so attractive and blond, you are somewhat striking. Such unusual beauty, and yet so strangely familiar. You must tell me your genealogy some time. Would you care to accompany me down to the Village Green this afternoon, my dear? It's Sunday and there should be cricket practice for the Villagers. I always enjoy watching that. So delightfully bucolic and traditional.'

She was just about to decline when it occurred to her that Yul might be there, so she agreed to meet him later in the porch.

The old professor hobbled slowly up the great staircase. He

headed for a locked room in a distant wing, where Stonewylde's oldest and most valuable documents were stored. He was in the middle of some interesting reading in the library but had to check this hunch first. He was sure there was a silver-framed photograph there, in that locked archive room, of Clip and Sol's mother Raven. He wanted to see if his memory was playing tricks on him. Or whether the wild, moongazy girl who'd wrought such havoc between his brothers all those years ago really had returned, in a new incarnation, to Stonewylde.

After lunch, Sylvie sat in the vast entrance porch waiting for the professor. The porch was bigger than the average family sitting room, and had an ancient vaulted roof. Tiny stained-glass windows were set all along the thick walls, and it was lined with stone benches big enough to seat two football teams. A jumble of riding boots, umbrellas and wellingtons lay under the benches. Being summer, the heavy oak front door to the entrance hall stood open, its thick wood bound and riveted with black wrought-iron. Opposite this, through the pointed stone arch, the gravel drive with its flanking lines of beeches glowed brightly in the hot afternoon sunshine, but it was cool and shady in the porch.

Sylvie gazed down at the floor's massive flagstones, worn down and shiny in the areas of heaviest tread. She imagined the feet that must have walked across those stones over the centuries. Hundreds upon hundreds of pairs of feet, slowly wearing away the stone. She thought of Professor Siskin's research and how she'd love to read what he'd written. Stonewylde's history must be unique. What other community had cut itself off from global and national influences in such a way and managed to keep itself completely intact?

She was awoken from her reveries by the arrival of the little professor, complete with panama hat and silver-knobbed walking stick. They set off down the long gravel drive leading onto the track to the Village, but their progress was slow and Sylvie wondered how they'd make it back up again. Siskin seemed to sense her concern and reassured her that Tom from the stables was sending down a pony and trap later on to collect him.

'I've just met your mother, I believe,' he told her. 'Fine young woman, hair the colour of chestnuts. English teacher, she tells me. A welcome addition to the gene pool, I've no doubt. But your father – who is he?'

Sylvie was a little thrown by his directness but replied with the same vague response she always gave. The old man shook his snowy head.

'You know, don't you, that you are Hallfolk?' he said. 'Whoever fathered you was beyond doubt one of us, and a close relation too. This morning I managed to locate our one photo of Raven, Sol's and Clip's mother. You're almost identical to her. The resemblance is quite extraordinary. Everyone here is inter-related and Raven must have had a great deal of relations, one of whom was undoubtedly your father.'

'I've been told before that I look like her,' Sylvie said. 'Mother Heggy thinks so, in particular.'

'Ah yes, the venerable Wise Woman. Haven't seen her for years, poor creature. Not too keen on us Hallfolk, especially not my generation. Understandable too, when one considers how she was treated.'

'So what's your relationship to Magus, Professor?' asked Sylvie.

'I'm his half-uncle, if there is such a thing. His father, Elm, was my half-brother. As was Clip's father, Basil. Both were older than me. Elm, Basil and I all shared the same father – the magus as was then, of course – but different mothers. Our father was . . . liberal with his favours, and fathered many children. Unlike our present magus, who's far more careful and selective about sowing his seed. My half-brother Basil was the eldest, and the one entitled to inherit Stonewylde. The rest of us were just excess siblings. Elm stepped in after Basil's death, and took over until Clip was old enough to don the mantle of magus. But he never did, and one can't really blame him given the weight of the responsibility and what he was up against. Sol was ever the dominant one, just like his father before him. It's fascinating to trace the family lines.

78

Not just Hallfolk but the Villagers too. So much inter-breeding, which is why Sol is keen to bring in new blood. He strongly encourages Hallfolk to go Outside for their partners. It's also why he's brought your mother here, I would imagine. As I said before, an addition to the gene pool.'

Sylvie was quiet at this. It seemed so cold and calculating, but she knew that Magus could be like that. The professor glanced at her, his wispy head in its straw hat bobbing about just like a little bird's.

'Not the only reason, of course. I should think that you, my dear, played a major factor in his making such an unusual invitation too. As the old saying goes – a moongazy girl is hard to find.'

Sylvie stared at him in amazement.

'How do you know I'm moongazy? Magus didn't even know about it when he invited us. He only found out recently himself.'

The old man smiled.

'It's your eyes, Sylvie. I remember Raven well, and you have exactly the same moonstone eyes. That girl drove those two half-brothers of mine wild with longing for her. There was something about her – a flash of quicksilver, a coolness of heart – that would not be warmed by their passion. They were both utterly obsessed with her to the exclusion of all else. I wonder if you'll have the same effect on men as you grow older?'

'I do hope not!' said Sylvie in horror. 'I'm not like that at all.'

Professor Siskin chuckled.

'Ah, but neither was Raven. She wasn't interested in the slightest, which made her even more desirable. All she wanted was to moondance, roam Stonewylde wild and free, and learn the craft with Mother Heggy. But anyway, that's another story which I'll tell you some other time. Don't let it trouble you, Sylvie. You may look uncannily like the poor girl but I'm sure you're very different inside. Raven was a strange little creature and you seem perfectly sane.'

They'd finally left the gravel drive and turned onto the track towards the Village. Progress was very slow but Professor Siskin shuffled along amiably, chattering like a bird and only pausing to catch his breath. After some time the trees thinned a little and the first buildings, their wattle and daub walls patterned with heavy beams, came into sight. Sylvie loved being down here in the heart of the community. The Hall was beautiful of course, but had a totally different atmosphere to the Village. She smiled as she saw the plump thatched roofs nestling in the distance and smoke curling from the chimneys. Even in the height of summer the ranges must be lit for cooking. The track became a cobbled way and a group of wild-haired children ran past chasing an errant chicken, a terrier yapping excitedly at their heels.

'I really love the Village,' she sighed. 'There's something so safe about it.'

'It's terribly old, you know,' twittered Siskin. 'We're talking Bronze Age, with evidence. There's been jewellery, a dagger, belt buckles and such-like dug up in the Village gardens. In fact I have a theory that the Village was here before the Stone Circle was built, which would make it Neolithic in origin. But there's no proof of that. Never been a proper archaeological dig here. Of course the river was a big factor in making it a habitable site, and the meadows so fertile, with woods too. Near the sea, but not exposed.'

'I don't understand. Why would the Village have been here before the Stone Circle? What makes you think that?'

'I've spent a lifetime researching that period, early peoples and their religions. The Village Green – this one at least – is the clue. A circular clearing in ancient woodlands was the very earliest form of temple. Woodland deities, with the tribe worshipping at the very trees themselves. The circular cleared area inside, allowing them to live and worship in the same place. Life and religion interchangeable to those people.'

Sylvie looked at him in puzzlement, finding his speech hard to understand. He spoke so fast and missed out many words in his sentences, assuming a level of knowledge in his listener that was often misplaced.

'Are you saying that the Village Green is what's left of an ancient woodland temple?'

'Indeed, indeed!' he cried excitedly, his small pointed shoes skipping on the cobbles in a shuffle of enthusiasm. 'Most people would see the Green and imagine maybe a meadow, with the trees planted around it for protection. But in fact the trees were there first, and the Green is an artificial clearing made in the middle. Not, of course, these trees themselves ... although the yew could be. Did you know the yew tree regenerates itself? Grows from the original root, out of the old bole and gives birth to a new bole? But the tree itself is as old as the root, and there's one in Perthshire, up in Scotland which is estimated to be about nine thousand years old. Many of the yews in churchyards are well over a thousand years old, often much older than the churches themselves ... most of which are built over pagan places of worship anyway.'

He paused for a second to breathe, beaming at Sylvie, then continued his rapid chatter.

'I don't know about our yew by the Village Green because I'm no tree expert, but it really could be thousands of years old. Especially given that Stonewylde didn't hack down every yew in sight to make longbows during the Middle Ages, or the Early Modern Period as we call it now. Far too sacred a tree for that, and anyway, even back then the Stonewylders didn't get involved in every battle and war raging in the Outside World. We've always kept ourselves apart. And of course, whilst we're talking trees, there's the funerary yew too, another ancient tree ...'

Sylvie stared at him in fascination. What an interesting man he was. She remembered her kiss with Yul under the yew tree. Knowing that the tree could be thousands of years old made that first kiss even more special. They'd finally arrived at the Green and saw a large group of Village men spread out in the familiar pattern of cricket.

'Let us sit outside the Barn for a while and watch,' suggested Siskin. He led the way around the grass to one of the wooden seats sheltered by the flint and stone walls of the Great Barn.

Sylvie sat down next to him and looked across at the figures on the grass. Her heart jumped when she recognised Yul – his very dark hair always made him stand out. He stood with a group of men, part of the batting team, and she noticed how much he'd grown. He no longer seemed a boy amongst men but was virtually one of them; in fact he was taller than some of them. She noted the brown skin of his arms, face and throat, the length of his powerful legs, and shivered. Siskin said nothing but smiled. All around them the Villagers relaxed in the warmth and peace of a Sunday afternoon.

'The other clue, of course, is the Village pub. Jack in the Green.'

'That must refer to the Village Green?' said Sylvie, eyes fixed on Yul as he swung his muscular arms in mock bowls. He hadn't noticed them yet and was entirely unselfconscious.

'Strangely enough, it doesn't,' said Siskin, 'although it would seem to. Jack in the Green is a medieval term referring to a May Day figure, the one who was encased in a green frame of shrubbery and boughs. The sacrificial male at the centre of the fertility dances and rites.'

'Oh yes! We saw him at Beltane, in the middle of the men's dance with sticks. He had his face blackened and he ended up completely trapped in a cage.'

'Indeed!' chuckled the old man. 'I wish I were still able to visit and see that lovely ancient custom in May. But in fact, you know, the Beltane reference was merely a later interpretation of something far, far older – namely the Green Man. Jack in the Green, therefore, actually refers to the Green Man himself. I'm sure you know that he is literally the embodiment of the spirit of the woods, the woodland deity – Lord of the Greenwood. Which is what this Village Green is all about – an ancient woodland temple!'

He beamed at her triumphantly and she smiled back, nodding her understanding. It was interesting, of course, but nowhere near as interesting as watching Yul in action. He was batting now and Sylvie, though she knew little about cricket, could see that he was good. He swung the bat strongly, whacking the ball with incredible power and precision. When he ran it was beautiful to watch; so fast and well co-ordinated. His team cheered him on as he ran, taking a risk, and made it to the crease just in time. Sylvie sighed.

'So who is he, that fine young man with the dark curls?'

Sylvie looked across at the professor sharply but he twinkled at her encouragingly.

'His name's Yul. He's a woodsman.'

'Of course, of course. A woodsman. What else could he be? And he feels the same about you?'

She nodded, a sudden lump in her throat.

'At least, he did. I'm not sure – something's gone wrong between us.'

Siskin patted her hand kindly.

'The course of true love never runs smooth. But it will be alright, my dear. Nobody could resist a moongazy girl like you. Look at him run! Poetry in motion.'

The Village Green was becoming quite busy as more people turned out to watch the cricket practice. Youngsters walked arm-in-arm around the edge of the Green, ignoring the game, whilst children raced about happily, many with wet hair. This puzzled Sylvie at first until she remembered the beach; they must have been swimming there or perhaps in the river. She realised that apart from the evening when she'd wandered down looking for Yul, this was the first time she'd been here for a normal visit without the Hallfolk as part of some festival or organised event. She felt, as she'd done when she'd blundered into the Barn that evening, conspicuous with her Hallfolk hair. Everyone else here today, apart from the professor, was Villager.

'Come, shall we have a glass of cider at the Jack in the Green?'

He rose creakily and Sylvie dragged her eyes away from Yul, still batting skilfully and running superbly. She walked slowly by the elderly man's side as they ambled around the edge of the Green towards the pub. Sylvie had never really looked at it closely before but noticed now that it was a beautifully maintained, very old building made of the same stone and flint as the Barn, with a lopsided slate roof. The building was long and low, the upper-floor windows tucked right up under the eaves. The entrance, too, was very low with a massive piece of ancient wood, practically a whole tree, forming the lintel.

There were benches outside where men sat watching the cricket and drinking from tankards. Professor Siskin raised his hat to them politely and they all nodded back, some touching their forelocks in time-honoured fashion. Sylvie nodded shyly, unsure of the protocol, and then looked up at the sign swinging on a post. It did indeed depict a Green Man; leaves sprouting around his green face, his hair a halo of foliage. It reminded her of Magus at Beltane with his face paint and leafy head-dress.

Sylvie and the professor entered the cool, dark pub and she looked around with interest. It was large and yet snug inside due to the low, heavily beamed ceiling. There was a long counter, its wood black and smooth with age. Tankards hung on hooks all along the walls and great barrels lined the space behind the bar. There were many dark bottles too and several smaller casks. The place smelt strongly of cider and mead. Small tables and stools filled the open area, and around the walls were benches and high-backed pews. The uneven floor was flagstoned and brought to mind the floor in the porch that she'd been studying earlier, for it too was very worn down in places. She could feel the age of this building, imagining that even before the present walls were built an older structure must have stood here.

They went to the empty bar and a burly Villager stood up from his dice game with a group of old men.

'Good afternoon, George,' said the professor, removing his hat from his damp head and fanning himself with it.

'Afternoon, sir,' growled the man. 'The usual?'

He moved round behind the counter and served Siskin with a tankard of cider and Sylvie a small glass of apple mead. They sat in a window seat and Siskin sipped at his cider appreciatively, smacking his lips.

'Nothing beats the taste of this,' he mused. 'I have imbibed the very best the Outside World has to offer, but you can keep your vintage wines and fine champagnes. Give me Stonewylde cider any day! Do you like the apple mead, Sylvie?'

'It's delicious! I didn't realise mead came in different flavours. I've only had the ceremony mead and it's nothing like this.'

He chuckled.

'Ceremony mead is something very different, my dear. Magus adds a special ingredient to that brew. But honey mead is one of the staple drinks here. You must visit the Meadery and see how it's made. And the Cider House too. The flavour of the mead depends on where the bees originally collected the nectar to make their honey – be it apple blossom, willow, clover, rose-petal or whatever. Then other fruits and flavours can be added before or after fermentation. So your mead is made with apple-blossom honey and mixed with some vintage cider, which gives it that lovely heady, apple taste. You'd like the cherry mead too, I expect, and blackberry. They're all delicious. I'll tell Sol of your new taste for mead and I'm sure he'd be delighted to bring some bottles up from the cellar for you to try.'

Sylvie felt very grown up but a little awkward, sitting in a pub. She wasn't sure if she should be here at all, but Professor Siskin assured her that nobody would mind on a Sunday afternoon. She was also fretting that Yul was outside and she wasn't there to watch him. Her dilemma was overcome when suddenly the two cricket teams burst in through the door and crowded around the bar, clamouring for cider. Sylvie immediately picked out Yul. He was handed a brimming tankard and stepped back from the bar to give the others room. He was very surprised to see Sylvie sitting in the window seat drinking mead and came over straight away, smiling as if his face would split in two.

'What are you doing here?' he asked, desperately trying to quench his thirst and be sociable at the same time. Sylvie watched his throat in fascination as he swallowed the cool cider in long gulps.

'We were watching the cricket practice and Professor Siskin here was explaining some of the history of Stonewylde to me,' she said. 'Come and chat with us.'

She moved up on the pew so Yul could sit next to her, and smelt him as soon as he got close. He was very hot and had been running fast; he smelt of fresh male sweat. The aroma made her feel quite weak with an almost animal recognition. She saw the beads of sweat on his forehead and upper lip, the way his dark curls clung damply to his flushed face. He seemed so much bigger next to her. She felt again that somersault of longing in the pit of her stomach, and was shocked by the intensity of her feelings. They alarmed her, belonging to another phase of their relationship for which she wasn't yet ready. She took a deep breath and tried to control the drumming of her heart.

'How do you do, Yul,' said Siskin. 'I hear you're a woodsman. No wonder you're so fit and healthy. And I remember now! You were the Herald of the Dawn at the Solstice. And a very fine job you made of it, I recall.'

Yul smiled at him politely, accepting the compliments but not accustomed to making small talk with Hallfolk. He wished the old man would clear off so he could have Sylvie to himself. She was still looking a little delicate, but nowhere near as fragile as the last time he'd seen her. He wondered if her recovery had anything to do with the fact that Magus was away at the moment.

'I didn't know you played cricket,' said Sylvie, smiling at him. Sitting so close, she was very aware of the heat he was giving off as his body cooled from such hard exercise in the hot July afternoon.

'Oh yes, I love cricket! But this is the first year I've played with the men and not in a boys' team. We're coming up to the big match at Lammas and I'm really hoping to be chosen for the Village team. We play against the Hallfolk. See Edward over there?'

He pointed across the pub to an enormous man with the stature of a mighty oak tree, who was busy downing a pint of cider.

'He's the captain and it's up to him. But he's pleased with the way I played today, so I've a chance.'

He finished his drink and stood up, noticing the other men

beginning to make their way to the door. He brushed Sylvie's shoulder longingly with his fingertips when he was sure Siskin wasn't looking, towering above her and staring deep into her eyes. She felt his love in that gentle touch. Her heart leapt as she was pulled into the intensity of his burning grey gaze. She poured her love back to him and hoped he read her message as clearly. His lips mouthed a tiny kiss and then he was gone, and the pub was suddenly empty around them.

'What a charming young man,' murmured Siskin. 'I can quite understand your attachment to him.'

Sylvie sighed, wishing Yul could've stayed longer. The sight and smell of him today had brought everything flooding back. Without him she was only half of what she was destined to be. Her heart ached for him. Why had they wasted their day up on Dragon's Back? It could have been perfect.

'Please don't mention it to Magus,' she said quietly. 'He's forbidden us to see each other and he's really got it in for Yul.'

'That doesn't surprise me,' chuckled Siskin. 'He has serious competition there and he's not the sort of man to take kindly to that. Now then, Sylvie, we ought to be leaving as well. Tom will be arriving to collect us soon. But before we go I want to show you something.'

They stood up and Siskin took her over to one of the back walls. Inlaid amongst the huge blocks of stone was a massive slice of wood. It was almost circular, well over a metre in diameter and clearly the complete cross-section of a once enormous tree trunk. Like the counter it was black and shiny with age, but Sylvie saw that it had been carved upon. It was dark at the back of the pub and she found it difficult to see exactly what was carved on the wood. She touched it gently with her fingertips and began to trace out the shapes – mostly leaves.

'Can you feel it, Sylvie? It's a Green Man, a Jack in the Green, a Lord of the Greenwood. Feel the face and the foliage radiating from it. And there's writing too, carved all around the edge of the circle. Can you see it?'

She bent and looked carefully, making out the face and some

letters, although she couldn't read what they said.

'It's written in Old English. Not much writing survives from that period for few people could write. And apart from stone there wasn't much to write on. That's why this yew tree bole is so unique. Translated, it reads, *"When the Green Man returns to this place, all will prosper and thrive"*. I've always felt it to be some kind of prophecy, a message from our ancestors.'

Sylvie felt a shiver trickle down her back at the feel of the wood beneath her fingertips. It was so ancient. All those hundreds of years ago, someone at Stonewylde had gone to such trouble to carve this message.

'Stonewylde is still waiting for its Green Man to return,' mused Siskin as he led Sylvie out into the bright, hot afternoon. 'Maybe then all will be right with the world.'

They blinked in the almost blinding sunlight outside and looked up the track, but there was no sign yet of Tom with the pony and cart. They wandered over to a great beech tree and stood in its cool shade.

'Are these trees really the descendants of the ancient ones?' Sylvie asked.

'More than likely, my dear. The people of Stonewylde would've collected the seeds and grown saplings, then eventually replaced the old trees as they died. Except for the yew, as I said, which reinvigorates itself in the most extraordinary, phoenix-like fashion. That splendid specimen over there could well be the original tree from the woodland temple. There could've been a woodhenge here too. A great circle of tree trunks erected into post holes, with lintels joining the uprights together.'

'Like Stonehenge?'

'That's right. A henge is simply an enclosed circular structure. Beyond doubt there would've been one here before the Stone Circle was built, for wood henges preceded stone ones. I've begged Magus to let me organise a dig, but he refuses. He doesn't want any Outsiders here, putting the place on the map, and a dig would certainly do that. There are many important archae-ological sites at Stonewylde, you see. The place is utterly unique and we'd be over-run by the media if the Outside World were to learn of what we have here. So until there are trained Hallfolk archaeologists, we'll have to wait to get our proof of a wood henge.'

Professor Siskin removed a large white handkerchief from his pocket and mopped his brow, adjusting his panama hat. He smiled kindly at Sylvie and patted her arm.

'I would dearly love to know if I'm right – just a small excavation would suffice. There must be a wealth of artefacts and evidence buried beneath our feet. But it's merely a dream and maybe Magus is right. He usually is in his decision-making where it concerns the care and protection of the community. One shouldn't desecrate a sacred place out of idle curiosity, or jeopardise Stonewylde's community to make an archaeological discovery. Remember this, though, Sylvie: whenever you're on this Green or under these trees, you are in a place of ancient worship and potent magic. You are in a place where the spirit of the Green Man is at its strongest.'

6

'Oh just look at this bed!' exclaimed Miranda, her eyes shining with excitement. Sylvie groaned, knowing full well what was going through her mother's mind as she stroked the carved wood of the antique four-poster. Harold and another servant dumped the last of their belongings in the sitting room and trooped off down the corridor. The suite of rooms was at the end of a long Tudor wing, which also housed a beautiful panelled gallery and several inter-connecting rooms that were kept for visitors, so remained empty for much of the year.

'And this room will be perfect for the baby,' said Miranda ecstatically, surveying the small adjoining room with pleasure. 'I wonder if Magus will mind if I re-decorate it? I've already chosen the new linen and some of the women have promised to help me embroider the crib covers. Apparently the Imbolc colours are white, silver and green, and it'd be nice to pick that up on the walls in here, maybe the curtains too. Though if the baby's born nearer the Spring Equinox, the colours are different of course. Yellows, I believe. Mmn ... I'm never sure about yellow. What do you think, darling?'

'Whatever you think best,' mumbled Sylvie, not caring one bit about the baby or its bedroom and thoroughly bored with Miranda's endless ramblings on the subject. She had a splitting headache and knew it was due to her terrible nightmares, which had resumed on Magus' return. The moon was growing fatter in the sky each night, and as the Hay Moon of July loomed closer,

Sylvie found her appetite waning and her fear increasing.

'Please don't sulk, Sylvie,' said Miranda. 'I know you liked Woodland Cottage but these rooms are lovely, and it'll be so much more convenient living here at the Hall.'

'If you say so.'

'This is such an exciting time for us, darling. Don't spoil it by being moody and difficult. Woodland Cottage was far too isolated and we weren't really part of the Hallfolk community there.'

'But I miss the privacy. I liked it being isolated. Everyone's on top of each other here.'

'Hardly! This is a real stately home, Sylvie, and it's enormous. Did you ever imagine, when we lived in that awful, cramped high-rise flat, that we'd end up somewhere like this? Not only do we have our own suite of rooms, with a private bathroom and sitting room, but we also have the whole of the Hall with all its facilities! I still find it hard to believe.'

'Well I preferred Woodland Cottage. I wish you'd let me stay there, Mum.'

'Don't be silly. You're far too young to live on your own and I enjoy your company, even if you don't like mine any more. And I'll need you around to help as my pregnancy progresses, and even more next February when the baby comes.'

'Great,' muttered Sylvie, wandering back through the sitting room and into her own new bedroom. Despite her misgivings, she had to admit that it was lovely. Situated at the very end of the wing, it was light and airy for a Tudor room with diamond-paned windows all around and her own fireplace. As well as her bed and dressing table, there was a bookcase, desk and chair and an armchair too, so she could shut herself away with her homework and reading and not have to be with Miranda and the baby in the sitting room all the time. This would give her a little privacy at least.

The best part of all, however, was the little pointed door in the corner which led straight onto a tiny stone staircase. This wound down to a heavy oak door at the bottom which opened straight into the garden, and it was this access to freedom that pleased Sylvie more than anything. Without it she would've felt completely trapped at the end of the long wing at the back of the Hall.

'Just cheer up and be grateful,' said Miranda briskly from the sitting room. 'You're a very lucky girl, and don't you forget it. Now stop moping about and come and help me unpack. I want our rooms to be cosy and inviting.'

'I wonder why?' said Sylvie under her breath.

Clip returned from his trip to Ireland and as Lammas drew nearer, the Hall began to fill once more with visitors. Uncomfortable facing so many people at every meal, Sylvie wished she could retreat from the bustle and noise and the obligation to be sociable at all times of day. She missed the peace of Woodland Cottage with a passion. Holly and her group continued to make her life unpleasant at every opportunity. Sylvie found she had no fight in her and avoided them wherever possible. Buzz was due back soon and she dreaded his return too, which could only make Holly worse. She longed to see Yul, but now she was living in the Hall there was little chance of that. As the end of the month drew closer, she became quieter during the day and ever more disturbed at night, her nightmares growing steadily worse.

Just before the full moon Sylvie had the worst nightmare yet. She woke in the middle of the night in the strange bedroom in a blind panic. Moonlight poured in through the latticed panes and onto her bed, shining straight into her eyes. She sat bolt upright, her body trembling and heart pounding with terror. For a moment she couldn't think where she was and stared wildly around the room. The shadows on the walls seemed sinister, but gradually, as the dream faded slightly, Sylvie remembered where she was.

She drank some water and lay down again, damp with sweat and too scared to go back to sleep in case the nightmare returned. It was all the more terrifying because she couldn't quite recall it properly. What had happened? She vaguely remembered being buried alive on the moon rock, unable to move or even breathe as a great weight of stones pressed down on her, crushing her lungs. And there was something else. Something sucking, leeching the life from her, a great snake with gaping jaws. It punctured her skin and coiled around her as it drank the moon magic from her, drained her dry until she was just an empty husk. But above it all, swimming in and out of focus, was Magus' face. His chiselled features were hard, as if carved from stone themselves. His silvery-blond hair glinted in the moonlight; his dark eyes glittered, cruel and implacable. He watched her suffering, her feeble struggle to breathe, and just stood and looked at her with a greedy smile on his face.

In the morning Sylvie awoke feeling exhausted. She didn't want to get up and face the world, and was overwhelmed with a sensation of dread. She knew that tomorrow was the full moon and thought desperately of Yul. He'd said he'd wait for her in the woods. More than anything she wanted to be with him, protected and loved, dancing around the Hare Stone in honour of the Bright Lady. But every time she thought about it a fog rolled over her, blocking everything out. All she could think of was her compulsion to visit Mooncliffe and give her magic to Magus. It was why she'd been brought to Stonewylde and she must do it without question. There was no doubt about it in her mind – only a deep sense of trepidation.

Sylvie dragged herself out of bed, gazing through the windows at the bright gardens below. It was a glorious day, full of bird song and blue skies, but her heart was heavy. She showered and got ready to go down to breakfast. Food was the last thing she wanted, but she knew she must look after her health. Miranda was still in bed feeling queasy with morning sickness as Sylvie left their rooms. She stumbled down the long gallery of the Tudor wing towards the upper landing, subdued and full of foreboding.

The first person she saw was Magus, glowing with vitality after an energetic early morning ride. He was making his way up the wide staircase as she was descending. His long legs in tight jodhpurs and highly polished boots took the stairs two at a time and he stopped on the stair below her as they met, still taller than she was. Sunlight shone through the great stained-glass window behind her, falling full onto his handsome face and bathing his silvery hair with royal red and purple light. His skin was golden from the summer sun and his dark eyes danced with energy; he looked glorious.

'Good morning, my moongazy girl!' he said, his voice smooth as mead. He couldn't see her face clearly for the light was streaming in behind her, throwing her into silhouette. He did notice that she seemed taller; no longer a young girl but now coltish and leggy. When had that happened? She was growing up so fast. He reached forward and took both her hands in his, surprised to find her trembling violently.

'Sylvie, what's the matter?'

He took a step up to the same level and turned her so the coloured light from the stained glass washed her face. The effect was quite uncanny; a masque of blue light fell onto her ashen skin and she seemed to go cold before him. He saw the strain and fear in her eyes, the way her lips quivered.

'What's wrong, Sylvie?' he asked softly. 'What's frightened you?'

She shook her head silently, unable to articulate her fears, her pale grey eyes enormous and pleading. Magus cocked his head, frowning at her.

'Has anyone hurt you? Upset you?'

'No,' she said. 'It's nothing, really. Just ... I had a dream. A nightmare.'

He stared at her, watching the expressions chasing over her face.

'Yes?'

'There were stones, rocks everywhere, crushing and suffocating me. It was horrible.'

He stroked her cheek gently.

'Just a dream, Sylvie. Forget it and it'll fade. Look outside – it's a beautiful day. Go for a walk and chase the darkness away. And you know it's the full moon tomorrow night? I've come back from London especially for you. You remember why?'

Her face clouded over immediately, like a shadow passing across her.

'You've come to take me to Mooncliffe,' she whispered. 'I want to dance on the stone for you.'

He smiled at her and bent to kiss the top of her head.

'And so you shall. I've been looking forward to it all month. See you later, Sylvie. Forget your nightmare. I'll never let anything hurt you.'

He patted her arm and bounded up the stairs, heading for his rooms. He needed a shower after his hard ride on the spirited Nightwing. Sylvie continued down the stairs feeling close to tears but not sure why. The hall below was full of people moving around, heading into or out of breakfast in the Dining Hall. Their loud voices and the greasy smell of food were overwhelming, and Sylvie felt sick and panicky. Rainbow stood at the foot of the stairs, her hand idly stroking the carved newel as she watched Sylvie intently with bright, sea-blue eyes. Sylvie found that her little appetite had now gone completely. Ignoring Rainbow's speculative look, she hurried outside into the balmy morning to find some solace.

Sylvie wandered around the grounds of the Hall gazing up at the great trees in their full July robes, their greenery at its thickest and best. She thought of the woodland nearby where Yul would now be working. She longed to go and find him, craving his company and security. She hadn't seen him since the cricket practice on the Village Green, when she'd felt that maybe things would be alright between them after all. But she had no idea where in all those acres of woodland he'd be, and she felt too listless and downcast to walk far today.

Instead Sylvie made her way to a beautiful sunken garden she'd recently discovered around the side of the Hall. Climbing down the uneven stone steps, she sat on a lichened bench carved into the rock walls and tried to let go of her tension. The secret garden was lined with dark grey stone, furred with emerald green moss. Every flower that bloomed down here was white: roses, lilies, jasmine, alyssum, clematis, marguerites, asters and even white snap-dragons. Great lush green plants and ferns offset the whiteness, giving the garden an exotic and luxuriant feel.

The scent of roses and jasmine and the soothing sound of water trickling from a mossy frog's head fountain in the wall caressed Sylvie's senses as she closed her eyes. She soaked up the warmth and languid calm and sighed deeply. Bees hummed drowsily in the somnolent peace. She tried to cast off the heavy sense of oppression that blanketed her mind, making her want to cry. The sunken garden was too beautiful for unhappiness.

'May I join you, my dear? With apologies for disturbing your reveries.'

It was Professor Siskin, who picked his way carefully down the mossy steps and into the warm enclosed garden. He raised his panama in greeting and lowered himself onto the stone bench next to her, gnarled hands resting on his ornate walking stick. He too closed his eyes in appreciation of the fragrance and heat.

'Ah, that scent! As one gets older, one better appreciates the simple pleasures in life. The Earth Mother is indeed bountiful with her favours. Blessed be!'

Sylvie sat in silence, still close to tears but pleased of his company. She felt an affinity with the elderly man and liked the way he'd spoken to Yul in the Jack in the Green. He hadn't shown the usual Hallfolk condescension, nor the automatic superiority they claimed as their prerogative. Yet given his close lineage to the old magus, Professor Siskin had more right than most to lord it over others.

'Are you feeling a little fragile, my dear? I noticed your absence at breakfast.'

She nodded and he patted her hand.

'Sol has that effect on some people. I don't know what's going on, Sylvie, but I would warn you to be very careful. To be on your guard.'

She turned and looked at him but he stared ahead, gazing at the white velvety roses.

'I don't understand, Professor. What should I be on my guard against?'

'I'm afraid I don't know. I wish I could help you but, sadly, I shall soon be leaving to return to Oxford. Lammas approaches and afterwards I shall have outstayed my welcome for another year.'

He glanced at her pale face for a moment, entirely in keeping in this hidden sanctuary of white petals and fragrance.

'But . . . Sylvie my dear, there is something in the air. I can feel it. And I know Sol of old.'

'Has he ever done anything to you?'

The old man shook his head, refusing to be drawn.

'That's all in the past now. But I watched him grow up. I saw him as a boy and then as an adolescent. He was . . . powerful, even then. He's always enjoyed exercising control and making others obey him, but when he was younger he was far less subtle about it. His father, my half-brother, was a nasty piece of work. Hardly a good role model for a young boy growing up and in need of guidance. Especially a motherless boy lacking any gentle, maternal influence or affection.'

'But Clip isn't like that, is he? He's always struck me as being far softer and kinder than Magus.'

'That's true. They do have different fathers, remember. Clip's father Basil was hardly a good man but he seemed almost an angel compared to Elm. Both of them, Clip and Sol, take after their fathers. Clip means well and he isn't a bad chap, but he's weak-willed and easily led astray. Whereas Sol . . . he's single-minded to the point of being obsessive, utterly ruthless – some would even say sadistic – in his determination to dominate. Sol has always had Clip under control. Clip jumps when he's told to jump and he's struggled to maintain any independence. I think it's why he goes away so much; to try to establish some sort of autonomy. But I've said more than enough, my dear. I'm very grateful to Sol for allowing me to return each summer. I don't wish to sound disloyal – I only meant to remind you to be aware of hidden . . . dangers, shall we say?'

'But it isn't disloyal to speak your mind, surely? After all, this was your home, it's where you grew up,' said Sylvie. 'You shouldn't have to feel grateful for being allowed to visit. Magus had no right to send you away in the first place. He's not even the owner, is he?'

'The estate belongs to Clip. Although it will be Sol's one day, I imagine. Clip has no children and is unlikely ever to.'

'Why not?'

Siskin raised his eyebrows delicately.

'I gather it wasn't originally from disinclination. But Sol discovered a weakness ... how can I put this? ... an insecurity in Clip and he exploited it, teasing and humiliating his brother until Clip found himself incapable of any act of passion. Completely impotent, it was always rumoured. And now of course Clip is the shaman, who must lead a celibate life if he wants to keep his powers strong. Clip was one of Sol's earliest victims of control and he's never managed to break free.'

'Yet Magus can be so kind too.'

'Oh yes, and that is part of his strength. He excites loyalty and devotion, even slavish obedience. The vast majority of people here are only too happy to serve him, anxious for his praise and approbation. It's not until you defy him that you come up against his steel. And then Goddess help you if you don't submit to him. He's not one to tolerate being crossed, or to ever accept second place. Ruthless doesn't even begin to describe him.'

He stood up slowly, leaning on his silver-topped stick.

'Just be careful, as I said, my dear Sylvie. Moongaziness is not necessarily a blessing.'

She nodded, aware of the heaviness still pressing down on her.

'I will be careful, Professor Siskin. But I feel I'm in a thick fog. I have no idea what's out there waiting for me.'

He looked down at her, his pale-blue eyes kind, and patted her shoulder.

'Maybe that's just as well, my dear.'

The day of the full moon dawned bright and clear. Yul sat crossed legged on the Altar Stone in the Circle facing the rising sun. As the golden disc cleared the tops of the standing stones and the shimmering warmth fell on him, he breathed deeply. He felt the now familiar surge of force flowing up through the stone into his body and tingled with the power; alchemy of earth magic and sun energy. The ancestors had known where to place their stones, how to mark the points where the dragon lines in the earth surfaced. They knew the places where the fecundity of the Earth Goddess rose up to meet the inseminating power of the sun. But it took a special conduit to make the magic happen; someone with the ability to channel the energy, to transform it within themselves. A magus, a wise one, a magician. Very few had these alchemic, transformative powers. Yul was one of the few.

He stayed there for some time in silent meditation, praying to the Earth Goddess that all would be well for Sylvie tonight. The sky turned from pink to blue and the sun rose higher. Yul opened his eyes and sprang lightly from the stone. Back home for breakfast, then off to work in the woodland. He'd wait for Sylvie tonight in the woods, but in his heart he knew that she wouldn't come to join him. Something had happened to her. Somehow she'd changed and now felt an allegiance to Magus. Why did she want to go to Mooncliffe with him rather than dance at Hare Stone where she belonged? Yul had felt a deep sadness fill his soul of late. Sylvie was slipping away from him and he didn't know how to get her back.

After the solstice Yul had thought that the world would be his. But apart from Alwyn's demise and his own growing strength, nothing else had changed. Magus was still in power. Sylvie was still out of his league. He was still a Villager in a society where that was not a desirable thing to be. Yul swore vehemently and ran as hard as he could back to his cottage.

Later that morning Magus called Miranda into his office. He was pleased with their new living arrangements. He now had Sylvie in the Hall close at hand so he could keep an eye on her. The fact that she was in a room with outside access was no accident, for he wanted to be able to get her in and out of the building every full moon without Miranda prying.

He'd organised the pieces of rock, taken from the great snake-carved stone overlooking the quarry, to be smoothed into egg shapes at the stone-carvers' workshop in the Village. These stone eggs were now ready up at Mooncliffe in a great sea chest. There were twenty-eight of them, one for each day of the month. Magus had no idea whether his plan would work; whether they'd hold the moon energy in the same way the great moon stone did. He'd had the rock analysed. The round stone at Mooncliffe and the tall stone overlooking the quarry were indeed identical, and were a very unusual form of oolithic limestone. The geologist who'd undertaken the analysis of the samples had been excited and had asked to visit the site to investigate further. Magus had refused, for he didn't want anyone snooping around. And particularly not near the quarry where the gang of immigrant workers were still tearing stone from the earth, working in conditions that didn't comply with any Health and Safety Act.

'Come and have a word in my office,' he said casually to Miranda, when he'd located her in one of the school rooms. Although the students didn't have a complete summer holiday there were fewer lessons at this time of year, with emphasis on personal study and coursework. Magus led Miranda into the wing overlooking the sunken white garden. She'd never visited this part of the Hall before and looked around with interest. She was impressed by the sheer size of his office and the old books and paintings that mingled with the very expensive, up-to-date-looking bank of computers.

She sat down on one of the leather sofas and Magus sat back on the other, surveying her. Pregnancy suited her; she was soft and curvy, her eyes bright. He smiled at her, noting her eagerness and thrill at being summoned to his presence. He found the energising effect of the moon stone had gradually worn off during the month, but when he looked at the woman before him he felt a surge of power. Miranda was completely in his thrall and would do whatever he asked of her. The baby growing inside her was his and would make her even more dependent on him. And maybe this baby would be as special as Sylvie. Next week, once this Moon Fullness and Lammas were over, he'd get to work on Miranda and find out exactly who Sylvie's father was.

And Sylvie herself – she'd knuckled down since the Summer Solstice. He remembered her arguing with him when Yul was at Quarrycleave, challenging him and disobeying him by bringing the boy back to the Village. He'd watched Sylvie this morning and couldn't imagine her ever standing up to him now. She was so quiet, her silver hair falling over her shoulders like a curtain that shielded her from the world. She looked delicate and meek, not strong at all. He knew that with a little help from Clip she'd obey him without question. Thinking of her now, and looking at her mother sitting before him, Magus felt that familiar melting sensation in his abdomen. He was in absolute control. Even that thorn in his flesh, Yul, seemed to have faded into the background. He was sure that Sylvie hadn't been seeing the boy. He smiled warmly; everything was working out perfectly to plan.

'Have you settled into your new accommodation?'

'Oh yes thank you, Magus. It's lovely. And wonderful to be here in the Hall, close to you.'

'Good. I knew you'd like that suite of rooms.'

'I was hoping you'd have visited me by now,' Miranda said diffidently. 'The four-poster bed is so—'

'Sorry, Miranda, you know I would love nothing better, but I'm very busy at present. In fact I have a call due any minute, and I just wanted to have a quick word about tonight. You know, the Moon Fullness.'

'Oh, that's tonight? I lose track.'

'Remember I said I wanted to keep an eye on Sylvie? I need to make sure she's not attempting to meet that boy.'

'I'm sure she wouldn't do that. She's changed recently. She's lost some weight, which is worrying, and she isn't herself. She's so docile and passive at the moment.'

'That's a good thing. She was becoming rude and defiant and I won't stand for that. As for her weight – well it's up to you to make sure she eats properly and rests. I won't be pleased if I find she's becoming weak again. Not after I've made such an effort to restore her health.'

'No, of course not. I'll keep a close eye on what she eats, I promise.'

'Good. Now, I shall take care of her this evening at the moon rise. I want to observe her again. Her apparent lunacy is rather worrying and I need to see exactly how the moon affects her. She's clearly distressed and psychologically disturbed when the full moon rises. I intend to care for her personally each month so you don't have to worry about her. All you need to do is make sure she eats, sleeps and generally stays healthy. Is that clear?'

Miranda gazed at him, loving everything about him. Magus really was the perfect man, strong and in control, and she was so lucky. She was sure that as the baby grew, their relationship would strengthen. Maybe one day he'd want to make a commitment to her and the child, if she could just keep him happy in the meantime. She knew he found her attractive and it was good of him to take such an interest in Sylvie and her problems; not many men would be so caring. She smiled at him and moved her head slightly, so her glossy auburn hair rippled over her breasts in a silky swathe. She leaned forward and looked deep into his dark eyes, willing him to love her as she loved him.

'It's really kind of you, Magus. I used to worry terribly about her behaviour during the full moon. She was so wild and strange. Thank you for taking this on. When we were in London I thought she was actually going mad, losing her mind. Will you keep her in the hospital wing under sedation or what?'

'No, no, I'll take her out in the open and watch her, as I did last month.'

Miranda frowned.

'What – let her free? Is it safe? I don't know about this dancing business. Are you sure it won't harm her? I remember how exhausted she was last time.'

Magus sighed, his mouth tightening.

'The reason she became so exhausted is because she's not

looking after herself properly and you're not doing your duty as a mother in caring for her. Why do you think I'm telling you to make sure she eats and rests? Use your brain, Miranda.'

She flushed and became flustered at his sharp tone.

'Yes, I'm sorry, Magus. I just thought—'

'Well don't! I'll do the thinking. All you have to do is to take her up to bed now and keep her there until tonight. I'll come and collect her at about eight o'clock. Make sure she's ready for me. And make sure she eats plenty of food today. I don't want her weak. Do you understand?'

'Yes, of course. And I'll come with you tonight, just to—'

'Absolutely not!' he snapped, his black eyes flashing. 'Clip and I will take care of her. The last thing I need is you fussing about.'

'But—'

'That's all, Miranda. Go and find Sylvie now and take her straight up to bed.'

Miranda stood up, feeling awkward and unsure of herself and ready to burst into tears at his curtness. The phone buzzed suddenly making her jump. Magus reached across and barked into it.

'What? *What?* The quarry? Well what sort of accident?'

He glanced across at Miranda. She hovered hesitantly, uncertain if she'd been dismissed or not. His face was hard and closed as he listened to the loud, rapid voice on the other end of the line.

'No! On no account call anyone. Drive back there and I'll come up right now ... I know, Jack, I do understand, but we can't have anybody seeing anything. That would be a complete disaster, wouldn't it? No, I'll meet you there. Do what you can and just hold tight till I arrive.'

He slammed the phone down and stood up.

'An accident?' asked Miranda. 'What's happened?'

'Never you mind! Just some trouble up at Quarrycleave. I have to go up there now, but I'll be back in time for this evening, whatever happens.'

'What about my classes today, Magus? Should I still teach or not? Sylvie will be fine resting on her own, I think.'

'No, cancel your lessons. Sylvie's far more important. Have meals sent up to your rooms and make her eat.'

'Okay, I'll do that. Thank you, Magus. I'm sorry if I annoyed you or . . .'

He shook his head impatiently, waving her away.

'Just make sure she's in a fit state for tonight, that's all I ask of you.'

7

As the afternoon wore on Miranda noticed a change in Sylvie. She'd been kept in bed all day despite her protests, and plied with food she didn't want. Miranda was still upset about Magus' attitude towards her that morning, which she knew was all Sylvie's fault for worrying him in the first place with her silly moon dancing. Miranda wasn't going to let this ridiculous business spoil her chances, especially as she had the nagging suspicion that Sylvie was somehow manipulating the situation and making a lot of fuss just to get attention. Miranda sat in their little sitting room reading and trying to prepare her next batch of lessons, but finding herself constantly doodling names in the margin of her notes. She must talk to Magus about names as he'd doubtless want the baby named in the Stonewylde way. She was fine about that as long as it wasn't something daft like Seagull or Foxglove. Although on reflection, Foxglove had a certain charm ...

Sylvie lay in bed all day staring up at the ceiling or out of the window, eating whatever she could force down. Miranda's flood of chivvying and scolding just washed over her, barely noticed in the turmoil that consumed her. She was filled with dread, her mind chasing round in circles thinking one minute of Yul up at Hare Stone and the next of her duty to dance at Mooncliffe. She felt torn in two, and utterly confused and frightened by the memories of her nightmare which crowded in whenever she dropped her guard. She recalled the sensation of being crushed by heavy rock and Magus' smiling face. It made her shudder.

As the afternoon passed, Sylvie began to feel the old, familiar rising of tension. She sat up in bed and started fidgeting.

'Lie down, Sylvie,' said Miranda, looking over from the chair where she sat reading. She'd positioned it so she could look in on Sylvie in her bedroom and keep a close eye on her.

'I can't. I want to get up.'

'Stay there and do as you're told. You know what Magus said.'

Sylvie lay down but within a few minutes she was up again.

'Please, Mum, let me get up. I can't keep still.'

'Why can't you just do as I tell you? Magus said you must rest. He'll be furious with me if you don't.'

'I have rested. I've been lying here all day. I'd like to have a bath. Please, Mum.'

'I don't think Magus would want that.'

'I don't give a damn what he wants!' cried Sylvie indignantly. 'Who the hell is he to say whether or not I have a bath?'

She flung the bed covers off and marched out of the bedroom, brushing past her mother and locking herself in the bathroom. She twisted the taps on and ignored Miranda's mingled pleadings and threats coming through the door.

When she emerged later, clean and refreshed, she took out the moongazy dress and put it on, remembering Yul's idea that she should always wear it for the Moon Fullness. As she thought of him she felt the sadness seeping in, overlaying the jitteriness. She had a sudden image of the Hare Stone and of walking up there holding Yul's hand. She thought of him sitting with his back against the stone, watching as she transformed into a moon angel. She remembered her sense of relief and fulfilment after the dancing and gazing were done; the joy of pouring her moon magic into the earth where it belonged, to mingle with the Earth Magic of Stonewylde. The Hare Stone marked the spot where this could happen, where the circle could be danced and the spirals of energy and force could interact. All of it flooded into Sylvie's mind as she put on the gauzy dress and stood brushing out her long, silver hair. She felt a renewed tingle of anticipation.

But then dowsing it, blanking it completely and utterly, came Clip's commands, rolling in like dark clouds blotting out the sunshine:

'You want to dance at Mooncliffe every Moon Fullness, Sylvie. You must dance for Magus and share your moon magic. It's what you were brought here for.'

The hair-brush fell to the floor and Sylvie sank down onto a chair, gazing blankly out of the window. When Miranda came in a few minutes later ready to do battle with her wilful daughter, she was delighted to see Sylvie had returned to her passive state. Miranda smiled and stroked her hair affectionately. Magus would be so pleased to find Sylvie ready, calm and obedient and he'd know it was all her doing. Maybe he'd stay when the moon dancing thing was over and he brought Sylvie back. Maybe he'd actually spend the whole night with her now she'd moved in here, and make love to her as he'd done during the May full moons.

Miranda was aware that Magus hadn't been near her since that night in the pouring rain on the cliff top when their baby had been conceived. One thing after another had seemed to conspire against it, not least the layout of the cottage and Sylvie's antagonism. But now, here in the Hall in these lovely rooms – or better still, in his rooms – Miranda hoped Magus would put their love-making high on his list of priorities. She planned to make herself irresistible to him, starting from tonight.

Yul felt the evening drawing in. Although not moongazy himself, he was very much in tune with the forces that underlay Stone-wylde and could sense the setting of the sun and the rising of the moon in his soul. He thought hard of Sylvie, trying to reach her with his mind.

Sylvie, come to me, my moongazy girl! Come to Hare Stone tonight. You belong with me, Sylvie, the darkness and the bright-ness together as one. Come dance with the hares!

But he felt no answering call, no tremor that might be her mind connecting with his. He felt only a black fog blanketing everything. He sighed and walked up the path past her old cottage into the woods. It was the gossip of the Village: the two newcomers had moved out of Woodland Cottage and into the Hall. Now he had no opportunity to see her unless she came to find him. And there seemed little chance of that, especially after he'd been so angry with her that day on Dragon's Back. He should've hidden it better; not shown how hurt he was. He felt bitterly sad for what had been lost, and lost for no reason that he could fathom. He also blamed himself for Magus' interest in Sylvie; it was he who'd betrayed her secret in the byre, and all for a mouthful of pie.

'Is she ready then?' asked Magus brusquely, walking in with a cursory knock.

'Yes, she's waiting in her bedroom,' said Miranda, jumping up. 'Magus, I—'

'Not now, Miranda. I must get on. She's eaten and she's rested?'

'Yes. But she insisted on having a bath, and—'

'That's fine. I'll take her down the stairs in her room and I'll bring her back that way too, so as not to disturb you. Don't wait up, Miranda. I really don't want to see you tonight when I get back.'

Her face crumpled.

'I'm sorry, Miranda – you know I didn't mean that the way it sounded. I meant you mustn't wait up when you should be sleeping.'

'But Magus, I really don't—'

'I absolutely insist. We must think of the baby. I'll come and see you first thing in the morning, I promise.'

'But I'm Sylvie's mother and I should—'

'The whole point is I'm taking this anxiety away from you. Remember you're *my* child's mother too. If Sylvie's tired when we get back, it's best you're not around worrying and upsetting yourself. All she needs is sleep, and I'm more than capable of making sure she's comfortable. So no fussing, please!'

'But Magus, I'd hoped—'

'Don't you trust me to take care of Sylvie?'

'Of course! I just wanted to spend some time with you, that's all. I was hoping we—'

'I've already told you, I'll come and see you tomorrow morning. Alright?'

'Yes, alright. I'm sorry.'

'No need to be.'

He pecked her on the cheek, ignoring her crestfallen face and drooping shoulders, and strode into Sylvie's bedroom, shutting the door firmly behind him. Sylvie still sat in the chair gazing out of the window, her arms and legs bare, the soft shimmering dress falling from the narrow silver straps over her shoulders. Her freshly washed hair hung like a curtain of silk around her face and down her back. She turned to him, her eyes enormous in her pointed face.

'I want to go to Mooncliffe and dance on the moon stone for you.'

'Good girl, Sylvie!' he chuckled softly, keeping his voice low. 'We're going up there now and you can dance for me all night if you want.'

He took her hand in his and led her to the little arched doorway. He lifted the latch and they climbed down the steep staircase. The outside door opened easily and they were out in the glorious evening, where the late July sun had begun its descent. Birds sang in the soft golden light as Clip stepped out from behind some trees to join them. Miranda watched in silence from the window above, the ache in her throat almost unbearable. Her beautiful daughter looked like a delicate silver flower fairy flanked by the two tall men. Their three blond heads disappeared round the corner of the building and Miranda turned away, trying to swallow her pain and disappointment.

'How are you this evening, Sylvie?' asked Clip.

'I want to dance up at Mooncliffe,' she replied, fixing her moonstone gaze on his. She seemed to be in another world, her eyes strange and face expressionless. She moved like an automaton.

'We want you to dance at Mooncliffe too,' he smiled. Looking over her head at Magus, he winked. 'Still working, then.'

'Certainly is,' Magus replied.

'I'll reinforce it again later on if necessary. I don't want her becoming upset, which can't be good for her. Much better to do this peacefully,' said Clip. 'She's so receptive and easy to command, and very obedient once it's in her subconscious.'

'Strange, seeing as how spirited she is normally.'

'That's her personality and conscious mind and something entirely different. But this is all linked to her magic, her ability to pick up signs and forces. You said you thought she had the sight, and that's why I can get her to do anything I want. She's incredibly compliant and open to suggestion.'

'Could be useful,' murmured Magus. 'I think I'll carry her up there. I want her as fresh as possible.'

He scooped Sylvie into his arms and she lay quietly against his chest, staring up at the sky.

'So tell me what happened at Quarrycleave,' said Clip as they walked along a back lane to where the cliff path began. 'I gather there was some kind of accident today?'

'It was awful!' said Magus. 'Jackdaw phoned down from the Gatehouse this morning in a panic. They'd been blasting and there was an unexpected rock-fall. A whole section came down that shouldn't have. Don't know if it was that bloody Portlander's fault or not – maybe just bad luck – but several of the men were trapped.'

'That's terrible. Was everyone alright?'

Magus shook his head, his face dark.

'No. We got a couple out and they were a bit mangled but alive. But three of them were buried – totally crushed. Not a hope in hell. That Portlander had disappeared by the time I arrived. Taken his truck and gone. The other men were hysterical. You know how emotional these foreigners can be.'

'Understandably so, given the circumstances. They must've been terrified.'

'But you should have seen them! Screaming and sobbing, refusing to set foot in the quarry again – and that's from men who weren't involved in the accident. Anyway, we dealt with the injuries as best we could and I didn't want Hazel involved for obvious reasons. Jackdaw's taken the minibus and got them all off the estate. He'll have dumped them in Dover by now, back where he found them.'

'What about the men who were buried?'

'They're still buried. They're not going anywhere, so they're best left where they are, under a ton of rubble.'

'Sol! I don't believe it! You can't just leave their bodies there!'

'The worst of it is I'll have to shut the quarry up again, for the time being at least. And just when it was going so well. It's a bloody nuisance.'

'Sol, that completely heartless, and if—'

'*It wants lives.*'

They both stared at Sylvie. She gazed up at the skies, her eyes faraway, her voice sing-song.

'What?'

'It's hungry,' she whispered. 'It wants more lives. Now you've fed it there'll be no end. It will not be satisfied.'

'What is she on about?'

'I know what she's talking about,' said Clip quietly. 'I've felt it too. It's the beast that stalks.'

'Oh please! Come on, Clip! That's just superstitious Village rubbish!'

In his arms, Sylvie shuddered. Even in her strange state she recalled the despair and the lure of whatever it was that walked the stone labyrinth at Quarrycleave. Those men had been crushed to death to feed its hunger. No saviour, no owl or raven to turn them away from the jaws of death. And if he'd stayed there as Magus and Jackdaw had wanted, Yul would now be trapped beneath a ton of rubble too.

*

Yul sat up in a tree in the woods. He still clung to the tiny ray of hope that Sylvie would come skipping up the path, her eyes strange and faraway, her body taut with the imminent rising of the moon. But his heart was heavy. He knew she wasn't coming tonight, and tried not to imagine her with Magus going up the path to Mooncliffe. It wasn't just jealousy. She'd insisted that she loved to dance on the great round stone, and yet he knew what he'd seen that night in June. She'd stood as if frozen until her legs gave way beneath her, nothing like her joyous dancing with the hares. And she'd been absolutely silent, not singing her strange, celestial music. Why did she prefer that to being with him at the Hare Stone? How had Magus persuaded her?

Up at Mooncliffe the sun was still visible, low over the hills. The great round stone glittered in the rosy light, all the tiny crystals within it picking up the dying sun's rays. It was a breath-taking sight, almost unreal. Clip stopped dead, gazing in wonder at the shimmering pink stone and its backdrop of silken water.

'Come on!' barked Magus, bumping into him and stumbling. 'No time for dreaming now – we've got work to do here.'

He sat Sylvie down on the grass facing the sun. She was passive and unresponsive, the antithesis of her normal behaviour so close to moonrise. Clip looked down at her.

'So how are going to do this?' he asked. 'Put Sylvie on the stone before the moon rises or what?'

'Yes I think so,' replied Magus. 'Last time she danced for ages on the grass. She must've wasted so much of the energy doing that. This time I want all of it fed into the stone, so there'll be no dancing around. Once she's on the stone she can't escape and we'll keep her there as long as we can.'

'Alright, but we must be careful, Sol. She doesn't look strong and we mustn't hurt her.'

'It won't hurt her – how could it? It may tire her a bit, but she can sleep for a week afterwards so there'll be no permanent damage. Don't go soft on me, Clip. You know how good that moon energy feels. We need as much of it as possible, and we're still learning how to get the best out of Sylvie. See the stone eggs I've had made?'

He showed Clip the chest full of the smooth, carved ovoids.

'Sacred Mother, how many have you got there?' exclaimed Clip. 'She can't possibly charge up all of those too!'

'There are twenty-eight, one for each day of the month,' said Magus. 'And she may be able to charge them all – we just don't know. Better to have too many than too few.'

'How will she charge them?'

'I thought perhaps put one in each hand? Or maybe we could lay her flat on the rock and place the stones on top of her? We'd get more done that way. I don't know, Clip. When the time comes we'll see what works best.'

'Look, she's standing up.'

The sun was sliding down behind the hills. The sky was beautiful, the few clouds on the horizon turning blood red and the higher ones a deep purple. Sylvie was washed in the pink light, her hair fanning slightly about her in the soft breeze as she watched the sun disappear. When it had gone she closed her eyes and started to shake. Magus and Clip began to unload the stones from the chest and lay them around the moon stone. As the dusk deepened they waited. Normally at this stage Sylvie would be restless and full of wild tension but tonight she seemed calm, although she still trembled.

At last there was that expectant hush at the moment before moon rise. They looked out to sea at the spot exactly opposite where the sun had set, where the full moon would rise. With the warm breeze wafting her dress and hair, Sylvie's arms began to rise slowly, like great angel wings. Her mouth opened, pouring forth the strange ethereal song. Both men stared, mesmerised by such unearthliness. Then Magus broke the spell.

'Quick, let's get her on the stone now before she runs off to dance.'

The two men lifted her up and placed her in the centre of the enormous disc. They stood on it together, one on either side of her, all three facing the sea. Sylvie's song had been silenced the moment she touched the stone and her wings had dropped. She stood transfixed, her eyes locked onto the horizon.

A soft pinkness appeared over the sea, turning the layer of low cloud draped along the horizon to flamingo-pink gold. Then there was a tiny sliver of deep pink which quickly grew. A strange noise came from Sylvie at the sight of the rising moon, a strangled mewing. Her trembling turned to a violent shuddering that racked her body, almost like a fit. Her hair rippled in silver waves, her eyes fixed wide open.

Then they felt the force coming up through the rock into their feet. It seemed as if the moon rock was moving beneath them, although they knew it couldn't be. The quaking was so powerful they felt they might lose their balance and fall, and both jumped off the stone feeling a little frightened at the intensity. Sylvie was rooted in the centre as the moon bloomed before her, huge and deep red-pink, hanging over the silver sea. Her body juddered and jolted, her hair flying around her, and then they noticed the light. It chased itself around her in tiny worm-like strands, flickering all over before heading downwards into the rock beneath her feet.

'I have never in all my journeys in this world or the Other, experienced anything remotely like this,' whispered Clip in wonder. 'It's something you have to see to believe.'

'Think of all that energy!' hissed Magus. 'This is much, much more powerful than last month and nothing's been wasted on dancing this time. Shall we get her to hold the eggs now?'

'No, I'd leave it for a bit,' whispered Clip. 'She's shaking so much I think she'd drop them. And I'm not sure about you, but I don't want to get close enough to touch her. She's jerking like there's ten thousand volts passing through her.'

The two men left her on the rock and sat down on the grass at a safe distance.

Yul, his back against the Hare Stone, watched the moon rise over the distant sea. The hares arrived from the long grass and the woods and started to run in a great circle around the stone, marking out the spirals. Bats flickered in the deepening darkness and then the barn owl appeared silently. Huge white wings outstretched in ghostly flight, it glided from the woods towards the stone calling plaintively in the moonlight.

'Oh Sylvie, why aren't you here where you belong?' whispered Yul, angrily wiping away the tears with the back of his hand. 'Why aren't you here with your creatures. Here with me?'

As the moon climbed higher and lost its pinkness, Sylvie's violent jerking lessened, settling down to a deep trembling shudder. Her mewing sounds had ceased. She stood fixed to the spot where they'd placed her, still staring at the rising moon, the stone around her feet glowing a luminous blue-silver. Magus picked up two of the eggs and knelt on the stone, wincing as the powerful force shot up through his knees. He crawled across and put an egg in each of her hands, curling her fingers around them, then felt his way back off the stone.

'I don't want to lie there right now,' he said softly. 'It's still much too strong a sensation, not pleasant at all.'

'How long's she been up there? Twenty minutes?'

'Don't know. My damn watch has stopped again. Must be something to do with the energy pulses. Last time I kept her up there until the moon was really high. We'll see how it goes. Oh look at the eggs! They're starting to glow already!'

He started a relay of egg holding that went on for a long time. As soon as they were glowing strongly he'd replace them with fresh ones and put the charged ones in the chest. He noticed it was taking longer as the moon rose higher. Every time he knelt on the rock to swap the eggs he received a blast of the energy, and soon he was buzzing with it. Clip lay on the grass with his long legs stretched out, feet just touching the moon stone so he too could absorb the moon power.

Sylvie only shuddered gently now, although the silver light still danced over her body and chased into the stone. She was becoming aware of her surroundings as the moon slowly turned bright silver and grew smaller in the sky.

'It's been a good hour,' said Clip. 'Shall we take her off?'

'What for? She's fine. The energy's still pouring through her into the rock. And besides, we've only done about half the eggs. No, she can carry on for a lot longer.'

Yul rose from the grass, his tears long since dried. He felt hollow with sadness. The hares had stopped their wild cavorting and sat upright, great ears laid back and lozenge eyes gazing up at the silver moon. They'd marked out the paths in honour of the Bright Lady and could now moongaze in peace. Yul stepped delicately around them and made his way down the hill through the boulders and back into the woods. He wondered whether Sylvie had enjoyed the Moon Fullness up at Mooncliffe with Magus. He hoped not. He hoped that by some miracle she would come back to him in August for the Corn Moon.

'I really think she's had enough,' said Clip. 'Look, the eggs are taking ages to charge up.'

'Yes, but they *are* still charging. She's alright, she can take it. Stop fussing.'

Clip shrugged. He wouldn't argue with his brother; there was no point. Sylvie's eyes blinked, and when Magus changed the eggs over again she gazed at him with the same beseeching look as last time.

'Let me go! Please!' she mouthed silently.

Magus ignored her and glanced down at Clip, who lay oblivious on the grass with his feet on the stone, soaking up energy and staring at the star-spangled sky above.

A while later Magus noticed tears on her cheeks, like diamonds in the bright moonlight.

'Please let me go,' she whispered.

'What was that?' asked Clip. 'Did she say something? She's done enough, Sol. It's been at least two hours. You must've got all the eggs charged now.'

'Not quite – still four to go. She can take a little more. Last time I left her up there until she fell down.'

'Yes, because you're cruel. For Goddess' sake, she must be exhausted. Haven't you any feelings?'

'You'll be grateful when you have these eggs all month to keep you buzzing with energy. Shut up and leave it to me, like you always do.'

Not long after this, Sylvie's legs gave way and she crumpled onto the stone.

'There, that's it!' cried Clip, jumping up in alarm. 'She can't take any more.'

'Hold on! She's okay. She's lying down now and there are only two more eggs to do. Just watch – she'll be fine for a little bit longer. She can take it, I know she can.'

He climbed onto the stone with the last two eggs whilst Clip wandered off to gaze across the dark water. Magus straightened Sylvie out so she lay on her back, arms by her sides on the stone and palms upwards. He placed an egg on each hand and sat back to watch. The silver threads still ran over her body, but faintly now. He could feel an immense swell of power pulsating in the stone beneath him. It was far, far stronger than last month's. His insides felt molten with energy and power. He felt as if he could jump off the cliff and fly. He laughed with exhilaration.

Sylvie's eyes turned in her head and locked onto him.

'I must get down from this stone,' she croaked. 'It hurts so much. Please let me go now. I've given you my magic.'

Clip came over and sat on the rock next to his brother, gasping in amazement as the force shot up into his body. But then he caught sight of Sylvie's huge staring eyes.

'What was that? Did she say something?'

'She's fine. Look, the eggs are just starting to glow. I want all the magic this month with nothing wasted. Just ten more minutes for these last eggs to charge and then we'll take her off.'

'Now!' she groaned. 'It hurts.'

'That's it, Sol,' said Clip, leaning across and sitting her upright. He cradled her in his arms as she lolled lifelessly, unable to support herself. 'You're being unnecessarily cruel. Poor girl! She's done more than enough.'

He lifted Sylvie off the stone like a little rag doll, and as he looked down at her lying in his arms, something inside him stirred. She was so vulnerable. What had they done to her?

'You really are an insatiable bastard, Sol,' he muttered, laying her down gently on the grass. 'Just look at her – she's exhausted. You've drained her completely. Why did you make her go on for so long?'

'Never mind that! You've lost one of the eggs, picking her up like that. It rolled off and I can't see it anywhere.'

'For Goddess' sake, Sol, stop it! She looks terrible. Look! She's unconscious. I can hardly hear her breathing.'

He laid his head lightly on her chest.

'Sacred Mother, she's barely breathing at all!' he cried. 'You greedy, selfish bastard! If you've killed her ...'

'Let me see,' said Magus harshly, pushing him aside and feeling her neck for a pulse. 'Stop fretting, she's fine. This is how she was last time. She'll be alright once we've got her home. You head back to the Hall with her while I padlock the chest. I'll have to come back in the morning to look for that missing egg.'

Eventually they climbed the stairs to Sylvie's bedroom and put her into bed. Her breathing was still shallow but steady. Miranda had left a glass of water on the bedside table and Clip tried to help her drink. But the water trickled down her chin and he gave up, lying her back down again and gently stroking the tangled hair off her face. She sighed and snuggled into the pillow.

'See?' said Magus. 'She's absolutely fine. A few days of rest and she'll be up and about and good as new. It was so much easier this time without her struggling. I want you to make sure she remembers the commands again, like you did before. Really drive it into her head. I want her to be desperate to dance for me again.'

Clip shook his head, looking at his brother with distaste.

'I can't believe you sometimes, Sol. You remind me of your father, you know.'

Magus shrugged. 'Well that's hardly surprising, is it? Are you coming now? It's getting late.'

'I know it's late; we've been out far too long. I'll stay here and sit with Sylvie for a little while. I'm still not convinced she's alright. What's the great rush?'

'Clip, it's the Moon Fullness! You know how I celebrate the full moon. And especially now I'm so charged up.'

Clip rolled his eyes and shook his head again.

'So you're going next door to visit her mother now?'

'Goddess no! Miranda's far too clingy and dull. I may visit her during the month to keep her happy, but certainly not tonight. No ... I've got one of our Lammas visitors waiting. Infinitely more exciting than Miranda, and she told me she's been waiting a long time for this. I mustn't disappoint her, and thanks to little Sylvie's gift, there's no danger of that!'

'You disgust me, Sol,' said Clip quietly. 'Close the door behind you.'

8

The brilliant morning sun sparkled on every surface in Sylvie's bright bedroom. It twinkled through the tiny diamond-shaped panes of glass and picked out the colours in the rug on the polished floorboards. In the corner, Magus, Clip and Miranda stared down at Sylvie lying motionless and ashen in her bed.

'She's just the same as the last time, only worse,' said Miranda.

'That's a contradiction in itself,' said Magus impatiently. He was in high spirits, bubbling with energy and verve, which only served to emphasise Sylvie's corpse-like state.

'I mean there was none of that restlessness or whimpering that she suffered back in May, when she'd been out with Yul in the woods. She's like she was last month when you took her up to the cliffs, only this time she seems even worse. I checked on her last night at about midnight and at first I honestly thought she was dead. I can't tell you what . . .'

She choked on the words, unable to express just how terrified she'd been. Clip patted her arm sympathetically but she gave him a cold glance.

'You see?' said Magus, his voice loud in the subdued room. 'You start fussing and then what happens? You must think of the baby, Miranda. That was exactly the situation I'd hoped to avoid.'

'Please don't be cross,' she pleaded. 'Really, Magus, I'm not fussing. It's just that—'

'I think we should get Hazel in to look at Sylvie,' said Clip. He took one of her lifeless hands in his. There was no response at all and her breathing remained almost silent. 'I'm worried, Sol.'

'For Goddess' sake!' exclaimed Magus. He shouldered Clip aside and sat on the bed next to Sylvie's supine body. He felt the pulse in her neck again, as he'd done the previous night, and placed his hand on her forehead. Miranda fidgeted by his side, longing for the courage to agree with Clip and summon Hazel but unwilling to anger Magus further. He frowned down at Sylvie, also in a dilemma.

'How do we know she isn't just putting this on?' he said. 'A bit of attention-seeking to get us all worried?'

'You can't fake a slow heartbeat and cold skin,' said Clip.

'Do you think she's cold?' asked Miranda anxiously, fiddling with the covers and trying to pull them up higher. 'I'm just not sure. Magus, I really do think we should—'

'For Goddess' sake shut up, Miranda!' Magus barked. 'Get out of here! You're driving me up the wall. Go down to the Dining Hall and find Hazel. Tell her we need her up here but it's not urgent. Let her finish her breakfast first. And stay down there and have breakfast yourself. I don't want to see you back here until you've eaten. Go on!'

When a dejected Miranda had left, he rose and turned to Clip.

'Do it now,' he commanded. 'Before they come back.'

Clip shook his head and Magus took a step towards him, frowning ominously.

'What the hell's the matter with you? We don't want her blurting anything out in front of the women! You must reinforce the commands and make sure she keeps it secret. Quick!'

'There's no point,' said Clip. 'I won't be able to wake her when she's like this. Don't worry – I doubt she's capable of speaking to anyone and if she does, they're hardly going to believe her, are they?'

'Mmn. I suppose you're right. But you must do it later.'

'You are the most selfish, unfeeling person I've ever come across,' said Clip with unusual temerity. 'Sylvie's ill because of what you've done to her, but all you can think of is covering your own back.'

121

'What *we've* done to her, Clip. You were as much a part of it as me. And she's tired, not ill. She'll be fine in a few days, you'll see.'

Clip shook his head again, his thin face miserable.

'You know what you need, Clip? A visit to Mooncliffe! I've been up there this morning and believe me, I feel on top of the world. Go and lie on the rock for a while and you'll stop this whinging. You'll realise that a little suffering on Sylvie's part is nothing if it means a constant source of moon magic for us. A small sacrifice on her behalf for the good of Stonewylde.'

Hazel was mystified at Sylvie's condition, and Miranda didn't help with her jumbled attempts to explain Sylvie's strange behaviour during the full moon. In the end Magus lost his temper and dismissed both Clip and Miranda. He needed Hazel to do whatever was necessary for Sylvie, but without knowing too much. She may be in his thrall but she was a doctor too; he didn't know where her loyalties would lie.

'Her pulse is slow but steady,' said Hazel, releasing Sylvie's thin wrist. 'Apart from being a little cold, there doesn't appear to be anything really wrong. She just seems exhausted, that's all.'

'Exactly!' said Magus. 'I knew those two were fussing unnecessarily. They've been behaving like a couple of old women and it's not helping Sylvie at all. What she needs is rest and warmth, just as I thought.'

'And fluids maybe, if she doesn't wake up. I could put a drip in later on if she's the same. But what happened to her? I've never seen her like this before, not even when she was so ill in London.'

'Hazel . . .'

Magus' dark eyes regarded her steadily and he gave a small smile. He watched Hazel's expression change under his glittering gaze. He held out his arms to her and she flew into them, to be crushed in his embrace. He bent his head and began to kiss her, slowly and very thoroughly. Soon the last thing on her mind was the sleeping girl lying only an arm's-length away.

'You didn't come to me last night at the Moon Fullness,' she whispered eventually, her body on fire. 'I waited for you all night, hoping you'd come.'

'I never promised, Hazel,' he said thickly, holding her head between his hands and looking intently into her soft brown eyes. 'You shouldn't wait unless I've told you to.'

'But after last month I thought—'

'Well you shouldn't have. You know how it is. I've always made it perfectly clear. Anyway, I was caught up in this.' He jerked his head towards the girl. 'I'll need your help with Sylvie. She has a strange kind of moongaziness, which is what Miranda was wittering on about. You may've heard of it before – how the women at Stonewylde can be affected by the full moon.'

Tenderly he removed the stethoscope from around Hazel's neck, kissing the soft skin where her blond hair brushed the collar of her pink linen blouse. She closed her eyes, her nostrils flaring, and took a ragged breath.

'I believe my own mother was moongazy,' he said softly. His hands brushed down to her breasts and Hazel opened her eyes wide, trying to concentrate on the conversation.

'Really? I ... I don't think I've come across it. I remember my parents saying something about your mother and the moon, though they're a little younger than she was of course. How strange.'

'I need your help, Hazel,' Magus repeated. 'Let me explain ...'

He guided her away from Sylvie's bed and over to the armchair by the window, where he sat down and pulled Hazel onto his lap. She fell against his chest willingly and he held her close against his body, his other hand tracing her collarbones with the lightest of touches. The thin material of her blouse parted as his fingers found the tiny buttons, one by one. Hazel's breathing quickened and a flush began to spread across her cheeks and down her neck. Magus continued smoothly, skilfully whilst Hazel dissolved into pure need.

'This moongaziness is all part of the magical forces at Stone-wylde,' he said softly, his voice deep. 'The effects are quite over-

123

whelming and it's cruel to keep a moongazy girl locked up when the lunacy is upon her. Poor Sylvie's desperate to dance when the full moon rises, and you know how over-protective Miranda is. She used to lock the girl in a small room to restrain her.'

'How terrible! I never knew that,' mumbled Hazel, shifting on his lap.

'It must've been very upsetting for Miranda, watching Sylvie to all intents and purposes losing her mind every month, and of course the doctors didn't have a clue how to help. So I'm trying a different, kinder tack – letting Sylvie dance to her heart's content out in the open air, which is what she wants to do as the moon rises.'

'I guess that's better, as long as she's closely supervised. Oh!' she gasped.

'I've taken on this responsibility to help Miranda, now she's expecting. The effects of moondancing are quite harmless I'm sure, though last night Sylvie danced for hours in the moonlight and today she's exhausted, drained of energy. But she isn't ill and I really don't want Miranda getting herself in a state about it, not in her condition. We don't want to risk damaging the baby's development in any way and we both know how Miranda's prone to worrying where Sylvie's health is concerned. Do you understand me?'

'Yes,' breathed Hazel, eagerly returning his caresses, her chest rising and falling rapidly. 'Yes, I understand perfectly.'

'I knew you would, Hazel. I knew I could count on you to help me. So just under-play it, would you? Sylvie will be fine. Put in a drip if necessary but make light of the whole thing to Miranda so she stops fretting. I'd be grateful to you, Hazel. So very grateful.'

The young doctor stared at him, mesmerised by the fiery intensity burning in his dark, velvety eyes. He crackled with it today; she could feel it in his touch, on his breath, and she shuddered with craving. He was charged with a different force that was irresistible. Her eyes were glazed with longing, her fair skin flushed with desire.

'Let's go for a walk up on the hills, shall we?' he asked, one long finger delicately stroking her bottom lip. 'I'm free for a couple of hours and I'd love to spend them with you, Hazel. I know a lovely spot smothered in sweet clover where the butterflies dance. I think you'd like it there, under the blue skies with the swifts and swallows flying overhead and the sun beating down on our skin. Just as magical as the moonlight. Unless you're busy, of course.'

'No, no,' she gasped, pulling her blouse together and scrambling off his lap to her feet. Her knees buckled and she nearly fell, but Magus reached out and steadied her with a knowing chuckle. Hazel's tousled hair fell about her red cheeks as she fumbled to fasten the buttons. 'I'm not busy at all. I can sort out the drip later – there's no urgency. You're right; Sylvie's fine, just tired. I'll put Miranda's mind at rest and make sure she understands that.'

'Oh Hazel,' he murmured. 'I knew I could rely on you to do the right thing for me. So . . . ?'

'Yes! I'd love to see the sweet clover where the butterflies dance. Take me there, Magus, please. Right now!'

He smiled as Hazel hastily crammed the blood pressure cuff and stethoscope back into her doctor's bag. He now knew exactly where her loyalties lay, and how to keep them there.

As the Hall filled with visitors and the Village bustled with Lammas preparations, Sylvie spent the next few days in bed. Hazel hydrated her with a drip and Miranda had to keep her warm even though the days and nights were hot and sticky. Under Magus' black gaze Clip hypnotized her again, reinforcing the same mantra as before. She repeated his words obediently, her moonstone eyes startling in her wan face. The dark shadows under her eyes emphasised their silvery softness as she dutifully reiterated how much she longed to give all her moon magic to Magus.

Privately Clip had his doubts whether she'd be able to take it again, particularly with the added burden of charging the eggs, which had taken every last drop of her energy. He knew that what he was doing was an abuse of his gift, but he'd always given in to Magus and this episode was no exception. Magus would take Sylvie's moon magic with or without his co-operation, and he told himself that his hypnotism made it easier for the poor girl. He tried to assuage his guilt by visiting Sylvie regularly, much to Miranda's annoyance. He liked to sit in her room, whether she was awake or asleep, and slip into meditation. He hoped that maybe he'd transfer positive energy to her just by being close.

The extent of Magus' concern was to barrage Miranda with instructions about feeding Sylvie and making sure she regained the weight she'd lost. Clip felt sorry for Miranda, who was losing her independence along with her figure. She was desperate for Magus' affection, returning like a puppy to be kicked again and again. Clip witnessed her humiliation on several occasions, but his admonishments to his brother had little effect.

'I hope you'll be joining us for the Lammas celebrations tomorrow?' asked Clip. He was sitting in Sylvie's bedroom with the windows open to the warm late July afternoon, and Miranda had just returned from the library. After three days she no longer felt that Sylvie needed to be watched constantly – all her daughter seemed to do was sleep or lie silently gazing at the ceiling – and she resented Clip's intrusion. Surely they were entitled to some privacy in their rooms?

'Lammas? Yes, I suppose so. What's involved? I don't need a costume do I, like at Beltane?'

'No, this is the celebration of the cereal harvest and most of the rituals focus on the crops and the Corn Spirit. It's not quite the same as the magic of Beltane and the Green Man, nor the holiday atmosphere of the Summer Solstice. But it's a lovely festival nevertheless.'

Miranda eyed him suspiciously from Sylvie's doorway. Why did he keep turning up like this? Sylvie didn't need babysitting and seemed to be on the mend now from the strange lethargy that had taken her over since the last full moon. Clip irritated her with his concern, and also hampered her attempts to entice

Magus to stay. Every time he came striding down the corridor to see how Sylvie was doing and Miranda thought to entertain him, there was Clip lurking about like a pale shadow.

'I'm sure I'll take part,' she said. 'Now if you don't mind, Clip, I ...'

He smiled at her and settled more comfortably in the chair.

'Please ignore me, Miranda. I'm happy just to sit here quietly and meditate. You get on with whatever you need to do. I'm preparing myself for the festival tomorrow.'

She frowned at this and came into the bedroom, fiddling with a jam-jar of wild flowers on the dressing table. The young lad Harold had brought them up earlier, saying a friend of Sylvie's had sent them for her. Several petals had fallen already onto the scrubbed pine surface, and Miranda brushed them into her palm.

'Preparing yourself in what way?'

'Focusing my energy. Concentrating on what Lammas really means. It's one of the Celtic cross-quarter festivals, part of the old farming calendar. Of all the eight festivals we celebrate here, it's perhaps the one most closely linked to our need to survive and the bounty of the Earth Goddess. And of course as a farming community, that's vital to us.'

'I see,' she said, rearranging Sylvie's things on the dressing table. Her daughter was asleep again, a little smudge of colour now in her cheeks, but otherwise still very weak and lacklustre.

'I know it's all still strange to you,' said Clip, his grey eyes gentle, 'but maybe it would help if you learned more about our customs here and what they actually mean.'

'Help?'

'Help you to really integrate into our community. Everyone at Stonewylde has grown up with this in their blood so it's second nature, but not for you. Take the corn dollies, for instance. For the past week or so, every child and many of the adults have been busy weaving corn dollies. It's something everyone does in the last week of July. Have you seen any of them yet? There are lots of different designs, from the simple little favours and knots to really complicated designs, spiral plaits and so forth. Our children understand the symbolism behind this straw-work, and why we weave and plait these tokens.'

'I'm sure I can appreciate the symbolism,' said Miranda stiffly.

'With your mind maybe, but not in your soul,' he replied. 'You need to feel it, not just know it. Tomorrow, if you come up to the Lammas field for the sunrise, I think you'll find it enlightening. Lammas is quite a low-key event and many Hallfolk don't bother too much with the sunrise ceremony. Some only take part in the picnic at lunchtime, and some only the evening ritual in the Stone Circle and the party afterwards in the Barn. But please do come at dawn and spend the day with the folk.'

'Doubtless I will, provided Sylvie's well enough to leave on her own.'

'Good!' smiled Clip. 'It's a shame that Sylvie can't come too, but she does seem to be making a little progress at least. I'm sure it'll do her good too, in the long run, if you're both fully integrated members of the community. That child you're carrying will be a born and bred Stonewylder and he needs his mother to be part of it too.'

'He? Do you know something I don't?' she asked sharply.

'He or she,' he corrected with a twinkle in his eye. 'A slip of the tongue.'

It was still shadowy as Maizie shut the door to her cottage and shooed four of her children along the lane that led up into the hills. They joined the huge throng of Villagers trooping along the stony track to the special place where the Lammas sunrise ritual was held every year. Maizie gazed with pride at her sons walking ahead as she fell into step with Rosie, both bundled in their shawls against the pre-dawn chill. The three little ones slept in the Nursery, and would join them in the Lammas Field later. Maizie watched Yul walk with a spring in his step, tall and strong, talking quietly to Geoffrey and Gregory. Both boys looked up at Yul as they walked, one each side of him, listening carefully to what he said.

Maizie thought back to Lammas last year, and how different

it had been. She recalled Alwyn's bad temper and how he'd cuffed Gregory hard, making the boy's nose bleed. Yul had left earlier, not walking up with the family so as to avoid his father, and had then felt guilty all day because his younger brother had suffered in his place. She remembered Rosie crying when Yul missed the picnic after Alwyn sent him back down to the Village on some trumped-up errand. Alwyn had been out of sorts, knocking back far too much cider, fumbling with the sickle when it was his turn to reap. She'd had to practically smother little Leveret when her grizzling enraged Alwyn; she'd feared for the child's safety and this had made the crying worse, as Leveret picked up on her fear. She remembered the humiliation of Alwyn, snoring loudly, being carried back to the Village in one of the carts normally reserved for the small children, the elderly and the heavily pregnant. She smiled to herself and thanked the Goddess for the happiness her family now enjoyed.

'Mother, do you think Robin will ask me today?' Rosie said quietly, not wishing her younger brothers to overhear.

'Aye, seems likely,' said Maizie. 'You been at the dairy a six-month now and 'tis plain the boy's smitten with you.'

'Oh, if he gives me his favour I shall wear it so proudly!' said Rosie warmly. 'Robin is my dream come true! And I've brought the one I made him to give in return, just in case. I'll be the happiest girl at Stonewylde if Robin asks me to walk with him!'

'He's a good lad, Robin, and from what I hear, turning out to be a fine dairyman too. You're old enough now, Rosie, for your first sweetheart. But young enough too to change your mind if he don't measure up.'

'Did you see our Yul last night, Mother? He was sat in the corner quiet, plaiting a favour too. I think he has a sweetheart!'

'No! Surely 'twas a knot for hisself? Just a decoration?'

'No, Mother, else why would he be so secretive? And he tied a scrap o' silver ribbon into it too, with a slip of yew! Whoever heard of that afore? Yew at Lammas?'

'True, 'tis rather odd,' mused Maizie. 'Fancy that, our Yul walking with someone! Though 'tis about time – the boy will be an adult this winter. We must watch to see who wears it then. Silver ribbon is different, and a pretty idea. Makes a change from the usual. But yew ... mmn, I wonder what that says?'

'I did ask him, but he near snapped my head off!' said Rosie. 'Well, we'll see soon enough. I do hope it's someone nice.'

They fell silent as the track became steeper, climbing up into the rolling hills. Hundreds of Villagers tramped along, the Hallfolk using a different route, more direct from the Hall. Many of them rode, and Tom had also organised several of the long, upholstered carts to carry the less energetic Hallfolk to the Lammas Field. These rather grand carts were normally used to transport Hallfolk back and forth to the Village events, and Miranda had been grateful for the chance to ride in one this morning.

Her absences in the Barn at Dark Moon had alerted everyone to her pregnancy and she was now treated with extra deference. She sat in the jolting open carriage with a group of visitors, thinking longingly of her four-poster bed back at the Hall. But Clip's words had resonated with her; the child she carried was Magus' and would be as firmly Stonewylde as everyone else around her. She needed to immerse herself in the customs and lores, which might bring her closer to Magus too. She just wished that these celebrations didn't involve quite so many early morning starts, especially when she felt nauseous. She turned to answer the visitor next to her, who was querulously bemoaning the fact that so many Hallfolk youngsters hadn't bothered to rouse themselves for this important ritual.

Bright dawn bloomed in the sky as the folk of Stonewylde gathered in the Lammas Field, high up amongst the hilltops. Under the pink sky the people stood strung out like a necklace around the rustling wheat, golden and heavy-headed. Everyone held hands around the perimeter of the large field and the giant human circle began to chant. Magus, glorious in his robe of gold, led the ceremony. Voices raised, they started to move widdershins, all facing outwards and looking out across the vast expanse of fields around them. There were crops growing and ripening as far as the eye could see; gold, ochre and burnt sienna in the clear light. This particular field was chosen for the Lammas ceremony because it commanded such magnificent views across the miles and miles of flourishing fertility that was Stonewylde in August.

As the red sun burned its fiery arrival above the horizon, the people turned inwards and began to move deosil, making another complete circuit of the field and chanting to the drumbeat. Overhead a pair of buzzards circled, their enormous wings outstretched, the air plaintive with their high-pitched mewing cries. Miranda was moved by the beauty of it all and wished that Sylvie were here to experience it too.

At a signal from the drums everyone released hands and stepped forward, each plucking a single ear of wheat from the crop. All was silent as the people reflected for a minute or so on the bounty of the Corn Mother who lived amongst the grain. Every year she sacrificed herself for the community, yet held within herself the seed for next year's abundance. The drums picked up a different rhythm and the folk plucked the grains off their ear of wheat one by one, thanking the Corn Mother for her generosity, throwing the individual seeds back onto the soil. Symbolically they returned some of her bounty to the darkness of the earth, where it would lie dormant through the long winter months until spring quickened it with new life.

The ritual struck a chord in the hearts of the people of Stonewylde. They were still in touch with a knowledge so simple and primeval that most others in the western world had long forgotten it. This knowledge was the very source of survival: without the Earth's gift of fruitfulness, all would perish. The ceremony ended with a final chant, and then the huge circle of people broke up, laughing and chattering, and crowded towards the entrance of the field.

The sun was by now well risen and everyone cheered at the arrival of two carts pulled by beautifully decorated horses, their manes and tails woven and plaited with red ribbons and corn favours. One cart carried wicker hampers of Lammas cakes, special flat cakes as big as dinner plates baked from corn, honey and butter and flavoured with nutmeg. The other brought great churns of milk, creamy and frothy, straight from the dairy. Robin walked by this cart, having helped that morning with the milking, and Rosie's heart skipped at the sight of him. She'd been disappointed to be relieved of her duties at the dairy in order to take part in the sunrise ceremony.

Breakfast was served and everyone tucked in hungrily to their Lammas cake and beaker of milk. Afterwards the younger men of the community were presented with sharp sickles decorated, like the horses, with red ribbons and favours. They stepped forward with a flourish and a few words from Magus, and began to cut the crop in time-honoured fashion. This was a ritual, for the combine harvesters reaped all the other fields. But at Lammastide this one field was reaped in the old way, just as their ancestors had done for thousands of years, ever since hunters became gatherers.

Many of the Village women and most of the Hallfolk went home at this point, after watching a little of the reaping. The women would be busy all morning preparing picnic lunches and also food for the feast tonight. In the Lammas field there was music and singing as the musicians took out their fiddles, pipes and tambours, and the old harvesting songs were played. Children ran around happily and the older men stood about gossiping of times gone by. The reapers worked steadily in relays. Their sickles sliced the stalks of wheat close to the dry earth, their hands grasped the bundles which were then laid to the side for the binders. The binders were younger boys and girls who tied the thick bundles into a sheaf with a long piece of reed. The stookers followed the reapers and binders, gathering up several sheaves at a time and stacking them into stooks, roughly pyramidal in shape. This took place all around the enormous field and everyone had their turn, for a while at least.

By mid-morning there were many stooks standing proudly in the blazing August sun, and the uncut area in the centre of the field was dwindling rapidly. Even for the hardy Villagers this was tough work, requiring a great deal of bending and stooping. There was water and cider available to quench thirsts, and as the morning progressed the atmosphere became increasingly merry. By mid-day there was only a small circle of golden wheat left standing in the middle, and it rustled and moved strangely. The boys got their nets and clubs ready to hand.

The band of Village women, all the small children and the Hallfolk returned up the track. Some came in the carts and some carried their own wicker baskets; all were laden down with the picnic lunch. Then, once they'd arrived, the last bit of the field was reaped. The boys hopped around in glee, as this next part was their special task. As the men cut into the wheat with their sickles, rabbits started to fly out, their final refuge no longer a haven. The boys were waiting. Nets were thrown and clubs whacked, and before long the stubble field became a rabbit grave-yard. Miranda turned away in horror, her Outside World sens-ibilities shocked at the carnage. The unfortunate creatures were lifted by the ears and flung into one of the carts. The Village women would spend the afternoon skinning and gutting and baking special Lammas rabbit pies, enough for the whole com-munity to feast upon tonight.

When the final handful of wheat right in the centre of the field was cut, it was carefully carried over to Magus. He stood waiting, the sunlight glinting on his gold robes, and wrapped it carefully in a poppy-red cloth. He then presented it to the Corn Mother, the girl who'd been chosen for the Lammas festival to represent the keeper of the Corn Spirit. She must take this last sheaf and during the afternoon, with the help of other women, weave it into a special, ornate corn dolly. This great dolly, sym-bolically harbouring the Corn Spirit, would take pride of place on the Altar Stone at tonight's ceremony in the Stone Circle.

Miranda had been told all this earlier and watched now with a catch in her throat. She longed to be the one standing by Magus' side, his queen and partner. She knew she'd look beautiful in the golden robes with the great headdress of corn and poppies on her red hair. She was pleased to see Wren was the Corn Mother, one of the rather silly teenagers she taught, and no competition at all; the girl was only a year older than Sylvie.

Now, with the whole field reaped, sheaved and stooked by so many willing pairs of hands, the picnic lunch could begin. Yul took his sickle and trudged over to the area where the women were spreading the cloths over the stubbly ground and laying out food from the baskets. His back ached, his arms throbbed, and he had a thirst on him that would've drained the duck-pond. But he was happy; it had been a good reaping and it was immensely satisfying to see the golden stooks stacked all over the field. This was the first year he'd been allowed a sickle; before he'd only been a binder or stooker.

Yul put the sickle into one of the carts where they were being collected and joined the queue by the cider cart. There were several barrels on board and some older men, no longer able to help with the reaping, handed out great tankards of cider to the thirsty workers. Tom was in charge of the carts and horses and greeted Yul with Lammas blessings as he was handed a brimming tankard. Yul stood gulping down the cool, tangy cider, his eyes shut at the pleasure of the liquid sliding down his parched throat. He was clapped on the back by Edward, the farm manager and cricket team captain, and nearly choked.

'Good reaping, Yul! Well done, lad. Let's hope you do as well tomorrow in the match, eh?'

'Yes, sir,' grinned Yul, feeling like a man amongst men. Since the Solstice, when Alwyn had been taken away, he noticed that people were treating him differently. He was now the head of his family and enjoyed the honour and responsibility. He refilled his tankard and found Maizie and the family already seated on their rug and tucking into the picnic.

'You two did well at the rabbiting,' Yul said to Geoffrey and Gregory, who were both experienced rabbiters. They grinned at him as they devoured their food. Gefrin and Sweyn poked at the ground as they ate, digging up insects with sharp stones and kicking each other. Rosie kept Leveret well out of their reach as the little girl ate her lunch and gazed dreamily up at the sky, watching the swifts darting and swooping overhead. Maizie poured everyone some redcurrant wine, diluting it with water for the younger ones.

Yul looked around at the other families enjoying their picnics under the brilliant blue August skies and felt a surge of happiness. For him, the only blight on the day was Sylvie's absence. He'd quickly established that she wasn't with the Hallfolk, although he noticed her mother was, and Harold had confirmed that Sylvie was still confined to bed. Yul was becoming increasingly worried about her. According to Harold she hadn't left her room since the last Moon Fullness. Yul knew something wasn't right but was at a loss as to what he could do. However, he'd devised a plan to visit her later on; besides being desperate to see her, he had something to give her as well.

Rosie was passing round little white currant tartlets to the children, pretending to be absorbed in the task, when Maizie nudged her sharply. Rosie looked up to see Robin standing diffidently at the edge of the rug.

'Welcome, Robin,' said Maizie. 'Bright Lammas blessings! Will you come and sit with us and share some of our food?'

'Thank you, Goodwife Maizie,' he said formally, blushing as Geoffrey and Gregory sniggered a little at his shyness. He sat down awkwardly and accepted a tartlet, which Rosie handed him with a dimple of a smile and a sweep of the eyelashes. Yul, who was the same age as him, nodded encouragingly, aware of the purpose of Robin's appearance. The poor lad seemed in a complete dither and Sweyn and Gefrin had just begun squabbling again, much to Rosie's consternation. She scooped Leveret away from them and bounced the child in her lap, hoping Robin would notice how very good she was with babies.

'Now that Father's been taken ill, I'm the head of the family,' said Yul, guessing the boy's dilemma. 'It's me you should speak to.'

Maizie smiled in agreement; this was as it should be. Robin nodded gratefully, his cheeks flushing again.

'Right enough, then.' He cleared his throat. 'Yul, I wish to walk out with your dau– sister, Rosie, and have brought my token to show my honourable intent. May I have your blessing to ask if she will accept my favour, and favour me in return?'

The words came out in a rush. Robin knew how things must be done properly, and had been practising this for a long time. Yul nodded seriously, suddenly feeling very adult. He knew Rosie had liked Robin for ages, and the boy was a good choice for her first sweetheart. Whether or not they stayed together beyond Imbolc, when all favours were returned to the earth, was another matter. But they would renew their intent then, if things had gone well.

'My family are happy for you to favour Rosie, if she so wishes,' he said solemnly. 'Lammas Blessings to you and your family, Robin.'

Rosie leapt to her feet with a radiant smile and Robin quickly followed. She led the way to the perimeter of the field, where many other young Village couples were walking arm in arm. All were exchanging favours and pinning them over their hearts to show the community they were walking with someone and their heart, for a while at least, was taken. Maizie beamed at the sight of her eldest daughter pinning Robin's favour to her breast, and tapped Yul on the arm.

'Your turn now, my lad! Who's the lucky maiden?'

But Yul merely coloured and turned his head away, and Maizie realised perhaps this wasn't a good topic to pursue. Maybe he'd been rejected, she speculated.

The Hallfolk sat together in a large group, not mixing much with the Villagers. Most of them had only come for the picnic lunch, sent up for them by Marigold and the kitchen staff, and hadn't taken part in the morning's reaping. Yul noticed the funny old man Sylvie had been with in the pub the week before; normally he never remembered the Hallfolk who came and went at each festival. The professor saw him watching and raised his panama in greeting. Yul nodded back, rather pleased to have been acknowledged so politely by a member of the Hallfolk.

Magus sat on a large rug with the Corn Mother, a special feast spread out before them. Yul knew that Magus tried to alternate the May Queen at Beltane, Corn Mother at Lammas, and Bright Maiden at Imbolc with girls from the Hall and the Village. He recognised Wren as one of Holly's silly crowd and scowled. Magus was making a fuss of her, feeding her titbits from the delicious picnic. Yul's stomach clenched with anger as he watched Magus in the distance, laughing and teasing the girl. Where was Sylvie? Why wasn't she here too, enjoying this glorious day? He was sure it was Magus' fault.

When the picnic was over, everything was packed up and carried back down to the Village. The Hallfolk left too and then the large farm carts arrived, pulled by the shire horses. Their manes and tails too were plaited and be-ribboned for the special occasion, their bridles and harnesses decorated. They trundled across the Lammas Field and men with pitchforks tossed the sheaves into the carts. It had been a long, hot summer and the wheat was dry enough for the Lammas threshing. Some years it wasn't, and this part of the ritual would be abandoned as the stooks remained in the field to ripen and dry out.

Yul worked with the men, flicking the sheaves expertly into the waiting cart with his pronged pitchfork, and then moving on to the next stook. A great buzzard perched on the gatepost watching the proceedings with golden eyes, his beautiful tawny feathers glowing in the blaze of the sun. Finally all the sheaves were loaded and the carts rolled towards the gate, heading back down the track to the Village. The buzzard launched himself from the post, the clumsy flapping of his immense wings belying the grace of his high altitude flying. Yul trudged with the men behind the carts, pitchforks over their shoulders, and felt quite light-headed from the cider.

Back in the Village the newly harvested wheat was taken to the Great Barn. Every year the women hoped the wheat wouldn't be dry enough for the threshing to happen, for they needed time to clean the Barn and lay out the food and drink for the evening.

But this year there wasn't a cloud in the hot sky and the threshing went ahead. It was another ritual that echoed the farming customs of their ancestors; before mechanisation, all grain had been separated from its stalk in this laborious way.

The men split themselves into teams of four, with four young-sters to help. Each man had a flail made from two pieces of wood joined with a leather hinge. The handle was made of strong ash and the beating piece was holly, which didn't split. Yul had helped cut the wood to make these tools himself. Each team had their own patch on the clean flagstone floor of the Barn, and several sheaves of wheat. The sheaves were loosened and then beaten with the flails, the team working in a peal, one after the other thrashing the wheat as it lay on the ground. As the grain became separated from the stalks, the youngsters would run in and pull away the straw, shaking it well to dislodge any remaining seeds. Then they would scoop up the grain into a pile to be put into a waiting sack. It was a fiercely-fought competition to see which team could fill their sack first, and the winners each received a specially brewed bottle of Lammas Mead.

Yul was delighted to be included in a team of men to thresh; last year he'd been one of the boys scooping up the grain from the stone floor. The competition began amidst much wild yelling and whooping. The Barn was alive with noisy beating as the wooden flails hit the stalks and stone, and the shouts and encour-agement of the boisterous men. The musicians played lively tunes and the dust rose in the air, golden in the shafts of sunlight and dancing with motes of husk. Slowly each team's sack of grain grew fuller until finally there was a triumphant shout and Edward, having inspected the sack to ensure it really was full to bursting, called a halt and announced the winners.

More cider was consumed to slake the latest raging thirsts, and then each team carried their sack on the strongest man's back down to the mill. The grain would be ground into flour at the old watermill where all the cereals were still milled under the ancient quern stone. The resulting flour from the afternoon's hand-threshing was given to the bakers that evening, and overnight they produced Lammas rolls in the shape of a plait, dusted with poppy seeds. They baked enough for every single person in the community, to be eaten the following morning for breakfast on the Green with butter and honey or new strawberry jam. This bread, when it was made from the hand-reaped and threshed Lammas wheat, was considered to hold almost magical properties; it was even customary to make a wish whilst eating it.

After this, the crowd of men and lads who'd taken part in the threshing would traditionally strip off and jump in the river near the mill. This was an expedient custom as there wasn't enough hot water at the Bath House for everyone to wash away the day's sweat. Although he was embarrassed, Yul thought his back was now probably alright to expose. So he joined in and tugged off his clothes, running and jumping into the river and the mill pond with everyone else, splashing about and making a great deal of noise. Nobody said anything but he felt the stares, and several times looked up to catch the expression on people's faces before they turned away. Everyone in the Village knew about the beating in the stone byre because Alwyn had boasted of it to anyone who'd listen. Yul was very pleased that Magus wasn't around to add to his humiliation. In fact there were very few Hallfolk about, which was a relief. He could imagine what Holly and her friends would've said.

After swimming in the river and cooling off, most of them went home for a rest before the evening's events. Everyone was exhausted after the reaping and threshing and the women were busy cleaning the Barn and preparing the feast for tonight. Yul trooped back from the mill to the Village Green, but when he got there he decided not to go home, where he knew it'd be noisy with his six siblings running around. Instead he flung himself down in the cool shade of the yew tree and lay thinking.

The thick dark branches almost blocked out the sky and it was very quiet under the canopy. Yul felt at once peaceful and yet stimulated. There was a strong aura of magic here and it wasn't just the memory of his and Sylvie's first kiss. He could sense something else, something magical that was part of Stonewylde's supernatural aspect and linked to the Earth Magic, the Moon Goddess and the Green Man. He felt its presence strongly today at this primeval festival, under the ancient tree of regeneration.

Yul closed his eyes and slowly drifted off to sleep, soothed by the enchantment of the yew. His young, strong body relaxed from the hard labour of the day as his soul danced in the magic permeating the woodland temple. Professor Siskin, sitting on a bench outside the Jack in the Green sipping cider, had seen Yul disappear under the spreading boughs of the yew. He nodded wisely, his heart more gladdened than it had been for many years. This was as it should be; the magic calls to its own.

9

W ren looked solemn and more than a little nervous as she stood on the Altar Stone in the Stone Circle. Her robes were green and gold, and on her blond head she wore a huge crown of woven cereals and poppies, radiating out like the sun's rays. She cradled the Corn Spirit dolly, a great spiralling neck of woven and plaited stalks almost phallic in shape, with a thick fan of wheat ears at one end, tied with red, gold and green ribbons. It was massive, longer than her arm, and heavy. The Corn Spirit lived in this dolly, safely housed now that the cereal harvest was under way. Wren held it rather gingerly but with a sense of grandeur, much to the amusement of her friends who stood amongst the crowds trying to catch her eye. Miranda watched her sourly, and smiled when a Village woman standing nearby let out a chuckle.

'That maid looks terrified of 'un,' she said. 'Does she think 'twill turn and bite her?'

''Tis not the dolly she should be fretting about!' said another. 'Maybe it's put her mind to what else she'll be dealing with later on tonight?'

They laughed at this, and Hazel, on Miranda's other side, diverted her attention from their ribaldry.

'Incredibly intricate, isn't it?'

'The corn dolly? Yes, and I hear she had to make the whole thing this afternoon?'

'That's the idea, though I doubt Wren actually did much of it herself. The Village women are far better at the old crafts. It really is beautiful – such a shame it's burned.'

'What a waste, all that effort up in flames,' agreed Miranda.

'Not tonight of course. It'll live in the rafters of the Great Barn for the next six months.'

'You'd think Wren would hold on to it as a keepsake of her special day.'

'Oh no, that wouldn't be allowed!' laughed Hazel. 'That's the whole point – its ashes are ploughed back into the Lammas Field to return the Corn Spirit to the land at Imbolc.'

'Imbolc – when my baby's due!'

'It's all very symbolic and primeval.'

But Miranda wasn't really listening, and Hazel joined her in gazing at the man standing on the Stone, holding everyone in his thrall.

Magus was magnificent as he led the chanting in golden robes that gleamed in the fierce flames of the bonfire. The sparks flew skyward as the people sang and Yul resented him bitterly, standing there glittering with bright energy and looking so pleased with himself. It was almost dark now, the sun having set, and Yul's stomach churned with excitement at his bold plan for the evening. If all went right, he'd be holding Sylvie in his arms very soon. At this wonderful thought a great thrill of anticipation pulsed through his body.

The ceremony continued and then came the sharing of mead and cakes. Yul made sure he was up near the front of the queue. This part of the ritual took ages, especially with all the extra visitors about. Even when the communion was over there was still the corn dolly drama to be enacted, with the Corn Mother and Corn Spirit and all the children. And after that, the procession down the Long Walk back to the Great Barn for feasting and dancing whilst the Rite of Adulthood took place up here. Nobody would miss him for quite a while if he were to leave early, but he knew he must first go up to the altar and receive the cake and mead. Magus might be looking out for him and notice his absence otherwise.

Yul bowed his head to Magus, glorious in his beautiful robes with the massive barley, corn and wheat crown adding to his stature. Magus looked down on Yul and smiled in satisfaction. It was rather amusing that not so long ago he'd actually perceived this boy, dressed in a simple tunic like all the other children, to be a threat. At the last ceremony Yul had confounded him by appearing on the top of the Solstice Fire with the crow on his shoulder, and the boy's clumsiness had made him drop the torch. But since then everything had changed. True, he'd felt an ebbing of the power he received at the Altar Stone. In fact tonight at sunset and the lighting of the Lammas fire, when normally he'd have received the Earth Magic, he'd felt nothing at all. But that was more than compensated for by the new energy he was getting from the round stone up at Mooncliffe and his supply of moon stone eggs. It was a different sort of energy, more thrilling and quicksilver than the deep, throbbing green Earth Magic.

Magus felt like a squirrel with a vast hoard of acorns stored up for winter, but best of all, his supply of eggs was a renewable resource. At the next Moon Fullness Sylvie would perform for him once again and he could drain her special energy every single month. It was evolution, he'd decided, when trying to understand why the Earth Magic no longer blessed him. He now had the moon magic instead and Sylvie was the catalyst for this evolution.

He watched as Clip ladled the measure of mead into the boy's open mouth, feeling a great bursting of power as Yul swallowed and bowed. He'd well and truly crushed this impudent upstart, and it felt good to see him lowering his head in complete subservience. Yul was unaware of this, keeping his face down to hide his euphoria as the power sizzled from the Altar Stone, finding its way to him even though he wasn't even touching it. In the flickering firelight Magus failed to notice the green flash as the energy merged with its host. Yul's almost daily visits up here, as Mother Heggy had advised, had strengthened his connection with the energy spirals. The Earth Magic now sought him out whenever he was nearby.

He relished the strong mead and the spreading heat as it hit his insides. As Yul held out his cupped hands to receive the ceremony cake he looked up, and in that split second caught Magus' eye. He felt another rush of exultation as the Earth Magic throbbed inside him. His cool grey gaze carried unmistakable challenge. He suppressed a grin as he saw the arrogance in Magus' black gaze turn to surprise and then anger as he read the look in Yul's eyes.

The fight's not over yet. You haven't beaten me and you never will.

Yul shuffled along in the massive queue away from the Altar Stone and then slipped out of the Circle through the throngs of people. He stuffed the cake in his pocket for later, knowing he'd need his wits about him. Still wearing his green and gold Lammas tunic with barley woven into his hair, he ran as fast as a leaf in the wind up to the Hall. Harold had told him which was Sylvie's wing, and of the fortuitous outside door and staircase leading straight up to her bedroom. He'd already visited at night to locate it and Harold had assured him the door was never locked. He'd seen Miranda at the Stone Circle looking enthralled at the celebration, so knew he was safe from bumping into her.

Now, out of breath but invigorated from his run, Yul arrived at the Tudor wing. He looked up to the softly-lit windows at the very end which he knew to be Sylvie's room. It was completely dark below as he opened the side door from the garden and crept up the worn stone stairs, silent and stealthy as an assassin. Carefully he lifted the latch of the arched oak door at the top of the stairs and found himself in Sylvie's bedroom, lit only by a soft lamp. She lay in the white bed, her long silver hair spread over the pillow and spilling onto the sheet. She was apparently asleep and he tiptoed over, gasping as he drew close enough to see her clearly. She looked like death.

In her tiny hovel the crone muttered to herself, peering through nearly sightless eyes into the piece of dark glass. She found scrying almost impossible now, but she grunted with satisfaction

144

as the black glass clouded over. A scene began to emerge beyond the smokiness. But as she squinted at the image, her heart grew cold.

'No, no, no!' she screeched, making the crow squawk in alarm. 'I never saw this! 'Tis happening all over again! Oh, dear Mother, not again!'

She shoved the dark glass away from her, rocking frantically in her chair while the crow scrabbled to maintain its grip on the chair back. After a while she calmed down but continued muttering to herself, shaking her wispy head. Then she turned and spoke to the crow. He hopped onto her shoulder and she craned to kiss him with her toothless mouth. With a flurry of black feathers he flapped across the room and out of the tiny open window to do his mistress' bidding.

Yul knelt by the side of the bed gazing down at Sylvie as she slept. It was now four nights since her ordeal up at Mooncliffe and yesterday Hazel had removed the drip, judging her to be improved. Her skin was still translucent and the violet shadows under her eyes remained deeply defined, but she had slightly more life in her now and could sit up in bed to eat and drink a little. She needed infinite amounts of sleep, and when she did awaken was often confused and disorientated. Yul knew nothing of this. All he saw was his beloved Sylvie, normally so bright with quicksilver magic, now as lifeless as a corpse.

Gently he stroked the hair away from her forehead and traced the contours of her beautiful face, still lovely despite its delicacy. His throat ached with sadness at the sight of her. He whispered to her, saying how much he'd missed her and how he thought of her every minute of the day. He sensed her struggling to surface from a heavy slumber.

'I'm here, Sylvie. Open your eyes.'

She recognised his voice and smiled slightly. Then her eyes opened and she smiled properly.

'Is it really you, Yul? Am I dreaming?'

'No, I'm here.'

She reached out to embrace him, pulling his head down and rubbing her cool cheek against his.

'Oh Yul, I've missed you so much. Don't leave me again, not ever.'

The crow flew over the Stone Circle, looking down with bright eyes at the people below spiralling in corn dances. The great fire sent forks of heat lancing up into the night sky. He flew on and finally reached the Hall where he circled for a while, then landed with a flap and a flutter on a window sill. He preened himself and peered through the diamond-paned window at the boy and girl inside, cuddling together in a gentle embrace.

Sylvie released Yul after a while and tried to sit up. He helped her, propping her against a mound of pillows and cushions, and passed her a drink of water. She smiled at him, trying to act normally, but it was obvious just how weak she was. Her eyes were enormous in her face, pale grey pools of suffering. It broke his heart to see her like this.

'What's happened to you?'

She shook her head.

'I don't know.'

'Was it anything to do with the Moon Fullness?'

A strange look passed over her face and she stared at him.

'I danced on the stone up at Mooncliffe for Magus.'

'And that's what's made you so ill?'

She shook her head and shrugged, her face screwed up in puzzlement.

'I can't ... when I think of it I feel muddled. It's not ... I don't understand what happened.'

'Can you tell me about it?' Yul asked gently, trying to hide his seething resentment.

'I ... I don't think I can ... but I love dancing on the stone.'

'How can you love it when it does this to you? Did he force you to go up there?'

Bewildered, she shook her head. He took her wrists and examined them for bruising, but this month there was none, only the marks on the back of her hand from the needle of the drip.

'If he didn't force you, why did you go? Why didn't you come to Hare Stone with me? You said it's where you belong. Why do you go to Mooncliffe when it makes you so ill, Sylvie?'

'I DON'T KNOW!!'

With that she burst into tears, sobbing piteously as if her heart would break. He held her in his arms, comforting her, stroking her hair, whispering to her that he'd help her. After a while she quietened down and sniffed into a hanky.

'I'm sorry, Yul. I'm just so frightened. I don't understand what's happening but I know something isn't right. I have these awful dreams . . .'

She shuddered violently.

'What happens in them?'

'I don't know! When I wake up I can never remember. Sometimes I remember just as I'm dropping off to sleep but then it's gone as soon as I wake up again.'

'Is it anything to do with Magus?'

He noticed that she shuddered at the sound of his name.

'I must share my moon magic with him. It's what I was brought here for and I have to do it. But . . .'

She shook her head in confusion and he frowned at her. Just then there was a tapping on the window and they both jumped, Sylvie clutching at him in terror. Yul walked over slowly and saw the crow. Laughing, he opened the window. The crow hopped inside and let out a polite *caw*!

'Look, it's only Mother Heggy's crow, Sylvie, come to say hello.'

She smiled wanly. He could see she was exhausted.

'I'd better go soon,' he said reluctantly, sitting on the edge of her bed. 'Someone could come back at any minute.'

For the first time she noticed his tunic and bare limbs, and the ears of barley and corn fastened in his hair.

'Why are you dressed like that?'

'It's Lammas! We've just had the ceremony in the Stone Circle. Now it's back to the Great Barn for the feast and dancing. I wish you were coming.'

'Me too. I'd love to be there.'

He took her thin hand in his and stroked it gently, then fished in the pocket of his tunic. First he brought out the ceremony cake, a little crumbled. He put this to one side and pulled out something else, which he concealed between his hands. He swallowed nervously.

'Sylvie ... we have a very special custom at Lammas. It's about walking out. Normally the boy asks the head of the girl's family for permission to favour her. But I can't ask anyone for permission to be your sweetheart. So I'm asking you directly, even though this isn't the right way to do it. I hope you understand that my intentions towards you are honourable. I love you, Sylvie, and I'd be honoured if you'd accept my favour and walk with me. In fact I'd be the happiest lad at Stonewylde if you agreed to be my sweetheart.'

Shyly he presented her with the little corn knot. Sylvie stared down at it, a long strand of her blond hair falling onto his wrist. The favour was three ears of wheat, with a little twisted loop of plaited stalks holding them together. A small silver ribbon was tied into a bow around the neck, where the loop flared out into the ears, and a tiny slip of yew hung amongst the wheat. Sylvie felt tears welling in her eyes, understanding that although she knew nothing of it, this ritual was very important to Yul.

'Oh Yul! It's lovely! I'm not sure of the words I'm meant to say in response, but I'm the happiest girl in Stonewylde to have this favour. And yes please, I'd love to be your sweetheart!'

She smiled at him, her soft grey eyes brimming with tears, and he took her gently in his arms and held her close. She felt so very frail and he pulled back, taking both her hands in his.

'So now we're a couple until Imbolc, when I hope we'll make a new promise to each other,' he said softly. 'It's sad that you can't pin my favour above your heart, nor can we walk around the Village Green together at twilight. But never mind, our time will come. '.

'It's so pretty, Yul, and I wish I could wear it. Maybe I could ...'

'No you mustn't. Everyone, even the Hallfolk, knows what wearing a favour means and they'd wonder who you were walking with. And it would attract a lot of attention – it's not quite the same as most favours.'

'Really? In what way?'

'Usually they have red ribbon. But I used silver because of your moongaziness, and I added the bit of yew because we had our first kiss there under that special tree.'

'Oh Yul, you're such a romantic,' she said. 'I love my special favour and I'll treasure it. What a lovely custom.'

He smiled at her, longing to crush her in his arms and kiss her hard and deep. He knew she wouldn't resist. But he couldn't be that selfish, not with the dark shadows under her eyes and her slow, almost painful movements.

'I really must go now, Sylvie,' he said, picking up the little cake and stuffing it back into his pocket. He didn't want Miranda noticing her daughter had had a visitor to her bedroom tonight. 'Make sure you hide my favour away somewhere safe, won't you?'

'Okay, but Yul, please come and see me again,' she said. 'I miss you terribly. I don't know what went wrong between us before, that day up on Dragon's Back, but I still feel the same way about you.'

He stretched over and kissed her cheek, wanting more than anything to kiss her properly.

'So do I, Sylvie. Remember that, whatever happens. I'd do anything for you. When you're well again we'll sort this out, I promise.'

'Thank you,' she whispered. 'I'm scared and I don't understand what's happening to me.'

'I promise I'll make it all better,' he said boldly, a fierce sense of protectiveness rising up inside him. 'I'll do anything for you, Sylvie my sweetheart. I'd die for you.'

She nodded weakly, stroking his tanned cheek with her delicate fingers. Unwillingly he rose to his feet and crossed to the arched door. The crow, who'd been sitting quietly on the dressing table by Yul's jar of flowers, hopped after him and then flapped up onto his shoulder. He blew Sylvie a kiss and shut the door carefully behind him, climbing down the stairs in the darkness.

The crow wouldn't get off Yul's shoulder and pecked his ear repeatedly, so he abandoned his original plan to join the feast and decided to pay Mother Heggy a visit. He'd seen her a couple of times since the Solstice but not recently, having been so busy with the harvesting of flax, fruit and vegetables and his extra responsibilities at home. He needed to speak to her about Sylvie's terrible condition and hoped she could help with a restorative potion. Yul skirted the Village carefully, not wanting it known where he was going. He carried on up the path leading to the cottage and the crow took off and flew on ahead. When he arrived, the door was already open and the wizened figure of Mother Heggy stood waiting for him.

Yul was pointed to the hard chair while the old woman fiddled about at the range, filling tiny bottles with various liquids from jars and saucepans. Every time he tried to speak she hushed him. She seemed agitated, muttering to herself and ignoring him. Finally he decided if she wasn't going to talk to him he might as well go to the feast – the thought of Lammas rabbit pie made him even hungrier. But she turned and glared at him.

'How did you let it happen, you stupid boy?'

'What?'

'The bright one – he'll destroy her if you don't stop him. The prophecy will never be fulfilled and you'll walk alone. Sylvie must be by your side if you're to take your rightful place. You should be guarding her but you let him take her.'

'I don't understand what you're on about, Mother Heggy. Do you mean the Moon Fullness and her moongaziness?'

'Aye, o' course I mean that! He's taken her to Mooncliffe and made her dance on the glittering snake-stone! And now he has strength again, just when he should be on the wane. The story repeats itself and you let it happen. She must dance with the hares, always with the hares, up high on the hill where the tall stone marks the sacred place.'

'I know, Mother Heggy, but it's not my fault. How can I stop her? She wants to go to Mooncliffe with him.'

'He's forcing her, like his father did to Raven. He's an evil man with a craving for power. Such a lust for power I've never seen, not even in his father. This one is worse, much worse. This one is the strongest, the cruellest. Aye, and the cleverest.'

'But Sylvie's told me that she loves to go there. He didn't force her to say that.'

'You're a fool, boy! I tell you, he forces her. Her heart cries out as she sleeps, yet nobody hears. Not till tonight would the dark glass clear and show me the truth, and then I saw it, the horror of it happening all over again. He drinks up her life, feeds on her magic until there's no more left to give. He's so greedy, this one. He'll never have his fill, always wanting more and more, bleeding her dry till he destroys her.'

'I don't understand. Sylvie *wants* to dance at Mooncliffe.'

''Tis a spell he's put on her. She speaks as a puppet.'

'But I didn't think he had any magic of his own. After the Solstice, the magic has become mine. I visit the Stone Circle every day and it's getting stronger. Magus has no power from there any more so how can he put a spell on her?'

She nodded at this.

'You speak true, boy. 'Must be the brother; he's the one who casts the spell. Beware of him. He creeps like a snake and you won't know he's about till you put a foot on him. Beware of him and his spells. He is powerful, and 'tis not earth or moon magic like yours and Sylvie's. His is a different sort, a wisdom he's learnt. He's a strange man; he has gifts and can walk with the spirits. And there's something else, some secret, something not clear.'

Yul nodded, remembering that night of the Story Web when Clip had invited him to touch the Rainbow Snake. The shaman had strange powers and could've put a spell on Sylvie, which would explain everything. But his more immediate concern right now was her health. He'd seen just how weak she was.

151

'I know, I know,' muttered Mother Heggy, before he could say anything. 'I have it all ready here.'

She showed him the little bottles she'd prepared.

'Morning, noon and night, a draught for each till all is gone. 'Twill help get her strength back. But the best thing, once she's up and about, is to take her to Hare Stone for the magic there. Come back next week and tell me how she mends. Here, put the bottles in this bag and mind you bring 'em back, boy. 'Tis not easy to get good bottles and corks.'

Quite when and how he'd get the remedies to Sylvie or take her up to Hare Stone, Yul had no idea. He ran back to the Village, and after concealing the bag at his cottage, joined the rest of the community in the Great Barn for the music and dancing. It had been a long and strenuous day and he needed to relax. He felt much happier knowing Sylvie was under a spell and not choosing to go with Magus. He could fight a spell, but he couldn't fight Sylvie not wanting him.

Yul stood chatting to Rosie as they watched their mother dancing around the Barn, free at last of Alwyn and his drunken possessiveness.

''Tis good to see her having such fun,' said Rosie. Her own cheeks were as flushed as their mother's as she too had been dancing. She looked very pretty and Yul felt proud of his sister.

'Where's Robin then? Not dropped you already?' teased Yul, sipping his cider.

'He's getting me some more blackcurrant cordial,' said Rosie. 'And anyway, Yul, where's your sweetheart? You never did tell us who she was.'

'She's not here,' said Yul sadly, eyeing the favour pinned to Rosie's blouse. 'I just wish she was. Hey, look at Mother now! She's dancing with Magus!'

They both watched as Maizie swung past them, her dark curls flying and eyes sparkling. She was linked to Magus, handsome in his festival clothes, who seemed to be enjoying the dance as much as she was. They made a striking pair and many people turned to watch them.

'Always did have a passion for each other, those two,' laughed a Village woman. 'Remember that long summer?'

'Aye, quite an item they were, as young 'uns,' agreed another. 'Alwyn was so mad and jealous, for he had his eye on her too. Remember how spirited Maizie was when she were just coming into her prime? Alwyn wanted her bad, but he had to play second fiddle, I recall. 'Twas Magus she'd set her heart on. Moonstruck for him, she was.'

'Aye, who could forget that? He'd come riding into the Village for her right under Alwyn's nose, and off she'd go with him, jumping up on his horse without a second glance or by your leave. She was a wild one, that Maizie, with her dark hair and rosy cheeks. Had Magus in her pocket for a while, no mistake.'

'And now Alwyn's safely tucked away, the first fiddle can come back and play another tune!'

'Get away with you! 'Tis only a dance, nothing else.'

Yul was shocked to overhear such gossip. He'd had no idea that Magus and his mother had once liked each other and the thought was repulsive to him. He turned to discuss it with Rosie but she'd joined Robin on the dance floor and he was left standing alone. Holly, Rainbow and a couple of other girls were now the closest people to him, and their giggling and shrieking was hard to ignore. He stayed in the shadows, not wanting any of Holly's attention. He disliked her all the more for having once found her attractive.

'Look at Magus tonight cavorting with another Villager! And an old one at that.'

Yul's fists clenched at this insult to his mother but he kept silent and out of sight.

'Well, he has to keep the peasants happy. I heard him say once that it's the main purposes of all these dances and things. It makes them work harder for the rest of the year. At least that stupid Sylvie's out of the way tonight.'

'Yes, else she'd be monopolising him. We all know the little cow's got her sights set on Magus.'

'I saw him kiss her on the stairs the other day.'

'No! And have you heard she was with him at the last Moon Fullness? You know, up at Mooncliffe.'

'But she's not an adult yet! That's not allowed!'

'Well she was definitely with him. Fennel saw them going up the path just before sunset. I don't know what they were doing up there but apparently she's been in bed ever since. So . . . what happened that night, I wonder?'

They giggled and Yul gritted his teeth feeling sick with suppressed rage. If they only knew the truth.

'And with any luck she'll be out of the way tomorrow too, when Buzz gets back.'

'Do you think she'll still be after him as well?'

'Well, you know how he was before he left, following her around like a little puppy dog. She's got him well and truly hooked, the bitch.'

'She certainly knows how to pull the men, doesn't she? And she looks so sweet and innocent too. You'd never think it. I hate her.'

'She'd better watch out with Buzz, though. You know he's got that . . . side to him. I'd laugh if she pushed him too far – that'd serve her right.'

'And he's back tomorrow for definite?'

'Oh yes, sometime in the morning in time for the Lammas cricket match, he said. Remember how mad he is about cricket? He's over the moon because he's on the Hallfolk men's team this year and he wants us all there, cheering him on. Apparently he's been practising all summer whilst he's been away. Oh, I can't wait to see him!'

'Will you go out with him again when he gets back, Holly?'

'You bet! With madam safely tucked away up in her tower, I'll remind him of what he's been missing all summer.'

The girls laughed at this and Yul slipped away, sickened by their talk, his evening spoilt. Sylvie and Magus, Sylvie and Buzz – he didn't believe a word of it. Sylvie was beautiful and special and of course she'd attract other men's attention; he'd just have to accept that. There was something so desirable and tantalizing about her, and naturally others felt it too. But she belonged to him, and him alone. Yul knew it deep inside, despite the apparent impossibility of such a thing. Mother Heggy had recognised it – the darkness and the brightness. And like any prize worth having, winning her wouldn't be easy. He'd have to fight for her.

Reaching his cottage, he looked up at the stars. Eternity was patterned in the sky and echoed in his soul. Yul knew without any doubt at all that he and Sylvie were destined to be together one day. An owl called from the woods nearby and he shivered suddenly. Tonight he'd told Sylvie he'd die for her, but that was only a part of it. Yul knew he'd also kill for her.

10

Yul left the Stone Circle once the sun had climbed a little in the sky. It promised to be a scorching day for the annual cricket match. Yul felt energised and strong and knew he'd need this today. He desperately wanted to play well for the Villagers' team and not let Edward down. At his age, not yet an adult, it was an honour to have been chosen to play with the men. Crackling with Earth Magic, both from this morning's sunrise and from the Lammas festival yesterday, Yul decided to go to Mooncliffe. Mother Heggy's words yesterday had been a revelation and he wanted to understand exactly what was going on up there. Clearly Magus had discovered how to drain Sylvie of moon magic, and it must be something to do with the disc of rock.

Luckily Yul moved silently up the path because when he reached the top, he was shocked to find Magus lying spread-eagled on the massive round stone. He'd taken off his shirt, revealing his tanned, well-muscled torso and the silver disc on a chain around his neck. His eyes were shut and his body relaxed as the sunlight glittered on the rock. Yul was reminded of a viper sunning itself on a stone to warm its cold blood. He crept off the path and hid behind the tall bracken that grew so thickly on the hill. His heart beat slow and hard as he watched the man glowing like a great golden god. This was the man responsible for Sylvie lying in bed, white, exhausted and barely able to move.

After a while, Magus sat up and stretched. His muscles flexed under the tanned skin.

'Sacred Mother, that feels good!' he said huskily.

He leapt off the rock and stood on the cliff edge looking out to sea. Yul hated everything about him; the way his silvery hair curled slightly as it reached his neck, the length and power of his legs, his smooth broad shoulders and the bronzed satin of his bare skin. The hatred rose unbidden and almost choked Yul with its violence and intensity. He had a sudden urge to run over and shove Magus hard in the back; to watch him fall down, down, until his golden body smashed on the sharp rocks below.

Yul swallowed, his throat painfully dry, and clenched his fists to stop the shaking. He'd never felt such hatred before, not even for Alwyn after his worst excesses. He wanted to destroy Magus and the feeling frightened him in its overwhelming passion. This man was so powerful – Sylvie so delicate. How could he force her to give him all her moon magic? How could he steal something so precious from a defenceless girl?

Magus chuckled to himself and turned from the sea. He strolled over to a large wooden chest that Yul hadn't seen here before. Taking a key from his pocket he unlocked it and looked inside, his face breaking in a smile of pure delight. He bent over and took out what looked to Yul like a large goose egg, cradling it in both hands against his chest. He groaned and at first Yul thought he was in pain. But then he heard what Magus muttered and realised that the man was actually in ecstasy. Yul frowned in bemusement. Magus locked the chest and picked up his shirt from the rock. As he turned, the egg caught the sun and sparkled.

In that instant, all became clear to Yul. He could barely swallow and had to steel himself against leaping up and attacking Magus there and then. As Yul watched, Magus grasped the egg like a ball and made a mock bowl, his arms rippling in perfect co-ordination. He chuckled again and tossed the egg in the air, catching it and laughing.

'Howzat!' he said softly, heading off down the path.

During the morning everyone was busy putting the final touches to the Village Green in readiness for the cricket match. This was a major event at Stonewylde and one of the few times that Villagers competed directly against Hallfolk. It was always a fiercely fought affair and evenly matched, as there was strength, stamina and skill on both sides. Yul could see both Magus and Clip on the Green and decided to risk a visit to Sylvie; he needed to deliver the potions from Mother Heggy that would help her recovery. He raced home to collect the bag and walked in to a major row. Leveret was cradled in his mother's arms, scarlet-faced and screaming, whilst Gefrin and Sweyn stood silently in the middle of the room looking down at the floorboards.

'Yul! Thank Goddess you're here!' cried Maizie. 'You sort this out. Rosie and the boys aren't here and I've enough to do helping get the cricket match tea ready without this.'

'What's happened?' asked Yul, wanting to face his responsibilities but anxious to get to Sylvie while he knew Magus and Clip were safely on the Green.

'Those two again!' said Maizie angrily. 'I don't know what's happened but they've done something horrible to Leveret and look at the state of her, poor little mite. She can't tell me o' course, and they're denying everything. Since their father's gone they've been terrible. You deal with them, Yul, and make sure it sticks. This isn't the first time they've hurt her.'

Yul glared down at the two little boys, both looking sheepishly at their feet. He felt a bubbling of anger. Sweyn, with his gingery hair and porcine features particularly annoyed him, and Yul knew why.

'Well?' he said. 'What did you do to your little sister? I want the truth now!'

'Nothing!' cried Gefrin. 'We didn't do nothing, Yul!'

'She's just a cry-baby,' muttered Sweyn, his jaw stubborn.

Yul took a deep breath. He had to get up to the Hall now; it really was urgent. Maizie had calmed Leveret down a little and watched her oldest son struggle to deal with the situation.

'Smack them, Yul,' she said firmly. 'They've obviously done something nasty to her.'

Yul rounded on his mother, his face white.

'I don't smack children,' he said quietly. 'Nobody in this house is to be smacked, or hit, or beaten. Not ever.'

She stared at him and swallowed. Leveret held out her arms to him and Yul took her, hugging her close. She clung to him, hot and tearful, her little body still shaking with the aftermath of sobbing. He turned back to the two boys who were eyeing each other hopefully. They weren't to be smacked. Maybe they'd get off altogether.

'If you won't tell me the truth, then you must've done something horrible,' he said. 'I won't stand for it. Smacking is wrong, but you'll be punished. I'm taking you down to the nursery and you'll spend the day there with all the babies. You'll miss both the cricket match and the tea. Daisy can keep you shut in the naughty room at the nursery for the whole day and that'll serve you both right. Don't ever do anything nasty to your little sister again. You should be taking care of her, not hurting her.'

He kissed Leveret and handed her back to his mother, then collected the bag of remedies from his room. Grabbing each of the boys by an arm, Yul marched them down into the heart of the Village to the nursery. Their legs could barely keep up with his long strides and both snivelled all the way. He saw Clip and Magus in the Barn and breathed a sigh of relief. With a final stern word to his youngest brothers, he bundled them into the care of Daisy and ran quickly towards the track leading to the Hall.

On the way he heard voices around the corner and dived into the bushes. He recognised Buzz's voice and didn't want to risk a confrontation now, not with the bag full of precious medicine for Sylvie. Soon Buzz came swaggering into sight surrounded by his old gang of friends, as loud and ebullient as ever. He seemed bigger than before and more adult. His face was freckled and his blond hair now cropped very short. Yul's skin prickled with dislike at the sight of him and the memory of the beatings Buzz had given him over the years. He had a score to settle with this large blond youth, and the sooner the better.

As luck would have it, he saw Miranda sitting outside on the long terrace as he skirted the Hall and made his way round to the Tudor wing. Quietly he climbed the stairs, knocking gently on the arched door at the top. Sylvie was sitting in a chair by the window and rose to fling her arms around him. He grinned at her, delighted to see her up and looking a little brighter today.

'Mother Heggy has sent you some of her potions to help get your strength back,' he said, showing her the bottles inside the bag. 'You must drink one – see, they're quite small – every morning, noon and night she said, until they've all gone. And keep the bottles and corks because she wants them back.'

Sylvie looked dubiously at the assorted glass bottles and their murky brown contents.

'Do you think it's safe?' she asked. 'It won't poison me, will it?'

'Sylvie, Mother Heggy is renowned for her remedies. She's a wonderful healer and I promise this'll make you feel better. Have one now.'

She did so, and felt the effect of the strange medicine as it slid down her throat. They hid the bag in the fireplace behind the decorative summer fire-screen. She smiled at him and sat down again in the chair.

'You're right – I feel different already.'

'Good! And Mother Heggy said you should get up to Hare Stone as soon as you're able. The magic there will help you get stronger. We'll go together if we can manage it.'

That sounds lovely. You look wonderful today, Yul,' she said softly. 'You're shimmering.'

'It's the Earth Magic,' he said. 'It comes to me now so strongly. Last night at the Lammas ceremony – I didn't even have to stand on the Altar Stone. It sought me out.'

'What about Magus? Did he notice? Isn't he angry that he doesn't get it?'

Yul's face darkened at the memory of what he'd seen on the cliff top earlier.

'No, he doesn't need it any more. And Sylvie, I know what's wrong with you now. It's all Magus' fault. It's that stone up at Mooncliffe. It . . .'

'No!' she cried. 'I don't want to talk about it! When I think of it all my head hurts. Please . . . just leave it, Yul.'

'Alright,' he said gently. 'We'll sort it out when you're stronger. At least you're safe from him until the next Moon Fullness. I'm sorry.'

He knelt before her and took her hands in his, gazing up into her thin face. She flinched, her eyes widening with shock, and pulled her hands away.

'What?'

'I can feel the Earth Magic in you, Yul! It's so strong. It feels the way it did when Magus healed me back in the spring.'

'Really? Then take it, Sylvie, take it now! Maybe I can heal you too!'

She looked uncertain.

'Are you sure? Magus said he had to be careful or it'd be too powerful. Can you control it?'

He shook his head. She looked down at him kneeling at her feet, his deep grey eyes full of concern for her. It seemed every time she saw him he'd changed. He looked so grown up nowadays, more a man than a boy. She thought back to the Yul who'd dug her back garden and looked at him now more closely. He was different; the thin defiant face now filled out into strong planes and hollows. He was so good looking. She reached forward hesitantly and stroked his angular cheek bone, tracing the thin scar.

'Just hold me,' she whispered. 'That'll be enough.'

He stood up and helped her to her feet, wrapping his arms around her and holding her tight. She felt thin and frail and he was careful not to crush her. Tentatively he tried to free just a little of the energy burning inside him and let it pass gently through his fingertips where they touched her. He felt her tremble but he held on and slowly felt the release. It was a strange sensation but not unpleasant, and he was pleased to be able to do something to help her.

Eventually she pulled away and held him at arm's length, looking deep into his eyes.

'Thank you, Yul. I feel stronger already.'

He saw a faint tinge to her cheeks that hadn't been there before, though whether that was due to his Earth Magic or Mother Heggy's potion he couldn't be sure. Her eyes sparkled slightly, no longer so dull and clouded, and she smiled. His heart filled with compassion for her. She was so brave, not complaining about what had happened to her, not making a fuss at all.

'I have to go, Sylvie,' he said reluctantly. 'It's the cricket match and I'm on the Villagers' team. Edward picked me after all. I'm so excited! That bastard Buzz is back and I'd love to bowl him out. I wish you could be there to watch and cheer me on.'

'Me too. Good luck, Yul. I'll be thinking of you.'

'I'll come and see you again soon, I promise, and you can take some more of the Earth Magic next time. I'll learn to control it properly and then I'll share it with you until we can get your moon magic back.'

She smiled and, reaching up, kissed him softly on the lips.

'The moon magic isn't mine to keep. I must give it all to Magus. It's what I was brought here for.'

The Village Green had been transformed for this one special day. The cricket pitch was marked out, with bunting strung around the trees in the colours of Lammas – green, gold and red. A platform had been erected for the scoreboard, the whole thing decorated with corn dollies and knots, and the great silver cricket cup stood up high on a plinth. Tonight the winning team would be drinking specially brewed Lammas mead from it to celebrate their victory. Chairs and benches were positioned all around and many families were staking claim to their places with rugs and cushions. Long trestle tables were set up for lunch and, later on, tea. Children ran around excitedly; when they started to get bored during the day, games would be organised for them on the Playing Fields with their own junior cricket match.

The two teams were changing into their whites ready for the match, Hallfolk in the School House and Villagers in the Jack in the Green. Yul was excited but nervous, and his hands shook as he tied his laces. Both Magus and Buzz were in the Hallfolk team and he'd love to beat them personally, but realised that was only a dream. His fear was that one of them would get him out at the very beginning and make him look a fool. He felt the energy rushing through his veins and prayed silently to the Goddess to help him play well today.

As the two teams were led out onto the Green, the community cheered and whooped. All the players wore proper whites and used best quality equipment, for this match mattered a great deal to Magus. He was very skilled at cricket and although his team didn't always win, he played well every year without fail. Yul stood out from everyone else with his dark curls, now almost shoulder-length again. Most of the Hallfolk team were very pale blond and the Villagers tended to be darker blond or brown-haired, so there were very few black-haired people in the community. Maizie and the children cheered especially loudly as Yul walked past, grinning at them. Maizie was so proud of her eldest son. He was turning into a fine young man, strong and hand-some, and she knew he wouldn't have been striding out confidently as part of the Villager cricket team if Alwyn had still been around. Rather than have the boy doing well and feeling good about himself, her husband would've taken pleasure in ensuring that Yul wasn't fit to play. Maizie shuddered at the thought and thanked the Goddess that Alwyn was no longer around to blight their lives.

The two teams stood beneath the platform and the captains climbed up the steps for the toss. Magus captained the Hallfolk team, and Edward the Village team. The Hallfolk won the toss and chose to bat second. Under the blazing August sun, the Lammas cricket match commenced. The Villagers batted well, scoring many runs. Yul himself scored a respectable forty or so before being bowled out. He felt he'd acquitted himself fairly well and his family cheered enthusiastically as he came off. Magus was in fine form, bowling superbly, and Yul was very pleased he hadn't had to contend with any of those balls. Buzz was so busy showing off to his Hallfolk gang that he missed several catches and often bowled wide. He was letting down the Hallfolk team and Magus was clearly annoyed. When play was stopped for lunch with two Villagers still in, Yul noticed Magus hauling Buzz off for a private word and smiled to himself. He liked the idea of Buzz being on the receiving end of Magus' wrath.

Everyone enjoyed a good lunch, and then a minor stir was caused when a Land Rover appeared. Clip, who was not playing cricket, got out and waved to everyone, then went round to open the passenger door. Yul stared in joy as Clip helped Sylvie out of the car and ushered her solicitously over to a comfortable seat near the platform. Magus seemed taken aback and strode over to talk to them.

'Hello, Sylvie! What a pleasant surprise! I hope you're well enough to be out?'

'She was desperate to come and watch and I thought it would do her good,' explained Clip. 'You're feeling a great deal better today, aren't you, Sylvie?'

She nodded. 'Yes, thanks. I think I'm getting over whatever was wrong with me. I feel much stronger.'

'Good, that's marvellous news,' said Magus. 'You're just in time to watch the Hallfolk bat. We're going to thrash the Villagers this year, I'm sure.'

'Now, now,' said Clip. 'It's the playing, not the winning, that matters.'

'That, dear brother, is why you're not on the Hallfolk team. Of course it's the winning that matters. Isn't that right, Sylvie?'

But Magus was in for a nasty surprise. There was some excellent bowling and fielding from the Village team and several Hallfolk were bowled or caught out in quick succession. When Buzz came to bat he swaggered onto the pitch, saluting the bevy of Hallfolk girls led by Holly who screamed and waved at him. He stood, bent in the batting position by the wicket, an expression of smug confidence on his face. He whacked the first bowl with a lazy swing and started to run. But he faltered halfway along as a great roar rose from the crowd. Yul had hared across the grass and, with an impossible leap, had somehow caught Buzz out. He sprang up from the ground and threw the ball into the air, whooping with triumph. Buzz's face flooded crimson as he stomped off the pitch, cursing loudly enough for many to hear. Yul looked across at Sylvie and saw her clapping wildly. He gave her a discreet wave and she beamed at him.

Magus liked to bat near the end and was becoming increasingly exasperated at the Hallfolk's performance. Their score was way behind the Villagers', which meant there was now considerable pressure on him. Magus knew how every person in the community looked up to him and felt he had a duty to play spectacularly, to show people that their admiration was justified. The game was stopped for afternoon tea just before Magus' turn to bat. Everyone enjoyed sandwiches and cakes and some late raspberries and cream. Magus ate heartily as his appetite had increased lately. As he ate he held a stone egg in his lap and could feel its effect pulsing through his body. He looked across at Sylvie nibbling on a sandwich. She seemed slightly stronger, not quite so pale and exhausted, which proved she was perfectly capable of recovering almost fully within a week or so. One week each month wasn't too much to ask of someone, not when it meant serving him in such a special way. Self-sacrifice was, after all, part of living in a community.

He looked around at the crowds of people, his people, and felt a swelling of pride. They were all here looking so healthy and happy because of his expert leadership. He glanced over at the Villagers, sitting on the grass on their rugs. He noticed Rowan, the delightful young May Queen who now carried his child, the fruit of their Beltane union. He caught her eye and she gave him a beautiful smile that lit her lovely face. He smiled back and saw her flush with pleasure.

Scanning across the crowd he saw Maizie with her family and she nodded at him, her pink cheeks dimpling. Magus couldn't see Yul's face for the boy had his back to him. He was holding the youngest child, little Leveret, and whispering into her dark curls. Magus frowned; Buzz should never have let the boy catch him out first ball. He'd been far too complacent about the whole match.

Magus's gaze moved on to the Hallfolk. Buzz was nowhere in sight and Magus imagined he'd gone back to the Hall in shame. The group he hung around with were particularly noisy and had clearly forgotten how Hallfolk should conduct themselves. He'd have to speak to them. Wren was with them and smiled across at him a little knowingly. He noticed Professor Siskin, sitting on a deck chair enjoying his cucumber sandwiches. The old man raised his panama in greeting and Magus nodded.

Then he saw Hazel sitting next to Miranda and smiled broadly. He knew Hazel would do whatever he asked. Both women were looking across at where Sylvie sat with Clip, and Hazel was talking earnestly whilst Miranda nodded. He was pleased with Hazel and must make sure he showed his appreciation. He knew exactly how to keep her happy. Someone was waving at him and he realised it was the charming young woman he'd visited at the last Moon Fullness. She'd be returning to the Outside World soon and he must visit her again before she left. Magus sighed as he bit into another scone – life was good indeed. He put his hand on the stone egg and accepted another cup of his favourite Lapsang Souchong from Marigold.

Tea over, the teams returned to the pitch. As Magus walked across the Green to bat, the whole community circling the Green stood up and cheered. He acknowledged the adulation with a slight incline of his head, his long legs in the cricket whites carrying him gracefully across the distance to the wicket. His blond hair gleamed in the sunlight and he nodded at the Village bowler to indicate his readiness. His face took on an expression of concentration; he intended to excel himself today.

Almost an hour later Magus was still batting. He looked magnificent; tall, powerful and shimmering with vitality. Yul knew where his strength had come from and felt a flash of white-hot rage shoot through him. Magus sweated in the heat, his bronzed face gleaming with perspiration. He was playing superbly, never better. He felt amazingly strong and wondered how much professional sports people would pay for access to such special energy. He smiled to himself. He hadn't thought of Sylvie's gift in terms of making profits, but here was another way she could be of use. He could make a great deal of money out of the eggs, the joy being that it was a renewable resource. Sylvie could be made to channel the moon magic every single month. Thirteen loads of eggs a year! She'd managed the twenty eight eggs fairly easily. With practice and training she could do considerably more. He smiled broadly and whacked the ball to score another six.

When Yul's turn came to bowl, Magus' features broke into a sardonic smile at the sight of a mere boy opposing him. In Magus' dark eyes, Yul read all the arrogance and superiority in which this man luxuriated. He truly believed that he was a god, that he was invincible. As he faced Magus across the cricket pitch, something deep within Yul snapped. With a tiny skip and a thudding heart, he started his run towards the wicket. Magus flexed his grip on the bat and narrowed his eyes in concentration, more than confident of dealing with anything the boy could offer.

The cricket ball felt like a missile in Yul's hand as he flew along his run, gathering tremendous speed, well-muscled arms and legs perfectly in synchronisation. He kept the gleaming, supercilious face in his sights as the ball launched hard from his hand like a rocket, flying in the fastest bowl ever towards its target. Magus seemed to move in slow motion. His eyes widened in surprise at the speed and velocity of the red ball hurtling towards him. He started to react, adjusting himself to intercept this unexpected and deadly marksmanship. But fast as he was, he wasn't fast enough. Yul's deadly shot had found its target. The bails went flying from the wicket in a great arc and the Villagers exploded into a roar of triumph that shook the trees and scattered the pigeons to the skies.

Across the expanse of grass, Yul's grey eyes met Magus' black ones. Yul nodded. Magus nodded back.

'Excellent bowling, young man!' he called down the pitch. 'I congratulate you.'

As Magus walked off in dignified style to great applause, Yul glanced again at Sylvie. She was laughing with delight.

The celebration in the Village pub that night was riotous. Yul sat amongst the group of men and felt on top of the world. The great silver trophy cup was filled to the brim with Lammas mead, brewed extra strong and heavy with the taste of malt. It was handed round from man to man, mouth to mouth, each sipping then passing it on. Very soon Yul felt the effects of the powerful drink. The speeches began and Yul became increasingly embarrassed by the over-effusive praise.

'But it wasn't just me!' he protested. 'We all batted well, and loads of you got them out when we were fielding.'

'Aye, but you caught out that puffed up Buzz on his very first ball!'

'Did you see his face? Hah! Cocky little bastard! That burst his bubble, right enough! Never did like him.'

'Didn't I always say Yul was something special?' shouted Greenbough proudly.

'And that ball you done at Magus! I never seen anything like it, lad.'

'Yes, but—'

'But nothing! Magus was on a winning streak, all set for another century. If you hadn't bowled him out the Hallfolk would've won.'

'Yet again! I hate it when the Hallfolk win.'

'Three cheers for Yul!'

Yul had never in his life received so much adulation. Even though at one point he fell asleep on a pew, when he woke up later it started all over again. The earlier rowdiness had calmed down a little and there was more chance to talk. Yul was pleased when Tom came over and patted him on the shoulder.

'Well done, Yul! A great catch and a great bowl!'

'Thank you, sir.'

'Tom, not sir. We're all friends and equals in this pub. None o' that cap doffing rubbish here.'

Yul grinned.

'Thank you, Tom.'

'You're very brave, lad, challenging Magus the way you do. Today you could've let him carry on scoring. Every year there's always a bother about getting Magus out. I seen men many a time deliberately fumble catches and give him easy balls because they don't want to be the one who gets him out.'

'Really?' It had never occurred to Yul not to do his utmost to get Magus out.

'Oh aye, and you did it on your first ball, like it were easy! It takes a good deal of courage to stand up to a man like Magus, especially after what he's put you through in the past. I reckon you're the only one at Stonewylde who'll do it. Can't think of anyone else, Villager or Hallfolk, who'd challenge him like that, and yet you have more cause than most to fear him. It ain't gone unnoticed, you know. People talk of what you've done, Yul. Talk and wonder at it.'

'They do? I haven't done much.'

'You've defied the man – look at the Solstice ceremony! He dropped that torch and 'twas you as picked it up and lit it again – I saw it. You used your fingers and nothing else. I saw the blue flames with my own eyes! You've got something in you and he don't like it. But we do, us Villagers. 'Tis about time somebody broke that man's power.'

Yul stared at Tom in amazement. He had never, ever heard anyone talking like this. He'd thought he was the only one who resented Magus' arrogance and domination.

'Anyhow, enough o' this,' said Tom, resuming the heartiness of earlier. 'You drink down this last bit of mead, my boy. You earned it. Right enough, everyone? Let's hear it again for Yul, the Villager who took on the master and beat him!'

It was very late when Yul finally decided he must go home to his bed. He said his farewells to much cheering and staggered out onto the Green, where he stood swaying slightly on the site

169

of his earlier glory. He remembered the two high spots of the match: Buzz's crimson face as he was caught out first ball, and Magus' expression of shock as he realised the ball flying towards him would bowl him and there was nothing he could do about it. Yul savoured those moments again and knew he'd remember them for the rest of his life.

He looked around the great circle of the Green. It was shadowy under the sparkling stars and tilted yellow moon and he felt the magic of the place, a different magic to that of the Stone Circle. This was a power from within, something deep in his soul emerging, a magic that the Village Green brought out of him rather than put in. He gazed at the great yew and thought of what he intended to do there one day, picturing himself and Sylvie lying entwined under the protection of the sacred boughs. Then, feeling a little uncoordinated from the strong mead, he headed along the track to his home. He wanted to lie flat on his bed as everything had now started to spin.

A fist flew out of nowhere and cracked him full on the cheekbone. Yul went flying into the hedge and lay sprawled and confused, his head ringing from the blow. His initial thought was that Alwyn had returned, but he shook his head. Alwyn was out of action; a living corpse up at the Hall. Then he was yanked out of the hedge by his shirt and shoved hard in the back. He fell face down onto the stony track and the weight of someone heavy thudded onto his back, crushing him. He felt an excruciating pain and vomited as the strong mead was forced out of his stomach.

'Oh shit, he's puking!' yelled Buzz, hastily scrambling off. Yul dragged himself up onto all fours and continued to heave. He was aware of a circle of feet surrounding him and judged there were five or six of them. He was sobering up quickly in the face of danger and being on the ground amidst all those feet was not a good position. Yul staggered upright, wiping his mouth with the back of his hand, surrounded by the gang of Hallfolk youths.

'I'm going to teach you a lesson once and for all!' growled Buzz. His speech was clumsy and his words came out garbled.

'I came back especially for that cricket match. I organised my whole summer holiday so I'd be able to play today. I never even had a chance to bat, thanks to you, you little bastard. You need to learn your place, boy. Isn't that right, lads?'

They chorused agreement. Yul smelt the alcohol on them and it was nothing that he'd ever come across at Stonewylde. Buzz must have brought it back with him from Outside. Yul tried to think straight; with all of them so drunk he was in considerable danger. If they got him down on the ground and started kicking, they might actually kill him. He had to escape, and fast.

'You're going to regret catching me out like that,' slurred Buzz. He shoved Yul hard into one of the others, who thrust him back equally hard. 'I'm going to beat the shit out of you! I'm going to smash you to a pulp, you ignorant bloody peasant! When I've finished you'll never play cricket again!'

They flung him back and forth across the circle, yelling insults and trying to unbalance him. As he was thrown around, Yul deliberately fell harder than he needed into each one. This made them step back each time, unsteady as they were, widening the tight circle a little. As soon as he saw a gap, he pretended to fall, then sprang out through the space between them and ran full pelt up the track.

'Quick, he's got away! Catch him!'

But Yul was much faster than any of them. He'd brought up the contents of his stomach and was feeling better than they were. Buzz in particular was out of condition after being away for much of the summer. Yul raced ahead into the woods, and soon lost them. He could hear them way behind him, crashing about in the undergrowth and yelling threats and obscenities at him. He ran lightly through the woods and decided to go up to the Stone Circle. All he wanted was to lie down and sleep, but he didn't dare head home in case they were waiting for him.

In the yellow light of the waning moon, now tipped very low on the horizon as it set, Yul approached the sacred stones. He felt the sheer grandeur and magic of the silent place. He apologised to the powers that walked there for his intoxication, trying to clear his thoughts as he entered the sacred space. He felt an almost tangible presence there – neither benign nor hostile, but immensely powerful. With a straight back and raised chin he carefully stepped onto the soft earth of the ancient arena and walked across to the great Altar Stone. He'd been coming here now almost every day for the past few weeks, but familiarity didn't make the place any less awe-inspiring. He vaulted up onto the waist-high altar and lay down. Immediately the force spiralled up around him; pure, green energy. All the places that hurt from Buzz's ambush throbbed less painfully.

He looked at the bright stars above, the familiar patterns in the sky. He picked out the great arch of the Milky Way, so beautiful it made the breath catch in his throat. Buzz and his friends faded into insignificance. Yul was acutely aware that he was just one tiny human being lying under such vast beauty. He felt the energy of the Earth Mother pouring up, greeting the starlit dome of the heavens with spirals of movement and power. He was caught in the glorious interaction of sky and earth, lying on one of the points where their forces met. Like Sylvie at the time of Moon Fullness, his body and spirit were in harmony with these forces; a perfect receptor and conduit through which they could pass. Yul fell asleep on the great stone as the stars danced their stately patterns above him and the Earth turned beneath him.

11

Yul was awoken long after sunrise the next morning. The sun was warm on his skin as he opened his eyes. He could see nothing at first; his head was muzzy and the light blinding, but then a dark figure moved and blocked the sun's brightness. The silhouette was unmistakably Magus and Yul's heart began to thud. He sat up quickly, blinking, scrambling upright. Magus moved round slightly and Yul saw his face. The man had obviously come straight from Mooncliffe for he was glowing with energy. Yul sensed it pulsating through him and wondered whether Magus in turn could sense the green energy swirling around him. They faced each other and Yul held his gaze, determined not to show any fear or subservience.

'Why are you up here asleep on the sacred Altar Stone?' asked Magus, his voice neutral. Yul was aware that Magus too may feel he had a score to settle from yesterday, but he might as well tell the truth. If Magus had already decided to punish him, nothing Yul said would make any difference anyway.

'I was hiding from Buzz and his gang.'

'Why?'

'Because they said they'd beat me to a pulp.'

'Why would they do that?'

'Because I caught Buzz out first ball and he wanted revenge.'

'I see.' There was an edge to Magus' voice that filled Yul with dread. 'And when did this happen?'

'Late last night. I'd been celebrating in the pub with the other Villagers and I was on my way home.'

'And was Buzz waiting for you, or was your encounter purely by chance?'

'He was waiting with his gang. They jumped out at me.'

Magus moved a little closer, his face expressionless but his eyes hard. Yul could feel just how much the man resented him. He steeled himself not to flinch at what must come next.

'I can see the bruise on your cheek. Have they done anything else to you?'

'No, not really, they just shoved me around. Buzz sat on me and made me throw up but I managed to escape before they could do anything else. They were very drunk and I was worried they'd go too far.'

As he spoke, Yul realised the futility of his words. This was the man who'd had him whipped so severely that he could no longer stand, and who'd then starved him for five days. He wouldn't understand the concept of going too far. But, to Yul's surprise, Magus looked concerned.

'That's plain bad sportsmanship on Buzz's part and he'll damn well apologise. He's forgetting the Hallfolk code of behaviour. Villagers must be allowed to win with impunity or there's no point in having the cricket match. Go back home and clean yourself up, and tell your mother that Buzz will be dealt with. You'll receive an apology later in the day.'

That afternoon Yul was helping the Village men dismantle the platform on the Green when they heard the clatter of hooves on the cobbles. Magus rode into the Village on Nightwing, accompanied by Buzz on a smaller chestnut horse.

'Here they come,' muttered one of the men. 'Watch yourself, Yul.'

They'd noticed the swollen bruise on Yul's cheekbone and heard about the previous night's events, and the Villagers were furious at what Buzz had done. There was a groundswell of feeling against the young Hallfolk and their arrogant ways, and Buzz was the least popular of them all.

Magus trotted over on the great black horse, whose eyes rolled at the sight of the group of men. Nightwing's mouth was foaming and he champed at his bit, sidestepping impatiently. Magus reined him in sharply and tapped the whip warningly against his neck. Nightwing tossed his head in defiance, flecks of foam flying. Buzz was astride a more docile horse who tried to crop the grass at her feet as they stopped in front of the Villagers. The men had closed protectively around Yul, shielding him from view. His performance yesterday had been spectacular and wasn't likely to endear him to the Hallfolk, especially not to these two.

Both Tom and Greenbough had spoken openly in the pub of all that had happened to Yul over the past few months. Everyone knew of Yul's ordeal at the quarry and the extra work he'd been forced to do over the Midsummer Holiday. It had become common knowledge that Magus abandoned his usual code of justice when it came to Yul, and the thin scar on the boy's cheek was a constant reminder of this. Yul was a popular figure in the Village, first something of a martyr after Alwyn's cruel abuse, and now a hero after the cricket match.

'Blessings to you all,' said Magus briskly.

'Blessings, sir,' the Villagers replied, nodding their heads in automatic deference.

'I believe you have Yul there. Come here, boy.'

The men parted reluctantly and Yul stepped forward. Nightwing bobbed his head and gave a little whinny of recognition. He tried to come forward but Magus reined him in viciously, cursing under his breath. The horse danced on the spot, haunches bunching up under him. Yul tilted his chin and looked up at Magus towering above him on the stallion.

'Yes, sir?'

Magus gazed down at him coldly, black eyes glittering.

'I was angry to hear that Buzz ambushed you last night on your way home from celebrating the Villagers' victory at the cricket match.'

There was an immediate murmur and grumble of disapproval amongst the men. All eyes turned to Buzz who stared at the ground, his face burning scarlet.

'You said it was he who bruised your cheek and made you sick.'

Magus shifted in his saddle, still trying to control Nightwing who pranced and shook his head, jingling his bit noisily.

'You told me Buzz was not alone but had a gang with him, and he wanted to punish you for catching him out at the cricket match. Is that correct?'

'That's correct.'

'Buzz, get down off that horse!' Magus commanded. 'Come here where we can all see you.'

Buzz dismounted and stomped round in front of Magus, still staring at the ground. Nightwing reared up slightly and one of the Villagers stepped forward to take the reins of Buzz's horse, walking it away so it couldn't upset Nightwing further.

'I will not tolerate bad sportsmanship,' said Magus curtly. 'Nor will I tolerate Hallfolk abusing Villagers.'

At this hypocrisy, Yul could barely contain himself. He glared up at Magus, grey eyes blazing, his nostrils as flared as Nightwing's. Magus regarded him with a black, steely stare.

'Buzz has seen the error of his ways and now wishes to apologise.'

There was a pause, the tension almost palpable. Yul's angry breathing was clearly audible as everyone waited for Buzz's words. Nightwing cavorted to the side and almost knocked Buzz over. Magus swore viciously, fighting to control the stallion. The blond youth stumbled and tried to get out of the great horse's way, frightened of the heavy hooves that drummed the ground in a tattoo of impatience. Yul stepped forward and reached up to Nightwing's bridle, holding him and stroking his long nose. Immediately the horse pushed his head into Yul's chest, rubbing against him and snickering with pleasure. Magus' mouth tightened dangerously at this but he said nothing. At least the horse had stopped fretting.

'Buzz?' Magus barked.

The youth looked up for the first time and Yul saw a long slash across his freckled cheek. The thin line was raised in a swollen red wheal just like the one Magus had given him, the skin broken and sore. Buzz's pale-blue eyes locked into Yul's. The Hallfolk youth shook and his lips trembled; the blood had drained from his face but the expression in his eyes was one of pure hatred.

'I apologise for attacking you.'

'And?' prompted Magus.

'And for my bad sportsmanship. The Villagers won the cricket match fairly.'

The speech had obviously been rehearsed. Yul held his gaze, a feeling of triumph welling up inside him at Buzz's public humiliation. He nodded.

'Apology accepted.'

He broke the gaze and cupped his hand under Nightwing's velvety nose, feeling the prickly whiskers beneath his chin. The men behind him nodded their satisfaction; justice had been done after all.

With a jerk of suppressed anger, Buzz turned away. Grabbing his horse's reins, he heaved himself into the saddle and kicked the horse away into a canter. With a final pat, Yul stepped back from Nightwing and Magus wheeled the great beast around.

'You see that I will not tolerate any Villager being unfairly treated. Now that's an end to the matter. Blessings to you all.'

With a squeeze of the thighs he galvanised Nightwing into action and left with a thudding of hooves and flurry of dust.

But if Magus thought he'd dealt with the matter, he was wrong. Buzz was too much his father's son to let it rest there, his ego dented and superiority in doubt. The revenge he chose against Yul was the one he thought would hurt most of all. A couple of days later when the Lammas holiday was over and everyone back at work, Yul was on his way to the hazel coppice. It was mid-afternoon, another sunny day, and Yul jogged along the woodland path shaded by the leafy canopy. He wore the usual woodsman clothing – a sleeveless jerkin, old trousers and leather boots, all an indeterminate shade of green-brown. He was hot and dirty, his curls full of bits of woodland. He'd been making hazel hurdles all morning and longed now for a drink. He knew that there was a large pottery jar of water nearby, one of many that the men had stashed all over the woodland for just such a need. He slowed down and left the path, stepping through the undergrowth of ferns and hart's tongues to the foot of a great lime tree where he knew the bottle to be laid.

The lime tree was ancient and beautiful. Its late blossom attracted the bees and it buzzed and hummed with life. The heart-shaped leaves clustered thickly but sunlight still dappled through onto the woodland floor, and Yul sank down with his back against the massive trunk. He sniffed the exquisite sweet fragrance of the lime blossoms, feeling sleepy from his hard work in the woods all day. He raised the stone bottle and drank deeply of the cool water, then splashed some onto his dirty face. The dirt and green lichen that coated his hands smeared all over his clear-cut features. He closed his eyes, savouring the moment, knowing that the lime was the tree of soothing justice, the generator of divine knowledge and truth. He felt peaceful here, in harmony with the spirit of the great tree. He drifted into a doze.

Yul was disturbed a little later by a sharp click, followed by another. His eyes shot open and he stared into the lens of a camera. It was Professor Siskin making the most of his last days at Stonewylde. The professor stepped around Yul, sprawled against the bole of the tree with his long legs spread out before him, sleepy in the heat. His slanted grey eyes watched the small man lazily and he smiled, his white teeth bright in the smeared green face. Siskin stopped and took another photo, gazing down at the boy intently.

'Extraordinary!' he muttered. 'Utterly extraordinary! Do you have any idea of your true identity? Who you actually are?'

'I'm Yul,' the boy replied. 'I'm a Villager and a woodsman.'

'Yes, yes, that is true. Just a simple boy of the woods, with the leaves and twigs in your hair, foliage all around you, and that green lichen on your face. You are truly sylvian.'

'What? Sylvian?'

'Of the woods. Like Sylvie – from the Latin.'

The white-haired man continued to stare, his conversation making no sense to Yul, who felt uncomfortable under the pale-blue gaze. He stood up, brushing bits off his trousers.

'I'd better be getting back to work, sir,' he said.

'Yes, of course. Yul – did you know that "Yul" means "the wheel"? And now it has come full circle, a revolution. We are back again at the beginning of it all, the wheel and the woods. The dance continues.'

'No, sir, I didn't know that. I must go or I'll be in trouble. Blessings to you!'

Yul stepped back through the undergrowth onto the path and continued on his way back to the hazel coppice, trying to banish thoughts of the strange little man and his weird ramblings. He'd been walking for a while when he heard cries. He stopped and listened intently. The cries of distress came from some way distant, in the direction of the track further along which ran parallel to the woods. Yul took off like a deer, cutting through the trees and leaping over undergrowth towards the sound. He saw the track ahead, the sunlight bright where the canopy was broken. The cries were loud now; a girl calling for help, pleading for someone to stop. With horror he recognised the voice as Rosie's.

He burst through the undergrowth and jumped down onto the track, looking around frantically. Then he saw her. She lay spread out against the mossy bank by the side of the track, her blouse pulled open and skirt bunched up, exposing her legs. Her hair was a tangled mess and her face scarlet, tears streaming down her cheeks. She was hitting desperately at the big, blond youth half lying on top of her, who held one of her hands pinned above her head whilst he tore at her clothing.

With a roar Yul sprang onto Buzz's back, pulling him with such force that a piece of Rosie's blouse, still clutched in his hand, was ripped away. Yul wrenched him off and sent him sprawling to the ground. Buzz looked up in wide-eyed astonishment; his freckled face flushed and mouth gaping in surprise at this unexpected attack. Yul leapt on top of him and punched him very hard in the face. He noted with satisfaction the clicking crunch his fist made as it hit Buzz's nose. A bright geyser of blood spurted out, spraying all over Yul's shirt. Buzz yelled, struggling to sit up. Yul grabbed a handful of his cropped hair and banged his head down hard on the stony track, whilst the other fist punched full force into Buzz's eye.

'What've you done to my sister, you bastard?' screamed Yul, white-faced and beside himself with rage. 'I'll kill you for this!'

Rosie was screaming too, trying to pull Yul off as he pounded again and again into Buzz, smashing his fist repeatedly into Buzz's face.

'Stop, Yul! That's enough! He didn't do anything – he didn't get that far! Stop, stop!'

But Yul wouldn't listen. He'd gone berserk and Rosie abandoned her attempts to stop him.

'I'm going to get help!' she cried, and clutching her open blouse together, ran off down the track towards the Village.

Buzz managed to push Yul off and stagger upright. His face was a complete mess; his nose a bloody pulp and both eyes swollen almost shut. A cut above one eye was bleeding profusely down his face, adding to the darker blood pouring from his nose, and his breath was ragged.

'You've done it now, you little shit!' he cried at Yul.

His voice was high and cracked and Yul realised that despite his aggression, Buzz was very scared.

'No, *you've* done it now, Hallfolk scum! You're going to get what you deserve at last!' spat Yul, his eyes ablaze with vengeance. 'Rosie's only fourteen – how *dare* you do this to her? How *dare* you attack my sister?'

They circled each other, fists clenched and legs slightly bent, ready to attack.

'I'm going to finish you this time!' screamed Buzz, finding it difficult to see through the veil of hot blood and puffed up eyes. His nose was excruciatingly painful.

'Come on then!' called Yul, his voice trembling with adrenalin but feeling very much in command of himself. 'Come on, you fat, lazy Hallfolk bastard! Let's see what you can do without your gang of friends to hold your hand! Let's see how you fight one against one!'

Yul launched his offensive in a frenzy of ferocity. He kicked Buzz hard in the stomach and twisted away fast, throwing a nasty side swipe at his head as he pulled back. Buzz staggered, doubled over in agony from the brutal kick. Yul leapt in again and punched upwards, his fist connecting with Buzz's chin. His lower jaw smacked sickeningly into the upper one and more blood sprayed everywhere. Buzz howled, spat and a tooth flew out with the mouthful of blood. Yul closed in, fists pounding relentlessly, thumping Buzz in the chest, stomach and shoulders.

Buzz tried to retaliate at first but he could barely see or breathe. His face was one livid mass of swollen tissue and he was winded. He slowly doubled over and sank to his knees, curling up, trying to protect his head. Yul flew in yet again, a whirlwind of snarling rage. His face was contorted with hatred as he roared and screamed abuse, kicking Buzz in the buttocks and kidneys. He knew very well where it hurt most.

'STOP!!'

At first the shout didn't register. Yul continued to lay mercilessly in to Buzz's crouched form, oblivious to his screeches and bellows of pain.

'I SAID *STOP*!!'

This time Magus waded in and grabbed Yul by the collar, hauling him off. Yul stood there shaking, panting and gasping for breath, his face white and hollow with the desire to kill. He was covered in blood. Rosie came running up with Maizie following breathlessly, and both stared at Yul in horror.

'What's he done to you, Yul?' cried Maizie, trying frantically to examine him. 'Where's it bleeding?'

Magus, surveying the scene, barked with laughter at this.

'I don't think Yul's bleeding anywhere,' he said. 'The blood is all Buzz's.'

He stepped over to where the youth crouched, huddled and squealing with fear, all self-control gone. He prodded Buzz disdainfully with the toe of his boot.

'Be quiet, for goodness' sake! You sound like a stuck pig. Stand up!'

Slowly, Buzz stopped his noise and tried to straighten up. He was in considerable pain and started to cry with loud, hoarse sobs. His tears mixed with blood and snot to form a cascade of red slime. Yul, his breathing now almost recovered, turned away in disgust. He had never, ever cried like that in all the years of beatings he'd taken.

'Are you alright, son?' Maizie asked him again, still looking for injuries.

'I'm fine, Mother,' he replied, shaking with the aftermath of fury but in control of himself. 'Is Rosie alright? What did he do to you, Rosie?'

All eyes but Buzz's turned to her. She clutched her torn blouse together trying to cover herself. Her hair was tangled and her hands and cheeks were scratched.

'He . . . he tried to force me,' she said in a small voice.

Maizie gasped. Yul took a deep breath and stepped towards Buzz again, his fists clenched ready for another go.

'Hold on!' commanded Magus curtly, putting out a hand to stop Yul. 'Enough, Yul. You've given him a beating he'll never forget. That's quite enough. Are you sure, Rosie? He wasn't just messing about?'

She shook her head, staring at the ground in shame and embarrassment.

'Can you tell us exactly what happened?' asked Magus, more softly. Maizie put her arm around the girl, who burst into tears.

'He were sitting on that stone, like he were waiting for me,' she sobbed. 'I was coming back from the dairy, as I come back this way every day. I saw him and I was a bit scared but I tried to be polite, and . . .'

'Tell us, Rosie,' said Magus gently. 'We need to hear the truth.'

'I was walking past him fast as I could,' she gulped, still staring at her feet, 'but he jumped up and grabbed hold of me and started kissing me. I thought he were just fooling about at first – maybe a bit drunk or something. But he meant it. He said he'd warned Yul what'd happen if he ever told tales. He said I was his revenge. He pushed me down against the bank there, and I tried to fight him off. I didn't give in, but he was so strong. I was trying to stop him but … but …'

'And that's when Yul arrived?' asked Magus, his mouth a tight white line of fury. 'Did Yul arrive before Buzz managed to do anything?'

She nodded, sobbing uncontrollably now. Maizie held her close and looked over her head at Magus. The bright spots burned on her cheeks.

'That's enough questions now,' she said, her voice shaking. 'Thanks to my son she weren't harmed. Though if Yul hadn't come along when he did, I'm sure that this … this animal would've forced her. I hope you deal with this proper, Magus. No sweeping it under the rug. 'Tis against the laws what he were doing and we all know it.'

Magus' face was tight as he surveyed the snivelling youth who could barely stand.

'Just so. Buzz will be dealt with appropriately. In the meantime I apologise on his behalf. Rosie was ill-treated.'

'And no punishment for Yul,' she said, looking straight into Magus' dark eyes. ''Tis plain he were only defending his sister. You can see that.'

Magus nodded curtly.

'As you say, Maizie. Yul was blameless in this incident.'

He flicked a glance to where Yul stood upright and taut, protectively close to his sister. Yul glared at him.

'I'd like to say something,' he said.

Magus' eyes narrowed.

'Well?'

'Buzz did this to get at me. Rosie's honour and welfare mattered nothing to him at all. So I want this known. If Buzz ever crosses me like this again I'll finish him properly.'

'Yul!' cried Maizie in horror. 'Don't say such things! I'm sorry, Magus. The boy's upset. He don't know what he's saying ...'

'Oh I think he does,' said Magus quietly. 'He knows exactly what he's saying. And he'd do well to curb his tongue before I do it for him. Take your children home, Maizie, but send Yul up to the Hall when you've cleaned him up. I want him checked over by the doctor. I think he may've damaged his hand.'

Yul had indeed hurt his hands; one finger broken, another dislocated, and a sprained wrist as well, all of which were strapped up. But as the doctor said, he would soon mend and it was nothing compared to Buzz's injuries. Hazel frowned at Yul, whom she remembered as a pleasant boy from their encounter in the cottage after Alwyn's seizure.

'It was a really vicious attack. Buzz is much heavier than you. How did you beat him so severely?'

Yul shrugged, shaking the dark curls from his face, his mouth hard.

'He's had it coming a long time. Those who stand against me will fall, one by one.'

Word spread around Stonewylde like wildfire. Magus had led Buzz back through the Village after the fight and many people had seen the state of him. At first, the Villagers thought it was Magus who'd beaten him and were horrified. But then the truth came out – Yul had done it defending his sister. People were shocked. Like the doctor, they found it hard to believe Yul had caused such damage to someone so much bigger than him, and virtually without injury to himself.

They didn't understand Yul had been fuelled by pent-up rage, his desire for revenge, his toughness and fitness and, above all, his first-hand knowledge of exactly where to hit to make it hurt the most. Buzz had never stood a chance. Yul was hailed as a hero for defending his sister's honour so bravely. That night he was carted down to the pub again and toasted with cider. People looked at him with a new respect; it was about time someone stood up to the Hallfolk. They waited to see how Magus would deal with Buzz.

'You bloody fool!' spat Magus, standing over Buzz's bed. The youth was now back in his own bedroom and in a terrible state. Both eyes were swollen almost shut, the puffy skin a deep, dark purple like a pair of plums. His nose was in a splint, having been badly broken, and his mouth was bulbous and raw. He'd lost a bottom tooth, although with his lips so swollen the loss hardly showed. He had to keep very still because of a cracked rib and was in agony from the deep bruising all over his body. He wasn't used to pain and made a great deal of fuss about it, whimpering in distress whenever the painkillers wore off.

'What the hell were you thinking of, having a go at a Village girl? And one not yet an adult? Have you *any* idea of the trouble you've caused me? I'd already had to deal with your previous incident, when you jumped Yul with your gang. Don't you understand how much I *hate* having to pander to the Villagers? Having to stand there and kow-tow to them, demean myself,' Magus ranted.

He banged his fist hard against the wooden shutter at the window, unable to contain his rage.

'It's the worst thing, the very worst thing in the world, to have that *bloody boy* looking at me like he's beaten me! Touching my damn horse as if he owns it, not showing me any respect in front of all those men, and then having to let the little *bastard* get away with it! I could have slashed his face to ribbons the other day on the Green. That was all *your* fault. And now *this*!'

He paused for breath, spitting with anger. His eyes sparked as he paced the room, his great body taut with controlled rage as he avoided looking at the pathetic wreck on the bed. Buzz moved a fraction, groaning, and tried to speak through bruised and puffed up lips.

'I'm sorry.'

'I should bloody well think you are sorry! Trying to force a girl – a child! – is one of the most serious offences there is. There

185

are only two punishments for it. Public whipping or banishment. I can't make it anything less.'

'No, no please, Magus,' he whimpered. 'Please don't.'

'You should've thought of that before you had a go at her. Why the hell did you do it? You can have any of the older Hallfolk girls you want. They seem keen enough on you. Goddess knows why, the way you behave.'

'It was because of Yul, to get back at him. You shouldn't have made me apologise to him. It's your fault.'

'MY FAULT?'

'For humiliating me in front of all those stupid, ignorant Villagers.'

Magus growled in exasperation and strode to the window, looking out over the sunny lawns. He saw a group of Hallfolk children running around playing a game and two gardeners working, bent over in the flowerbeds. He turned back to the pulpy face before him.

'*You* are the stupid, ignorant one, Buzzard. I'm ashamed to admit you're my son. How can you be so bloody dense?'

He sat down on a chair next to the bed, visibly trying to calm himself down.

'Look, you idiot boy, do you really not understand how Stonewylde works? The whole community here only functions because of the Villagers. They grow all the food, provide all the labour, keep everything running smoothly. They make our lives very comfortable indeed and we need their goodwill. There are more of them living here than there are of us. They may not realise it now, but it only takes a couple of bright ones and there could be a revolution just like in Russia, in France. You know your history.'

'You're not scared of the Villagers, are you?'

'Goddess, you are *stupid*! No, I'm not scared of them, but I put a great deal of effort into ensuring they're happy, that they respect me and actually *want* to serve me. They consider it an *honour* to bend their backs for me and they'd all willingly do anything I asked, just to please me. I've worked very hard, both here and Outside, to ensure that Stonewylde is a perfect society

186

and that everyone shows me the proper honour and obedience, not because they fear me but because they respect me. And I'm not going to let an arrogant young fool like you destroy everything I've achieved over the past years with your thoughtless, selfish actions.'

He shook his head, looking disdainfully at his son. Buzz struggled to sit up a bit.

'But I didn't actually do it. So you don't need to punish me.'

'You intended to! And with the beating Yul gave you, every person on the estate knows about it. It can't be hushed up, and once again, he's the bloody hero. Have you seen yourself in a mirror? How could you let him do this? He's given you a professional work over and you didn't even scratch him! There's not a mark on him, other than his knuckles and wrist, and they're only damaged because he hit you so hard.'

'He's a madman! You should banish him, not me. He's vicious and violent and a danger to the community. He's inhuman.'

'Oh come off it! He's only fifteen and he's nowhere near your weight. You should've at least put up a fight. I don't think I've ever seen such a pathetic display of cowardice before.'

'He didn't give me a chance to fight back. And he knew what he was doing, exactly where to hit me.'

'Yul learnt the hard way from his father. I've had several run-ins with that boy over the past few months and I thought I'd broken him, but clearly not. He's even tougher than I imagined and I'll have to deal with him again, once and for all. But even so, to be honest I can't blame him for beating you. He was only defending his sister's honour and he had every right to. More importantly, that's what the Villagers will think and they'll be after your blood.'

'I still don't see what all the fuss is about. She's just a stupid Village girl and I didn't do anything to her!'

'But you meant to. You deliberately assaulted a child! You know how important it is to wait until a girl is sixteen. Nobody at Stonewylde *ever* breaks that rule.'

'But what's the big deal? She may be fourteen but she's *not* a child. I've seen her at the festivals chatting with the boys. In the Outside World lots of people do it before they're sixteen and I should know – I spend time out there every year. Why have you got such an obsession about sixteen?'

Magus sighed and stood up, moving to the window again. He'd calmed down, his anger turned to exasperation and disdain. It was baking hot outside and the brilliant light fell on his face, etching the lines around his mouth, the hollows under his cheekbones. His deep brown eyes gazed at the rolling parkland that surrounded the Hall from this view. The raucous rooks caught his eye, circling above their old nests in the trees, gossiping like a queue of noisy women. He recalled Sylvie once laughing at the way they stole each other's twigs.

'Girls do grow up quickly and look older than they are. But there has to be a cut-off point, a time up until which they're treated as children and are off limits. Otherwise mistakes can happen and a young girl could end up being coerced before she's ready. That's one reason, and it's as valid in the Outside World as at Stonewylde.'

He came over to the bed again and stared down at the disfigured young man. Buzz obviously believed that Magus would smooth it all over for him. He wasn't in the least contrite.

'There's another reason I'm adamant about observing the Rite of Adulthood and making everyone wait until they're sixteen. If there were ever even the *slightest* whiff of underage sexual activity here, however common it might be in the Outside World, we'd see the end of Stonewylde. Can you imagine what the gutter press would make of a sex scandal here with underage girls? The police involved, questions asked ... we'd all be arrested, every child here taken into care and there'd be a complete witch-hunt. That's why I'm so unwavering in upholding that law and why I can't forgive what you've tried to do.'

'But I didn't—'

'Don't take me for a fool, Buzz. We both know that if Yul hadn't intervened you'd have raped that girl, knowing full well that she was only fourteen. You'd have jeopardised our entire way of life and you deserve everything that's coming to you.'

His stare was unrelenting and cold, showing no sympathy whatsoever for his badly injured son. Buzz's voice cracked with self-pity and fear and his swollen eyes oozed tears.

'Please, Dad, *please* don't have me publicly whipped. Don't banish me. You always said that one day I'd be magus after you. Don't let that little bastard Yul spoil everything. It's all *his* fault anyway. Please!'

Magus looked at him with cold distaste, his lip curling.

'For Goddess' sake, stop your snivelling – you have no backbone whatsoever! And I've never once said that you'd be magus after me. You may have wished it or assumed it, but I've never said it. As for this being Yul's fault – you need to take responsibility for your actions. Like he does.'

'But—'

'I'll be dealing with Yul once and for all before the next solstice, but that's in connection with other matters and nothing to do with you. This is entirely *your* fault, not Yul's. You need to face that fact and deal with it. You may've reached adulthood, Buzzard, but you're certainly not yet a man.'

With a final look of contempt, Magus turned and left the room. Buzz simply didn't get the point, but he had a while to decide on a course of action as Buzz was in no fit state to be up and about. He'd see how opinion stood in the Village, and maybe it would all blow over. He'd have to lay off Yul for a while too. The boy was something of a hero at the moment and that's what really made him angry. Yul was once again getting ideas far above his station and needed to be brought to heel. The way he'd proprietarily handled Nightwing during Buzz's apology still rankled. Magus had warned him before about the consequences of touching the stallion, but in his arrogance Yul had ignored it. Magus smiled grimly as he strode down the long corridor towards the stairs. He'd have to bide his time, but Yul's insolence on the Green in front of all those Villagers would not go unpunished.

189

12

The talk amongst the Villagers was all of Buzz and his expected punishment. There was much speculation about which Magus would favour; whipping or banishment. Most agreed that whipping was more likely, for Buzz hadn't actually forced Rosie and he was after all Magus' eldest son. Yul had his doubts and wasn't convinced that Magus would do anything at all, despite his reputation for justice. In which case, Yul decided, he'd have to take matters into his own hands. Amongst the young Hallfolk the sympathy naturally lay with Buzz, particularly after the beating he'd received at the hands of a Villager. Buzz had locked himself in his room, taking his meals in there and seeing only Fennel.

'I think it should be both,' said Marigold firmly as she dished up the servants' lunch early one afternoon. 'A good whipping and then banish him. What that young man done was terrible.'

'You're right, my dear,' said Cherry, sitting at the head of the table. 'Why should he get off lightly?'

The sun streamed into the cavernous kitchen, gilding the heads of the troupe of servants as they ate. The enormous scrubbed table was packed as everyone enjoyed a hearty shepherd's pie, their morning's work done. With Lammas over the atmosphere was more relaxed; nobody had time to chat during the festival periods when the Hall was crowded with visitors. Copper pots and pans gleamed on the walls above the enormous cast-iron range. Pots of lavender lined the windowsills to keep the flies at bay during the hot weather, and the huge door was open onto the sunny courtyard outside, where some servants had taken their lunch. Most however preferred to squeeze in at the table and join in the gossip.

'They say 'tis not the first time Buzz has had a go at a Village girl,' said Meg, one of the chamber-maids.

'Wouldn't surprise me,' said Cherry. 'He's got no manners at all, that one. Reminds me of his grandfather.'

'Aye, Magus' father was the same. Any girl that took his fancy.'

'We're lucky that Magus isn't like that,' said Rowan warmly. 'He'd never force anyone.'

'Wouldn't have to, would he, Rowan?' said another laundry maid with a sly grin. 'Not with girls falling over themselves to bed him. Girls just happen to bump into him every time he turns around.'

'Now, now!' said Marigold. 'None o' that sort of talk at my table, thank you.'

'And what about the beating Yul gave him!' said Harold, his eyes shining with admiration. 'Have you seen the state of Buzz? Yul did him over good and proper!'

'Aye, Yul put him in his place, right enough,' agreed Cherry.

'They say if Magus hadn't turned up when he did, Yul would've killed him,' said Harold. 'They say our Yul were like a mad bull and he'd lost his reason altogether.'

'Well, 'twas about time our Yul got his own back on them that've bullied him all his life. When they were younger, that Buzz used to . . .'

'That's enough of your idle gossip!'

All eyes turned to the door where Martin stood glaring at the sea of faces around the table. He walked into the great kitchen and stood with his arms folded, a grim look on his dour face.

'We was just saying about Buzz and—'

'I heard what you were saying, Marigold. 'Tis not our place to question the business of Hallfolk. Magus is the judge and we can be sure that he'll be just.'

191

'Well of course!' said Cherry, a little pink. 'We know that. We was only saying—'

'I think you've said far too much! I'd like a word with you two women after lunch, in my office.'

'Silly old fart!' muttered Marigold as she and her sister made their way to the cubby-hole by the pantry that Martin liked to call his office. 'Who does he think he is?'

'Always been like this, though,' said Cherry. 'Never hear a word against any Hallfolk. Goddess knows why. He's more cause than most. 'Tis plain as your face he's a Hallchild – everyone knows 'twere Master Clip's father, Basil – but look at him! Never given any Hallfolk treatment – just a servant like you and me, sister.'

When they entered the tiny room, Martin stared sternly at them and indicated for them to sit down. They squeezed their ample bulk onto two chairs squashed into the corner and crossed their arms over their bosoms in unison, their mouths obdurate.

'I was very unhappy to hear the way you were both talking today. You have positions of authority here, as the cook and the housekeeper. 'Tis our duty as the senior servants to set a good example,' he began.

'As we do!' said Marigold indignantly. 'There's no need for you to get so pompous, Martin.'

'Aye, Martin. You'd do well to recall we two've been serving here at the Hall even longer than you,' said Cherry. 'A good many years longer. We know our duty well enough.'

'Your tone was disloyal,' said Martin.

'We said nothing against Magus!'

'But you spoke badly of Master Buzz. It's the same thing.'

''Tisn't the same thing at all! What Buzz did was wrong and we can say so if we want.'

Martin tapped his pen on the desk.

''Tis not our place to sit in judgement. We know nothing of what led up to his ... involvement with the girl.'

'Rubbish!' cried Cherry. 'What he did was wrong whatever

way you look at it. 'Tis against the laws to force a girl, and against the laws to go with a girl under the age of sixteen.'

'We don't know he forced her,' said Martin. 'And besides, everyone knows what that family's like.'

'What do you mean by that?' demanded Marigold, her jowls quivering in fury.

'Oh come on – we all remember Maizie as a girl. I expect her daughter's the same.'

'Ooh, sour apples!' mocked Cherry.

'Aye, I remember you had your eye on Maizie yourself!' said Marigold. 'And she weren't interested in you. Or maybe you've forgotten that, Martin?'

He ignored this, although his ears burned red.

'All I'm saying is, Master Buzz is Hallfolk, Magus' son no less. Whereas she's just a Village girl, a dairy-maid with her face in a cow's flank all day. It weren't so long ago that we wouldn't even be discussing this. I really don't know why there's all this fuss – the girl should feel honoured.'

'That's the biggest load of pig-swill I've heard in a long time!' said Cherry.

'Aye! Just because your mother was tumbled by Hallfolk when she were a maid don't make it right now.'

Martin stood up and turned on them both, his narrow face furious.

'My mother was honoured to be chosen. How dare you speak of it in that way!'

'Your mother Violet was hoping to be the Wise Woman back then, all those years ago,' said Marigold. 'I was a young maid and I remember it well. Mother Heggy was teaching the craft to Raven, but Violet always wanted to learn too. Once Raven was taken by the magus, Basil, and expecting the first baby, Violet were over the moon thinking she'd be trained instead.'

'Aye,' said Cherry. 'I remember it clear as spring-water. Violet vowed to anyone as would listen that she'd never be handfasted, would never lie with a man, just as it must be for the Wise Woman. And next thing we know – she's expecting too! There went her chances of ever taking over from Mother Heggy.'

'That's all in the past,' said Martin quickly. 'My mother was proud to find she was carrying me. And her skills have been put to good use for the community, especially since Old Heggy went so mad after that Winter Solstice. My mother bakes all the ceremony cakes and she makes remedies for us all. It never made any difference that I was born.'

'Pah! Old Violet's never had any real powers. And anyone could bake those ceremony cakes,' said Marigold. 'If Magus gave me the special ingredients I'd do a better job of it than she does. Mine would melt in the mouth, not stick in the throat.'

'Anyway,' said Cherry firmly, 'I have work to do, Martin. You keep your nasty old-fashioned ideas to yourself. I don't want any of my maids hearing such rubbish and thinking they should put up with any nonsense from Hallfolk men. Magus'll punish that boy of his, you'll see. And I hope it's banishment, because that Buzz isn't worthy of being magus one day. And I don't care if you don't like me saying so.'

That evening, Martin took the supper tray up to Buzz's room himself.

'Thanks, Martin,' mumbled Buzz. 'I hope it's something soft I can manage. My jaw's still so painful and I can hardly open my mouth.'

'Of course, sir,' said Martin, placing the tray on a side table and helping Buzz sit up in bed. He plumped the pillows and poured some more water for him.

'What's everyone saying?' asked Buzz, eyeing the tray with little enthusiasm. 'Are they all laughing at me for getting beaten up by that bastard Yul?'

'No, no, sir, of course not. Nobody's laughing at all. 'Twas shocking what happened. Yul should be punished for what he did.'

'Well he won't be,' said Buzz morosely. 'Magus said it was my fault.'

'Maybe he doesn't know all the facts, sir,' said Martin. 'Whatever happened, a Villager should never be allowed to get away with doing this to Hallfolk.'

'You're very loyal, aren't you, Martin?'

'I believe in the natural order of things, sir. I was born to serve the Hallfolk, and especially the magus. To be his right-hand man. My loyalty is of course with you, as Magus' eldest Hallfolk son. I would always stand by you and help you in any way you asked.'

Buzz smiled grotesquely through swollen lips.

'You're a good man, Martin, and I'll remember that.'

Whilst Buzz recuperated alone in his room, Sylvie made every effort to get back to normal after her ordeal at Mooncliffe. Wandering around the Hall one day, deserted because of the hot weather and lack of school lessons, she found herself in the Galleried Hall. She sat down on an oak settle against the wall and stared up at the vaulted ceiling. It was very high, carved in dark wood that curled and swept in curves. There were many stained-glass windows set up in the walls near the roof. The sun poured through the beautiful windows in coloured shafts, illuminating the motes of dust dancing like gnats in the light. She craned her neck to study the designs illustrated in stained glass.

She was particularly struck by a great window that glowed green and gold, depicting the Green Man. It reminded her of the carving Professor Siskin had shown her on their visit to the Jack in the Green pub. Looking around the Galleried Hall, she realised just how often the motif was repeated. Many of the ceiling bosses held tiny leafy faces staring down at her. There were faces surrounded with leaves carved into the stone above the arched doorways, and all around the vast room more leafy faces were carved into the cornice of the dark-oak panelling that lined the walls. These had been picked out with gilt, and the leaves burned gold in the bright sunlight.

'I see you've discovered the Lord of the Greenwood carvings,' called an unmistakable voice from high up in the gallery overlooking the hall. Sylvie smiled up at Professor Siskin, pleased to see him again. He kept himself tucked away most of the time, buried in his research.

'There are so many of them,' she called back. 'It's a forest of Green Men!'

'Indeed it is! Wait there, my dear, I'm coming downstairs to join you.'

He disappeared from his vantage point and reappeared a few minutes later through a door opposite her. He hobbled across the flagstones and sat down stiffly on the settle next to her, looking around him with pleasure.

'This is the oldest part of the Hall still standing,' he said. 'It's probably thirteenth century in origin, with later additions, of course. The floor itself is undoubtedly even older.'

They looked down at the large, worn flagstones, and Sylvie shook her head.

'I find it hard to imagine just how many feet have trodden this floor. I was thinking the same thing in the porch the other day. The Hall is so steeped in history.'

'Indeed, which is why it holds such fascination for me. I've devoted my life to history and all because I was lucky enough to be born here. Of course there's my history of Stonewylde too, my own small contribution to posterity. And don't forget, Sylvie, it's not just the Hall. Remember we talked about the Village Green and my theory of the woodland temple? I think the oldest thing on the whole estate of Stonewylde, including the standing stones, dolmen and barrows, is the yew tree on the Village Green.'

Sylvie smiled at the thought of that yew tree.

'I'd love to read your book when it's finished, Professor.'

'Indeed you shall, my dear,' he said delightedly.

'I was wondering – has Stonewylde always had a magus?' she asked. 'A lord and master who lives here in the Hall?'

'I believe there's always been a magus, and of course Stonewylde's always had a lord. But it's only in fairly recent times that the two roles have been held by the same man. Do you know what "magus" means?'

'I thought it meant the master, the ruler?'

'Not at all, although a common misconception. A magus is a magician, a wise one, a learned one. As an Outsider here, you may remember the magi of the Bible, the three wise men who visited the infant Jesus, bearing gifts? It's the same word. Magi is the plural of magus. Stonewylde has always had its magus, the one who receives the Earth Magic, the single one who can channel the power. So the magus would be the one leading the ceremonies, while the lord was the person who ran the community. Not the same person doing all of it.'

'That's interesting.'

'Yes, and I've recently re-read some fascinating accounts from early Tudor times describing the ceremonies up at the Stone Circle. Sol must've read them too, for when he took over he revived the celebrations. Thanks to his father and grandfather, the ancient traditions of Stonewylde as a pagan community were almost lost and forgotten. We've a lot to be grateful to our present magus for.'

'I suppose so,' agreed Sylvie, shivering at the thought of him.

'But interestingly enough,' continued the professor, delighted to have someone to share his discoveries with, 'the documents I read spoke of how the magus channelled the Earth Magic during the festivals and shared the power and force with the folk of Stonewylde. He passed the energy on to everyone, but that's one practice our magus hasn't continued with. Instead he gives us the feeling of well-being with mead and cakes.'

'They're amazing. You feel so good after them.'

'That's the idea, I believe,' said the old man with a twinkle. 'Sol is a clever chap indeed.'

'So why doesn't he channel the Earth Magic and share it with everyone?'

'Who knows? Maybe he feels that he alone needs the energy in order to run the community so effectively. It can't be an easy job. But whatever the reason, he ensures that the people leave the ceremonies with a feeling of euphoria. As an act of mass socialisation, that's crucial to the community. Ah yes, he's a clever man.'

Sylvie stood up and stretched. She helped Siskin stand, for his joints were stiff.

'Yul gets Earth Magic from the stones,' she said casually.

'*What?*'

Siskin sat down again abruptly and blinked up at her.

'Say that again, my dear. What do you mean?'

'Yul goes up there most sunrises and sunsets if he can and stands on the Altar Stone. He comes back charged up with power, full of it. And at the festivals it's even stronger. At the Summer Solstice he made sparks shoot from his fingertips to relight the torch when it went out.'

'But it's not possible for two people to receive the magic! It'll only go to one person, the chosen one who has the ability within them to channel it. According to the history, there've been times when there's no magus at all. But *never* two. How extraordinary! Unless . . . unless it has ceased going to Magus. I wonder . . .'

'I think you're right. I don't think Magus receives it any more. That's what Yul says anyway.'

The old man sat there in the dusty sunlight and gazed up at the ceiling.

'Well I never. The Green Man . . . and now this. I hadn't imagined . . .'

He shook his head in bewilderment. Sylvie glanced at him; he seemed to have disappeared into a day dream. Then he turned and smiled at her.

'These are exciting times for Stonewylde, my dear. I wish I could be here to witness what is about to unfold.'

'Why? What's going to happen?'

He shook his head again.

'Time will tell. I'm only speculating and best keep it to myself, I think. But I do wish I weren't leaving.'

'Will you be back soon? Do you come back for the Winter Solstice?'

'No, my dear girl. I wish I did, but I'm only permitted to stay from the Summer Solstice until Lammas, and that's much longer than most get. Sol's been very good to me this year, allowing me to stay on a few extra days, but I'm leaving tomorrow.'

'I do wish you weren't going,' she said sadly. 'I have so few friends here, and you're one of the best. Can we keep in touch when you're back in Oxford? Do you use e-mail?'

'Of course, my dear! I might be old but I'm jolly good on my computer. A wonderful invention, the Internet. Invaluable for research. I'd love to correspond with you electronically. You can keep me informed of events ... as they unfold.'

They sat in peace for a while longer, the professor in his old velvet jacket gazing around wistfully. Sylvie felt so sorry for the elderly man who'd been sent away from the home he loved. She sighed and looked up at the ceiling again, noticing this time another motif repeated around the gallery.

'What's that one?' she asked. 'The three ... rabbits? Or are they hares?'

'Ah, the triple hare motif! Yes, another favourite; this Galleried Hall is positively teeming with hares. See how they chase each other in a circle and share the same three ears? A clever stylistic device, creating a triangle in the centre like that. It's a very popular symbol and the research surrounding it is really quite fascinating. There are many churches throughout the country, but especially in Devon, where the triple hare symbol can be found. Mostly in ceiling bosses, stone or wood, but sometimes in stained glass or floor tiles. And not just this country either!'

Sylvie smiled encouragingly at him. He was so enthusiastic and full of knowledge.

'It's been discovered in churches all over Europe – France, Germany, Switzerland – and even further afield.'

'The same symbol?'

'Exactly the same symbol! The three hares in a circle with a triangle of ears linking them. An Iranian coin from the thirteenth century, a Russian reliquary casket, thirteenth or fourteenth century. But the most exciting of all – our triple hares have been discovered in a Buddhist cave temple in China! Dating to the Sui Dynasty, circa the sixth century. Isn't that extraordinary?'

'It's incredible! ... so what does the symbol mean?'

'We don't know. Experts think that it was perhaps brought to Europe along the Silk Road, when the Mongol empire opened the trading route for silk from the Orient. But I don't know ... I sometimes wonder if it was here all along. The fact that we haven't discovered any older examples in Britain doesn't mean it didn't exist here. Maybe there are examples yet to be unearthed. It could be a universal symbol. The hare is a sacred animal, after all, and linked to the Moon Goddess. Even the ancient Egyptians had a hare god, and that's going back a great deal further. The hare is a magical creature indeed.'

Sylvie nodded, thinking of the hares that danced with her up on the hilltop. But then her head began to cloud and throb, and she tried to dismiss the memory.

'Ah well, that's enough of the history lesson for today, my dear Sylvie. I hope I haven't bored you? I do get a little carried away in my zeal.'

'No, I find it fascinating. I wish you were around for longer to tell me more.'

He stood up slowly, a groan escaping his lips.

'I don't mind getting older but I do wish my body still worked properly. Make the most of yours, my dear, while it's young and supple. Now before I leave in the morning I wanted to give you something. I have it in my room and I think you'll like it. Will you accompany me there?'

They left the mediaeval hall with its blazing stained glass and dark carvings, and made their way into the corridor leading to the entrance hall and the main staircase.

'Why are there so many Green Men in the Galleried Hall?' asked Sylvie, as they slowly climbed the wide stairs.

'He's a popular motif everywhere. Many churches have a Green Man tucked away up in the roof or hidden in a corner, since many of them were built on sites already used for pagan celebrations. The builders – stone-carvers and woodcarvers – would've felt uncomfortable abandoning their woodland deity completely for the new Christian one. So the Green Man pops up everywhere.'

'It's strange, the idea of such a pagan symbol in churches.'

'Ah, but some symbols are universal and transcend the boundaries of religion,' he explained, pausing to catch his breath. 'The ones here at Stonewylde are in the "foliate head" style, where the head of a man is surrounded by a halo of leaves. This indicates the Lord of the Greenwood. Others you'll see elsewhere, and particularly in churches, show branches and leaves sprouting from the mouth, nose and ears. They're "masque feuillu", or the "sprouting head". Sometimes they symbolise death and sometimes they're to ward off evil spirits.'

'But I still don't understand why there are so many of them in the Galleried Hall.'

'The religion here in mediaeval times when the Galleried Hall was built was not only the cult of the Earth Goddess but also the woodland deity, the Green Man. He's the spirit of virility who impregnates Mother Earth and makes her bountiful and fruitful. He's the male counterpart to the female Goddess, for nature always seeks a balance. So it's natural he'd appear in the early architecture at Stonewylde.'

They'd climbed the main stairs and were now making their way down corridors into a wing at the back where Sylvie had never been before. She'd easily get lost on her own in this vast place. They started to climb another, narrower staircase. Professor Siskin was wheezing and took it very slowly.

'The Green Man isn't important here anymore, is he?' said Sylvie, waiting for the professor to catch up. 'I know he's celebrated at Beltane, but apart from that nobody seems to mention him much.'

'Well observed, my dear!' gasped Siskin, halting at the top of the stairs as he struggled to breathe. 'The Green Man was also part of a sacrificial cult, I believe. It's possible the Jack in the Green – the man encased within boughs of greenery in a type of cage – is reference to this. Generally it was a Beltane custom, but not necessarily at Stonewylde. I've uncovered some fascinating references to a very old, dark practice here of an annual sacrifice of the Green Man at the time of the Winter Solstice, to ensure the vitality and renewal of the sun and the life force for the coming year.'

'Sacrifice? Do you mean *human* sacrifice?'

'Indeed. I believe it took place at the quarry, for there's mention of it in several documents. The Place of Bones and Death, it's referred to. Rather eerie, I thought. I imagine that's why the custom of deifying the Green Man fell out of practice, for, after all, who wants to give up their life?'

'Yes, they'd have to choose someone to be killed every year. That's horrible.'

'Exactly, and a rural community needs its strong men. So you're right, the cult of the Green Man has fallen from popularity but it's a shame really. I don't mean the sacrifice of course, merely the veneration of such an ancient god, because I personally feel at my most spiritual in woodland. There's a definite feeling of a deity present, don't you think?'

'Oh yes,' she agreed. She'd felt that tingle in the woods, knowing there was an unexplained presence watching her. 'I really can't wait to read your book, Professor!'

He chuckled, and finally opened a door at the end of a corridor. It had been a long trek for him, and once inside Sylvie was surprised at the meanness of his room. Surely Magus could've made him more comfortable during his stay?

'My needs are simple,' he said, seeing her disapproval as she looked around the small room. 'And my rooms at Oxford are splendid, so this is only a temporary privation. Sit down, sit down my dear.'

He indicated the lone chair, where she sat whilst he rifled through a stack of papers.

'I have it here and I know you'll treasure it. I made you a copy especially. Here!'

He presented Sylvie with one of the photos he'd taken in the woods. It was a close-up of Yul's face smiling out at her, his slanted grey eyes drowsy in the golden sunlight. His face was smeared green and brown, his almost classical features clearly defined. His hair was a wild riot of dark curls, and surrounding his head was a great halo of green leaves and ferns where he lay in the undergrowth against the beautiful lime tree.

Sylvie stared at the photo in surprise.

'Why, it's the Green Man!' she exclaimed.

'Indeed it is,' agreed Siskin. 'I knew you'd understand. Yul is our very own Lord of the Greenwood.'

After Professor Siskin had left Stonewylde, Sylvie finally cast off the shadow of illness that had hung over her since the last full moon and went walking every day. She found Hare Stone to be a place of healing, as Mother Heggy had said it would be. Lying on the grass by the tall stone amongst the vetch and harebells filled her with a sense of calm and peace. She loved it up here. When he managed to join her, Yul was very careful not to put Sylvie under any pressure. He'd mentioned the Moon Fullness once and she'd become agitated and upset. The next full moon was still a week away and he hoped Mother Heggy would be able to break the spell before then.

Yul wasn't the only one worrying about the next Moon Fullness. Miranda was concerned and quite sure she didn't want Sylvie going up to Mooncliffe again. But when she broached the subject with Magus he lost his temper.

'Sacred Mother, as if I haven't got enough to worry about at the moment without you interfering! The girl wants to go there, she enjoys going there, and we're on hand to take care of her, so leave it be. I don't want to hear any more about it.'

'But Magus, she comes back so ill. It can't be good for her if it makes her weak and exhausted. She was almost comatose for a week afterwards and she's only just about back to normal now.'

'Have you thought about how ill she might be if she *didn't* go up there? I don't want to hear another word about it.'

'But I think—'

'I don't care what you think! Enough!'

He glared at her, black eyes flashing and mouth severe. She was frightened of him and wanted to give in. But a spark of her former self – the girl who'd stood up to her parents and fought to keep her baby from being adopted, who'd struggled against the odds as a teenage single mother and succeeded through sheer determination – suddenly reignited.

'I'm sorry, Magus. I'm her mother and I say she can't go. And *that* is the end of it.'

She turned and almost ran out of the room, terrified of what he might say or do next. Up in her room she sat on her bed and cried. If she made him really angry would he throw them out of Stonewylde? What about the baby? He had all the power here and his word was final. What had she done?

An hour or so later, by which time she'd worked herself into a terrible state, there was a gentle knock on their sitting room door. Magus was calm, and as handsome and charming as ever. He walked straight over, took her in his arms and kissed her; a long, passionate kiss such as he hadn't given her for some time. She melted in his embrace like snow in the glare of sunshine.

'Don't say another word about it, Miranda. You were absolutely right. You're Sylvie's mother and of course you're concerned for her welfare. Please forgive me for my anger earlier. Come and sit down here with me.'

He held her in his arms as they sat on the sofa together and rested his hand on her belly, already starting to swell slightly. He began to caress her slowly.

'How could I ever be cross with you? I'm such a fool,' he murmured, his face nuzzling at her neck. She closed her eyes in contentment, loving him with all her heart, becoming aroused by his knowing touch.

'You must understand, Miranda,' he said, continuing his caresses, 'that I only have Sylvie's interests at heart.'

'I know, Magus, but—'

'No buts. I really do know about this. Moongaziness is something that happens at Stonewylde, and my own mother was moongazy. I have experience of it, and so in this case I know what's best for Sylvie.'

'Yes, but—'

'Come on, Miranda,' he whispered, his lips brushing her collar bones. 'Stop fighting me. You know you want to please me and you know how happy I can make you. Humour me in this matter – let me decide what's best for Sylvie.'

'Oh Magus, I do want to please you,' she breathed, her eyes half closed with pleasure. 'But I really don't want her going up on that cliff.'

'You really will anger me if you don't agree,' he murmured. 'And I don't want to be angry with you, Miranda. I want you to stay at Stonewylde and have our baby here, with me to care for you. I want you living under my roof and close by, so I can make love to you. Why are you fighting me?'

'I'm not fighting you,' she said tremulously. 'You know I love you, Magus. I'd do anything to please you.'

'Don't defy me then. Give me the responsibility to decide what's best for Sylvie. This is your chance to show me how you trust my judgement.'

'But I don't want her getting ill again. I love her and I can't bear to see her so weak. That's why I can't let you take her up there.'

He sighed and pulled away from her slightly.

'You've brought this on yourself,' he said, his voice now cold. 'You were given the chance to comply with my wishes. You disappoint me, Miranda.'

'Please, Magus,' she said desperately, 'please let—'

'Clip!' he called sharply.

The door opened immediately and the thin, long-haired brother walked in. He came straight over to the sofa where they sat and knelt on the floor in front of Miranda.

'What on earth are you doing?' she cried in alarm.

She struggled to sit up but Magus held her firmly.

'Sit still and do as you're told. It's really not a good idea to go against my wishes. My brother would agree with that, wouldn't you, Clip? Everybody here obeys me and you, Miranda, will be no exception.'

Clip ignored him and leant forward, looking into her green eyes.

'Miranda, look at me. Look at me.'

'No! What are you doing? Stop it!'

She tried to avert her gaze but Magus held her firmly and then she relaxed suddenly, her eyes locked into Clip's.

'Ah that's it, well done. Listen carefully to me, Miranda. When I tell you to wake up, you will do so immediately. Do you understand me?'

'Yes.'

'Good.' He turned and looked at Magus. 'Well she went under quickly. What do you want me to say? I'm getting fed up of being used like this, you know. I'm a shaman, not a bloody party trick.'

Magus laughed, releasing Miranda and stretching back on the sofa lazily.

'It's easy for you to do, Clip, so stop complaining and just make her obey me. I don't want her interfering with my plans for Sylvie.'

'Alright, but I've had enough of this, I warn you.' He turned to Miranda again. 'Miranda, listen to me.'

'Yes.'

'You must obey Magus. He has Sylvie's interests at heart and you mustn't interfere. Magus knows best. You'll let him do whatever he wants. Do you understand?'

'Yes.'

'Good. Tell me what you'll do?'

'I must obey Magus. I won't interfere. He knows best.'

'Well done, Miranda. Don't forget what we've agreed. Now I want you to wake up.'

She blinked and stared at Clip in confusion. Magus stood up briskly.

'Sorry, Miranda, I have to go. Clip just came in to get me.'

'Oh, right. Yes.'

'Thanks for your apology. I knew you'd agree with me when you'd thought about it.'

'I'm sorry? I don't know ...'

'About taking Sylvie to Mooncliffe next week. You said I must do whatever I wanted because I know best.'

206

Miranda frowned and rubbed her forehead.

'Yes, Magus, of course. I'm feeling muddled. But I know you only have her interests at heart. I'm sorry I disagreed with you.'

'Just don't do it again, Miranda. I may not be quite so forgiving another time,' he said silkily. 'See you later.'

The two men strode down the long gallery leading out of the Tudor wing and Magus chuckled.

'I wish I could do that. I'd have such fun!' he said. 'You don't realise the power you have.'

'Yes I do realise the power I have, which is why I'm not going to repeat this, Sol. It's a gift, a wisdom, and I'm abusing it. Don't ask me again.'

'Oh lighten up! It's no big deal. You know we need Sylvie to go to Mooncliffe every month and work her magic, and I can't have Miranda constantly interfering. That's all.'

'Well I think she's right. I don't think you should take Sylvie up there either. It's obviously damaging the poor girl.'

'What?'

Magus turned on Clip angrily, grabbing hold of his brother's shirt in a swift movement.

'Let go of me, Sol!' he cried, his face blanching. 'We're not boys now. You won't win with violence anymore.'

Magus released him abruptly.

'I'm sorry. It just makes me furious when you talk such rubbish. Of course it's not damaging Sylvie. She's absolutely fine and you know how I need those eggs charged up. Actually, I was thinking of trying some smaller pieces of stone, to be worn around the neck. I could use—'

'NO!' Clip shouted. 'I draw the line at that!'

'I don't understand your problem,' said Magus tersely. 'You're happy enough to share the moon magic, aren't you?'

'Yes, up to a point. I agree that Sylvie was brought here for this. We always knew it wasn't simply coincidence that you found her. But it's one thing sharing the gift of her moon magic when she channels it into the rock at Mooncliffe – that's a natural phenomenon – and it's quite another, exploiting her in this way. You're so greedy, Sol!'

'Greedy? What's wrong with trying to—'

'Exactly! You can't even see it, can you? There's a big difference, and I have a conscience even if you don't. So *if* I help you take Sylvie up there this month, it's just going to be for half an hour or so on the round moon stone. She's not going to charge up all those eggs, nor anything else you've brought along. She's not strong enough to do it again so soon. You can threaten me all you like, Sol. But if you try to force me to do this, I'll reverse the hypnosis on both of them and then you'll find it impossible. Just for once in your life, you have to do what *I* want.'

13

It was the last week of August and the day of the full moon. The summer had been long and hot and most of the crops were now harvested. The fields were a patchwork of deep brown, ochre and sienna, stubbly and bare, many already ploughed. The flax had been retted and some of it bleached; now the Village women spent every available moment spinning the long fibres ready for weaving. The cobnuts ripened in thick clusters on the hazel trees, green and frilly, whilst the great tufted heads of sweetcorn, zipped in their green jackets, were almost ready for harvest. In the orchards the trees were laden with apples, their boughs heavy, and the early types of apple were already being picked. The swallows were still around but beginning to gather in the skies and there was a sense of sadness, of the summer nearly gone but no sign yet of beautiful autumn to cheer the heart.

Yul left the Stone Circle after his sunrise ritual. He was tanned a deep golden brown, his clear grey eyes striking against his skin. He'd managed to keep himself out of trouble since his big fight with Buzz, who was skulking around the Hall avoiding people. Magus had let it be known that he was deciding his son's punishment whilst he recovered, but people wondered when it would be announced. The Villagers were still very angry that one of their girls had been attacked by a Hallfolk man; Magus was aware of this anger and knew he must act soon.

Yul ran down the Long Walk as fast as he could. Legs pumping, he enjoyed the animal pleasure of the exercise and the green coolness under the ancient trees that lined the processional walk. He sprang and cavorted like a young stag, laughing out loud and shouting like a wild thing. Then he saw a figure at the other end standing in the shade, silhouetted against the brightness and his heart leapt. He ran full pelt towards her and she smiled as he approached, loving his darkness and wildness.

'I thought I might find you at your stones,' she said. 'Can you come with me to mine now?'

They cut through the woods and made their way up the hill to Hare Stone. As they got closer Sylvie felt the familiar tranquillity enfolding her. She touched the stone with her cheek before lying on the grass next to it. The moon magic of the place soothed and nourished her and she closed her eyes. Yul sat next to her on the grass gazing down at her, his heart melting. She was so very beautiful, so ethereal and perfect. The dark shadows under her eyes were now gone and she'd lost the haunted, suffering look that had veiled her beauty after her ordeal at Mooncliffe. Her fair skin was tanned to a pale gold, her silvery hair exquisite. He loved the arch of her lips, the tiny line each side of her mouth that crinkled when she smiled. He noted the delicate veins at her temples and the way her white-blond hair started to grow there like down, feathering back into proper hair. He saw the pulse in her throat beating like a tiny creature. Her small hands, their fingernails bitten, were spread on the grass, her thumbs idly stroking the ground. He bent over without thinking and kissed her mouth; soft kisses like angel wings.

Her eyes flew open, pale-grey glass within her dark-ringed irises, and then they dreamily fluttered shut again as his kisses became more insistent. She kissed him back, loving the feel of his mouth on hers, the emotion she sensed just under the surface. His lips were soft but demanding, his tongue firm but gentle. She felt herself spiralling away into heaven and wrapped her arms around his neck, pulling him down closer, her fingers twined in his curls.

Their kiss was shattered by a very loud *CAW*! Sylvie looked up and saw the crow fidgeting on the stone above them. Yul's eyes were smoky with passion, his dark lashes drooping.

'Damn crow!' he muttered. 'Perfect timing.'

But then they heard a voice calling from down the hill.

'Sylvie! Sylvie! Are you up there?'

'Oh no, it's my mum!' cried Sylvie. 'What on earth's she doing here? What shall we do?'

'It's alright,' said Yul softly. 'I'll just go over the brow of the hill. Don't worry, she won't see me if I keep low. Sylvie, I ... Sylvie ... You were ...'

He gazed down at her and bent his head again. She laughed and pushed him off.

'Go! There'll be so much trouble if we're found here together. Go!'

'And the Moon Fullness tonight? Will I see you here?'

'I love to dance on the great moon stone at Mooncliffe,' she told him, the dancing light in her eyes suddenly extinguished. 'I must do it for Magus.'

'No, Sylvie!' he groaned, scrambling away over the hilltop.

Sylvie sat up, hastily smoothing her hair, hoping her face wouldn't give her away. Now she was upright she could see her mother climbing the hill, red hair gleaming like conkers in the sun.

'I'm up here, Mum!' she called, waving. Miranda waved back and continued to make her way around the boulders littering the hillside. Sylvie hoped that Yul was safely out of sight. Her mother finally reached the great stone.

'Phew! I'm really out of breath!' she panted. 'That's a steep climb.'

Sylvie thought of how she and Yul liked to run up the hill together and smiled. Her mother sat down on the warm grass beside her, exactly where Yul had been stretched out only a few minutes earlier.

'This is a lovely surprise, Mum,' said Sylvie brightly, trying not to think of the kiss she'd interrupted.

'Well, I haven't been out for a walk for a while. I need to keep fit for the baby's sake. What a lovely spot!'

'How did you find me?'

'You've talked so much about Hare Stone, so I thought you might be here. I asked one of the Villagers and they directed me. Didn't seem to know it was called Hare Stone, though – just the stone on the hill, they said.'

Hare Stone must be Yul's own special name for the place. Thinking of the moonlight and hares made her feel strange, and she remembered what he'd said. It was the Moon Fullness tonight. She thought of how wonderful it would be, dancing up here in the warm August moonlight with Yul watching over her. But then the black fog rolled in over her mind, blanking it out. She saw an image of moonlight over water, snaking a path towards her. She saw a great disc of rock where she must stand and send her magic deep within, so the snake could coil in contentment. There was a man, two men, laughing with pleasure and delight. And the pain, the weariness, the sadness. No hares or moon angel wings or singing heavenly songs for the Triple Goddess. She hung her head in sorrow.

'What's the matter, darling?'

'It's just tonight, Mum. I must go to Mooncliffe and dance.'

'Oh yes,' agreed Miranda. 'I've been so worried about that. But Magus says it's what you must do, and he does know best. Did you know that his mother was affected by the full moon too? Apparently some people at Stonewylde are. He'll take care of you. I mustn't interfere.'

She lay back in the grass and closed her eyes, her thoughts a little jumbled. She sighed; it was so peaceful up here.

'I love you, Mum,' said Sylvie suddenly, squeezing her mother's hand.

Miranda turned her head on the grass and looked into her daughter's clear grey eyes, so beautiful and strange.

'I love you too, Sylvie, my special girl.'

'Mother Heggy, you've got to help me!' Yul stood in the doorway of the hovel and the smell billowed out to hit him. She glared at him from her rocking chair.

'Brought back my bottles and corks, have you?' she squawked. 'No! And you didn't come to see me, did you? But now 'tis the Moon Fullness and you realise you have none o' the knowledge yourself, oh aye, *now* you come here with your tail between your legs!'

She glared at him, although he doubted she could actually see him at all.

'I'm sorry,' he said, worried that she'd turn him away. 'I've been so busy with the harvesting and helping at home. I thought you'd be able to undo the spell before this Moon Fullness.'

'Did you now? Well come in and shut the door!' she snapped irritably.

He sat down opposite her, trying not to recoil from her stale odour. How could Sylvie not be repulsed by her? She cackled, and too late he remembered her uncanny knack of reading his mind.

'Can you sit still awhile so I can read you? Or must I make you as stone?'

He remembered the potion she'd given him on his first visit and quickly shook his head.

'No, I promise I'll sit still.'

She cackled again and pushed him back in the seat with a bony claw. She hunched forward in her chair and regarded him intently. He felt the tug of her milky eyes, and then of something deeper, something powerful.

'Quiet now,' she whispered hoarsely. 'Quiet and still. Let your mind float free. Let the white swan glide in the misty waters.'

He felt his heartbeat slow down, his mind relax and slip away to the place between waking and sleeping where all is hazy and everything is possible. His breathing became deeper; his eyelids drooped shut. She took his hands in hers . . .

His head was filled with a sudden vision of crimson and black swirling in a vortex, a silver light glistening, and then feathers everywhere, black feathers falling and falling, a tiny, white baby and a crow on the cradle. Mother Heggy snatched her hands away, muttering sharply. His eyes flashed open and he stared at her, jolted back into reality. He saw how the shadows had moved across the room and knew she'd been reading him for quite some time.

'Well, well, so much has happened. Poor Mother Heggy. Not many visitors nowadays, nobody to tell me what is abroad. But now I've seen all that has passed. I understand the spell they put on the bright one.'

'Can you break it, Mother Heggy?' he asked urgently. 'Tonight – she'll go up there tonight if you don't do something.'

She nodded, sucking her gums and rocking.

'Aye, I know that, boy. But I cannot break the spell for tonight. You must go to Mooncliffe and see what is happening with that evil man. 'Twill be hard for you. You must watch your girl suffering and you must do nothing. Don't try to stop it tonight for the time is not yet right and you would fail. You must watch but you must be hidden. When you came at Lammas I was afeared. The dark glass showed me what he did to her. I feared for her life, like my precious Raven before her. But now I see more clearly. There's danger, real danger, but you're far stronger than I'd thought and I have faith in you, my young Holly King. The Goddess has chosen wisely. The magic will be safe with you.'

Magus and Clip strode into the rooms at the end of the Tudor wing as the sun was dropping in the sky. The nights were beginning to draw in, dusk coming earlier as summer came to an end, although tonight it was very warm indeed.

'We've come for Sylvie,' said Magus briskly, walking straight through the sitting room and towards the bedroom.

'Of course,' said Miranda. 'She's rested and ready, as you said.'

'Glad to hear it,' said Magus.

Clip gave Miranda a little salute, which she ignored. Sylvie was sitting on her bed, her eyes vacant. Tears rolled down her cheeks but she was silent. She wore the moongazy dress and her hair floated around her bare arms and shoulders in a silver cloud. As the men walked in she raised her eyes to them. The tears spilled over and caught on her dark lashes.

'She's so very lovely,' said Clip softly.

'Never mind about that,' said Magus. He took her hands from her lap and tugged her upright. 'Come, my moongazy girl. It's late and you've work to do tonight.'

Yul was hidden behind the bracken alongside the path. Gnats danced on the cliff top and swallows swooped, feasting while they could before their long journey ahead. The stone disc was rosy in the setting sun's rays, the brightness also reflected on the opposite horizon where the moon would rise, tinting the whole sky. It was a bloody sunset, the sky a burnished gold, and the heat pressed down, stifling and close. The still air was oppressive and Yul was sweating. He was scared; not of Magus, but of being unable to control himself. Mother Heggy had stressed how important it was not to act yet, but could he bear to watch Sylvie suffer at Magus' hands?

He heard them coming before he saw them.

'Goddess, we're late.' It was Magus' deep voice. 'Look, the sun's set already. Come on, Clip, hurry up!'

Clip led the way with Magus behind him, carrying Sylvie. Yul's heart wrenched at the sight of her lying in his arms, her head resting on his shoulder and her hair hanging down. Magus reached the top and put her down quickly. She stumbled as she tried to find her feet and then stood like an automaton. Yul remembered how she usually behaved at this time, just before moon rise; full of energy and fidgety, jittery with anticipation.

'Remember what I said,' said Clip, talking as if Sylvie couldn't hear them. 'No eggs and not too long on the stone. No more than half an hour.'

'Oh come on, she can do a few eggs. Just to replace the ones I've used.'

'Absolutely not, Sol – we agreed! She's just not strong enough this month. You were too greedy last time and she can't take it again so soon.'

'You're being ridiculous, Clip. She's fine now. Look at her – of course she can take it.'

'She's been ill for most of the month! I'm warning you, Sol, you'll damage her if you overdo it and then there'll be no moon magic at all.'

'Alright, alright. We'll compromise. Just one hour with six eggs and then we'll let her off the rock. But you must promise me she'll do the full load next month, whatever happens. I've got some people interested in the eggs. Is that a deal?'

'Oh I suppose so,' sighed Clip. 'But six eggs at the very most, and if she gets distressed then I'm taking her straight home.'

Yul was sickened by the way Magus spoke as if she were nothing, just a commodity to be used. How could the man be so heartless? While they were distracted arguing, Sylvie had slowly turned towards the sea, gazing out at the pinkness that heralded the first glimmer of moonrise. Her arms began to lift but it was her singing that roused them both.

'Quick! It's rising!' shouted Magus, grabbing her round the waist and almost throwing her up onto the disc. Again she stumbled and he jumped up next to her, pulling her into the centre. Her arms had dropped and she stared at the horizon, making a strange, horrible mewing noise. It was nothing like her ethereal singing at Hare Stone.

'Are you coming up too?' Magus asked Clip.

'No, it was too strong last time,' he replied. 'I'll wait till the moon's risen a bit and she calms down.'

'Well I'm going to try and stay on this time. Here we go!'

The pink rim of the moon was just visible and Sylvie had begun to shake and vibrate, her body jerking uncontrollably, her face contorted. Yul had to close his eyes. He thought of her tip-toe dancing, leaping with the hares, skipping around in the grass, and then this – standing on the hard stone, being pounded and shaken by a force of immense magnitude pouring through her body. He understood what was happening straight away; the great stone was wrenching the moon energy from the night sky, dragging it down hard through her frame and into the rock at her feet. She took the full force of it and couldn't move; she simply had to endure. Yul felt the tears hot on his cheeks and fought down the sob threatening to fly from his throat. This was far worse than he'd imagined. He'd have done anything to stand there instead and take the pain for her.

Magus stood next to her, blasted with the force that came back up through the stone and into his body. He shouted in exhilaration as if on a roller-coaster ride, his arms outstretched and head thrown back. But a few moments later he jumped off the stone.

'Sacred Mother, that's too much! I thought my heart would give out. That is *so* powerful!'

Clip lay on the grass with his toes touching the stone, an expression of ecstasy on his face. Magus unlocked the chest and brought out six stone eggs, which he placed next to the disc of rock.

'I'll load her up in a minute, when it's less intense,' he said, joining Clip on the grass. Yul could feel Sylvie's suffering; the sharp, shooting needles that darted through her and down into the rock below her feet. He saw her glowing, the silvery threads chasing over her skin. She'd closed herself away, retreated into some tiny, hidden place where the pain couldn't touch her so badly. Yul tried to embrace her in his mind, tried to comfort her. He too almost drifted away from consciousness in his fierce attempts to reach Sylvie in her hiding place.

He was brought back to reality by Magus' voice.

'I think she's ready to charge the eggs now.'

'Alright, if you're sure she's okay. How long have we been here?'

'I've no idea. My watch always stops up here at moonrise. But it's fine – she's doing well so don't worry.'

He climbed up onto the stone and put two of the heavy eggs in her hands. Yul could see how they started to glow almost immediately as the force shot down through her arms into the greedy stone. Her severe jerking had stopped now the moon had risen above the horizon and lost its pink-gold colour; instead she merely trembled and shuddered. Yul closed his eyes, wishing desperately to relieve her of such pain.

Magus changed the eggs over after a while and both men climbed up onto the stone, spreading themselves out on it. Sylvie remained standing, staring up at the moon with unseeing eyes. Yul was sure that an hour had passed and he felt his anger, clamped down tightly inside, begin to bubble up. When Magus changed the eggs again, Yul realised he'd never had any intention of keeping to the agreement. Clip, for all his earlier solicitousness, appeared to have forgotten about Sylvie and her suffering. He was having too good a time soaking up the moon magic. As Magus put the new eggs in Sylvie's hands, she turned her eyes to him. She'd left her hidden place and felt the pain shooting through her body. Her arms and fingers ached terribly and Yul willed her to drop the eggs, but her fingers were frozen into position.

'Please let me stop now,' she whispered to Magus. He smiled at her in the moonlight, his hair shimmering almost as brightly as hers. He shook his head and put his finger to his lips, glancing down at Clip.

'*You bastard!*' thought Yul, longing to leap out and hit him over the head with his stone eggs. But Clip heard something, for he opened his eyes and sat up.

'Goddess, I must've been in a trance,' he mumbled, staring around him in the bright moonlight. 'I meant to keep a close eye on Sylvie this time but that moon magic just sends me off to another realm. I'm sure we've been here longer than an hour, Sol. Why didn't you wake me?'

'Don't be a fool,' laughed Magus. 'See, she's fine – much better than last month. Your hypnosis really helps her, so no need to worry yourself.'

'That's good. Come on then, let's get her down and take her home.'

'Just five more minutes,' said Magus. 'Remember, she does love to dance at Mooncliffe.'

He laughed again and Yul found it almost impossible to control his pure, white-hot hatred.

*

Later, Yul followed them back to the Hall at a distance. Sylvie was delivered to her bedroom via the private staircase and both men left. Yul saw her mother moving around in the dimly lit room upstairs. He knew there was no point going home and trying to sleep as he was boiling over with anger. He seethed with it; a molten rage that ran through his veins like poison. He knew that if he were to bump into Magus now, he'd try to kill him. He wasn't rational in any way. He'd had to endure watching Sylvie being abused by Magus, used for the man's own gratification and then laughed at in her weakness. It was more than he could take.

Yul ran from the Hall and headed for the Stone Circle. In the light of the brilliant silver-gold moon, now riding high across the night sky, he could see perfectly. He pushed himself to his limit, trying to blot out the images of Sylvie's suffering. His legs pumped like pistons as he raced up the hill. The great stone dance was silhouetted against the silvery night sky, the dark shapes blotting out the stars. He slowed down just before he reached the circle and tried to calm his emotions, knowing he should enter the sacred space with reverence. But he couldn't. His hatred for Magus was too intense and all-consuming to be pushed aside so soon. He stepped into the arena with his heart pounding from the punishing run, his veins pulsing with fury and the desire to kill. He stood in the centre of the circle not wanting any energy tonight from the Altar Stone. He already seethed with an excess of energy that chased around his body searching for an outlet. As the moon poured quicksilver into the circle Yul raised his face to the bright disc and howled.

The rage and frustration, hatred and blood-lust came cascading from him in a torrent. It hung in the hot night air, eddying about with nowhere to go. Then, slowly, Yul started to move, pacing around the edge of the circle. He prowled silently and purposefully, circling inside the circumference of the great stones still adorned with corn dollies and images of the Corn Mother. Gradually he picked up speed, loping round and touching each stone as he passed. Moonlight and shadow flickered on him as he ran faster, light and dark, silver and black, like a strobe on his face flashing into his soul. Round and round he raced, his pain and rage spiralling into the centre of the Circle. A great vortex of emotion started to build, a flickering carousel of anger and passion.

He didn't see the inky clouds piling in from the west. They rolled in fast, building and climbing on each other, great towers of swollen blackness growing in the sultry August night. Still Yul ran, his body slick with sweat, curls stuck to his head. He wrenched off his restrictive damp clothes as he ran. The night air clung to him, oppressively hot and heavy against his bare skin. The hair on his body tingled. He felt a strange lifting in his heart as if his breath itself was charged with particles of rage.

He raced one final, mad circuit of the Stone Circle, stirring the power and energy into a maelstrom of wild and uncontrollable passion. He felt it building inside him, climbing, towering, piling up. With a shout he broke away from his track and lunged full pelt for the Altar Stone. He sprang onto the great stone with a mighty leap and turned to face the moon, his body thrumming and throbbing with a dark, negative charge. He roared and roared, the sound pouring from him in a blind flood of wrath. At that moment the heavy black clouds billowed across, blotting out the moon and plunging the arena into utter darkness.

There was an earth-shattering crack as the skies and the boy released their fury in unison, all the elements as one. A great pillar of lightning slashed down to earth accompanied by an explosion of thunder strong enough to rouse the dead. Yul screamed in wild glory and again the lightning forked down, hitting the hills in the distance. Flash followed flash, the blue-white light blindingly intense, searing the eye. Pure volts of vicious energy discharged themselves from the skies and blasted the earth below with their violence.

Completely exposed to the elements, Yul stood astride the stone with his arms outstretched to the heavens. His dark curls corkscrewing with static, he threw back his head and laughed. He shouted, screamed, yelled, bellowed – his tiny sound drowned by the great anger of the elements, the rage of the thunder as it

220

rolled and rumbled around Stonewylde. And then came the rain. It hit Yul's hot skin like burning nails, driving hard into every inch of him, bouncing off his skin with such force that he felt punctured. He raised his face, tipping his head right back and letting the needles of water wash away the sweat. It ran in torrents through his curls, down his body, washing and cleansing him with its fierce drumming. He was caught in a waterfall of rain. Gradually the downpour turned cold as the heat and energy of the storm dissipated, its force spent. Yul's roars turned to cries and then to sobs, and he howled once more into the drenched night. Howls of pain and sorrow, howls of anguish and torment for the girl he loved but couldn't protect from the man who abused her.

Just before dawn, the cold boy lying crumpled on the Altar Stone was awoken by a pecking on his arm. He opened his eyes blearily, unable to focus properly, and saw the crow perched next to him. It blinked and let out a loud *caw*. He pushed himself upright, his head spinning and his body wracked with tremors. Slowly he levered himself off the stone, stumbling as his bare feet hit the wet earth below. The crow flapped off and he followed it, falling and tripping, as it took the short cut to the sanctuary of Mother Heggy's cottage.

After the night of the Corn Moon Sylvie rested in her Tudor bedroom for a few days, spending most of her time asleep or sitting by the window in a daydream. She wasn't as weak as the previous month, having been allowed down from the stone before she collapsed. Miranda took care of her and Magus looked in to check she was alright, pleased that Hazel wasn't needed this month. Clip too was delighted that she seemed stronger than the month before, but he still irritated Miranda with his frequent visits to sit with Sylvie.

Yul, however, was not safely tucked up in his bed. When he'd arrived in the grey light of the misty August dawn, falling through her front door and shivering without his clothes, Mother Heggy had been waiting for him. She'd wrapped him in a mouldering blanket and laid him on a narrow truckle bed at the back of the cottage. She made him drink from her stone mug and then left him to battle it out. He had a high fever but she knew he was strong and in good health. He tossed and turned for two days and nights, his black curls plastered to his head, cheeks flushed and eyes glassy. He was delirious and unaware of where he was. Mother Heggy took good care of him. She forced him to drink, sponged him down with tepid water, covered him when he shivered with cold. She sent a message with a passing Villager to Maizie telling her of Yul's whereabouts. On the fourth night Mother Heggy judged him recovered from the chill and let him leave, wrapped in the blanket and with stern instructions to bring Sylvie to her well before the next full moon.

September began as warm and balmy as August had been. The sun was hot, and in the afternoon Sylvie decided she felt strong enough to go outside. She'd recovered so much quicker from her ordeal this time, although she still felt a little weak. She wandered around the lawns and flower gardens, watching the newts in the great ornamental pond for a while. Then she went to the formal garden with its raked gravel paths and clipped hedges. She'd never been here alone before and strolled around looking at the stone ornaments carved to represent mythological creatures.

Sylvie was deep inside the maze-like garden when she heard the gravel crunching behind her. She turned to see Buzz approaching and her heart sank. She'd managed to avoid him so far as he'd been keeping to himself because of his injuries, which were the talk of the Hall. But it was now a month since the fight with Yul and he was on the mend. His nose was out of the splint, although swollen and unsightly. The bruising around his eyes had faded to a nasty yellow and his split lip was almost healed. The tooth was still missing; soon he'd have to face the dental work necessary to restore his smile.

He quickened his pace and waved for her to stop.

'Hello, stranger! I saw you coming into this garden from my bedroom window. I've wanted to catch you alone for ages.'

'Hi, Buzz. Are you feeling better?'

'Yes thanks, though it's taken me a long time to recover. I expect you've heard all about how I was viciously attacked by that Village thug? He thought I was having a go at his bloody sister, though she was willing enough, believe me. I mean, do I look like I have to force myself on girls? But he hasn't heard the last of it ...'

'Really? I thought we were all waiting to see what punishment Magus decided on. It's a serious crime, trying to force yourself on anyone, but especially an under-age Village girl.'

He looked at her sharply.

'No, Sylvie, that's just malicious gossip. It's a horrible mis-understanding and I know Magus'll sort it out. That boy has got it in for me and it was all his doing.'

He ignored her look of scepticism and put an arm around her shoulders, giving her a hug.

'Anyway, forget about that half-witted bastard. Did you hear about my exam results? I got straight A's!'

'Congratulations. But Yul's not a half-witted bastard. From what I've seen he's very intelligent.'

'You're not still keen on him after all he's done? I warned you about his violence before, remember? And the consequences of getting involved with a Villager. Do you know what my father did to him in June, while I was away sitting my exams? That proves just how far Magus will go to keep him in line, and that's why I know he'll sort this mess out. He won't take Yul's side over mine.'

Sylvie shrugged miserably. She'd been worried about exactly that outcome.

'And how can you say he's intelligent? Pig ignorant, more like. I wonder how many A's he'd get, if he was even capable of taking any exams. He's illiterate, for Christ's sake.'

Sylvie turned on him angrily.

'And just why is he illiterate? Because your father doesn't allow Village children to learn to read and write! If he'd been educated properly, he'd outstrip you in every way. Leave me alone, Buzz! I don't like your attitude or your values.'

He stopped and looked at her hard. Then he shook his head and took her elbow quite gently.

'I'm sorry, Sylvie. I always seem to go crashing in and upsetting you. Can we start again? Forget Yul and what he did to me and let's talk about something else. Please?'

Against her better judgement, and mostly because he looked so ugly with his broken nose and missing tooth, Sylvie nodded.

'Let's go in here, shall we?' he said smoothly. 'I like this part of the garden – it's very private.'

He led her into a hidden section of the formal garden she'd never seen before. It was concealed behind a tall yew hedge with a trick entrance and exit that fooled the eye into the illusion that it was solid. Inside, the dark hedges were tall and impossible to see over. There were more alcoves with benches and she could hear the sound of water. It was a maze within a maze. They walked around the endless short paths, hemmed in by the high, over-powering hedges and Sylvie felt trapped. She glanced at the large stone ornaments that decorated this inner maze.

'Oh!'

She blushed scarlet. The statue was obscene, and so was the next one. Buzz laughed at her embarrassment.

'Great, aren't they? I believe my grandfather or maybe great-grandfather had them carved. They were both rogues, apparently, and loved their wine, women and song. I think I must take after them!'

She grimaced, wanting more than ever to get out of the horrible place.

'Come on, we're almost in the middle and there's an incredible fountain I'd like to show you. I bet you've never seen anything like it! I hope you're not a prude, Sylvie – you're far too gorgeous for that. And I've heard all sorts of gossip about you since I got back at Lammas.'

'What gossip? And I'm not a prude but I really don't like vulgar or obscene things.'

'Let's sit down here then,' he said, patting a large, comfortable

224

bench. 'Come and tell me what you've been up to lately, since I last saw you in May. I can't believe it's September already.'

She sat down reluctantly, trying to keep a distance between them. He placed himself close, trapping her in the corner of the bench.

'Nothing much. I haven't been very well for some of the time.'

'Oh? Holly tells me you've been spending a lot of time with Magus.'

She began to tremble.

'No, not really.'

'Holly said you were keen on him. She said you've been going up to Mooncliffe with him at the Moon Fullness. Is that right?'

'Yes,' she replied, shuddering, 'I love to dance on the stone for Magus.'

He laughed at this and it was not a pleasant sound.

'I bet you do! You're a dark horse, Sylvie. You seem so sweet and innocent, but there you are – my mistake. And I thought you were fifteen at the Summer Solstice, not sixteen. Or am I wrong about what goes on at Mooncliffe with Magus at the full moon?'

She looked away, her cheeks burning again.

'I don't know what you mean. Can we talk about something else? Tell me what you've been doing in the Outside World.'

'Oh, this and that. I stayed with my mother after the exams and we went abroad – I hadn't seen her in ages. It's odd when you leave here and go into the Outside World. Everything's so different and I always find it hard to adjust when I come back here again.'

'And what are you planning to do now?'

'Well, begin study for my next exams of course, as I certainly intend to go to University one day. I'm very excited about the subjects I've chosen – can't wait to get stuck in. And we'll all go skiing as usual this winter, after the Solstice, so that's something to look forward to. You'll come, won't you?'

'I don't know ... I've never skied before and Magus hasn't mentioned it,' she said doubtfully.

'Don't worry – I'd love to teach you! We stay in a gorgeous, very grand place in the Alps and have a ball. Superb skiing and snow-boarding there. Stonewylde's grim at that time of year, cold and grey, and it's a relief to get away and have some fun. Leave it to the peasants to toil away in the mud while we hit the snow, that's what we always say. Give me the piste any day.'

'I think I'll be getting back now,' she said tightly, moving to get up. He pulled her down on the bench.

'Don't go yet, Sylvie – we haven't even started. I really missed you when I was away. I thought about you a lot, and I've never done that before over any girl. I've been looking forward to picking up where we left off.'

His arm on the back of the bench slid down around her shoulders, his hand stroking her arm. She noticed the bristly blond hair on his thick fingers and a new signet ring to match the heavy gold bracelet. He was sweating and she could smell his anti-perspirant as he squeezed her warmly. She'd forgotten just how insistent he was and bitterly regretted allowing herself to be persuaded into this situation. She should never have come into this secluded part of the garden alone with him. He was bigger than ever and had that gleam in his pale blue eyes which she remembered of old. She began to feel frightened.

'Did you miss me, Sylvie?'

'To be honest, Buzz, no I didn't. I—'

'Oh come on, Sylvie, stop playing hard to get! You know I want you. I meant what I said – I really have been thinking of you. It's been hell stuck up in that bedroom and not being able to see you. I've been dying to spend some time with you and tell you how I feel.'

'I'm sorry Buzz but I don't feel that way about you at all.'

'That's okay, give it time. I know you like me and that's a start.'

'No! No, I don't even like you. I'm sorry.'

She felt him stiffen next to her and swallowed hard. Maybe she should just pretend until they were somewhere less isolated. She glanced at his battered face and shuddered as he glared down at her.

'I see – so you're after the bigger fish, eh? You're a scheming one, Sylvie, and I misjudged you there as well. Well let me tell you this – you might've set your sights on Magus and he may seem interested now, but it won't last.'

'No!' she said, her cheeks burning. 'I don't—'

'Just hear me out please! Magus never stays with one woman for long, not ever, and by the next full moon he'll have moved on to someone else. But I'm different. One day all this will be mine and you'd do well to remember that. You and I could have a future together if you play your cards right.'

'No! I can't—'

'Oh Sylvie,' he groaned hoarsely, reaching to stroke her silky hair. 'Please stop saying no to me – I'm crazy about you! There's something about you – something special. I want you more than I've ever wanted anyone or anything. Just give me a chance, please!'

She shook her head and tried again to stand but his arm held her fast. He shifted his weight so she was wedged even more tightly into the corner of the bench. With his free hand he turned her head towards his and clamped his lips onto hers, trying to thrust his tongue between her teeth. She pulled backwards but there was nowhere to go. His hand began to roam over her T-shirt, grasping and kneading at her. She struggled and hit out at him but he was heavy and persistent and she couldn't push him off. She tried to scream but he took the opportunity of pushing his tongue deep into her mouth. She started to gag, repulsed by him, and as he pulled back she bit his split lip. He jerked away, eyes blazing with a strange light.

'You little bitch – that hurt! What are you playing at?'

He put his hand to his mouth and it came away covered in blood. Again she tried to get up and make a dash for it. He grabbed her and pulled her down, shoving her hard against the bench and thrusting his hand roughly up the front of her T-shirt.

'Bite me again and I'll hurt you back! Really hurt you. We can both play rough if that's how you like it. Now kiss me properly,

Sylvie. I don't care if I'm covered in blood – that's your own fault.'

He closed in on her again and the taste of his blood made her retch. He pushed her onto her back on the seat, using his weight and bulk to pin her down, easing himself on top of her. He was crushingly heavy, his breathing hoarse, his hands insistent. Sylvie punched up at him wildly and caught him hard on the nose. An arc of blood spattered across her, hot and wet on her face. He yelled with pain and closed his hands round her neck as he shook her, screaming at her frenziedly. She shut her eyes against the horror of his face so close, blood streaming from his nose and mouth, his pale blue eyes manic. This, thought Sylvie, was the last thing she'd ever see. He'd lost control and there was nobody to stop him squeezing her soft throat, squeezing hard . . .

14

Buzz sat white-faced in Magus' office, a towel on his lap to catch the blood that still oozed from his nose. His hands trembled and his head hung in despair. Magus sat opposite in a large leather chair, his mouth curled in disdain at the spectacle before him.

'I'm formally banishing you from Stonewylde, Buzzard. You've an hour to pack your belongings and then you'll be driven to your mother's house, where you'll make your home permanently. Your mother will receive a single, generous payment that will sever any need for future contact between us. I'm formally cutting all family ties between us. You're no longer a member of the Hallfolk, nor part of the community of Stonewylde, and you'll never be permitted to return here.'

Buzz began to cry; piteous, mewling sobs which made everything bleed more.

'Please, Dad, please!' he snivelled, his voice cracking. 'I beg you, don't do this! It was all a misunderstanding.'

'Whatever your previous actions, there's no misunderstanding about this latest assault. You tried to strangle Sylvie. Maybe I should call it attempted murder rather than assault. If those gardeners hadn't heard you and stepped in so quickly, you could've killed her.'

'But she led me on! She—'

'No she did not,' said Magus coldly, his expression implacable. 'Sylvie would never do that.'

'Alright, she didn't. But I wanted her so badly! I've wanted her since she got here and she couldn't stand me. She treated me like I was dirt.'

'I'm not surprised. You are dirt.'

'No I'm not – I'm your son! Anyway, if you can have her, why can't I?'

'I haven't had her, as you so crudely put it. She's still a child. I thought I'd made it clear how important it is *never* to break that law.'

'But you take her up to Moo—'

'Don't you *dare* suggest such a thing! You're the one who's done wrong,' barked Magus, his face twisted with distaste. 'She's not for you and never would be. Sylvie's very special and she's out of your league.'

'But she's Hallfolk! You said I mustn't have a go at Village girls, but Hallfolk were alright. You said—'

'Oh be quiet, Buzz,' Magus said wearily, shaking his head. 'You don't have a clue. We do not force ourselves on any woman, be they Villager, Hallfolk or Outsider. Not ever. We don't need to.'

'Don't tell me you've never forced anyone!'

'Of course I haven't! Why would I? Now that's enough – you sicken me. Go and pack. You've only got an hour and I really can't wait to be shot of you for good.'

Buzz started to cry again. Magus hauled him roughly out of the chair by the back of his collar, propelling him to the door.

'No, Dad! Don't do this! I'll do anything—'

'Get out of my sight! You're pathetic and disgusting. When I look at you, I feel ashamed to have fathered something so worthless.'

'But I'm your son! You must love me!'

Magus laughed harshly at this, pausing at the door where Buzz tried to cling to the frame, his face convulsed with weeping and blood still flowing down his front.

'For Goddess' sake, stop this blubbering and have some dignity!' spat Magus. 'And don't you dare get any blood on the Aubusson carpet!'

He bundled the towel under Buzz's face, wrenching his hands away from the door-frame.

'Please, Dad! I beg you!'

But Magus opened the door, his face contemptuous.

'I'll tell you something, Buzz; for all that boy Yul has been a thorn in my flesh, he's worth ten of you. I've seen him take more punishment than I'd have believed possible, yet I've never once seen him cry like this. Yul has something that you utterly lack – he has pride.'

The talk in the Village pub and on the Green was all of Buzz's banishment. The Villagers were delighted that Magus had acted so strongly, particularly as Buzz was his own son and the rules could've been bent. Some would've liked to see him publicly whipped too, because Buzz had not been popular. He was arrogant and rude, and many in the community had been slighted or upset by him in the past. Rosie was hailed as a heroine for standing up to him and fending him off. Yul was everyone's hero for beating the Hallfolk at cricket and then for thrashing Buzz so soundly in his sister's defence. And Magus was once more the benign master who could always be relied upon to mete out justice fairly.

When Yul met Sylvie a couple of days later in the woods, he told her how happy he was that Magus had taken the matter of Rosie's assault so seriously. He'd never expected Magus to actually banish Buzz and was impressed by his decision. Sylvie looked at him sadly.

'Sorry to disillusion you, Yul, but I don't think that's why Magus banished him at all. You obviously haven't heard what happened, and I think it's being hushed up because Magus told me not to talk about it to anyone.'

'What? I don't understand.'

'Buzz attacked me too – look.'

She wore a silk scarf round her neck, not something he'd seen her wear before. She undid it to reveal deep purple bruising around her neck.

'Sacred Mother! Buzz did that to you?'

'Yes. It looks worse than it is because I bruise so easily, but I thought he was going to kill me. I wasn't co-operating with him, just as your sister wouldn't. He tried to force himself on me but I fought back and then he went completely mad and tried to strangle me. Luckily some gardeners heard and pulled him off just in time. A few seconds more and it may've been too late.'

Yul grimaced as he stroked Sylvie's damaged throat with gentle fingertips. His face was white.

'And then Magus banished him?'

'Yes, apparently within about ten minutes Buzz was hauled into his office and told he had to leave. An hour later he was gone.'

'So he attacks a Village girl and almost a month later he's still here, unpunished. But he attacks a Hallfolk girl and he's banished within ten minutes?'

He shook with rage, barely able to contain himself.

'This is one more thing in a long line of things that Magus is going to pay for,' he said ominously. 'Nobody in the Village will think the banishment is because of this attack even if I tell them what's happened, which I can't without giving away that we've met and you've told me.'

'I'm sorry, Yul,' said Sylvie gently. 'But at least Buzz has gone for good.'

'Yes, but everyone believes he's been kicked out on our account, because of what happened to poor Rosie. Because Magus is so just and fair, so caring towards his Villagers, such a kind master who puts our welfare above his own son's. They're all praising him and saying how well he treats us. That man is so bloody clever! Goddess how I hate him!'

Drowsy and golden, September was the month of the great apple harvest at Stonewylde. Yul, along with many others, was pulled from his normal duties and sent to the orchards to pick fruit. Working from the misty dawns until the mellow dusks, the Villagers arrived daily in the vast orchards filled with apples of every variety. The gnarled old trees groaned with heavy fruitfulness waiting to be harvested, and this was overseen by two men: Stag and Old Bewald. Eating apples were taken to the fruit and vegetable store house, a stone building almost as big as the Great Barn. Cool and dark inside, it was full of different levels and racks where vegetables, fruit and potatoes were stored. Cider apples were carted straight to the Cider House, where the maunds were hauled up by a winch and pulley into the apple loft, ready for the mill.

The apple gathering was overseen by Stag, although anyone less stag-like would be hard to imagine. He was in his fifties, small and wiry, with skin like leather and a permanent squint from screwing up his eyes against the sun. He was in charge of the orchards and under normal circumstances was grumpy and morose. At this time of year he became a complete tyrant. The apple harvest was vital to the community; Stonewylde without cider would be unthinkable. The Cider House was the domain of Old Bewald, an ancient, wizened man who'd worked with cider all his life. Stag and Old Bewald didn't see eye to eye at all. There was constant friction between the two about which varieties should be harvested next and when the apples were truly ready for picking.

The grass in the orchards, which had grown tall and lush with wild flowers to provide nectar for the hives, had been scythed for hay in June. It had been cut again for silage at the end of August and was now short around the trees so that all windfalls could be easily collected. The ladders were stacked every night near the trees, and just after dawn the tribe of Villagers gathered to begin their day's work. Yul and his younger brothers, Geoffrey and Gregory, arrived with a group. Rosie was needed at the dairy, and Maizie was busy harvesting her own back-garden produce and making chutneys and preserves. Her jams were all done; row upon row of jars sat on shelves in the pantry all neatly labelled with a picture of their fruit. Maizie would bring down lunch for her children later, after she'd visited the baker's to collect their daily bread.

The younger Villagers were back in school or the nursery, but anyone over the age of eight or so helped to bring in the harvest. Picking up windfalls was easier for children, who could also climb up into the thinner branches which wouldn't hold an adult's weight. They ran errands and helped with other autumn harvesting; the hedgerows glistened with ripe blackberries waiting to be picked, and juicy elderberries clustered thickly on elder trees all over the estate. The sloes weren't quite ready, but cob nuts were just beginning to fall and needed to be gathered before the squirrels had their fill.

The band of Villagers stood in the soft light waiting for orders. The shadows were long and the air hazy with early morning gold. Old Bewald and Stag were away over the far side of the orchards in heated discussion about which trees were ready for today's harvest. Yul sent his brothers to collect mushrooms in the dewy grass where the blackbirds hopped. Maizie would be pleased, and if they weren't picked now the mushrooms would be trampled by the harvesters. While he was waiting, Yul strapped a wicker basket tightly round his waist and adjusted the harness on his shoulders. He was still sleepy for he seemed to be working even longer hours than was usual for harvest time. Edward, who orchestrated the labour at this time of year, was piling the duties on him, expecting him to work in the Cider House every evening after the day's picking was done.

'Come on!' grumbled one of the men. 'Them two, like a couple o' women the way they nag and scold at each other.'

The carters put nosebags of oats onto the horses' heads whilst they waited, and people joined Yul in strapping themselves up with a picker. Eventually Stag came stomping over to the group, whose number was growing all the time as more workers arrived. Old Bewald hobbled out of the orchard towards the Cider House muttering incoherently under his breath, a battered clay pipe clamped between his teeth and foul-smelling smoke hovering around him. Stag began to direct the workers to different areas of the orchard, growling out the names of the apples that were to be gathered today. The warm September sun rose higher, the dew started to dry and the day's work commenced.

Yul was sent over to the far side of the orchards and took a stack of large wicker maunds with him. He and his group began to collect the apples; the children gathered the windfalls, being very mindful of wasps, the adults picked the ripe fruit from the lower branches of the tree, and Yul set the ladder against a strong branch and climbed up to pick from the top. As an agile woodsman he was useful at the apple harvest. He shinned up and down the ladder with the full picker, tipping it into the waiting maunds, which were loaded onto the cart when it came over on its rounds. It was thirsty work and several times Yul sent one of his brothers over to fill his water bottle from the barrel.

Yul was up the tree stretching towards a branch almost out of his reach when Magus rode into the orchard. He greeted his people warmly, encouraging them and praising their efforts. On the great prancing horse he trotted over to the tree where Yul was working with his team and sat watching from the saddle for a while. Yul felt uncomfortable under his scrutiny. Magus looked up at him through the foliage and caught his eye. The man's face hardened, his eyes cold.

'I hope you're working hard, boy!' he called up. 'No fooling about.'

'No, sir,' replied Yul, smothering his irritation.

'You're putting in the hours in the evening too, at the Cider House?'

'Yes, sir.'

Yul had been right then; he was being given extra work. And of course it was Magus who'd ordered it.

'Good. There are many extra jobs to be done and I plan to keep you busy from the moment you wake up until you go to bed at night. You've been a damn nuisance for the past six months and it's going to stop. You're going to be so bloody tired you'll have no energy for more mischief.'

'Yes, sir.'

Yul kept his eyes lowered, the dark hair falling over them, but his nostrils flared and his mouth clamped tight to stop it quivering. Although he was happy to work for the good of the community, he resented being singled out for added labour. September was a lovely month and he'd have liked a little free time to enjoy it; to walk up on the ridgeway, or go fishing in the evening on the beach with the other Villagers. Not to mention seeing Sylvie.

Magus turned and trotted Nightwing back through the trees to where Stag was supervising the loading of maunds into a cart.

'There'll be a group of young Hallfolk coming up after lunch, Stag,' he said.

Stag suppressed a grunt of annoyance at this, and managed to arrange his features into an expression of mild pleasure and anticipation.

'Right enough, sir.'

'I want them to do their bit to help with the harvest. The Villagers work damn hard at this time of year and Hallfolk youngsters should do the same. They're a lazy bunch, most of them. So make sure they work, won't you?'

'Oh aye, sir,' said Stag, thinking ahead as to how he could get rid of them as quickly as possible. Hallfolk were useless at this sort of thing. They had no idea what was required, they couldn't take orders, and they had no stamina. All they did was get in the way, but Magus' commands were not to be questioned.

Yul and his team made their way back to the centre of the orchard at mid-day, along with everyone else. Maizie was waiting with a basket of food for her hungry sons, and little Leveret skipped about chasing copper-coloured butterflies. When the food and cider were finished, Yul lay back in the grass. He laced his hands behind his head and gazed at the blue skies through the branches, drowsing in the golden September heat. He was tired and would've liked to sleep. All around him people chattered and gossiped, happy with the weather and the way the apple harvest was going. Someone had brought a fiddle and started to play a harvest song, which many people sang along to. After a while Stag hollered at them all to get back to work or he'd tan the nearest arse. Reluctantly they packed up their lunches, brushed themselves down, and headed back to their assigned trees.

Yul and his team were hard at work when they heard the group of Hallfolk coming towards them through the orchard.

There was a ripple of discontent amongst the Villagers. The young Hallfolk seemed to be worse than ever each year, becoming ruder and less co-operative. Yul eyed the bunch approaching and groaned at the sight of Holly and her crowd. That was all he needed. He didn't notice Sylvie trailing behind them, keeping herself apart. She didn't see him either, up in the branches with only his boots visible from below.

'Is this the tree he said? Silly old fool – they all look the same to me.'

'Don't suppose it matters, does it? One apple's much the same as another and if they're ripe, they're ripe.'

'I don't see why we have to do this anyway. That's what the Villagers are for. Since when did we have to supply manual labour?'

'Magus has a bee in his bonnet about us not doing enough for the community. It'll blow over and then we'll all be back to normal.'

'It's not fair! I wanted to ride this afternoon.'

'Well I was in the middle of watching a really good film and then we were going to have a swim, so you're not the only one to have their plans ruined. Come on, let's just choose any old tree and get on with it.'

The Villagers picking below Yul's feet exchanged glances and rolled their eyes in disbelief. Hallfolk could be amazingly dense.

'Which tree did Stag ask you to pick?' asked one of them politely.

The Hallfolk regarded him with disdain.

'If we knew that, we wouldn't be confused. Not that it matters, surely – they're all pretty much the same.'

'It does matter, sir. Some are for cider, some for eating, and some aren't ready yet. It's important to pick the ones Stag has chosen, else all the apples'll get mixed up. What was the name of your apple?'

'Some ridiculous name – he said it was near your tree.'

'Well that tree's the Onion Redstreak, and those ones over yonder are the Catsheads.'

'Neither of those.'

'This here one is a Foxwhelp, and—'

'Yes, that's it! Foxwhelp.'

'There you are then, miss – that's your tree there. 'Tis important to pick up the windfalls first so they don't get trodden underfoot, and then start on the lower branches. Apples should fall into your hand if you cup and twist. There's the ladder to use for the upper branches.'

'Yes, alright, thank you. We do understand how it's done.'

The peaceful golden afternoon with its gentle rhythm of reaching and picking, reaching and picking, whilst chatting desultorily or humming softly, was now spoilt. The young Hallfolk were strident and treated the event as a game. They messed about, throwing apples to each other, swinging on the branches, shrieking and laughing. Sylvie kept her head down and worked steadily, filling her picker and tipping it into the maund before starting again. She was acutely aware of the Villagers' disapproval and felt embarrassed to be classed as a member of the poorly behaved Hallfolk.

Holly was on good form. She insisted on dragging the ladder over and positioning it against the twisted trunk. It looked precarious; the tree split and divided into branches and there was no good resting place for the top of the ladder. Wearing a skimpy T-shirt, short skirt and trainers, she acted provocatively, tossing her shoulder-length hair about and flaunting her bare legs. As usual, the boys in her group pandered to her ego. The other girls seemed to find it hilarious, which encouraged her further. Sylvie kept as far away from them as possible, picking from the spreading branches on the other side of the tree.

Holly climbed halfway up the ladder, making a big deal of the boys looking up her skirt. She began to pick apples and throw them down, trying to hit people. She made a lot of noise and Yul, up his tree, was sick of it. He and the other Villagers had been working for many hours now and he was in no mood for Holly and the Hallfolk. His picker was full so he climbed down the ladder and went across to the maund, where he unstrapped it and gently tipped the apples onto the steadily increasing pile.

At that point he looked across and saw Sylvie reaching up into the branches above her, unaware of his presence.

He paused to admire her as he re-buckled the picker, noticing how she'd become taller and willowy in recent weeks. His mouth went dry and he felt a surge of excitement at this unexpected encounter. He was on his way over to her to say hello, trying to be unobtrusive, when one of Holly's apples hit him on the chest. Without thinking he caught it and threw it back. It bounced off her leg and she shrieked with exaggerated pain. Then she noticed who'd thrown it.

'Yul! You great oaf! That hurt!'

They all turned to look at him and he glared back sullenly, hair in his eyes. Sylvie turned around too, her heart beating faster at the prospect of seeing him. She'd imagined he'd be working in the woods as usual, not the orchards. He stood by the maund, chin raised and contempt on his face. His bare arms were well-defined with muscle and the picker strapped tightly around his waist emphasised his lean height and the breadth of his chest and shoulders. When had he turned from a boy into a man? It had happened so gradually and yet so quickly. Sylvie longed for him and shivered at the intensity of her emotions as she stood in the sunshine amongst the ripe apples, grappling with the temptation he aroused in her.

He looked away from the group of Hallfolk and straight into her eyes. His deep grey gaze flared with emotion and she read all his love and longing in that look.

'Oi! Yul! Come here! I want a word with you!' shouted Holly, still halfway up the tree. He ignored her, but with all eyes now on him thought better of going over to see Sylvie. Instead he returned to his own tree, climbing it swiftly and disappearing amongst the foliage. The last thing he wanted was a run in with Holly and the Hallfolk, bringing down Magus' displeasure. The Autumn Equinox festival was close now and he was determined to enjoy it this year.

But Holly couldn't let it rest. She remembered how keen he'd once been and his complete indifference now only fuelled her interest. With Buzz gone, she was at a loose end. None of the Hallfolk boys of suitable age took her fancy; they'd all been Buzz's satellites and were now directionless and dull. She was surrounded by blond, soft people; Yul was their complete antithesis. He'd grown up so much since the spring and she'd always recognised his promise.

Holly climbed higher up the ladder and then off it altogether, getting right up into the boughs amidst a great deal of commotion. The Villagers were now ignoring the Hallfolk, for the afternoon was well under way and they needed to move on. Their tree was almost picked and they must check with Stag where to go next. There were several maunds sitting on the grass, all full of apples. Yul climbed down from the tree and told one of his brothers to run over to the nearest horse and cart and ask them to come over for a collection. He removed the ladder and laid it on the ground, then unstrapped the picker from his waist.

Sylvie noticed and discreetly made her way around towards him. They managed to stand close together, shielded by the low-hanging branches of the tree, now bare of apples but still covered with leaves. He caressed her slim bare arm with his fingertips, looking into her silvery eyes.

'How are you, Sylvie?'

'Better for seeing you.'

'Me too. I miss you and I wish I could be with you every day, every minute. I think about you all the time, Sylvie.'

She nodded, her heart drumming at his proximity and gentle caress. He moved a little closer and his hand slid round her waist, pulling her to his side. His touch burned her skin through the thin cotton of her dress.

'All I want is to hold you and kiss you!' he whispered.

Sylvie's legs weakened at the desperation in his voice. She felt at once powerful and yet also completely in his thrall. Their snatched intimacy was shattered by a shriek from Holly, high up in the Foxwhelp tree.

'I'm stuck!' she wailed at the top of her voice. 'I can't get down! Someone help me!'

One of the Hallfolk boys climbed up the ladder and tried to persuade her down through the branches and onto the upper rungs.

'No! I can't move! I'm completely stuck!'

'Holly's awful!' whispered Sylvie with a groan. 'She's such a show-off. I can't stand her.'

Fennel said that he certainly wasn't going up there and Yul grinned at this, remembering how wobbly Fennel was on ladders. July tried to rescue Holly too, shouting at her to just put her foot on the rung and stop being so silly. But Holly wouldn't budge. Then she started shouting for Yul to come and rescue her. Yul stiffened. He closed his eyes in dismay at the sound of Holly repeatedly yelling his name, insisting he was the only one who could rescue her.

'You'd better go and help her,' said Sylvie, her voice small and quivery. 'She'll just go on and on and make it worse.'

'I don't want to help her. I can't stand her either.'

'I know, but she won't stop until she gets what she wants. That's what she's like. Just get her down, Yul.'

Sylvie moved away from him and resumed her picking.

'Yul! *Yul!* Come here and help me!'

All eyes, Villager and Hallfolk, were turned on him. Reluctantly he stepped forward and stood at the foot of the ladder looking up. She was high in the tree, perched uncomfortably on a branch and holding on tightly. Her bare legs dangled down and her face was a mixture of imperiousness and discomfort at her situation. Yul shook his head.

'What a stupid thing to do,' he said.

'It's not my fault!'

'Yes it is. There aren't even any apples up there. You climbed that high for no reason other than to show off. Didn't you, Holly?'

'No! Just shut up and rescue me, Yul.'

'Not until you see how stupid you've been. Else you might do it again. I'm far too busy to waste time rescuing silly girls who don't know their own limits.'

The Villagers and Hallfolk alike laughed, many pleased to see

Holly getting her come-uppance. Everyone was looking up at her and she flushed.

'Come on, Holly,' said Wren. 'It was stupid. Just admit it and he'll come and get you. I've had enough of this apple picking.'

'Me too. Just agree with him, Holly. He's right; you are stupid sometimes,' said Rainbow.

'Okay, I was stupid,' yelled Holly. 'Now get up that bloody ladder, Yul, and help me down!'

He climbed up and edged towards where she was perched, until his head was level with hers. Her knees brushed against him and he pulled away. His face was closed and cold as he looked around, working out the best way to get her down. She gazed at him speculatively.

'Since when did you become so masterful, Yul?'

He shrugged, not even bothering to reply.

'Did you enjoy humiliating me just then? You're so unfriendly nowadays. I remember how you used to be at the ceremonies and in the Great Barn afterwards, dancing and messing about with me. Do you remember?'

'That was all a long time ago.'

'Not that long ago. In fact it was the last Equinox, as I recall. I went off with Buzz and his gang and you got upset. And then they beat you up and you got into trouble with Magus.'

At this he looked her full in the face, his grey eyes blazing. She recoiled slightly, quite shocked at his intensity. She noticed how handsome he was, with his high cheekbones and chiselled nose and jaw.

'I remember, Holly. I remember your part in it all, and how you found the whole thing so funny and flattering, with no thought of the consequences for me. And now I'm grateful to that moron Buzz for showing me what a waste of time it was. Even the punishment from Magus was worth it, to see you for what you really are.'

She flushed at the insult of his words and the contempt in his voice.

'Shut your mouth, you stupid Villager, and get me down from

this bloody tree!' she hissed. 'And don't you *dare* speak to me like that again! Remember your place or Magus will hear about it and then you'll suffer.'

He shrugged at this, indicating his disdain for both her and Magus.

'Slide along the branch here and then slip off and stand here, where I am now. You can't go down the ladder facing that way, so, as you slip yourself off, twist around and I'll guide you down.'

He edged away giving her space to move along. Down below the onlookers had lost interest. The Villagers were loading their maunds into the newly arrived cart. The Hallfolk were now busy picking again, as the cart driver had brought a message from Stag. Magus had left instructions that they couldn't go home until they'd picked at least one tree. The only person still watching was Sylvie. She couldn't quite hear what they were saying up there but she could see them looking into each other's faces, and Holly's bare legs touching Yul. Sylvie's throat was tight and aching and she had an urge to climb the ladder herself and give Holly's ankle a hard tug.

As Holly slid her bottom off the branch, Yul braced himself to balance her. He put his hands round her waist, ready to twist her so she faced the right way. As he touched her Holly gasped and stared into his eyes, now only centimetres from hers. She felt the energy inside him; the pull of his being and the sheer magnetism flowing through his strong fingers. There was something in him – something powerful and thrilling. She could sense it dancing just behind his eyes. She was washed with a wave of desire for him and wobbled on the branch. He grasped her more tightly, thinking she'd fall. His body pressed against hers, both of them balancing precariously on the branch. She closed her eyes and swallowed.

'Yul, Yul, please.'

'What's the matter?' he said coldly. 'Hold on to the branch for Goddess' sake or you'll fall. Hold on! Stop leaning into me.'

'I can't help it,' she whispered. 'I want you. I'm sorry, Yul, sorry for everything. I was wrong. I made a mistake about you and I want to go back to how we used to be together.'

'You made a mistake alright, but there's no going back now, Holly. Let's just get down to the ground.'

'Wait!'

He'd started to move away, now that she was facing the right way. He planned to guide her from below onto the rungs of the ladder and get down as fast as he could. The last thing he wanted was Holly making a play for him, especially with Sylvie watching. He caught a glimpse of Sylvie's face down below them, white and pinched. He couldn't blame her. He knew how he'd feel if he was on the ground watching her and Buzz up in a tree.

'Hold on a minute, Yul,' Holly said quietly. She closed her fingers around his wrist, looking at him with an expression he'd never seen her wear before.

'Let me go,' he said. 'I'm not interested, Holly. That was in the past.'

'Please listen, Yul. I've just made a decision. It's our Rite of Adulthood at the Winter Solstice and it's only three months away. If I can't have Magus, I want you to be my partner at the ceremony.'

She gave him a little smile and cocked her head. He stared at her, a dangerous glint in his slanted eyes.

'Oh really? Well understand this, Holly. I don't take second place to anyone, not even Magus. Besides which, I have other plans for the Winter Solstice and they certainly don't include you.'

She gasped at the harshness of his words and the pitiless look in his eyes. She recalled the fun-loving Villager from six months ago, the boy who loved to leap high during the dances in the Stone Circle and gallop around with her in the Great Barn afterwards. The boy who used to show off and try to impress her with his antics. She'd never seen this side of him and she shook her head, bewildered by his curt rejection.

'I don't understand, Yul. You've changed. You used to be such fun and you've always liked me. Remember how we'd play together and get up to mischief at school, before I went to the

Hall School? We used to be friends, Yul – a bit more than friends, even. Why are you so cold to me now?'

He sighed and gazed up through the branches above their heads, not even wanting eye contact with her.

'It's hard to know where to begin and I really can't be bothered anyway. Just accept that I'm not interested and leave it at that. Now let's get down from this tree. You're fooling around and I should be working.'

As his feet found the upper rungs of the ladder and he began to climb down, she spoke once more in a voice which quivered dangerously.

'No I won't leave it at that! How dare you treat me like this? You should be honoured that I'm favouring you. I'll speak to Magus about it and then, believe me, you *will* partner me at our Rite of Adulthood.'

'Only in your dreams, Holly,' he said, with a harsh laugh. 'Remember what happens to Hallfolk who try to force Villagers? Now get on the ladder and stop wasting my time.'

He grasped her ankles quite roughly, not wanting his actions misinterpreted, and pulled her foot onto the rung. He slid down the ladder quickly and stood below, watching her descent. But when Holly was only halfway to the ground she stopped and turned around precariously, now facing outwards. She smiled down at Yul, and they both remembered when he'd done the same thing in the Stone Circle climbing down the bonfire.

As the thought raced through his head he took a step back, but then, without warning, Holly launched herself off the ladder and leapt straight at him. He caught her full on and staggered under her weight, only just managing to keep his balance. She clung to him, her arms around his neck and her bare legs wrapping around his hips. She kissed him hard on the mouth. He pulled his head back sharply but she clung to him like a limpet. Then she let go and sprang back from him, landing lightly on her feet, and he remembered how agile she'd always been.

'Thank you for rescuing me, Yul,' she said brightly. 'I owe you.'

15

Yul was aware that Sylvie had turned on her heel as Holly clung to him, and was now disappearing amongst the apple trees. He was desperate to run after her and stop her, and stood indecisively as Holly began throwing apples straight into the maund. The Hallfolk were picking away at their tree and putting in a little more effort now. He turned back to his own tree and found the Villagers had finished and were now following the cart back to find Stag and ask him where to go next. Yul decided Sylvie was worth getting into trouble for, should Stag notice his disappearance.

'I'll be back soon!' he called to the rest of his group and hared off through the trees and the other apple gatherers. The orchard was very busy, full maunds on the grass, ladders and people everywhere. Horses and carts trundled about and children skipped around, their work mostly done for the day. Yul dodged through the lot, but by the time he caught up with Sylvie she was almost out of the orchard. There were so many people about and he despaired of talking to her alone.

'Sylvie!' he called. He slowed down as he approached her, not wanting to attract too much attention. 'Sylvie!'

She turned slightly and saw him, but carried on walking away.

'Wait! Please stop!' he said, catching her up and touching one of her wrists. He longed to grab her and spin her around to face him but could only risk a surreptitious tap. She shook him off and marched on grimly.

'Just leave it, Yul,' she snapped. 'I'm going home. I've got a headache.'

'Please listen, Sylvie. Just listen and then you can go home.'

Reluctantly she stopped and turned to him, but stared down at the grass. Her face was tight and closed and she stood stiffly. Yul was acutely aware of all the people milling around them. If they'd been alone he'd have taken her in his arms and kissed her jealousy and anger away. As it was, his hands were tied and there was nothing he could do. She wouldn't even look him in the eye.

'Sylvie, I understand why you're cross, but believe me, I wanted nothing to do with her. I can't stand her.'

'I know.'

'I hated having to rescue her. I never wanted to go up and help her.'

'I know.'

'I told her I wasn't interested in her.'

'Oh, so you discussed it then?'

'Well, not exactly . . .'

He decided it wouldn't be wise to tell her about Holly's plans for their Rite of Adulthood, or that he'd once liked Holly.

'I just want to get home, Yul. Forget what happened here, as I intend to.'

'But you're angry and upset! I swear to you, Sylvie, there's no need for it.'

'I know. Really I do.'

'Good. What happened with Holly was nothing.'

'Well, hardly nothing. In fact it was pretty full on.'

Her cheeks were now flushed and her mouth grim. She fiddled with a strand of her hair, wrapping and unwrapping it tightly around a finger.

'Yes, but—'

'And she was so intimate with you up in the tree, so close to you, all that whispering to each other and—'

'And I hated it! I nearly fell out of the tree trying to get away from her.'

'Well you obviously didn't get the message through, did you Yul?'

'Oh Sylvie, you're being silly now. I didn't encourage Holly – how can you think that? You couldn't hear what we were saying, and if—'

'Whatever it was, she feels in your debt now. "*I owe you!*" And I'll bet she's just longing to pay up!'

'Sylvie, why are you being like this? Nothing happened, I can't stand Holly, and it—'

'But the way she wrapped herself around you when she jumped down, and then she kissed you ... How d'you think I feel? I'm not even allowed to talk to you in public, but Holly can kiss you whenever she likes!'

'But I didn't want her to! It was horrible. Please don't be upset.'

'I can't help it. I asked you at Beltane about Holly, and you said there was nothing between you. Now it seems there was something after all, and she obviously thinks there still is, the fuss she was making about you today.'

'That's ridiculous! I swear to you, Sylvie, that—'

'Alright, I believe you. Now let me go – I've had enough.'

'Just show me you're not angry with me. Please, Sylvie.'

But she couldn't bear to look at him.

'All I want is to go home, but you're making a big deal about this when I just want to forget it. Leave me alone, Yul, and keep out of her way.'

She marched off, close to tears, her annoyance with Yul all the worse for knowing that her jealousy was unwarranted. He gazed at her retreating back with dismay and exasperation.

'Yul! What are you playing at? Get your arse back over here, boy! You ain't finished yet.'

'Sorry, sir. I was just coming.'

With a sigh, Yul stumbled over to where Stag stood by the horses and carts puffing on his clay pipe, his face screwed up sourly.

'Course you were. Get down the Cider House now and put in a couple o' hours on the apple mill. Woodruff's been up there all afternoon. You can knock off to eat when the others go home for their supper but mind you come back straight afterwards. Edward said I can have you all evening if I want, so you'll be working in the Cider House again. The old cheese needs taking apart tonight. You know how to do that?'

'I think so, sir. Unscrew the press and pull out the old sacking and pomace.'

'Aye, but make sure you do it proper. Those apple cheeses are rock-hard once the juice has been squeezed out of the pomace. You need three bins – one for the straw, one for the sacking and one for the dried up pomace. Don't mix 'em up, boy, and make sure you leave it all clean and tidy. I want it done tonight so when Bewald comes in first-light tomorrow morning 'twill be ready to build a new one. I don't want the old bugger moaning at me. You don't go home tonight till that cheese is completely cleared and make sure you do a good job of it. Understand me, boy?'

'Yes, sir,' said Yul wearily.

Nearly three hours later, Yul stopped to go home with the other Villagers for a meal. He was bone tired, his body shaking with exertion and fatigue. He'd fed hundreds and hundreds of apples into the mill, scooping them down from the apple loft into the large funnel that led to the mill. Turning the great iron handle that operated the mill, crushing and chopping the apples until they were macerated into a lumpy pulp, was hard work. The muscles in his arms, chest and shoulders screamed for mercy. He'd been up and down the ladder continuously, pulling a barrel in place, opening the valve to let the mashed-up pomace slide out, scraping out the mill, and then starting the process all over again. The mountain of apples in the loft that had greeted him on arrival was now considerably smaller. He surveyed the many barrels of pomace he'd made, which would sit for a day or so before being packed into a new cheese. A job well done, Yul thought, and nodded to himself in satisfaction. Neither Stag, Old Bewald nor Magus himself could accuse him of slacking.

He was very pleased to drag himself home and be greeted by a smiling Maizie and a hot supper waiting on the range. The three younger children were already asleep upstairs, and the two older boys were in the Village School with their friends making new rabbit nets. The atmosphere in the cottage was peaceful and calm, and Yul enjoyed sitting with his mother and sister listening to their chatter. Rosie had put the ordeal with Buzz behind her and was much happier since he'd been banished.

'Not walking with Robin tonight?' Yul asked.

'No, I'm helping Mother with the spinning,' she replied, rummaging in the dresser. 'And he's busy too, helping his father make a new pig-pen. One of their pigs made an escape the other day – must've realised we're coming into autumn already!'

'Ask Robin round for tea on Sunday,' said Maizie. 'I like the lad and now you're sweethearts, 'tis right he should spend some time with your family.'

'I will, Mother,' Rosie smiled, her pretty face dimpling. 'His family have invited me to visit too, and I were going to ask if that's alright by you.'

Maizie nodded, adding, 'If it's alright by Yul, o' course?'

'Yes, it's the proper way,' he said. 'I saw Robin's brother in the orchard today and we had a quick word.'

'And what about your sweetheart, Yul?' asked Rosie. 'We never did hear who you—'

'There's nothing to hear,' said Yul sadly, recalling Sylvie's anger today at their enforced secrecy. He hated denying his feelings for her like this when he wanted to shout about them from the rafters. 'It came to nothing.'

'But Yul, I thought—'

Maizie shot her a warning glance, picking up Yul's empty plate and tidily brushing his scattered bread-crumbs onto it.

'Stop being a nosy little sparrow, Rosie, and leave the lad be,' she said firmly. 'Yul will tell us in his own good time. Now come on, girl, the spinning won't do itself.'

Yul rose from the table unenthusiastically, every muscle aching. It was hard going back to work after sitting down and relaxing. All he wanted to do was slump in the armchair and rest his tired body. The thought of dismantling the old cheese filled him with despair, for his arms were already painful first from picking apples all day, and then milling for three hours. He had a horrible feeling that Stag expected him to do the job alone this evening. Maizie couldn't understand why he had to do so much extra work and had offered to speak to Magus about it. But Yul had asked her not to, on any account, hoping that if he kept his head down and did as he was told, Magus would eventually lose interest.

Maizie and Rosie had set up the spindles and stools for an evening of flax spinning, and had a great bundle of long silky fibres ready. It was fine flax from the retting pond rather than the coarse dew-retted fibres, and would be woven into the best quality linen.

''Tis for you, Yul,' said Maizie, stroking the pale flax tresses. Yul recalled the back-breaking hours he'd spent in July pulling the flax crop and then gathering it up for the retting. He was pleased to know that he'd benefit from all that hard work.

'What are you going to make, Mother? You've already sewn me some new clothes for the Equinox celebration.'

''Tis for your Rite of Adulthood – only three months away!' she said. ''Twill become the linen for your robe. You must decide soon what image you want woven into it. Have you any notion yet what you'll choose for your totem?'

He smiled, suddenly excited at the prospect of having his own robe at last instead of the childish tunic.

'I always thought I'd like a hare,' he replied slowly. 'You know how I love hares, and for years that's what I wanted. But now I'm wondering about the Green Man instead.'

'Ooh, that sounds nice!' said Rosie smiling at her brother. 'And unusual too.'

'Aye,' said Maizie, scooping up some fibres and twisting them expertly. 'I don't think anyone else uses that totem and 'tis just like you to be different from other folk, Yul. Well, you don't have to decide quite yet, but I'll need to know the colours soon so I can dye the thread afore I start the weaving. Shades of green, perhaps?'

'Yes, and maybe some gold and brown too. Do you both think

251

the Green Man would be a good totem for me? Would it look right on my silver disc, on the other side to my sprig of mistletoe?'

'Well, my boy, you're not Beltane-born but you're a woodsman, and you've always loved the trees. Old Greenbough says you're a natural-born man o' the woods such as he's never seen afore,' said Maizie 'Tis a good idea in my opinion.'

'I think it'd be perfect for you, Yul,' said Rosie. "The Green Man and mistletoe – they seem right together.'

'Good – that's settled then,' said Yul happily, feeling the rightness of his choice in his bones. 'And now I must go in case Magus decides to check up on me.'

He left the comfort of the cottage and walked down the track leading into the heart of the Village. The sun had vanished in a soft haze of gold and the twilight was deepening. Yul walked through the warm night, greeting several Villagers on their way to the pub. On the Green the bats swooped and dived, hunting for gnats. Light and laughter spilled out from the Jack in the Green, and the Great Barn was also lit. Through the open doors Yul could hear the musicians practising the harvest jigs that folk loved so much, ready for the Equinox dance. The drummers would be in there too, waiting to go through the rhythms for the Stone Circle ceremony.

Sweethearts wandered together on the Green where the Villagers' courtships mostly took place. There were plenty of sheltered spots under the great circle of trees that clustered around the perimeter, just right for kissing and cuddling and making promises. Unattached youngsters sat on the benches outside the Barn or further on by the pump, chatting and joking together and eyeing up likely partners. Yul felt a pang, realising all over again that he'd never be part of this. His sweetheart must be kept secret and their relationship must be furtive and snatched. He could never court her openly like those around him now, sauntering arm in arm in the balmy autumn night under the golden moon, kissing and laughing. She was forbidden to him and any liaison had to be clandestine.

Although he knew he should hurry, Yul made a detour to the

great yew tree. He slipped under the low boughs into the dark cavern of its shelter and breathed in the magic he always felt in this place. He was pleased there were no couples here, in the spot where he and Sylvie had shared their first kiss on the eve of the Summer Solstice. He remembered that night in exquisite detail and closed his eyes, his breath catching in his throat. He cautiously opened the lid on the treasured memory and was blown apart as always by the explosion of joy it detonated in his soul.

This was their special place and Yul hated the thought of others intruding here. Yul was unaware that nobody else ever came under this tree for their assignations because they found it too dark and sinister. Its association with the Yew of Death down in the valley made other people feel uncomfortable around it. He and Sylvie alone felt the pull of the dark magic in this ancient place.

Yul dragged himself away reluctantly and jogged slowly along the track leading to the Cider House. He was so tired, yawning hugely as he opened the door. It was pitch black inside and the smell of apples was overwhelming. He felt around for the lantern that lived on the shelf near the door, and groping for the matches, lit it carefully. The soft candlelight illuminated the immediate area but left everything else in shadows. He lit another lantern over by the cider press where he'd be working and looked woefully at the machinery. He had a mammoth task ahead of him. The great screw was clamped fully down, the flat press as low as it would go. Beneath it was the old apple cheese, a huge cube of woven straw and hemp sacking filled with layer upon layer of compressed pomace from which all the apple juice had been extracted. It would be a deep brown and quite solid; very different from the fresh pulpy pomace he'd been making earlier.

Tonight he must unscrew the press, which was a heavy physical job, turning the great wheel above that would slowly release the press and make it lift off the cheese. Then he could begin the task of pulling the cube apart and separating the materials as Stag had instructed. Yul dragged three bins over and then climbed up above the press where the heavy iron wheel was situated. Turning

253

the wheel to lower the press onto a new cheese was a two-man job, for there was great resistance. Raising the press, as he must do now, was slightly easier, but he'd be doing it alone.

With a grimace, Yul gripped the rim of the wheel and put his back into it, trying with all his strength to move it. The wheel turned a few centimetres; the press didn't budge. He tried again, and after a minute of straining as hard as he could, the press seemed to move slightly up the giant screw. Yul paused and took a deep breath, wondering if he'd actually be able to manage the task. Was it Magus, Edward or Stag who'd decided he should do this alone? But there'd be trouble if he didn't, so he heaved and strained, knowing that tomorrow every sinew would be pure agony.

Unbeknown to him, somebody had slipped into the Cider House whilst he wrenched at the wheel, and now stood silently in the shadows watching him sweat. She kept absolutely still, her heart beating fast as she saw him toiling away on the platform, his brown arms pulling for all their worth, sinews and muscles bulging with the strain. His legs were braced and his hair fell into his eyes. In the gleaming candlelight she saw the sheen of sweat on his face, his determination and concentration as he wrestled with the heavy machine, knowing that at all costs he must raise the press.

She shivered as she watched him working; watched him pushing his body and strength to the limit, grunting with the effort. Eventually, with a roar, he swung the wheel round and the press was fully raised. He shouted in triumph, flipped the lock on the wheel to hold it in position, and jumped down from the platform. The curls were stuck to his face and his chest heaved with exertion. He went over to the tap, where water was piped in from the springhead, and filled a bowl. He drank deeply and let the cold water wash over his sweaty face. Then he went back and surveyed the great apple cheese, knowing he must start now to pull it apart back into its three components.

But just as Yul was about to pull off the first layer of straw and hemp sacking, Sylvie stepped out noiselessly from the shadows. He jumped with surprise, then his face lit up at the sight of her. Her silvery hair hung down around her bare arms, almost reaching her waist. She smiled at him, beautiful in the soft candlelight.

'Are you really here?' he whispered, echoing the words she'd spoken not long ago. 'Or am I dreaming?'

She laughed and came forward, taking his hands in hers.

'I've been feeling guilty all evening about how I treated you today. I knew what happened in the orchard wasn't your fault and I was being unfair. I was just so jealous, seeing you touching Holly and whispering up in the tree with her. I couldn't bear it, but I behaved really badly and I'm sorry, Yul.'

He smiled down at her, noticing that although he'd grown so much, she was barely a head shorter than him. He looked into her silvery-grey eyes with their startling dark rims.

'You never need to feel jealous of Holly, I promise.'

She nodded, letting his hands go.

'Maybe you don't know, but I haven't made any friends here and lately it's all been quite nasty. Holly doesn't like me and I think she's turned everyone against me. So I probably over-reacted today because it was her – if it was anyone else it wouldn't have been so upsetting.'

'Oh Sylvie, I'm sorry. She can be nasty, I know. There's a spiteful side to her that she never had when we were children. I don't like her at all, and that's why she behaved so badly today. Holly wants to be liked and be the centre of attention and today she realised I couldn't stand her.'

'I overheard her tonight at dinner talking about you with her friends. She was saying how you didn't want to know, and how rude you were to her up in the apple tree. She's very angry about it. But Yul, then she said something horrible. She said she wants you for her partner at the Winter Solstice, for her Rite of Adult-hood. She said she can make Magus agree to it too. You won't do it, will you?'

He gazed deep into her eyes.

'The only person I ever intend making love to is you, Sylvie. I know exactly where I want our first time to be, and it's not in public up at the Stone Circle, believe me. I shall be giving that a miss. It's my Rite at the Solstice too but I'll wait until you're old enough. And until you feel ready.'

He watched the expressions flit across her face; embarrassment, relief and something else, which he hoped was excitement at the thought of making love with him. He smiled at her, loving her openness but realising that her inability to mask her emotions and bury her feelings deep away from prying eyes made her vulnerable. She'd yet to learn the lesson he'd been forced to learn this summer.

'Good,' she said. 'Because I'd have killed her rather than let her have you first! Or have you at all, for that matter.'

He laughed out loud at this uncharacteristic outburst.

'I'm not joking!' she said. 'I hate her. But let's forget about Holly. I can't stay long. I'm meant to be in the Great Barn with a couple of Hallfolk who came down to practise the drumming. I said I needed some fresh air and I knew you'd be here because I heard that grumpy old man ordering you about. Why do you have to work so much harder than everyone else, Yul? It's so unjust. It's a beautiful evening and they're all out there relaxing and enjoying themselves.'

'Magus' orders, to keep me so constantly tired that I can't get up to any tricks, he said.'

'He's so cruel to you. He's completely abandoned that deal I made with him at Midsummer. He's on your back all the time, isn't he?'

'Yes, but remember what Mother Heggy said. I've just got to bear it and hold on. It won't be forever.'

'Poor you,' she said softly. 'Why can't things ever be easy for you? "*Some are born to endless night*" . . .'

'What?'

'It's from a poem by William Blake. About injustice and inequality, I believe. Oh Yul, life is so unfair . . .'

'It seems unfair now, but it won't be in the end,' he said.

'That's what Blake thought too,' she smiled.

They stood in the shadowy candlelight, acutely aware of each other. Yul knew he must get on with his work or he'd be here all night dismantling the old cheese. Sylvie knew that the Hallfolk in the Great Barn would be wondering where she'd got to. Their time alone together was so precious, but the very fact that it was snatched and secret made them both feel constrained.

Sylvie looked around the cavernous building with the two cider presses and the enormous apple mill. There were bins and barrels everywhere and piles of sacking and straw. Then she noticed another room leading off, dark and shadowy.

'What's in there?' she asked, wanting only to prolong her time with him but feeling awkward being alone together in the old Cider House. She could see many barrels inside arranged in rows and walked in, looking around the shadowy depths. Yul followed her inside, also feeling a desperate need to keep her there for as long as possible, even though their time together had to be short.

'This is where the apple juice is stored when it's fermenting. See these barrels have no bungs in them? They're fermenting now. They need constant topping up with juice to keep the air out. Usually they rack them after the first fermentation – that means transferring the juice to a clean barrel. They let them ferment a bit more, then put the bungs in and leave the cider to mature. Those ones at the far end are last year's cider, waiting to be moved to the cellars in the Jack in the Green.'

'I see,' said Sylvie, interested but more interested in the proximity of Yul as he stood beside her in the near darkness. The strong smell of apple juice and cider was in her nostrils but she could smell him too. Every tiny hair on her body was aware of him standing so close to her, taut with control as he kept himself apart. Her fingertips brushed his bare arm longingly. She drew breath sharply as he tensed like a bow-string at her touch.

'Yul,' she whispered. 'Yul, I ...'

His body hit hers so urgently she was thrust back against a barrel with a thud. He bent his head and his mouth locked onto hers. Twisting his hand into her long hair, he held her tightly to him and released all the frustration and anger of the day into his kiss. Sylvie kissed him back with equal intensity, her lips crushed against his and desperate. Jammed with her back to the oak of the cider barrel and his body pressed up hard against hers, she felt a flood of longing melt her bones. She pulled him even closer, wanting to lose herself in this intense pleasure. His mouth was demanding but so giving too. He kissed her until she was on fire for him, feeling as if her heart must explode ... She twisted her head away, gasping for breath, her legs quaking. She could make out the brightness of his eyes in the shadowy darkness and sensed rather than saw the trembling excitement in him too. With a small cry she plunged back in, her mouth seeking his.

Then they heard sounds from outside that made them both freeze in terror – the jingle of metal and the snicker of a horse. Yul jerked away, abruptly releasing her from the fierce embrace, his breathing audible in the silence.

'Sacred Mother, that's Nightwing!' he hissed. 'Magus has come to check up on me!'

She gazed at him in mute terror, aware of the consequences if they were found like this.

'There's an outside door at the end of this store,' he whispered urgently. 'I'll go back into the press room and talk to him. You get out and run like the wind back to the Barn. Sylvie, be very careful – don't make any noise.'

She nodded and began to tiptoe into the deeper shadows of the barrel room towards the far end. He dashed into the other room and started to pull frantically at the straw of the apple cheese, flinging great handfuls of it into one of the bins. The door opened and the two lanterns flickered slightly. Magus' blond hair shimmered in the soft light, his dark eyes fathomless in the shadows. He stood in the doorway, tall and broad-shouldered, surveying the scene. If he noticed Yul's quick breathing and nervousness, he said nothing. He walked in and shut the door behind him, tapping his boot with his riding whip.

'Good evening, Yul.'

'Good evening, sir.'

Yul stopped ripping at the straw and turned to face Magus. He concentrated on not looking into the dark doorway of the barrel room, doing nothing that could give away Sylvie's presence. He needed to mask any sounds she might make in her exit, so he nudged the straw bin with his foot. It shifted loudly on the stone floor.

'Stop fidgeting, boy. I dropped by to make sure you're not slacking, and just as well, it seems. You haven't got very far, have you? Stag told me you're dismantling this cheese tonight, but you've barely started. Do you have any idea how late it is? You'll be here half the night.'

'I'm sorry, sir, it was the press. It was difficult to turn the wheel to release it by myself and it took me a long time.'

Magus frowned at him, the lines around his mouth sharp.

'I find that hard to believe. One thing that's struck me recently is how much you've grown.'

He stepped forward and reached out to feel Yul's bare upper arm, squeezing the muscles with iron-grip fingers. Yul steeled himself not to recoil from Magus' touch.

'Well, well! Even stronger than I'd imagined. I don't believe you had any trouble raising the press. Far more likely you've just been dawdling about. Don't let me keep you, boy. You've a good couple of hours' work ahead, and you must be up early in the morning so I suggest you get on with it and stop wasting time. You're going to be very tired tomorrow with so little sleep.'

He smiled at Yul and raised his whip to stroke the thin white scar on Yul's tanned cheek.

'I see you still bear my mark. Let it be a constant reminder to you, Yul, of what happens if you defy me. You may be free of Alwyn now, but you're not free of me. Whatever you do I shall be watching and waiting, ready to correct you if you stray in any way whatsoever. I'm taking a personal interest in you, Yul, so be very careful. One step out of line and I shall come down on you hard.'

He tapped his boot again with the whip, his meaning clear.

'Goodnight, Yul.'

'Goodnight, sir.'

16

The Autumn Equinox was approaching and Yul was particularly looking forward to the festival as he'd been working at full stretch all month. A couple of days before the Equinox, Edward, who'd co-ordinated the harvest labour, took Yul to one side and told him to go back to Old Greenbough in the woods where he was needed more urgently. Yul grinned in relief at this news for he was sick of the sight of apples.

'You've worked really hard, lad,' said Edward, clapping him on the back. 'I'm proud of you. Magus told me to give you an extra heavy load and so I have done, but you've borne it well and not complained once. It's certainly built up your strength, hasn't it?'

Yul nodded, knowing this was true. Greenbough would appreciate the change in him.

'When are you an adult?' asked Edward.

'Winter Solstice, sir.'

'Well you've done the work of two men this harvest-time so you won't have any problems. Is your mother coping alright without your father? I been worried that with him up in the hospital and you working every hour of the day for Magus, she might be struggling.'

'It's difficult for her, sir. There's lots of work to be done at home and I've always helped with it, but this year I'm barely there at all. Rosie's busy at the dairy, and my two brothers are still too young to do the heavy stuff. And there're the three little ones to cope with too. She's finding it hard.'

'In that case I'll stop loading you with extra duties in the evening. I'll let Magus know, so don't you worry about that. You'll be working hard at home and he can check on that if he wants to. 'Tis not fair that your mother and family should suffer because Magus wants to punish you. I'm sure he never intended that. What had you done anyway?'

Yul shrugged, as ever at a loss of words to explain the antipathy that Magus felt towards him.

'He's just got it in for me. He doesn't need a reason to punish me.'

Edward frowned down at him and shook his burly head.

'I don't like the tone of your voice, lad. Magus is always just – sometimes hard, I'll give you that – but always just. You show the proper respect for him or you'll feel the weight of my hand. He's a good master and a truly great man. You should be giving thanks to Magus for his generosity and his bounty.'

Yul bit back the retort that it was the labour of the Villagers and the bounty of the Earth Goddess that ensured their comfort, not Magus' generosity. He liked Edward and didn't want to make an enemy of him. Unlike Tom and Greenbough, whom Yul had sensed were becoming disillusioned about the true greatness of Magus, Edward was very loyal.

'I'm sorry, sir. I meant no disrespect,' he said, backtracking quickly. 'At some point in the past I displeased Magus. He doesn't need to justify punishing me whenever he wants, if he chooses to do so. That's what I meant and I'm sorry if it sounded like I was speaking against him.'

The giant of a man looked down at him and ruffled his hair.

'Fair enough, lad, fair enough. And you're right, he doesn't need to justify himself to us. We must just obey and not question. The master is the master after all. But I stand by what I said – you stay at home in the evenings and help your mother.'

*

Greenbough was delighted to have Yul back again.

'Thought you'd become a farmer, boy!' he growled, giving Yul a great slap on the arm. He knew what a hard life Yul had led and felt affection and respect for the dark-haired boy who took whatever was dished out and still kept his chin up and the light in his eyes blazing. And Yul was a damn good worker too.

'We got the bonfire up in the Circle to start. We're going up there now and most likely tomorrow too, and 'tis the Equinox the day after. Then it's the oak woods and pigs to organise. Bloody pannage! The bane of my life every autumn, them pigs are, rooting up everything with their snouts. I'd sooner collect up the acorns and give 'em each a bucket-full than have 'em messing up my woodland, and I says so every damn year.'

Yul grinned at this. Greenbough's grumpiness during the pannage season and his contempt for pigs was legendary, although he enjoyed his ham, bacon and blood pudding along with the rest of them.

Yul started to shake as he and the group of woodsmen approached the Stone Circle. With his increased workload he hadn't been up here for almost three weeks, and had felt an ache deep in his soul. The green magic called to him, needing him for its release from the dragon lines in the Earth. The other men headed straight for the site of the bonfire at the opposite end and stood around waiting for the horse and cart to bring the wood. Yul took a deep breath to steady himself and walked with a straight back towards the Altar Stone. Fortunately the painters who decorated the stones hadn't yet arrived and he was alone in this part of the circle.

He approached the stone and felt an immense pull, a surge of the force snaking towards him, seeking him out. As he drew close there was a mighty flash of green and he felt something leap inside him. The energy poured into him, drenching him, flooding him. He sprang up onto the horizontal stone, his feet barely able to make contact with the rock. He groaned aloud, overwhelmed by the sensation. He'd never known it this strong, and closed his eyes in silent thanks to the Goddess. With her magic inside him he could face anything.

Then the cart arrived and the woodsmen began building the bonfire. Although still agile and now throbbing with new strength, Yul found that he was no longer able to slither up the framework like a squirrel. He'd grown too tall and heavy. A young lad who'd joined the woodsmen at Lammas was now the one who'd be sent up to the top of the bonfire with the bag of brushwood strapped to his back.

Yul stood watching the boy climb the first timbers and felt an unexpected moment of sadness. He'd always longed to be a man, wanting the size and strength that maturity would bring so he could stand up to Alwyn and look after his family. And now at last he'd realised this ambition, but the blitheness of boyhood was lost, gone forever. In that moment, Yul understood one of life's hardest lessons: nothing is truly gained without something being lost.

The artists arrived soon after and a group of Villagers began to clean the stones of the Lammas symbols. A horse and cart had brought the buckets of water, tallow soap and scrubbing brushes, along with the ladders and paints. Merewen the potter's daughter was in charge as usual, gathering the painters around her and discussing the patterns and symbols they'd use this festival. Once the stones were dry, they began to sketch the Autumn Equinox designs in chalk and charcoal. The acorn was the main symbol, to signify the fruit of the harvest and the seed of new life already produced, ensuring the never-ending cycle of growth, death and new growth. All around it they drew blackberries, apples, hazel-nuts, and corncobs and the creatures of autumn: the squirrel and dormouse, the leaping deer and the hedgehog.

Busy constructing the frame of the bonfire, Yul felt happy to be working with wood once again. Harvesting was all very well, but it was wood and trees that he loved best. The day passed quickly as there was much to be done in preparation for the festival. Yul was aware of the painters working all around him, and kept well out of the way of the Hallfolk among them. Fennel seemed worse than usual, and Yul guessed he was enjoying a new sense of power with Buzz gone. Rainbow, Fennel's younger sister, was in the painting group for the first time, but rather than encouraging her Fennel constantly criticized her work. Yul felt a flicker of sympathy for the girl and was glad when Merewen stepped in. Rainbow was taken to the largest upright stone that stood behind the Altar, and Merewen told her to begin sketching out the design. It was an honour to paint this stone, the focal point during the ceremony.

'Take no notice of him,' said Merewen gruffly, patting the girl's shoulder. 'He's just jealous. You've far more talent than him, Rainbow, and he knows it. He doesn't like the fact that you've been coming to me for lessons either.'

Rainbow smiled at the dark-haired Village woman, one of the few who seemed to command Hallfolk respect. Merewen took no nonsense from anyone, and as a gifted artist she enjoyed an undisputed status at Stonewylde. She left the girl roughing out the great cornucopia that always adorned the largest stone during this festival. Glancing over every so often, Yul could see that Merewen was right; Rainbow was talented and deft. The design grew quickly under her sure hand, the cornucopia spilling out its harvest bounty in a cascade of abundance.

The sun was low in the sky when Greenbough decided to call it a day.

'Come on, men, home we go. Don't know about you lot, but I got a tasty rabbit pie waiting for me.'

They packed up their tools, leaving them stacked ready for the morning, and trooped towards the Long Walk leading from the Stone Circle.

'I'll see you tomorrow, sir!' called Yul. 'I'm going to stay up here a bit longer.'

'Right enough, son. See you back here in the morning.'

Yul glanced at the sky, and then impatiently at the painters who were also packing up their things and leaving. Soon it would be sunset and he wanted to be here alone. Fennel wandered over to where Rainbow was fiddling with the first coat of paint on her design.

'We're off now,' he said. 'Are you coming or what?'

She glanced at him and shook her head, turning back to the great horn of plenty she'd spent the afternoon creating.

'Suit yourself. It's no good sulking, Rainbow.'

'I'm not sulking. I just want to finish this base coat. Merewen's really pleased with it.'

'Well of course she'd say that. She's only trying to make you feel better about your first bungled attempts. You'll see – in the morning she'll come and add her own images until yours are almost hidden underneath. I've seen her do it before to new artists, so don't kid yourself, Rainbow.'

He sauntered off, joining the others who were leaving the Circle. Rainbow stood back from the stone looking at it critically. Then she scrambled up onto the Altar Stone to get a different angle. Yul cursed silently. The sun was a golden ball, sinking rapidly in the sky. He needed to get on the stone himself. He glanced around and realised that everyone else had gone. Frowning, he came out from behind the bonfire where he'd been waiting and went over towards the girl on the stone. She stood dejectedly.

'It's beautiful,' Yul said, and she spun round in surprise.

'You really think so? You're not just being kind?'

'No, it's one of the best cornucopias I've seen. Some years they're really ordinary. Yours looks like its bursting with goodness. And I love those half-hidden dormice.'

She smiled at him.

'That's nice of you. You're Yul, aren't you? Holly's been going on and on about you.'

He shook his head and groaned. Rainbow laughed and jumped off the stone. She quickly rinsed her brush and picked up the basket of materials.

'Well, she's one of my best friends so don't be nasty, will you? All I can say is, she's very cross with you, but if you're playing hard to get then it's worked. She's talked about you non-stop since you were so unfriendly in the orchard. I wish I'd heard what you said to her. Not many boys would turn Holly down – they wouldn't dare!'

With a little wave, she turned and walked off towards the darkening tree tunnel of the Long Walk.

Yul breathed a sigh of relief. He stood alone at last in the ancient circle. The sun was burrowing into the west, glittering gold in the pink sky. He could hear the soft, soothing call of woodpigeons in the oak woods nearby. The Altar Stone pulled at him, urging him to come. Yul closed his eyes and breathed deeply, feeling perfectly in harmony with the earth and the sky, the moon and the sun, the five elements and all the stars. He was part of the fabric of life and at peace with himself and the world. With a run and a leap, he landed on the stone and faced the setting sun, his arms raised to the heavens and his head thrown back. As the sun disappeared, the Earth Magic spiralled up and enveloped him. He laughed out loud with the glory of it.

Rainbow worked quickly, her soft pencil capturing the lines perfectly. She perched in the shadows of the Long Walk on one of the low stones that lined the way, sketch book balanced on her knee. She didn't understand what she'd just witnessed, but her picture told the true story. The lines of Yul's taut body arched backwards in ecstasy, the radiance about him, the joy on his upturned face. She'd caught the essence of his blessing by the Earth Goddess without even realising it. She smiled and stood up. Holly would love the picture, she knew. Not that she planned to part with it – she rather liked it herself.

Many of the community gathered in the Stone Circle in the grey light before dawn at the Autumn Equinox. The birds in the woods sang gloriously. Overnight a myriad of spiders had visited the Circle and left their Equinox gift; silver gossamer threads shimmered in cascades of silk from the stones, catching the light and dew to form a glistening skein across the soft earth floor. The drummers had been playing softly, but as the sky lightened their intensity increased. The beats bounced around the stones, leaping off the hard surfaces and into the bodies of the people of Stonewylde. Magus chanted as he stood on the Altar Stone, facing east where the sun would soon appear. Yul smiled to himself. He felt the energy; tendrils had been seeking him out ever since he arrived in the Circle. He doubted whether Magus was feeling anything at all.

As the sun appeared for this day of equilibrium between light and dark, the drumming reached a crescendo. Magus lit the kindling in the brazier and the blue flames fizzed up. All eyes were on him, but Greenbough, standing near to Yul, felt the blast of energy that shot through the boy. Yul staggered as he took the full force of it, and the old man stared at him in wonder. His gaze was speculative as the ceremony finished and the people began to make their way back to the Village and the Hall for breakfast. Greenbough knew that he'd seen something special, something of which only a few were yet aware.

The day was perfect, with that misty softness peculiar to September. The skies were mackereled with wispy clouds, and as Yul lay on his back on the Village Green looking up into the bright blueness, he felt completely happy. Sylvie was about, and just knowing she was close by made him feel good. They barely managed to speak a few words to each other, but both were acutely aware of where the other one was at all times. Sylvie watched him, looking taller and more handsome than ever in his new clothes. He seemed to be constantly surrounded by a flock of girls, and every so often he'd catch her eye and grimace.

Lunch in the Barn was a true Harvest Festival for everything served today had been grown and harvested at Stonewylde. There was a primeval pleasure in knowing the harvest had been a good one, and the Village Stores were brimming with produce. Nothing of Mother Earth's bounty was wasted; the hedgerows with their glistening treasure of blackberries, elderberries, sloes, and rose-hips were still being plundered, and the walnut and hazelnut trees daily loosed a little more of their fruits. The Meadery was working flat out to cope with the massive honey yields that had poured in all summer long, whilst Old Bewald in the Cider House said he'd never known a year like it for apples. The coopers were struggling to keep up with demand for new barrels, whilst the Store was crammed with produce for the winter ahead. It had been an exceptional harvest and the folk of Stonewylde enjoyed the festival to the full.

During the afternoon the community relaxed and enjoyed the warm sunshine on the Village Green, at the beach, and along the river banks. Magus himself was in fine fettle. Morale amongst the Villagers was high thanks to the excellent harvest and Buzz's banishment, which had reaffirmed the people's faith in Magus' justice. He was fired up on the moon eggs and his energy knew no bounds. He sparkled and thrilled with it and Yul watched him covertly, noticing how he pulled the community together and bound the people in a web of goodwill and contentment. But like the spider who wove the web, his intent was to create a cocoon that would entrap his prey and allow him to feed.

Yul realised in a flash of understanding that Magus needed the folk of Stonewylde far more than they needed him, despite their apparent dependence on his leadership. Fired up himself on the great doses of Earth Magic he'd received over the past few days, Yul felt powerful and wise. A revelation kindled inside him, quickly taking hold and blazing in his heart.

I could lead Stonewylde for the good of the Villagers, the true folk. And I'd do a better job of it than he does.

A large group of people headed off for the beach as the afternoon had become very hot indeed and the sea was at its warmest now after the long summer. Yul noticed Sylvie sitting under the walnut tree on the Green tucked almost out of sight. She was watching him and beckoned him over.

'I've just seen Mother Heggy's crow,' she said, smiling up at him. 'And Yul, I have to tell you how gorgeous you look today. Although doubtless you've already been told.'

He pulled a wry face and sat beside her.

'Are you sure it was Heggy's crow? Not just any bird?'

'No, definitely hers. I can tell.'

'In that case, we'd better get ourselves over to her cottage. The crow's her messenger and she sends it to summon me. And you too. I expect she wants to speak to us urgently.'

Inside he rejoiced; now must be the time to remove the spell. He'd become increasingly worried as time was running out.

'Why does she want to see us?'

'Let's go and find out. We'll leave separately in case anyone notices and I'll meet you by the rowan tree just before the path forks to her cottage. You go first, Sylvie.'

As they approached the hovel, Sylvie slipped her hand into his and squeezed it, smiling at him happily. He felt a pang of guilt for deceiving her about the purpose of their visit. Sylvie was delighted to see the Wise Woman again and kissed the crone on her withered cheek.

'I'm so sorry I haven't been to see you lately, Mother Heggy. I've been ill quite a lot and everyone watches me. It's hard to get away unnoticed.'

'I know, I know, my little one. But you're stronger now, and 'tis why I had to see you. Do you trust me?'

She nodded. 'Of course I do.'

'Then you must believe me when I tell you this: you're under a spell.'

'What? A *spell*?'

Yul and Mother Heggy knew from her incredulity that she didn't believe it. They caught each other's eye.

'Clip put a spell on you, Sylvie,' said Yul gently. 'It's to do with the Moon Fullness, and it's why you don't come up with me to Hare Stone anymore.'

'You must be joking. A spell? With a magic wand?'

'No, no, a spell to make you obey. A spell that speaks to your mind but not your soul. You do what he's commanded without question,' said Mother Heggy. ''Tis an old trick and Clip has the wisdom for it. He's done the same to your mother. Mother and daughter both spellbound by that evil pair o' half-brothers.'

They could see Sylvie still didn't believe them. Yul took her hand in his and looked into her startled eyes.

'Sylvie, every time I speak to you about the Moon Fullness, you say exactly the same words. It's like you learnt them off by heart and you must obey them.'

She frowned as something stirred in her mind. She thought of the rising moon and the first thing that came to mind was Hare Stone. But then the fog came rolling in and she nodded.

'A black fog that blanks out everything. That's what I see when I think of the full moon.'

'Aye! A black fog is right, covering all. Smothering your own desires like a blanket over the face so you no longer breathe freely. Do you know what he forces you to do at the rising of the moon?' asked Mother Heggy.

'I ... I ... I like to dance on the round stone at Mooncliffe. I must share my moon magic with Magus. It's why I was brought here.'

'That's the spell!' cried Yul. 'You always use those same words!'

'Do I? But it's true. I do like to dance at Mooncliffe.'

'Sylvie, listen to me, you don't dance there at all! They put you on the rock and you stand frozen there like a carving. I saw it all last month and it nearly killed me to watch you suffering like that. I could feel your pain. The moon energy pours through you into the rock and they make you stay up there for ages, holding heavy stone eggs to charge them up. There's a whole crate of them. They feed off your moon magic and that's why you're so ill afterwards. They bleed you dry.'

She shook her head.

'I don't remember any of that. But really, I do like to dance at Mooncliffe.'

'So now we must unlock the spell,' said the old woman. 'Sit down, my bright one. Sit down and look at Mother Heggy. You must trust me, Sylvie. And trust your sweetheart here. We'd do you no harm and you know that in your heart.'

Sylvie nodded reluctantly, her eyes scared. She looked at Yul and he put his arm around her, holding her tightly as she trembled.

'I'd never hurt you, Sylvie. I love you. They're leeches, those men, feeding off your magic. This is for your good, I swear to you.'

Sylvie sat in the chair opposite Mother Heggy and Yul kept a reassuring hand on her shoulder. The crone took Sylvie's hands and looked into her eyes, and within seconds Yul felt a change in her. She was somehow more rigid, less conscious, although she didn't look any different. He remembered the power he'd sensed inside the old woman; a power all the stronger for being so well disguised in the withered, feeble frame.

'You're a blessed moongazy girl,' she began, in her high, sing-song voice. 'Blessed by the Triple Goddess at the rising of the Moon Fullness. You are hers – she calls to you and you must come. She calls to your heart and your soul. She's in your eyes, your moonstone eyes, and she gives you wings to fly and a tongue to sing in her honour. This is what you must do at the Moon Fullness, my little one. Listen to the Goddess calling you, as she's done since you were born, and obey only her commands.'

She paused, tiny and hunched in her chair, and Yul marvelled again at the power inside such an ancient body.

'The stone at Mooncliffe is of another power,' she continue, her voice cracked and reedy, 'the evil power of the serpent at Stonewylde. In your heart you know 'tis a place of suffering and malevolence and you don't truly want to dance there. You must go where the Goddess herself calls you. At the Moon Fullness you must honour the Bright Lady in her special place on the hill with the hares. You must dance only where you feel 'tis right, not where others force you to go.'

She looked over Sylvie's head at Yul, her eyes cloudy.

'Will it work?' he whispered.

'Let's hope so,' she replied. 'She *must* be at Hare Stone for the Harvest Moon. She needs that red harvest magic if she's to face the dangers that lie ahead.'

The evening party in the Great Barn was riotous. This was the festival for serious cider drinking and as the next day was a holiday, everyone let themselves go. The cider had been brewed the previous autumn for just this event and was particularly potent. Yul had in past years been especially wary of Alwyn at the Autumn Equinox celebrations. The man was renowned both for his prowess at cider consumption and his brutal aggression afterwards, and this year was the first Harvest Festival where Yul could truly relax and enjoy himself.

After the evening ceremony at the Stone Circle the party got underway in the Barn. There were traditional country dances involving circles, lines and arched arms, and Sylvie found herself galloping round the Barn with several different partners. She'd hoped to be able to dance with Yul but he was monopolised the whole evening by girls, both Hallfolk and Villager, who wouldn't leave him alone. Even when he did break free of them he didn't dare make any move towards her. Instead he sought refuge with his family whenever possible, and had to content himself with meaningful looks across the floor at Sylvie.

When Magus arrived in the Great Barn a little later, his add-itional rituals in the Circle over, the atmosphere became even more charged. The apple games, involving bobbing, peeling and passing apples down the line without hands, were a great leveller. Hallfolk mixed freely with Villagers, all laughing riotously as they made fools of themselves. Soon afterwards the children were taken off to bed, then the musicians struck up a lively tune, and the dancing started all over again. It was hot inside the Barn and the great doors were flung open to the starry night. A waxing gibbous moon hung overhead, whilst the bats flickered in the night air devouring midges. People wandered in and out of the Barn to cool off when the dancing and cider became too much, and several people lay outside on the grass completely oblivious.

Magus was on top form. His energy knew no bounds and he dominated the Great Barn, the focus of all attention. He was working his way around the dance-floor and Sylvie's heart sank as he approached and asked for the next dance. He was very hot, his tanned face sheened with perspiration and his distinctive cologne wafted around him, released by the heat from his body.

His grip was firm and he smiled down at Sylvie, dazzlingly handsome.

For a moment she almost forgot all she'd learnt that day. His charisma worked its magic even on her, despite knowing the truth about him. His teeth gleamed and his dark eyes danced as he looked deep into hers. Close up like this, in physical contact with him, she felt an inkling of why every woman was so enthralled by him. He exuded an animal lure that was almost overpoweringly sensual, even to a girl as innocent as Sylvie. As he held her to him, his strong hands on her spine and her face close to his great chest, she felt his aura enfolding her, drawing her into its gravity. Her hands were awkward on the back of his damp shirt, trying not to touch him. She trembled as her body and mind sent different messages. But then he brought her back to reality with a jolt.

'You're a special girl, Sylvie,' he murmured, taking advantage of the softer music now playing to hold her close and speak to her as they danced. 'Truly unique. I'm so pleased you came to Stonewylde. Are you still happy here? I haven't had a chance to talk to you for ages, have I? You've been quite poorly lately, what with one thing and another.'

She stiffened at this, knowing the only thing that made her ill was his greed.

'Yes, I'm still happy, thank you.'

'Delighted to hear it. Did you know it's the Moon Fullness in three nights' time?'

She shuddered at the mention of it and suddenly a clear memory flooded into her mind. The moon rock and the silver snake of moonlight on the water. The endless needles of pain and the heavy stones in her aching fingers. She trembled violently.

'Sylvie? What must you do for me at the Moon Fullness, my moongazy girl?'

She looked up and met his eyes; her grey ones were filled with fear, his black ones were piercing. Just in time she remembered the spell.

'I love dancing at Mooncliffe,' she said quickly. 'I want to share my moon magic with you.'

She saw his expression change to one of lazy confidence. He smiled down at her, then bent and kissed her head.

'You're a good girl. I'll let you dance to your heart's content and you may give me all your moon magic. You know it's why you came to Stonewylde.'

Sylvie found her knees almost buckling at his words, Yul's explanation now fully confirmed. This man was evil and she knew without doubt that she was in danger from him. As the music drew to an end, he hugged her tightly, wrapping his arms around her. His scent was overpowering.

'You really are special, Sylvie. There's no one else at Stonewylde who can give me what I need. I shall have to take very good care of you.'

When he finally released her, Sylvie stumbled towards the doors of the Great Barn and into the cool air outside. She still shook, overcome with dread at what Magus had in store for her in three evenings' time. Yul and Mother Heggy had promised they'd prevent him taking her to Mooncliffe but she wasn't convinced, and was terrified of both Magus and his intentions. He appeared so charming and benevolent but underneath was as cold and cruel as sleet. He manipulated and controlled and fooled everyone. She sank onto a bench outside the Barn and closed her eyes, breathing deeply to calm the trembling. She wanted to cry but knew she must be brave. Everyone around her was having such a good time and if Magus noticed her upset, he may guess the spell had been broken.

She felt the caress of fingertips on her shoulder and looked up into Yul's smiling face.

'At last! I thought we'd never get a moment together! Come on, let's go and find somewhere quiet.'

'Oh Yul, we can't, people might notice. Just sit down a minute here and talk – it'll seem innocent enough.'

He did as she said, but looked at her in consternation.

'What's wrong, Sylvie? If it's because of Holly, I promise that I don't—'

'No, it's nothing to do with her. It's Magus.'

'Why? What's he done?'

Yul had tensed and his eyes flashed as he stared at her. She felt him bristle with anger.

'He talked about the Moon Fullness and Mooncliffe, and I pretended I was still under the spell. Yul . . . I'm so scared.'

He reached across and took her hand in his.

'Don't be. Mother Heggy has said she'll sort it out. Whatever happens I'll make sure you spend Harvest Moon up at Hare Stone with me, Sylvie. I promise you that.'

She gave him a little smile.

'I know and I do believe you, but I'm still scared. The way he spoke about it . . . my moongaziness, how much he needs me. He's so strong, Yul, so powerful and relentless. It's as if he owns me and I'm only here to serve him. It was terrifying.'

'Oh Sylvie, you mustn't be terrified! Please, let's go under the yew tree—'

He was interrupted by a shriek. Holly appeared with July and Wren in tow.

'There you are! We wondered where you'd got to! You must have one dance with me, Yul – you promised earlier on and this is it! You always loved the Flying Sheaf. It was your favourite last Autumn Equinox, remember? Come on!'

She grabbed both his hands and pulled him off the bench, the other girls tugging at him too, almost dragging the shirt off his back. They were flushed and intoxicated, their eyes over-bright and their voices shrill. They hadn't even noticed Sylvie sitting next to him. He looked back apologetically over his shoulder as the girls manoeuvred him back inside the Barn. Sylvie sighed and wished that Holly would trip over her Flying Sheaf and break an ankle.

17

After breakfast the next day, Magus summoned Miranda to his office. She entered the room with some trepidation; there'd been times of late when she felt he didn't really care for her at all, that he found her dull now she was pregnant and so desperately in love with him. He'd danced with her in the Barn, but then he'd danced with every woman at Stonewylde it seemed, so that meant nothing.

'You're looking radiant, Miranda,' he said, patting the leather sofa by way of invitation. She sank down next to him, her heart quickening hopefully. 'Pregnancy really suits you. I meant what I said last night at the dance – I'll have to keep you constantly pregnant. Would you like a string of little blond haired children? Seven, as so many of the Village women have? I'm sure it could be arranged!'

She laughed, slightly embarrassed, and snuggled up against him.

'I think I'm a little old now for seven more children.'

'Not at all! You've plenty of fertile years left and you obviously find it easy to conceive. One a year and you'd still be under forty. You're in full bloom, Miranda, like a luscious fruit ripening.'

He'd thrown an arm around her and his hand idly stroked her breast, fuller than usual because of her pregnancy. He spread his other hand across her belly, pressing firmly.

'Have you felt the baby move yet?'

'Not yet.'

'It shouldn't be long now. I was thinking about you in bed this morning, Miranda, and—'

'Were you really?' She flushed with pleasure at this.

'Yes, I was thinking that it must've been about the time of the Autumn Equinox that you conceived Sylvie, if she was born at the Summer Solstice.'

She nodded, laying her face in the strong hard hollow between Magus' arm and chest, breathing in his scent. She craved his affection more than anything else in the world; she longed to captivate and enthral him so he wanted her and no one else. He felt so solid and powerful, almost vibrating with energy. When she was close to him like this she felt herself drowning in a dark well of want and need. She loved him with blind obsession – nothing else really mattered. His frequent indifference to her only fuelled her longing and made her more desperate for his attention. Being cuddled up to him like this was pure, utter bliss.

'I think, Miranda, that the time has finally come for you to tell me all about it,' he murmured.

She tensed.

'I think I have a right to know. So tell me now – who was Sylvie's father? How did you fall pregnant so young?'

'Please, Magus, I really don't want to talk about it. It upsets me and—'

'I think you're forgetting something,' he said very softly, his fingers still fondling her breast. 'I know best and you always obey me. Remember?'

She nodded again and swallowed.

'You never defy me or go against my wishes.'

She shook her head miserably.

'No, of course not, Magus. It's just ... I've kept everything buried inside for so many years and I really can't *bear* to talk about it. I've never told anyone exactly what happened.'

'But I'm not just anyone, am I, Miranda? And you don't want to make me angry again, do you?'

Miranda felt herself splitting inside; a new force had entered the sphere of her resistance and pulled at her free will, compelling her to obey.

'No, Magus,' she whispered. 'I only want to please you and make you happy.'

'Good,' he said smoothly, stroking her collar bones and the soft skin of her throat with a rhythmic touch. 'That's as it should be. So tell me about Sylvie's conception; I want to know the whole story, every detail. This is not a request, Miranda, it's an order.'

Falteringly, she told him everything she could remember about that night, sixteen years ago, when she was taken into the woods by a stranger. There wasn't much to tell because the whole incident had happened so quickly. Magus listened carefully.

'The red full moon must've been the Harvest Moon. And you didn't see his face at all?'

'No, he wore a mask like everyone else at the party. It was a big charity function at a country house, a masked ball in aid of a Third World fund-raising trust or something. I don't think I ever knew why we were going – my parents never explained things to me. I was just expected to do as I was told, speak when I was spoken to, that sort of thing.'

'There's a lot to be said for the old-fashioned ways,' he said, thinking of the rude behaviour of the young Hallfolk recently. 'Anyway, it was a big party, you say?'

'Oh yes, there were lots of businessmen there, colleagues of my father's I suppose, and their wives of course, but no children. It wasn't that sort of a party, more of a formal thing. My parents always dragged me around with them like a little mascot – I was never trusted to be left on my own. Anyway, everyone at the party was in fancy dress or at least masked. The man who ... the one who took me into the woods wore a sort of bird mask, like an eagle or a hawk.'

'And he definitely had blond hair?'

'Yes, a silvery blond like yours. Like a lot of the Hallfolk.'

'And he didn't say anything to you at all? Not even afterwards?'

'No, not really. He just told me to lie down on the leaves ... murmured, rather than told me. That's why I didn't resist him. He was kind, so gentle and his voice was soft and deep. I didn't realise what ... And afterwards, when it was over, he said nothing, only smiled and stroked my hair. I started crying, I remember, and my mask was wet with tears. I couldn't quite believe what he'd done. He helped me up, brushed the leaves off me and put my clothes straight again. I just stood there in my fairy costume sobbing, trying to hide my face. I felt so ashamed. He was still so very gentle then, I remember, and he said something ... I don't recall exactly. Something about me being beautiful and fulfilling his dream at last ... I'm not sure. Then he took my hand and led me back to the party. He left me by the open French windows and disappeared into the night. My mother assumed I'd been to the ladies' room and told me off for disappearing without telling her, and then soon afterwards we went home. It was as if nothing had happened. In fact I even wondered, until I knew I was pregnant, if it had all just been a dream.'

She fell silent, her head bowed. Magus glanced at her and frowned, shaking his head.

'I don't understand why you're still so upset about it,' he said. 'It was such a long time ago, and you weren't hurt or brutalised at all.'

'I know. But my parents ... they were religious, real pillars of the community and very moral and judgemental of others. This was the worst thing that could've happened to them, an absolute disgrace and a scandal. When they discovered I was pregnant and made me tell them what'd happened, they said it was all my fault. That I must've encouraged the stranger. But I didn't! I'd been so innocent – I had no idea what he intended to do, and once he'd started I had no chance to try and stop him. It happened so fast and he was gentle, almost reverent, the way he laid me down and touched me; the way he took my virginity. It really didn't seem like rape until afterwards, when I was bleeding and alone. Of course it wasn't consensual and if he'd asked me, I'd have said no, but I didn't feel as if I'd been violated because he hadn't actually used any force, hadn't hurt me.'

'Exactly! That's what I meant.'

'But my parents never let me forget how wicked I'd been, how dirty and disgusting and sinful. The way they treated me all through the pregnancy, practically locking me away so nobody would see me and guess, and then washing their hands of me after the birth when I wouldn't give Sylvie up for adoption ...'

She began to cry quietly and Magus stroked her hair, gazing absently through the French windows.

'It had to be one of the Hallfolk,' he mused. 'Too much of a coincidence that it was a full moon and he had our blond hair. There're so many of us out there in the Outside World. After I took over here I sent a great horde of Hallfolk away, told them to make their own living in the world instead of leeching off Stonewylde. Something like a business charity function is just the sort of thing they'd go to – a networking occasion. And one of them obviously couldn't resist the chance to do what comes so naturally to us at the Moon Fullness. Sylvie does seem to be one of us, don't you think?'

'Yes, Magus.'

'I know it was difficult for you at the time, Miranda, and your parents were wrong to make you feel so ashamed. But I'm sure that you appreciate what a gift Sylvie is and you wouldn't want to be without her. So you could forgive the father now, couldn't you? Lay it all to rest?'

'I suppose so. If you think I should.'

'I do – no more guilt. Sylvie is a true blessing and who can blame a man for wanting you under the Harvest Moon? At Stonewylde we know how the full moon can affect ones normal judgement. The Villagers call it moonlust, and it makes you throw caution to the wind. I've felt the effects of moonlust myself, in fact, and I've behaved very irresponsibly on more than one occasion.' He chuckled and squeezed her in a comforting hug. 'I'm sure you were as lovely as a young girl as you are now as a woman, a temptation impossible to resist. It's not as if he hurt you or used brute force. It was wrong of course – there's no excuse for taking any girl like that – but he was clearly carried away by the whole enchanted dream of it. A beautiful young woman dressed like a faerie queen in the woods under the red harvest moon, a girl who perhaps seemed willing ... at first anyway. It's understandable how these things happen. Could you to see it more in that light, and less as rape? You need to forgive and accept.'

Turning on the sofa towards her, he brushed away her tears with his thumbs, then bent his head and started to kiss her full on the mouth. He kissed her deeply, running his hand through her long red hair and caressing her rounded curves.

'Mmm, you're delicious,' he muttered, his chest rising and falling. 'There's a lot to be said for a woman in full bloom.'

She responded readily, drawing him closer and kissing him passionately. He chuckled at her enthusiasm, resisting her mouth and eagerness.

'Enough of this! No, stop tempting me, Miranda. I can't – I don't have enough time to enjoy you properly. You know how I hate to rush these things and unfortunately I have to be off within the next hour or so.'

He pulled away from her and leaned back into the soft leather of the sofa, his eyes dark and heavy, the lines around his sensuous mouth etched sharply. Miranda gazed up at him dreamily, her breathing deep.

'Off? You're not going away again?'

'Yes, I have to go to London on business for a couple of days. It can't be helped, but I'll be back for the Moon Fullness. That's what I really wanted to say to you. Make sure Sylvie's ready, won't you? I've an important appointment in the morning and then a lunch engagement, so I can't leave London until early afternoon, but that's still more than enough time to be back here before sunset. Just make sure she rests from now until then. I want her kept in bed and given plenty to eat so she's strong enough for her moon dancing. Do you understand me?'

'Yes, Magus.'

'She's not to go out during the next couple of days or do anything at all other than rest, sleep, and eat. Make sure she's bathed and ready before sunset. Is that clear?'

'Yes, Magus. I'll make sure.'

'Good.'

He kissed her briefly and stood up from the sofa, stretching contentedly like a great cat.

'I'm not promising, but I might come and visit you afterwards when I've finished with Sylvie. It's the Harvest Moon and maybe I can help finally lay those ghosts to rest for you. That's all, Miranda – you may go now.'

Magus searched for Clip before he left for London, anxious to make things right between them. They'd had an argument a few days earlier about the coming Moon Fullness, when Clip had baulked at reinforcing the hypnosis and coming up to Mooncliffe again to help with the eggs. Clip had been avoiding his half-brother ever since the argument, but Magus hunted him down in his circular tower playing his gongs. The incredibly complex waves of successive sound travelled down the spiral stairs to greet Magus as he entered the ancient tower. He climbed until he reached the room at the top where Clip spent much of his time, surrounded by his books and precious objects.

Clip, dressed in a golden silk robe, stood with his back to the staircase. In his hands he held a pair of huge, soft-headed beaters, and before him, hanging from upright stands, were the gongs. Clip's arms moved in gentle and fluid motion, coaxing and burnishing the great gongs into mystical vibration. The beautiful, shimmering sound resonated around the cornerless stone room, filling it with layer upon layer of reverberation. The music was invasive, not an exterior noise that was heard through the ears, but something more corporeal that burst in waves into the whole body and settled there, flooding every cavity and cell with its energy. The sound from Clip's gongs was immense and impossible to resist. Despite his need to leave for London, Magus found himself calming and centring as the magical sounds entered his body and drove all thoughts from his head.

Magus stood transfixed by the gongs' power, until eventually Clip became aware of another person in the tower standing behind him. He eyed Magus warily but his grey gaze softened as he recognised Magus' altered state. His arms slowed and gradually the massive, encompassing dome of sound diminished, until the circular room was almost silent save for a whisper of vibration that hung in the air. Clip laid down the beaters and turned to face his half-brother, dressed in city suit and gleaming shoes.

'I'd forgotten how powerful that is,' said Magus softly, his body still reverberating slightly. 'We should use gongs at the ceremonies to welcome the sun.'

'Yes, I'd love to hear the sound in the Stone Circle,' agreed Clip. 'I've never taken the gongs there but I think it'd be absolutely magical.'

'Shame they're not indigenous though,' said Magus. 'Sun gongs from China – not really quite the thing for Stonewylde perhaps.'

'Oh I don't know,' said Clip thoughtfully. 'They're made of bronze, finely beaten and hammered – I like to think that perhaps our ancestors, when making their circular shields, also discovered the joy of creating music with them. Sound is universal, and people the world over honour the rising of the sun. I don't think it matters where the instrument originates, if the intent is global.'

'Maybe you could play them at the Winter Solstice then,' said Magus. 'An appropriate festival perhaps for sun gongs, and they'd certainly create a stir.' He nodded at Clip's battered old sofa. 'May I?'

Magus sat down, and Clip watched him guardedly, knowing the euphoric effects of his gong playing wouldn't last long on this impatient, purposeful man. Magus carried a biscuit tin which he placed on the old chest that stood between them, doubling as an occasional table.

'Are you planning on spending the Moon Fullness in your dolmen?' he asked quite gently, remembering his mission but feeling far less aggressive than when he'd entered the tower.

'Yes I am. Don't try having another go at me, Sol, because I won't change my mind. I need some time alone. I'm out of touch with everything that matters to me, thanks to you.'

'I'm sorry, Clip. I appreciate all you've done to help me and I know it's not your style. I wish I had your natural abilities but I don't, and that's why I need your help sometimes. You were lucky to be born with such powers – I just wish I'd been. Anyway, no hard feelings, I hope. I've had these made especially for you as a peace offering – your favourite ceremony cakes, and we've added a new ingredient. I think you'll find these really special.'

Clip's eyes lit up; he adored the cakes. Only Magus and Violet, Martin's mother, knew the recipe, which was a closely guarded secret. They'd certainly help with his shamanic journey during the full moon.

'Thanks, Sol,' he said delightedly, his thin, rather tired face relaxing into a smile at the sight of the little golden cakes nestling in the tin. 'Ooh, and so many – I'll be well away on these. No, no hard feelings I suppose. Have a good trip to London. You'll be back for the Harvest Moon?'

Magus chuckled.

'Yes, of course! You were right though; I can manage Sylvie on my own. She's easy enough to handle and she told me only last night how she wanted to give me her moon magic. She's still compliant, so I'll be fine up there alone with her. I've told Miranda to keep her in bed from now until the evening itself and to feed her up, which will hopefully strengthen her. I'll get her to do all the eggs this time because she seemed absolutely fine last month – up and about again in no time. I expect it'll get easier for her, as I said before, with some training and practice. It's probably fairer to make sure she does all the eggs every month so it's not such a shock to her system. She'll get used to it and I may even be able to gradually increase the amount she can take. Don't you agree?'

'Yes, I suppose so,' said Clip distractedly, nibbling at one of the cakes. 'Just don't overdo it, will you? Take care of Sylvie and don't exhaust her.'

'Of course, Clip. Actually, while I'm in London I'm seeing a couple of people about the eggs. I'm sure there'd be a huge market for them and it's an exciting prospect.'

'Mmn, very exciting,' mumbled Clip through a mouthful of cake. 'These are superb, Sol! I've never tasted anything like them – they're so powerful! You should be selling these too.'

Magus laughed and stood up, a stark contrast to his gold, silk-robed brother in the dark business suit.

'Somehow I don't think they'd be legal in the Outside World.'

Yul worried all day. He nearly chopped off his fingers with an axe, and later let a whole load of logs roll from a cart, which he then had to reload. He swore fluently and started again, tossing them onto the cart at top speed, anxious to finish and get away. How on earth could he stop Magus forcing Sylvie up to Moon-cliffe that evening? He knew Mother Heggy had said she'd stop him, but what was the plan? Did he need to help?

'Sir, could I finish after this, please? Mother Heggy said she wanted me to drop by with some provisions today.'

Old Greenbough looked surprised, but nodded.

'Course you can, lad. I didn't know you still called on her – 'tis good of you. I feel sorry for the old thing; used to be so respected, she was. Delivered all the babies, brewed all the remedies and everyone looked up to her. But then Magus brought doctors to live in the Hall and opened that hospital wing and nobody needed old Mother Heggy anymore.'

'It must've been difficult for her.'

'Aye, I reckon so. There was trouble, years and years back, and since then she hated Magus, and she never hid it like some do. 'Twere all on account of a girl who lived with Mother Heggy, a strange, wild maiden. She were the mother o' Magus, and o' Master Clip too, and she died up at Mooncliffe one Moon Full-ness. Mother Heggy reckoned it were the old magus' fault. She never forgave him and she blamed our Magus too though, to be fair, I don't see how it could've been his fault as well. He were only a scrap of a boy when she passed on.'

Yul listened intently, shocked at this revelation. So Raven had actually *died* at Mooncliffe? His heart clenched at the thought of what Sylvie had to go through up there. Had the same thing happened to Raven? Did Elm, Magus' father, feed on her moon magic too? Why had she died? He needed to know, but Old Greenbough had little more information than that.

'All I know is when our Magus brought in the doctors, he told us we weren't to go to Mother Heggy no more. Made out she were a useless old biddy and may even harm us with her remedies seeing as she'd gone soft in the head. Can't blame him really for she were very rude about him, and openly, and he can't have that. She was a powerful woman with a great deal o' the old knowledge and I suppose he couldn't abide someone else having such power. I wouldn't dare cross her myself, though. You've finished, lad, so you go on now and give her my respects.'

Yul found Mother Heggy hunched in her rocking chair with the crow in her lap and an ancient book open on a stool beside her. She looked up crossly when he arrived at her door.

'I'm busy!' she snapped. 'I don't need disturbances. Go away.'

'But Mother Heggy, how am I going to stop Magus taking Sylvie up to Mooncliffe tonight?'

'Stupid boy! Didn't I say *I'd* stop him! Leave me in peace or 'twill be too late. He's already well on the road.'

'But . . .'

'All you need to do is take the girl up to Hare Stone tonight and let her drink her fill o' the red Harvest Moon. That evil one won't be back in time for the moon rising. You must be ready to take her at sunset and that's all. Now go!'

Yul turned away reluctantly, unable to trust the old woman could do it.

But it seemed Yul had been wrong to worry. He slipped in through the outside door and climbed the stairs to Sylvie's bedroom before sunset, having spotted Miranda in the sitting room from the garden below. He fully expected to find that Magus had already taken her, but Sylvie was pacing the room, alive with jitteriness and jumpiness.

'Yul!' she whispered frantically, springing on him as he crept through the arched door. 'Where've you been? I'm going mad.'

'Good – it shows the spell's well and truly broken. This is normal, isn't it?'

'I suppose so, but please let's go now! I've got to get out!'

She flung her arms round him, her body rigid with tension, and kissed him hard on the mouth.

'It's so good to see you, Yul.'

He grinned at her.

'And you, Sylvie – I've missed you at Moon Fullness. And tonight it's the Harvest Moon which is really special. We need to get going, the sun's low already. Where's Magus?'

'I don't know! Not back from London yet I suppose. I've been stuck in this room for three days and I've no idea what's going on. What about Mum?'

'I think she's sitting in the other room – I could see her through the window. Let's just go, Sylvie, and by the time she realises you're missing, hopefully it'll be too late. She won't come chasing after you, will she?'

'No, but what about Magus? Won't he come and find us at Hare Stone?'

He shrugged.

'Mother Heggy said she's taking care of him and she's been right so far. We've just got to trust her. Come on!'

They tiptoed down the stone staircase and ran across the gardens. Then they hurried along the track to the woods, alive with bird song. The sun was setting as they climbed the hill, the evening warm and still. The sky was a soft pink; tiny golden clouds speckled the horizon after the sun had slipped away. The light grew thicker and the birds stopped singing. The hares appeared from the woods, loping up the hill to sit long and upright, their ears raised, looking about them. The leverets, now well grown, hopped around nibbling grass and playing like kittens.

Yul sat in his familiar place, his back to the great stone and his legs hugged up to his chest, chin resting on his knees. He breathed a sigh of relief; it was almost moon rise and Magus couldn't possibly make it to stop them now. He shook the dark curls from his eyes and glanced across at Sylvie. Wearing the beautiful moongazy dress that clung to her slender curves, she stood a little way off facing the horizon where the moon would rise. She looked well, not so thin and pale now, and he was pleased. His own stomach growled but he ignored it – plenty of time for food later.

Mother Heggy crouched on the filthy flagstones of her cottage. Clutching a short, smoke-darkened hazel wand, she poked at some dried lichen, fungi and herbs which burned acridly in the little pot-bellied fire-cauldron on the stone floor. She muttered unintelligible words to herself, rheumy eyes fixed on the distance, hunched-up body swaying and rocking. In her other shrivelled hand she held the dark glass into which she peered every so often. Her crow was missing.

The crow sat on the bonnet of Magus' car and cawed. The front of the sleek sports car was crumpled to half its size. The radiator grille was wedged against a large stone in the ditch and steam poured from beneath the twisted metal. Magus was trapped in the driver's seat. Apart from a few bruises he was unhurt, but the damaged door wouldn't open, the air bag wedged him in his seat and his safety belt was jammed. He cursed vehemently at the police officer who stood nearby.

'I'm sorry, sir. You can swear all you like, but there's nothing more I can do until the fire-fighters arrive with their cutting equipment. They reckon at least half an hour as they're busy at the moment with a rick fire and you're not hurt or in immediate danger. Don't fret, sir, please. We'll have you out in an hour or so.'

'That's not good enough! The sun's set and I need to get home *now*!'

'Oh no, sir,' said the police officer, shaking his head. 'We have to get you checked over by the paramedics first, once we've cut you out. And how do you intend getting home? This car won't be going anywhere, will it? And I need to take a statement. I know you haven't been drinking from the breathalyser, but I need details.'

'I *told* you! It was that bloody crow over there! It came out of nowhere straight into my windscreen. Look at it!'

The large black crow blinked its bright eye at him. Then with a clumsy flapping of wings it took off into the darkening skies.

Now I can spread my wings and fly the spirals! Together they dance, earth and moon in harmony. Come, Bright Lady – I am here!

As the rim of the enormous red moon peered over the edge of the earth, Sylvie rose up on tiptoes, spread her moon-angel wings, and began her dance with a joyful song. Her gossamer silk dress floated around her, the silver beads that tipped the pointy hem flying out as she moved. The barn owl called across the silence; an eerie sound to accompany the rising of the blood-red moon. It glided in on silent white wings, round black eyes staring from its pale heart-shaped face as it perched on the stone. Yul leaned his head back against the stone and smiled to himself. Mother Heggy had done it!

Much later Yul roused Sylvie from her moongazy reverence on the grass, where she'd been kneeling surrounded by many hares. Yul stood, tall and strong, looking down at Sylvie with eyes full of love. He helped her stand, and as she rose to her feet, still gazy and dazed, it was natural to fall into his arms. The moon had now lost its deep red tint and sailed high above them as they kissed in the soft, silvery light. Sylvie felt the power of the red Harvest Moon glowing inside her, calling to his green and gold Earth Magic. The quicksilver enchantment of the sacred place sparkled all around them and she clung fiercely to him, excited by the steely restraint she sensed beneath his passionate kisses. Eventually he pulled away and held her at arm's length, his face hollowed in the moonlight.

'We must get back, Sylvie. Magus may be back by now and out looking for you. He'd try Mooncliffe first, but then he'd come here and we mustn't let him catch us. I need to get you home safely, my moon angel.'

'I love you, Yul,' she whispered, her eyes full of moonlight. 'I wish we could stay up here all night and be together.'

'I love you too, Sylvie,' he replied, kissing her tenderly. 'And one day we'll have all the time we need. But not tonight – not yet.'

They hurried through the woods together and arrived at the Tudor wing. The pointed roofs and gables were silhouetted against the moon-washed skies and a light still burned in the sitting room window. Yul quickly kissed her goodbye and she raced on tiptoe up the stairs, heart pounding with fear. Her room was dark and empty and nobody waited for her in the shadows. She jumped straight into bed and pulled the covers up to her chin, trying to calm her breathing. She couldn't believe they'd got away with it. Where on earth was Magus?

She found out in the morning. He was like black thunder, shouting at everyone and upsetting the entire household. When he questioned Sylvie about the previous night, his dark eyes flashing ominously, she smiled guilelessly and told him how she loved to dance at Mooncliffe. That was all she'd say, endlessly repeating it until he almost slapped her. As he turned away in exasperation, she smothered a smile. Poor Miranda was shouted at brutally for not knowing what had happened. Miranda, it turned out, had fallen asleep on the sofa after she'd got Sylvie ready and had slept through the whole night. She hadn't a clue whether Sylvie had been out moongazing or not. She burst into tears when Magus yelled at her and spent the next few days moping around in abject misery. Clip had been oblivious to the world all night, on a long cake-induced shamanic journey in his dolmen. He'd felt a pang as he saw the deep-red moon rising, thinking of Sylvie, but his mind had been too muzzy to dwell on it for long. He couldn't help Magus either as to Sylvie's whereabouts, merely shrugging vaguely when interrogated.

Sylvie smiled in her school room as Magus stormed around the Hall, furious with everybody, yelling at anyone who got in his way. His beautiful, expensive sports car was a write-off. He'd also been delayed even longer than expected once the fire-crew finally cut him free from the wreckage; the person summoned from the Hall to collect him had run out of fuel in the middle of nowhere. He'd had no phone with him and had to walk miles along the back-roads to find help. Then they'd had to wait ages for the breakdown service to bring fuel, and it had been very late indeed when Magus had finally returned home. It was as if someone hadn't wanted him to reach Stonewylde that night.

18

October had come to Stonewylde and the leaves were changing colour. The hedgerows were bright with haw hips, scattered like blood-red garnets along every lane. The field maples glowed brilliant yellow and the beeches a deep gold. Everywhere the trees released their fruits to the waiting earth: conkers, beech nuts, chestnuts and acorns. It was a new experience for Sylvie, brought up in a city with only exhaust-dusted trees and fenced-in parks. She loved the different colours, textures and smells of autumn at Stonewylde. Yul and the other woodsmen were busy splitting and chopping from dawn to dusk, getting the loads of logs into the Village and stored away for winter. He found the log chopping easier this autumn and realised how much muscle he'd acquired during the spring and summer. Greenbough was proud of him and delighted that he could now trust Yul with a man's full workload.

Sylvie was in the woods one misty morning, working on a biology project. She'd chosen to study fungi, and was trying to identify different types from her book. She walked slowly through the trees carrying a camera, sketchbook and a basket for collecting specimens. She loved this type of practical learning, especially as it allowed her to be outside in the glorious autumn morning. Birds flitted all around her, darting from tree to tree, and squirrels scampered everywhere making a surprising amount of noise as they rustled in the fallen leaves.

Her foray proved quite successful and Sylvie identified a

number of different fungi which she photographed and sketched, picking a specimen of the more plentiful ones. As she added another one to her basket she was struck by the beauty of the mushrooms; the delicate blue sheen of the Wood Blewit, the pinky-brown tinge to the recurved scales of the Shaggy Parasol, the purple-lilac of the Amethyst Deceiver. She had a giant white puffball that she'd almost tripped over and a great orange-red bracket of Beefsteak Fungus which she'd climbed a tree to retrieve. She loved the names too and was pleased that she'd chosen this fascinating topic for her project. She wished Yul was with her; he'd have known all these species and many more.

She heard the faint sound of axes thudding into wood, and her heart raced. Yul might be nearby. Since the Harvest Moon a week or so ago, her feelings for him were running deeper than ever. She thought back to the sight of the enormous deep red moon rising, the Triple Goddess wearing her red harvest robes as she walked in beauty. Sylvie now thrummed with a deep red energy which coursed through her veins; she no longer felt frail or delicate, but empowered.

She wandered along an overgrown path off the track, heading towards the sound of axes on wood, all thoughts of fungi forgotten. Up ahead she spotted a group of men working in a clearing. Then she saw Yul and her breath caught in her throat. He wore old trousers and work boots and had taken off his shirt. The mist was clearing into a sunny day, and Yul worked in a pool of hazy sunlight filtering down through the golden leaves. He was deeply tanned from the summer, and although the stripes still criss-crossed his back, the sun had helped camouflage the scars. The muscles in his arms, shoulders and back rippled as he wielded the heavy axe, his movements precise and rhythmic. His chest was well-defined with muscle, his stomach hard and flat. The axe bit into the wood as he swung it powerfully, putting all his strength and energy into the task. His black curls were stuck down with sweat and the rest of his torso gleamed too, golden and smooth. Sylvie watched him with a strange tingling and felt herself dissolve inside at the sight of him. But after a while she turned away and decided to look in another part of the woods for her fungi. She was too embarrassed to approach him, knowing he'd recognise the dark hunger in her eyes.

A while later she sat on a mossy bank for a rest, enjoying a drink of water and a quick look at her pictures and notes. Sylvie closed her eyes, remembering how Magus had once told her to use all her senses in the woods. She smiled sadly as she recalled his kindness when she'd first arrived. So much had happened since then; had she really been so naïve when she came here? She knew that this summer she'd left the innocence of childhood behind and started the rocky transition to womanhood. It wasn't easy and she wished she were still close to her mother, but Magus had spoiled that as he had everything else. Her mother was a different person now, obsessed with him and the new baby, and Sylvie no longer felt she could rely on her. She sighed and then jumped as she heard voices approaching.

A strange duo came into sight along the path. Two old women hobbled side by side, both wrapped in grimy shawls and carrying battered wicker baskets over their arms. Their heads bobbed as they talked; they were deep in conversation and didn't notice her sitting on the bank.

'Good morning!' she called, not wishing to startle them as they drew nearer. Their heads shot up and both glared at her, whiskery chins jutting belligerently. They peered with beady eyes and she recoiled from the animosity in their look.

''Tis the Newcomer!'

'Aye, sister, you speak right. The Newcomer on the bank, right by our little crop o' Fly. She better not've touched 'em!'

'No, she better not've. They're ours, them Fly. Always pick 'em, every year 'tween Equinox and Samhain, this crop.'

Sylvie had no idea what they were on about but recognised their hostility. She put her things back in her basket, anxious to be off. These were the first Villagers to show outright unfriendliness towards her and she was unsure how to respond to them.

'You stay put, girlie!' muttered one of the women. 'Stay there – we want a good eyeful of you.'

'Aye, sister, a good eyeful. We seen you afore, at the ceremonies, but never so close. You stay put, young maiden.'

They'd stopped before her as she sat on the moss, both staring down at her, and she felt awkward under their scrutiny. They nodded, pursing their wrinkled mouths.

'Moongazy as they come, ain't she?'

'Aye, moongazy as that one afore her. And I'll bet he loves it too.'

They cackled in unison and Sylvie felt the hair on her arms prickle.

'Well, Raven, you're home again to roost.'

'Aye, and roosting up at the Hall in luxury this time around.'

'I'm not Raven,' said Sylvie, her throat constricted. 'I'm Sylvie.'

'Aye, right enough. But we know, don't we, sister? We know what comes around.'

Sylvie started to get to her feet, but one of them stepped forward and pushed her back with a shrivelled hand.

'No, don't you go yet. We want to speak with you, get the feel of you. We mean no harm.'

'No harm at all, young maiden, so bide your time. What've you got in your poke?'

She peered into Sylvie's basket.

'Been gathering, girl? Gathering the fruits of the woods?'

Sylvie nodded.

'I'm doing a project for biology.' She realised the futility of that sentence as soon as it was uttered. 'I mean I'm learning about fungi and I've been looking for different types.'

'And you found our Fly!'

They pointed along the bank, where a group of brilliant red toadstools flecked with sugary white spots glowed against a backdrop of emerald-green moss. Sylvie wondered how on earth she'd missed them.

'No, I hadn't seen them. They're beautiful.'

'Aye, beautiful for dreams and wanderings. Beautiful for helping the spirit travel far. They're our Fly Agaric – you ain't been at 'em?'

Sylvie shook her head quickly.

'Raven always was one for the mushrooms, weren't she, sister? Always one for the gathering.'

'Pah! I could've shown that Raven a thing or two. Too busy moongazing and singing to notice what was right under her pretty nose. Too busy dancing around with all the men in her thrall crawling after her. Never would've made Wise Woman, that one. Moongazy and feckless with her bare feet and that mass o' hair.'

'Aye, sister. You were always the wiser. She never had her heart in it, not after they got their hands on her and took their fill.'

They cackled again, clutching at each other's arms in glee.

'Who are you?' asked Sylvie, her mouth dry.

'Who are we? Who are we? There's a question!'

'You've been here a six-month – you should know by now. You've ate my cakes, girl.'

They glared at her again and the older of the two shuffled to the bank. To Sylvie's dismay she lowered herself stiffly onto the mossy top.

'You've ate my cakes and you seen my son, Martin. I'm Old Violet, the Wise Woman of Stonewylde.'

Sylvie was puzzled by this. Martin the major-domo at the Hall? It seemed such an unlikely relationship. Closer up, she saw the women weren't quite as old as she'd originally thought. Their lined faces were ingrained with grime which made them appear more wrinkled than they actually were.

'I thought Mother Heggy was the Wise Woman,' said Sylvie.

The women spat in unison.

'You're wrong there!' hissed the one still standing. 'My sister Violet's the Wise Woman. That crone Heggy has no power left in her broken old bones. She's worthless as wet firewood.'

'If you've had dealings with her,' said Violet, 'then you're in for a spell o' trouble. She's a danger to all who come to her, that one. She'll drag you into her web of lies and spit you out when she's done. You mark my words, girl – you'll rue making a friend of her. You should've come to Old Violet. I'd look out for you;

I'd help you find your way. Here, give me your hand and let me read you.'

Violet grabbed her hand before she could snatch it away. She now sat with it clutched between hers, rubbing Sylvie's palm with her filthy thumbs and peering at it intently, her bony nose almost touching it. She rocked slightly as she held on tightly and Sylvie was wafted by her sour odour. It repulsed her in a way that Mother Heggy's strange scent never did. The other sister sat down too, wedging Sylvie between them, and fingered a long strand of her silver hair. Sylvie felt trapped.

'Well blessed be!' muttered Violet. 'Blessed be. 'Tis the maiden and the mother, but not the crone. Oh no, not the crone.'

'Do you see, sister?' cried the other woman. ''Tis clear?'

'No, Vetchling, 'tis not clear. Like moonlight through dark clouds – only glimpses. She'll suffer, this one, how she'll suffer! Her heart will be broken. The place of the hares, that's part of it – moonlight and the black zigzag on silver. Three of 'em joined, chasing around in the dance and never finding what they seek. Not until 'tis too late, not until 'tis far too late to save her.'

Old Violet released Sylvie's hand abruptly and wiped her own dirty ones on her shawl as if Sylvie had somehow tainted her. She shook her grizzled head, staring into Sylvie's eyes, and in their black depths Sylvie saw something that shocked her. She saw pity.

'Just look at her, acting as if there's nothing wrong! I'd like to go over and slap her.'

'Don't be silly, Holly,' said Dawn. 'I feel sorry for her. She's all on her own – maybe I should go and sit with her.'

'Don't! She's on her own for a good reason – nobody likes her. And I'm not surprised after what she's done. Poor Buzz! We all knew it was coming. He can only take so much teasing and then he flips. It's all her fault!'

'Come on,' said Dawn. 'You're being unreasonable, Holly. Sylvie says she always made it clear she wasn't interested.'

'Oh yeah!' said Rainbow. 'As if we'd believe that! Remember that time they were caught cuddling in the music room? I've seen them together messing about on the lawns too. And if she wasn't interested, why did she go into the maze with him?'

'True, that was a bit stupid,' said Dawn.

'I don't know about stupid – asking for it, more like,' said Holly bitterly.

The girls sat around on the squashy cushions in the Great Barn, ostensibly sewing patchwork hexagons together for quilts. But this Dark Moon, Holly's group wasn't getting much work done. Although Buzz had been gone for some time, the incident had been raked up again that morning by an e-mail Fennel had received from him.

'I can't believe he wants a photo of her,' said Holly. 'Why? Somebody tell me that!'

Dawn shrugged, trying to keep her stitches small and even.

'He's obviously still crazy about her.'

'The bitch! How does she do it? Goddess, I hate her!'

July and Wren came to join them, flopping down on the cushions.

'You're not still on about the photo?' groaned Wren. 'Get over it, Holly. It's no big deal.'

'But I miss him! It's so boring here without him. I've hardly seen him since May when he went off to do his exams. I've e-mailed him since he was banished, but all he ever wants to know is how Sylvie is, and now he's asking for a photo! I hope nobody sends him one.'

'I thought I might send him a sketch,' said Rainbow. 'I've got a few in my book.'

'What? Why on earth do you want to draw *her*? Are you mad?'

'She's beautiful,' said Rainbow. 'And there's something about her that's hard to catch; I'm determined to get it.'

'You're so talented, Rainbow,' said Dawn. 'You must go to art school when you're old enough.'

'Maybe, but I don't see it could be any better than studying here at Stonewylde. Merewen's a brilliant artist and she's also a great teacher. I'm learning a lot from her and once you get past her gruffness, she's really kind. I don't think any boring old art teacher in the Outside World could be better than her. But I'll tell you what, Holly – just to cheer you up I'll scan my drawing of Yul and print you a copy.'

'Really? Have you got it here now? I thought you said you'd never part with it.'

'A copy won't hurt. Here, it's somewhere in the middle of the book. But be careful – no grubby fingerprints please.'

The girls huddled around Rainbow's sketchbook and located the drawing of Yul on the Altar Stone, his body arched and arms outstretched for the sunset.

'You've captured him perfectly,' said Dawn. 'Hasn't he changed over the past few months?'

'He's gorgeous!' breathed Holly. 'Although I hate him too. Did you see the way he was at the Equinox dance? Just didn't want to know. When I think back to the Spring Equinox – I had him wrapped round my little finger back then. He was all over me, and he even had that fight with Buzz because of me! Why doesn't he want me anymore?'

'Maybe he fancies someone else,' said July.

'What, some stupid Village girl? I don't think so – he's always seemed a bit too . . . special for some gormless girl in a shawl, and he wasn't with anyone at the dance, was he? No, I don't think it's that.'

'He was sitting with Sylvie, wasn't he?' mused Wren. 'When we found him for the Flying Sheaf? They were outside the Barn on a bench together.'

'No way!' shouted Holly, ignoring the stares from other women. 'No – surely not? She can't have got her claws into him too!'

'I'm sure she hasn't,' said Dawn soothingly. 'Wren, don't start stirring. You're speculating – just leave it.'

'Well look at her now!' exclaimed Rainbow. 'That's Yul's sister isn't it? Going over to sit with Sylvie?'

Sylvie sensed someone approaching. Feeling awkward and self-conscious, she'd been huddled in a corner trying to hide herself away. She wished her mother was here so she'd have somebody to talk to now the Hallfolk girls were openly ostracising her. Dawn was the only one who still talked to her and even she kept away when the gang were about. Sylvie knew they all blamed her for Buzz's banishment. Normally she didn't let it bother her and she could avoid them at the Hall, other than in the classroom. But in the Barn for the Dark Moon menstruation gathering it was impossible to act as if nothing were wrong. Sylvie tried to sew her patchwork pieces and pretend she didn't care, but the day stretched ahead emptily, and tomorrow did too. She hoped maybe Dawn was coming to sit with her after all.

But she looked up to see a pretty Village girl approaching and knew that this must be Rosie, for she had the same dark curls and slanted grey eyes as her brother. Sylvie smiled shyly, delighted that someone was prepared to talk to her at last.

'Come and sit with me,' she said warmly. 'I think I know who you are.'

The girl sat on the bench next to her and smiled back, picking up Sylvie's hexagons and examining them.

'Oh no, please don't look! They're terrible – I'd never sewn anything before I came here. I'd love to sew properly but nobody has shown me how and I just can't get the hang of it. Don't look at them – it's so embarrassing!'

Rosie laughed.

'I only came over to say hello, miss. I think we went through the same nightmare with a certain person.'

For a moment Sylvie thought she meant the moondancing with Magus, but then she remembered Buzz and nodded with a grimace.

'Please – I'm Sylvie, not "miss". And yes, I heard he attacked you first. It sounded awful.'

'I was so frightened,' said Rosie, shaking the curls from her eyes in a familiar gesture. 'There was something mad about him, more than just a lad wanting a bit of fun. He were so vicious about it, like a dog gone crazed.'

'He was the same with me – terrifying. I think if those gardeners hadn't come in time he'd have killed me! I'm so grateful to them. Magus said he didn't want me to talk to anyone about it but I think everyone knows now, don't they?'

'Oh aye, 'tis common knowledge that Buzz attacked you too. Now they're saying that's why he were banished and 'twere nothing to do with forcing himself on me. But I reckon it were because of both of us, and anyhow, makes no difference why he's gone. I'm just pleased he has.'

'Yes, it's a relief knowing he won't be coming back, isn't it? But I'm not very popular with them now. They say I encouraged him, led him on.'

Sylvie nodded towards the group of Hallfolk girls spread out in the centre monopolising the large cushions.

'Oh, they're not worth bothering about, stupid Hallfolk,' said Rosie, then gasped and put her hand to her mouth. 'Oh miss, I'm sorry! I didn't mean ...'

Sylvie laughed. 'It's okay. I'm really not one of them. I can't stand them either and you're right – they *are* stupid.'

They smiled at each other and then Rosie looked away in embarrassment.

'I hope you don't mind me asking, miss, I mean, Sylvie. It's just ... do you know my brother Yul?'

Sylvie found herself blushing scarlet, and Rosie giggled into her hand.

'We been wondering, Mother and I, who's this girl he's hankering after. He's so secretive and won't tell us a thing, so I guessed it must be someone a bit different and I thought it might be you. He used to like that nasty Holly but he's over her, thank Goddess.'

Sylvie felt a sharp stab of jealousy.

'So it's true then – he liked Holly once?' Sylvie's throat went tight and her voice came out wrong. 'Buzz told me there was some fight between him and Yul over Holly, but when I asked Yul he said he couldn't stand her! I just can't imagine anything going on between them as she doesn't seem his type at all – she's so spiteful.'

'Oh don't you worry – it were a while ago, before you came here, and it was nothing like he is about you. He just used to dance with her at the ceremonies up in the Circle and back in the Barn afterwards. They made a good pair, both very quick on their feet, but that's been over a long time since.'

Sylvie stared at her in consternation, fighting the tears that prickled behind her eyes. Why had he never admitted that when they'd discussed it? Was he hiding something? Rosie glanced at her and frowned.

'Honestly, miss, he never really liked her, not like he feels about you. I never seen him like this before. Yul's completely moonstruck for you, and that's what I really wanted to talk to you about. I hope you won't mind me speaking plain, but I'm worried, you see.'

She took the piece of material now lying idle in Sylvie's lap and began to sew, her stitches deft and tiny.

'I'm worried about what will come of all this. Yul's led a horrible life. I expect you know some of it but I'll bet you don't know the half of it. There are some things he'd never talk about and you probably wouldn't believe it if he did. But he's suffered so much ever since he were a little boy, no older than our Leveret is now. Our father was a hard, brutal man, and when it came to Yul he never had any self-control . . . Well, 'tis over now, all that terrible cruelty to my poor brother.'

She sighed, finishing the hexagon and biting off the thread. Sylvie nodded, not sure exactly how much Rosie knew.

'I heard some of it, and I can certainly see the difference in Yul since your father was taken ill.'

'Aye,' said Rosie quietly. Her face was shadowed as she stared down at her hands, and then she looked up at Sylvie, her lovely dark grey eyes brimming with tears. 'This is the first time Yul's been happy in his whole life and I don't want to see him hurt. He truly loves you, 'tis plain to see, but you're Hallfolk and he's just a Villager. Where's the future in that? 'Tis against our laws for you two to be walking together as sweethearts. I don't know how you feel about him, whether 'tis just a bit of fun for you or something deeper to match his feelings, but please, miss, I beg you – don't hurt him, will you? Don't break his heart.'

During October, as the land began to draw back into itself for winter, Sylvie learned of how Stonewylde dealt with its dead. At breakfast she heard people discussing how Old Humphrey had passed away during the night peacefully in his own bed, in the cottage where he'd lived all his life. He'd been a farmer and right up until the end had continued doing whatever odd jobs he could manage, making himself useful around the Village and playing his fiddle at the dances. Humphrey had an enormous family and was a well-liked member of the community. The funeral was set for the following day, there being no reason to delay, and Sylvie and Miranda were invited to attend along with the rest of the community. Sylvie was nervous; she'd been ill enough in the past to have felt the cold draught of mortality but had never been to a funeral before and had no experience of death.

Late afternoon the next day the resident Hallfolk walked together down the long drive, everyone dressed smartly but not in black. Clip, wearing a dark green cloak and carrying a staff, fell into step beside Sylvie and Miranda and smiled at them both.

'This is your first Passing On, isn't it? I'll stay with you during the ceremony if you like. You'll find it very unlike anything you've experienced before.'

'I'm amazed at how many Hallfolk are going,' said Sylvie. 'I wouldn't have thought they'd go to a Villager's funeral.'

She was pleased Clip was with them. Even though Mother Heggy had insisted it was he who'd put the spell on her and she knew he'd been at Mooncliffe with Magus for the Moon Fullness, somehow he didn't fill her with the same fear and dread as his half-brother. There was something gentle about Clip, an inner core of kindness where Magus had only cold steel.

'Humphrey was a popular chap and, being so old, he's been around for most people's entire lives. Hallfolk and Villagers usually attend each other's Passing On. We may live different lives and I expect you've noted how segregated our worlds are, yet actually we do integrate at certain points in the year and certain times in our lives. Festivals, hand-fastings, funerals – we all join together for these and share in the ceremonies as they're such an important part of our culture. We're a community and you're never alone in a true community.'

'So what should we expect at this funeral?' asked Miranda coolly, irritated that Clip had attached himself to them.

'It's a cremation, not a burial,' said Clip, 'and it takes place outside.'

'Why do you call it a Passing On?' asked Sylvie.

'Because that's what we believe death is. Your soul passes on to a different place.'

'Like heaven and hell?'

'No!' laughed Clip. 'Absolutely not – that's a Christian concept! We call it the Otherworld and it's the next stage in your soul's journey. Your soul spends some time in this world and then it passes on to another world when your time here's finished. Our ceremony honours the person's life and offers a send-off to the next world. We need to dispose of the body, of course, and comfort those who remain behind, but we don't see death as the end, nor as an opportunity for divine punishment or reward.'

They walked some way further and instead of forking into the Village, headed towards the higher woods surrounding the Stone Circle. They didn't go up the Long Walk but turned off at a path marked by two carved stones. Sylvie saw that the images carved in relief were crows, and she shivered. The crowd of Hallfolk had fallen silent now as they walked along the stony path. They were surrounded on either side by dead bracken of a deep gold and bright silver birch trees, their leaves yellow and trunks papery white. All around in the undergrowth Sylvie saw different types of fungus and mushrooms and thought what a good place this would be for her research, although she wouldn't like to come here alone.

'Clip, where are we going?' she whispered. Miranda walked in front of them, for the path wasn't wide enough for three abreast. He bent his head to answer her.

'To the Yew of Death. Are you alright, Sylvie? You're pale.'

She nodded although her hands were shaking.

'I'm okay thanks. It's just a bit daunting.'

He patted her shoulder.

'Don't be scared. Death isn't frightening. I've seen the other side, the Otherworld, and it's a good place to go when your time here's done. The only thing that's frightening is the unknown, and the idea that death is the end. It isn't, believe me. I promise you, nothing you'll see today will give you cause for fear.'

The path continued for some time and gradually the silver birches gave way to oak trees. Acorns clustered thickly amongst the leaves, just beginning to turn ochre. Squirrels scurried up and down the trunks, leaping between branches and bounding across the ground. The oaks were dense around them, overhanging the path which now led downhill into a secluded valley. Sylvie had never visited this part of Stonewylde before and looked around with interest. The route was marked with waist-high stones, many of them carved with crows and some with skulls. There were lanterns on each stone to mark the way, although there was still some murky daylight. Sylvie heard the soft beat of drums coming from the valley below and the hair on her arms began to rise. Still the procession walked on in silence, travelling down deeper into the woods, and at last they came to a great clearing.

Sylvie gasped at the sight before her. At the far end of the huge open area stood a yew tree, bigger than any tree she'd seen in her life. It had many twisted trunks all rising from a single massive bole, covered with pink-brown scaly bark. The bole was hollow, creating a huge open cave of contorted wood, and she could see dark figures inside. She remembered what Professor Siskin had told her about the yew tree regenerating itself, and how yews could live for thousands of years. She wondered how old this one was. Its dark green spiky slips made a huge canopy, and in places the gnarled branches hung low. The ground underneath the yew was strange; soft grey and powdery, and covered with pebbles.

What really drew the eye, however, was the funeral pyre in the centre of the arena. It was built of a series of criss-cross rafts of wood, and stood chest high to a man. On top was a bier covered with slips of yew, forming a dark green bed upon which Humphrey's body lay, dressed in his ceremony robes. His shock of white hair was bright in the gloom. His arms were crossed on his chest and he looked peaceful, as if he were sleeping. The clearing was full of Villagers in their best clothes or ceremony robes, and the long procession of Hallfolk pouring into the circle mingled with them. The drums still beat softly, the rhythms weaving in and out of each other and making a strangely comforting background layer of sound. Clip stayed close to Sylvie and she was glad of his presence beside her.

'The yew's wonderful, isn't it?' he whispered to her.

'Yes! It's massive, even bigger than the one on the Green,' she whispered back.

'It's special because it's the tree of . . .'

'. . . life and death and rebirth,' she finished for him, smiling.

'Well done! Who told you that?'

'Yul,' she said, without thinking.

'Did he now? Are you still hanging around with him?'

'Oh no!' she said, shaking her head vehemently.

He looked down at her with raised eyebrows, then pointed to the oak trees all around them.

'Look, Sylvie. See the birds?'

She was shocked to see the trees' branches clustered with hundreds of black birds, mostly rooks and crows. They perched in silence, fidgeting slightly, and she felt a little spooked.

'Why are they here? I've never seen so many birds all together in one place.'

'The crow is one of the emblems of the Otherworld,' explained Clip. 'Humphrey was a lovely chap and well-loved, and that's why there's a good turn-out of birds here today.'

Sylvie frowned at him – surely he was joking.

'Humphrey was brought down here at dawn and his body placed on the bier; his family and friends have been with him all day. They'll have had a picnic and spent the day thinking of him, talking about him and his life; all that he's done, all that he was, and taking their leave of him. In a minute Magus will start the ceremony and as the sun sets, the family will light the pyre. We believe that then, as his body burns away in the twilight, his soul leaves this world and enters the Otherworld.'

Sylvie shivered suddenly and Clip looked closely at her.

'You're sure you're alright?'

She nodded and looked around, trying to locate Yul amongst the great crowd. She could feel him there and knew he was watching her right now. She scanned the faces and then her eyes locked into his, feeling the jolt of fire behind the deep grey. She drew breath sharply as she gazed at him and Clip, watching her carefully, bent down close to her.

'You'll have to give him up, Sylvie,' he whispered. 'For his sake, if not your own. Magus won't tolerate a relationship between you.'

She was saved from replying by the appearance of Magus in a long grey cloak emerging from the depths of the yew, stepping from beneath the boughs and out into the open. As he turned and the cloak swished, she saw the great crow with outstretched wings embroidered on the back, defined with golden stitching. Beside Magus walked another dark-cloaked figure carrying a burning torch, who wore a mask of black feathers with a long protruding beak. This transformed his head into that of a crow's, reminding Sylvie of the sinister beaked doctors of the Great Plague.

Magus strode towards the funeral pyre, the crow man following, and the drumming changed beat. More instruments joined the music and suddenly the whole community burst into song. Sylvie and Miranda both jumped and clutched each other's arms at the unexpectedness of it. The sound was strange – a sort of eerie serenade, almost an ululation, which filled the clearing. The birds shifted in the branches, preening and watching.

'Who's the man in the bird mask?' asked Sylvie, noticing the blond Hallfolk hair beneath it.

'Martin, from the Hall. He always assists Magus at funerals.'

It was too cloudy to see the sunset but Magus seemed to

anticipate the moment. The light had been steadily fading from the grey skies, and at his signal, five men brought forward a large piece of heavy hemp cloth embroidered with a pentangle of green and gold.

'Do you know about the pentangle?' whispered Clip. 'It represents the five elements and it's a sacred symbol to us.'

Sylvie was about to reply when the music quietened and Magus began to speak. His deep voice rang out in the clearing, his words unhurried and beautifully spoken.

'Blessings, folk of Stonewylde!'

'Blessings, Magus of Stonewylde!' chorused hundreds of voices in perfect unison.

'Great Earth Mother who gives life to us all, in your sacred presence we gather to honour our friend Humphrey, who was a beloved member of our community. His time with us is now over and his soul is ready to leave our world and enter the Otherworld. We come to say farewell at his Passing On, to wish his soul good speed through the veil, and to comfort those who will miss him most.'

Every face was turned towards Magus; everyone was rapt and still. Even the birds were unmoving in the branches.

'Humphrey was a good man, a much-loved son, brother, husband, father, grandfather and great-grandfather, held in great affection by everyone. He was a true Villager who loved Stonewylde and served our community well. He loved the land, he worked hard all his life, and he honoured the Earth Goddess in every way. His special gift was music, and we'll always remember Old Humphrey for his lively fiddling at every dance in the Great Barn.'

Magus stood gazing at the white-haired old man for a moment and Sylvie felt a catch in her throat.

'We say farewell to you, Humphrey,' Magus continued, 'with thanks for your life, but sadness that you'll no longer be among us here. We will remember you, especially at Samhain when the veil is thin. We send your soul now to pass on to the Otherworld, under the green symbol of the five elements that are the fabric of life itself. Earth! Air! Fire! Water! Spirit! We say farewell to you under the boughs of the Yew of Death, the great tree of rebirth. As the yew is reborn from death, so too may your soul be reborn in the Otherworld. May you ever walk with the Goddess, she who is life itself. Farewell, Humphrey!'

As the five men draped the green cloth over the body, high up on the bier, the community spoke in one great voice.

'Farewell, Humphrey! Goddess speed your soul to the Otherworld!'

The drums took up a gentle beat and Magus nodded to an old woman who stood nearby, flanked by her family. She took the burning torch from the crow-masked man and bending stiffly, lit the kindling at the base of the pyre. Sylvie swallowed hard and felt Clip's arm slip comfortingly around her shoulders. There was a whoosh as the flames caught hold, and the resin-soaked pyre very quickly became a crackling mass of red-hot fire. Everyone stepped back and, as the fire burnt, the music played and the people swayed gently, many with tears rolling down their cheeks.

Sylvie felt incredibly moved. Her tears flowed freely as she thought of the old man she'd seen but never even met, who'd been so loved all his life and would now be so missed. She felt part of something special; a coming-together of human kindness and love. As the pyre burned, people held hands or hugged for comfort and the music was gentle and calm. The body under the hemp cloth seemed to have been consumed already; there was a strong, spicy smell in the air and ashes floated upwards. Suddenly, and with no warning, the birds rose from the trees together in a great black cloud. The music stopped immediately and the air was full of dark wings as if black confetti had been scattered over the silent clearing. There was a collective sigh and everyone raised their arms, holding them outstretched to the darkening sky. They stood transfixed gazing upwards, all attention focused on the sky and the birds.

Then, after a minute, it was over and people began to talk almost normally.

'His soul has gone,' said Clip. 'Did you feel it? Whatever the essence of Humphrey was, it's no longer here with us in this world. The birds know the moment when the soul passes on.'

'That was amazing,' said Sylvie, wiping her eyes. 'Wasn't it, Mum?'

Miranda nodded, also clearly moved by the experience.

'The most beautiful funeral I've ever seen,' she agreed, blowing her nose. 'All I remember of the last one I attended was the plastic flowers and the stink of air freshener. I'll never forget this moment. Magus does things so wonderfully, doesn't he?'

'What happens now?' asked Sylvie.

'We all go back to the Great Barn. We share some mead and a bite to eat, and that's it. His immediate family will probably stay in the Barn together this evening, and in the morning they'll come back here and sweep the ashes under the Yew of Death. They'll also place a pebble under the tree to represent Humphrey's presence at Stonewylde. The next boy to be born into the family will be named after him.'

Back in the Great Barn Sylvie sipped at a glass of mead and looked about her. The bakers had been busy; great basketfuls of fresh rolls sat on the tables, each one dusted with black poppy seeds and baked in the cruciform shape of a flying crow. There were bowls of butter and chutney, many round cheeses, several huge, pink hams and baskets of apples. Everyone milled about, talking and eating, and the fiddlers played softly. Sylvie found herself standing next to Cherry, whom she saw often enough but rarely to talk to. It was frowned upon to be sociable with servants at the Hall, although was more acceptable at festivals and ceremonies. Cherry was always so busy but Sylvie remembered her kindness when they'd first moved in to Woodland Cottage. She welcomed this chance for a chat, although she found it hard to get a word in edgeways.

'May I say, miss, how tall you've grown lately? I remember when you came here barely a six-month ago, a scrawny little scrap, and now look at you! Still much too skinny for my liking, mind, but you're so tall and leggy now.'

'Thank you, Cherry. I'll take that as a compliment.'

'Well, 'tis a blessing you've lost that nasty scaly stuff on your skin too. Told you our wholesome food would do the trick, didn't I? You're happy at Stonewylde, aren't you m'dear? Not planning to go back to the Outside World, I hope?'

'Oh no!' said Sylvie quickly. 'I shall never leave Stonewylde – I love it here! That funeral ... I mean, the Passing On, was wonderful. They don't do it like that in the Outside World at all.'

'Aye, 'twas a fine ceremony today, lots o' birds. He'd have liked that, old Humphrey. The Village'll seem strange without him around, sweet old soul that he was. But never mind; we go when the Dark Angel summons, and not before nor after. And Humphrey knew his time on this earth was finished – he were ready.'

'The Dark Angel?'

'Why the angel of death, m'dear. You must have him in the Outside World too. How else is a person to know when they must pass on? He appears when death is close, and if he summons you, your spirit must follow. We all obey him, even the magus himself. Nobody cheats the Dark Angel.'

Later, as they walked slowly back up to the Hall, Sylvie reflected on the funeral. It had been simple, with no drawn out speeches or tributes, no prayers, hymns nor dogma, yet all the more effective for its simplicity. The community had despatched Humphrey's soul with love and sadness, disposed of his body respectfully and comforted his family. Sylvie thought of what she'd said to Cherry about never leaving Stonewylde. If she stayed, one day she'd end up under the Yew of Death as a handful of ashes with only a simple pebble to mark her presence at Stonewylde. The thought made her shiver and she took Miranda's arm in the darkness. Sylvie felt in need, all of a sudden, of her mother's protection.

19

The community began to prepare for the next festival in the pagan calendar celebrated on the last day of October. Samhain was a major event at Stonewylde as it was the festival of the dead and also the end of the old year. Sylvie was expected to take part in a dance-drama performed by all the young people, Villager and Hallfolk, and must make her own costume and mask. She'd been given the materials and sat alone in the window seat of one of the downstairs school rooms carefully stitching the seams, glancing outside every now and then at the misty lawns. A cluster of gardeners worked steadily, raking dead leaves into large piles for composting into leaf mulch.

Sylvie, sitting alone in the gloom with the black material draped around her, felt the death of the year approaching and a sadness creep into her soul. She looked up as the door opened; her heart sank at the sight of Magus. He came over and sat down next to her, examining the fabric of her costume and then looking intently at her, his dark eyes searching.

'All on your own, Sylvie? Don't you want to sit with the other girls to do your sewing?'

She shook her head.

'They don't like me very much. I'd rather be on my own anyway.'

'That's a shame, but to be expected in a way. You're different, like a pearl amongst pebbles. You're not one of them and I like the idea of your not mixing too much with the other girls; I think you're right to keep yourself apart.'

He continued to watch her, his proximity and the scent of his fragrance making her nervous.

'Sylvie, I need to talk to you about the Moon Fullness next week.'

Sylvie kept her head down over her sewing, knowing he was testing to see if she were still under the spell. She tried to remember the exact words. She looked up directly into his deep brown eyes; they bored into her as if he were entering her soul.

'I want to dance at Mooncliffe. I want to give you my moon magic.'

He smiled at her and put his hand on hers, stroking it gently with his long fingers.

'You're a good girl, Sylvie. You know how much I need it, and you know it's why you were brought here.'

She forced herself to smile in return and carried on stitching, her hand shaking slightly under his touch. He turned to gaze out of the window.

'Unfortunately you didn't give me any of your magic last month, did you? So this month it'll take longer and afterwards I expect you'll be a little more tired than usual. I need to take extra special care of you now, so the effects won't be quite as tiring for you.'

'Thank you, Magus,' she said quietly, trying to sew and hide her fear.

'I want you strong and healthy; you know how important your well-being is to me. Remember how I healed you, Sylvie? If you wish to moondance for me every month, you need to conserve your energy.'

'Yes I will.'

'I'm sure you will, but I'm taking no chances, not with your health at stake. So I've decided that you can be excused the demands of school until after the Moon Fullness. You're not to leave your rooms at all next week, and I want you to stay in bed quietly. All you must do is rest and eat. Is that clear?'

'But I don't want to go to bed for a week,' she protested, her heart sinking even further at the thought. 'I like school and I'll be bored if—'

'No arguments, Sylvie. Your health must come first.'

'But please, Magus, I really—'

He sighed, and took the sewing out of her hands. He laid it on the window seat and put his hands on her shoulders, twisting her so she had to look at him. She felt the full glare of his relentless will as he shook her very slightly, his fingers digging into her bones.

'I may have to ask Clip to speak to you again if you don't co-operate. And I may even get Hazel to sedate you. Do you understand, Sylvie? This isn't negotiable so don't make me angry – just be a good girl and do what I want without a fuss. Take your sewing and go to your room right now. I'll send your mother up to look after you.'

She nodded slowly, her mind racing; the last thing she needed was Clip intervening. The thought of losing her free will again was terrifying, as was the idea of being medicated by Hazel. She had no choice but to co-operate and not arouse any suspicion. But her heart seethed with anger; Magus was confining her to bed for a week *before* the Moon Fullness, and then she'd probably be ill for another week afterwards. He couldn't steal away her life like this, two weeks a month just to satisfy his need. How could she avoid it this time – surely Mother Heggy couldn't arrange an accident for him every month?

Sylvie miserably made her way to the Tudor wing and tried to talk to her mother about it. She came up against the spell Mother Heggy and Yul had spoken of straight away, and understood why they saw it as magic. Sylvie knew little about hypnosis, though she recognised what Clip had done, and she was shocked at Miranda's complete subjugation. It was frightening to hear her mother, the one person in the world who should be protecting her from predators like Magus, parroting that she'd always obey him and that he knew what was best for Sylvie.

Confined to bed even though she was perfectly well, she'd

314

now have no chance of getting help from Yul or Mother Heggy. Over the next few days of enforced bed-rest Sylvie realised just how very vulnerable she was, and became increasingly frightened about the ordeal Magus had planned for her up at Mooncliffe.

A couple of nights before the full moon, Magus asked Clip to come into his office for a chat. They sat down and Magus rang for coffee. As they drank it, surveying each other on opposite sofas, Magus produced a tin of cakes.

'Almost forgot I had these in here. Would you like one?'

'Are they ...?'

'They certainly are – help yourself.'

Magus watched as Clip devoured the cake, eyes closed in bliss. He didn't have one himself.

'Absolutely scrumptious! May I have another?'

'Have as many as you like, Clip.'

When he saw that Clip was relaxed and amenable, he set to work.

'I need your help this month with the Mooncliffe business.'

Clip waved airily.

'I'll help if you want, but you really don't need me. The hypnosis hasn't worn off, has it?'

'No, I've checked and Sylvie's still under, but there're other things that could go wrong. After missing it last month, the moon energy's gone completely from the big stone at Mooncliffe. There're only a couple of charged eggs left and it's Samhain in a fortnight. For some reason I'm not getting anything from the Altar Stone any more so I *must* have this power next week. You know what Samhain's like – I really need the extra energy. So if something were to go wrong at the next full moon and I'm up there all on my own, I'd be stuck. I need your help, Clip.'

'Well, it's nice to be wanted. Mind if I have another little cake? They're so more-ish, aren't they?'

He sat eating the cake slowly, savouring each morsel.

'I'll help you,' he mumbled, wiping crumbs from his lips, 'but Sol, I don't want Sylvie kept up there for hours and weighed down with all those heavy stone eggs. It's cruel and I can't stand it.'

Magus sighed and shook his head slowly.

'I wish there could be some other way of taking the moon magic but regrettably there isn't. Sometimes, Clip, to be part of a community one has to make sacrifices and this is Sylvie's sacrifice in return for all that we give her. At the moment she's the only one we know of with this ability to channel the moon's energy. Sadly it takes some of her own energy to do it but she does recover fully, and I think she overdoes the suffering just a little, don't you? It can't hurt that much surely. I think there's something of the teenage martyr about her and she enjoys wallowing in it. She needs to toughen up a bit, don't you agree? And it's not as if she gives anything else back to Stonewylde after all. Here, have another cake.'

'Well, possibly. But her distress on the rock is genuine.'

'Oh no doubt it's a little uncomfortable for her, but this time we'll lie her down after a while so it's not such a strain and more of her body will be in contact with the stone. She can even sleep if she wants and she'll barely notice it then. Are you happy with that?'

'Alright, alright, you've persuaded me, just like you always do,' laughed Clip, his pupils dilated. He waved his hands expansively. 'Just don't be cruel, will you? I hate it when you're cruel, Sol, and you so often are.'

'I think the cakes have affected you, Clip,' said Magus smoothly, his eyes gleaming. 'I'm not cruel at all.'

'Come on Sol, I've known you all your life, remember? I understand what you're capable of, and it's why I have to leave sometimes. I can't cope being around you for long – you're too demanding, too overwhelming. In fact, I might as well tell you this now – I've decided to leave Stonewylde after the Winter Solstice so you'll need to find someone else to help you out with the ceremonies and things.'

'I expect I'll manage until you come back – I usually do.'

'No, you don't understand. I'm planning an extended stay in the Outside World this time, not just a quick trip.'

Magus looked hard at him.

'This is a very bad time for you to be away for a long period, Clip. There's so much going on and I need you – we agreed this.'

Clip closed his eyes, blotting out his brother's handsome face and the ruthless eyes that bored into him so relentlessly.

'No we didn't! You know how I get when I'm trapped in one place for too long, Sol – I need to get away. That's why I handed everything over to you in the first place. I don't want the pressure and responsibility of Stonewylde. You can't make me stay! You know I can't take it.'

His voice had started to crack. He'd only found the courage to stand up to his brother because of the cakes, and even their effect was limited. Magus watched him carefully, eyes narrowed, gauging how far he could push.

'Don't get upset, Clip,' he said soothingly, his voice soft. 'I'm sorry – don't even think about it now. We'll talk another time. It's just that with all my plans for expansion there're going to be some big changes at Stonewylde in the New Year, and you're so good at getting difficult people to comply with my wishes.'

He sighed, gazing through the window at the huddle of gardeners still raking up the endless fallen leaves on the misty, dew-soaked lawns.

'I don't know, Clip, I do my best for these people and sometimes I wonder if it's all worth it. I've such dreams for Stonewylde, but does anyone appreciate my efforts? I'm going to build another school to accommodate all the children, and more cottages in the Village, larger ones for the bigger families. Do you know the average Villager family now has seven children, and that's risen every year?'

'Maybe you should encourage more birth control,' said Clip glumly, toying with another cake.

'Oh no, on the contrary – I've been urging the women to produce more children,' said Magus. 'There are some really large families now and that's what I want. We need more labour and skilled craftspeople for the future if Stonewylde's to expand, and we've plenty of food to feed the extra mouths. No, I want lots more Village children and I shall be offering lovely new cottages with loads of space and extra amenities as an incentive to women to keep on having more babies. They're all so healthy and fertile, and just imagine how rapidly our community will expand when this new generation starts to reproduce! We'll have to do something about the gene pool then, but I've some good ideas about how to bring in fresh stock.'

'We'll be over-run with Villagers,' murmured Clip, rolling his eyes.

'Not over-run – supported by their labour and skills. And I intend to build a complex of holiday homes up here for Hallfolk so we can get all of them to stay more frequently. We need to keep their money pouring into the coffers and holiday homes will generate excellent revenue. The wind farm will have to be expanded to cope with the extra power needed. And then there's the quarry – I really need that stone. Jackdaw proved to be an excellent site manager back in the summer and got so much work out of those men before that damn accident. I'm planning to re-open the quarry properly next year, with experienced workers this time. So you can see just how much I've got on my plate and that's why I really need your support. You're my right-hand man, Clip. There's no one else – please don't leave Stonewylde.'

Clip gazed helplessly at his younger brother, so vibrant and determined. He felt worn out and frail just looking at him and knew that he must stick to his plan or Magus would talk him round, as he always did. But it was so difficult to stand up to him and go against his wishes; Magus commanded obedience.

'You don't get it, Sol. I hate all that. I just want to live in a simple hut in the hills and devote my life to my calling. I'm a shaman not a businessman. All this empire-building stuff – I hate it, so please don't look to me to get involved. You need to find someone who shares your passion and who'll want to help build it all up – that's certainly not me. And obviously I won't be having children either, so it's up to you to pass it all on. I know you were considering Buzz; that must've been a disappointment to lose him.'

Magus' face darkened.

'Buzzard was a complete waste of time. He'd no backbone at all, the snivelling wretch, and he cared nothing for Stonewylde. I'm better off without him.'

'Are there really no others? I know you abstained from procreating for years, although you've two on the way now, haven't you?

Magus shook his head.

'There's nobody. After Buzz, I . . . well, I decided to wait a few years. It would've been tempting to father children all over the place of course, but that would've been irresponsible and a genetic nightmare too. I just hope that either Rowan or Miranda's baby proves to be a worthy heir, although I probably won't stop there. But that's all years away – they're not even born yet.'

Clip sat up suddenly, his face brightening.

'Of course!' he said excitedly. 'Why didn't we think of this before? I always forget about him, but what about the Village boy Yul? They don't come much tougher than him and he seems bright and intelligent, from what I've noticed. There's something special about him, something steely there. I know he hasn't been brought up as a Hallchild, but—'

Magus glared at Clip, his black eyes glittering.

'Yul? Why mention him of all people?'

'Because he's yours, isn't he? I remember he—'

'You're mistaken, Clip – he's not my son.'

'Come off it, Sol, of course he is! It's obvious! I know he's as dark-haired as his mother, but in all other ways—'

'I repeat: Yul is *not* my son. I've been through this with you before and he can't be my son, so just leave it, Clip. We *don't* talk about this.'

'But you *know* he's yours! Your grand passion with his mother all those years ago, not long after you'd taken over here – your lovely little dark-haired Maizie, with her pretty grey eyes and joie de vivre. I remember it so well. That Moon Fullness – it was a Blue Moon too! You took her up to Mooncliffe and the stone and you couldn't stop talking about it the next day, in far too much detail as I recall. What a night for her first time! It was that spectacular Blue Moon – you *must* remember it! The moon had the most enormous moon-bow arched around it, absolutely huge and glowing – remember? And everyone was saying it was a special sign from the Triple Goddess in her blue robes, and you and Maizie—'

'Nothing came of that union,' said Magus in a dangerous voice. 'Maizie did *not* conceive that night.'

'Of course she did – she had Yul!'

'Oh for Goddess' sake, she *didn't* conceive that night! She couldn't have because she was already pregnant.'

'Already pregnant? But you know that's not true! She was a very popular girl, being so pretty, but you were the only one she had eyes for. That night was her initiation, *you* told me so. She was mad about you and you were pretty keen on her too, I recall. She'd only just reached adulthood and she'd been with no one else. She couldn't possibly have conceived before that Moon Fullness.'

Magus regarded him coldly.

'You're completely wrong, confused. She was very popular, as you say – I hadn't appreciated just how popular. And Alwyn was always in the picture, sniffing around her and trying to muscle in. Maizie lied to me – Alwyn had her first. I thought at the time that I was her first, but in fact she was already pregnant with his child when we made love during that Blue Moon. She must've been; Yul was born eight months later. *Eight* months, not nine, at the Winter Solstice. He was born on the Solstice itself.'

'Oh yes! It was so long ago but it's coming back to me now! It was a full moon that Solstice too, and a total eclipse at that. A blood-red moon, so dark, and the owls calling and calling, all that wild noise echoing around the Circle. Remember, Sol?'

Magus shook his head, refusing to look his brother in the eye. Clip continued excitedly, cake crumbs flying as he gesticulated.

'It was very potent magic – solstice, full moon and total eclipse all in conjunction. An auspicious time for a baby to be born, especially in the middle of the ceremony with the Earth Magic at its most powerful. I remember Maizie giving birth in the Circle right up by the Altar Stone. *Blue and red, blue and red*, Mother Heggy kept screeching it out like a mantra, with poor Maizie squatting on the ground groaning and pushing. Her labour lasted only as long as it took the moon to be completely shadowed. *The blue moon and the red moon – conceived under the one and born under the other.* Out came the baby and Old Heggy held that tiny boy up to the eclipsed moon, and said that one day when your son reached adulthood, he would—'

'WILL YOU SHUT UP!'

Magus' face had turned white and he sprang up from the sofa, his hands trembling as he raked them through his hair.

'*We don't talk about that!*' he shouted. 'I told you years ago to *never* mention it! It's all rubbish anyway, just a crazy old biddy's rantings that no one ever believed for a moment. Enough, Clip! Yul is *not* my son, he's Alwyn's! Maizie was pregnant before I had her and Yul was *not* conceived under that Blue Moon. Heggy's mad, her insane prophecies are pure nonsense, and Yul's just a stupid, ill-bred Village boy. He's no threat to me; never has been and never will be!'

Clip regarded Magus warily, shocked by his reaction. He'd never seen his brother quite so shaken.

'If you don't believe the prophecy, Sol, then why are you so scared? Why do you hate the boy so much if he's nothing more than an ordinary Villager?'

Magus glared at him and sat down again, taking a deep breath.

'I'm not scared! But I've had enough of Yul's bad behaviour, his defiance and disobedience. He's got above himself in the past few months and he's over-stepped the mark once too often. I intend to finish him off before he reaches adulthood.'

'Finish him off? What ... *kill* him? Surely even *you* wouldn't go that far!'

'No, not kill him – don't be ridiculous! I don't go around killing members of my community.'

'And you couldn't even if you wanted to, could you, Sol?' said

Clip slyly. 'Now I remember! Mother Heggy put a binding spell on you that night.'

'ENOUGH!' snarled Magus, his face once again dangerously pale and pinched. 'I don't—'

'If you killed Yul before he reached adulthood, the Dark Angel would take you too!' Clip continued gleefully, enjoying this rare opportunity to gain the upper hand over his brother. 'Even if you organised his death indirectly, you'd die yourself, and—'

He stopped abruptly as Magus snatched up one of the empty coffee cups and smashed it down full force on the table. Magus looked nearly as shocked as Clip at this unexpected act of violence. His dark eyes locked into Clip's pale ones in a look almost of supplication as he tried to bring his ragged breathing under control. His hand trembled as he began to carefully gather together the shattered pieces of bone china that now lay all over the coffee table and carpet.

'What I meant, Clip,' he said shakily, 'is that I'm going to crush the boy completely. There's no place at Stonewylde for someone who defies me the way he does. I am the magus and if he can't accept my absolute authority, his days here are numbered. I'll take pleasure in subduing him once and for all, or banishing him forever.'

'Surely,' said Clip quiet and sober now 'rather than trying to destroy him, it'd be better to have him on your side? Heggy may be wrong. Her prophecy may never happen. If you had Yul as your ally, working by your side, maybe none of it will happen as she predicted. Maybe, when he reaches sixteen, he won't rise up against you. Think about it, brother.'

'I have,' said Magus shortly. 'I've thought about it a great deal. There's something about Yul ... some dark flame burning in him that I have to snuff out. He and I could never work together and I will never, ever let him become magus after me. Consequences or not, I'd see him dead first.'

Sylvie was scared. Restricted to her bed, she could think of nothing but the approaching full moon and almost wished she were still under Clip's hypnosis and living in blissful ignorance. She was virtually a prisoner since Magus had locked the outside door leading to the garden, and her mother never seemed to leave the sitting room, through which she'd have to pass to leave their rooms. She deeply resented having to stay in bed when there was nothing wrong with her. She wasn't sick or weak; she felt absolutely fine and had already lost far too much of her life to the sick bed to accept this enforced and unnecessary bed-rest now. The moondancing at Hare Stone had restored her fully and she teemed with the dark red energy of the Harvest Moon, feeling stronger than ever. Lying in bed all day, even with books to read and studying to do, was driving her mad. And the food! Magus had trays of it sent up every meal time and she was expected to eat it all, but had no opportunity to work up an appetite.

Her mother was driving her crazy with her blind adherence to Magus's instructions, constantly repeating how they must both do what he wanted and keep him happy. The worst of it was that Sylvie suspected her mother would act like this even without the hypnosis. She seemed to have lost every last shred of her former independence and objectivity. Sylvie was becoming increasingly anxious to see Yul and plan how to escape on the night of the Moon Fullness, which loomed ever closer.

Yul was frantic with frustration too. He plied Harold with questions and was told that Sylvie was kept locked in her room with all her meals sent up. It explained why he hadn't seen her out and about, despite having hung around at every opportunity in all the places he might find her. He visited Mother Heggy, desperately hoping that she'd be able to help again. He was disappointed.

'This Hunter's Moon he'll take her to the stone and there's nought I can do.'

'But why can't you stop him again? It worked so well last time.'

She wheezed at him, pouring him a mug of some concoction.

'Sit down, boy, and stop fidgeting. Drink this – no, 'tis just a drink. You've grown, Yul, did I tell you that? A young man now, as the Solstice comes closer. 'Tis as well, for you'll need a man's qualities soon enough.'

She sat rocking back and forth, peering at him fondly as he downed the drink impatiently. The crow hopped along the table, pecking at scraps of meat with its black beak whilst a battered black cat crouched under the table twitching its tail.

'Please, Mother Heggy, you *must* help! Sylvie can't go up there again.'

'If there were a way clear, I'd follow it. Do you think I want her to suffer? But 'tis not yet time for the conflict, and till that day comes, he still rules and he still gets what he wants. Bide your time, boy, and have faith.'

'But Mother Heggy, it's dangerous!'

'Aye, true enough, but she's strong now. 'Tis why I made sure she had the Harvest Moon at Hare Stone. With that red magic in her she'll be strong enough for the Hunter. She can take it.'

He leapt up and banged the table hard with his fist, making the crow flutter aside and the cat growl.

'I don't *want* her to take it!' he shouted, his face dark with anger. 'I can't bear her to go through that again! If you could see how she suffers . . .'

Mother Heggy nodded her wizened head, rocking fast in the creaking chair.

'I have seen. Not your bright one, but my Raven, my poor little girl – I saw how she suffered. Every moon, every single moon, she were up there for years and years. I watched her getting weaker as first one man, then another fed off her magic, bled her dry. All that life draining from her, month after month. So don't you think I don't know! I know better than any what snake-stone does to a moongazy girl.'

'But couldn't you have stopped it? You were powerful, Mother Heggy, you were the Wise Woman with magic at your call. Why didn't you stop it?'

She laughed harshly at this and pulled her shawl closely around her withered body, her eyes faraway.

'Do you think I didn't try? Do you think I stood by while they took my little one away? Of course I fought them! 'Twas not so bad with the first one, with Basil. He were softer and he cared for her in his own selfish way, despite the forcing. He only wanted to lie with her at the Moon Fullness, and at first he took her into the woods or down to the river under the willows. But after the baby was born he came across the secret of the snake-stone at Mooncliffe and there was no stopping him then.'

'Couldn't you have hidden her away somewhere?'

'Aye, I did everything I could to hide her, but then he captured her, kept my Raven in the tower at the Hall so's I couldn't see her. Locked my girl away when she had to roam wild and free. 'Twould kill her to be in captivity so I got her out, one Dark Moon. I cast my circle and I got her out. But then the other one, Elm, he found out the secret too. He saw what went on at Mooncliffe and the magic my girl could draw down to that stone. He saw it one Moon Fullness, and Basil were dead within the month.'

Yul stared at her in astonishment.

'You mean Magus' father, Elm, he killed Clip's father?'

She shrugged, plucking at the frayed shawl with bony claws as she rocked.

'I saw nothing. But one moon Elm discovered the secret of the rock, the snake within that feeds and holds the magic deep in its coils. By the next moon Basil were dead, fallen sick and wasted to death in his bed. There were dark magic afoot there, and not my magic either. Somebody else's hand, somebody who bore a grudge and wanted Basil dead. 'Twas the Destroying Angel as finished him, and I know who brought *her* to the feast. There was only one other with knowledge enough.'

'You mean he was poisoned by mushrooms – the Destroying Angel mushrooms? Does Clip know?'

'He were only a babe-in-arms at the time. If anyone knew then they kept their silence. Elm was not to be crossed, and once he had the power of the moon magic in him too there were no stopping him. He took the mantle of magus and he took my

Raven too, every moon, up on that rock. He were an evil man much like this one now, cruel and hard and only looking out for himself, never for others. Wanting everyone to worship and obey him and destroying anyone who defied him. This one now, he hides it better. He can make people believe he's a good master, however black and deadly his heart is underneath. But Elm – if he wanted something, he took it without planning and scheming as this one does. He knew I had some power and would stop him if I could, for he were far crueller to my girl than his brother afore him, rough and violent with her and I couldn't bear her to be hurt. So he made a pact with me. If I let him bring Raven to Mooncliffe every Moon Fullness so he could take his fill, he'd let me keep her here all the other days of the month.'

'But I still don't see why you didn't hex him, like you did my father at the Summer Solstice.'

The crow hopped from the table onto the chair-back and the old woman turned to whisper to him. He dropped onto her lap and hunched there, staring at Yul with his beady eyes.

'I told you he were clever, that Elm. He had these papers writ and they were kept in the Outside World, locked away somewhere safe. Should anything happen to him – anything at all – the papers would be read. They told of Raven, of her moongaziness, but they twisted it. He read them to me so I knew. They spoke of her strangeness at the rising of the moon, of how she were wild and magical, but they made her sound a danger to folk. They said she were a madwoman, and Elm said that men would come from the Outside World, if they read them papers, and take my Raven from Stonewylde. They'd lock her away in the Outside World and she'd never be free again. So I could do nought for fear o' them papers. 'Twas like a binding spell – he had all the power and my magic was as nought.'

Yul shook his head. It was just the sort of thing Magus would do – clever and cruel.

'I'm sorry, Mother Heggy. I didn't realise.'

'Aye, history repeats and the wheel turns. I know well how you feel, my Yul. You want only to protect her from his evil, but

Sylvie will survive this. He forces her to feed the snakes in the rock but nought else – it could be far worse.'

'I was worried because I heard that Raven died up at Mooncliffe, and I thought . . .'

Mother Heggy nodded, her eyes gazing unseeing at the fireplace.

'Aye, she died there, 'tis true. 'Twas an eclipse and the moon magic is strange at times such as that. Different, more powerful, yet tainted and dark. Well, she lay on the rock as always, the moon was high and he'd done with her. I came up the path for her, same as every month, for she were too weak to walk alone after he'd taken his fill. Then the eclipse began, and the bright moon grew darker and darker as the jaw moved across, devouring it. My Raven started to groan with the pain of it. I tried to reach her, to pull her off the rock where the snake drank so greedily of this new dark magic, but the evil one held me back. He wouldn't let me near her – he said he wanted to see her moongaziness under the eclipse. She moaned and she cried, like a hawk riding the winds she sounded, high and keen. But then, when the Bright Lady was all dark, all devoured, the crying stopped. My girl had gone.'

Her shrivelled hands caressed the crow in her lap and she sighed heavily, the breath rattling in her old lungs.

'After a while he prodded her and saw she were dead. He cursed and cursed, ranting and raving, calling at the dark powers with every foul name, howling at the blood-red moon. He dragged her poor little body off the rock and threw her at me. I had to get her down from there, carry her all the way down the cliff path on my own.'

'Mother Heggy, that's awful. I'm so sorry.'

She got up and poked at the fire fiercely.

'Aye, well, 'twas a long time ago and he got his justice in the end. And 'twas as well she passed on when she did, for her life was nought, just a vessel to be used by him for his greed. I hated that man, just as I hate this magus. They have the same lust in them, the same desire for power. I see it clear in this one and he'll get worse, just like his father did afore him. That power, that stolen moon magic, is a canker. 'Twill eat into his soul and turn him bad, like a maggot in an apple, spoiling and rotting him. So, my Yul, never believe I don't want to help. When the time comes, I'll fight for you as I've done before. Every last drop of my magic will be yours when you need it. But 'tis not yet time and I know the bright one can take this, though it hurts her. She'll survive the Hunter's Moon – Raven survived years of it.'

Yul stood up and the crow fluttered from her lap onto his shoulder, pecking at his ear.

'Alright then,' he said sadly. 'I'll have to accept it, unless I can think of a plan.'

'No! You mustn't force a battle yet! No plan, Yul – the time isn't right and the wheel hasn't yet turned full circle.'

'But *when* will it be time? How much longer do I have to wait before I can destroy him? I feel strange at times, Mother Heggy, I feel this great need in me, this stirring of power and knowledge growing inside. There are things I must do and Stonewylde calls me to do them. I feel it at the Altar Stone when the green magic comes, but I feel it at other places too, in the woods, on the Village Green, at Hare Stone, by the river – everywhere! I feel Stonewylde calling to me. It must sound strange, but I know that I'm here to guard and protect Stonewylde and Magus isn't. He's forgotten what being the magus means. He thinks only of his own power and glory, not what Stonewylde and the folk need, and not what the Earth Mother wants of him. That's why she no longer gives him her Earth Magic. When will his rule end, Mother Heggy?'

'The Winter Solstice, my boy, that's when. *Under blue and red, the fruit of his passion will rise up against him with the folk behind, at the time of brightness in darkness in the place of bones and death.* Be patient, Yul, and bide your time for 'tis almost come and some of us have waited long for this. Remember what I told you. If we do it right, if we can keep on the path, those who stand against you will fall, one by one.'

20

Sylvie stood in her room looking through the window. It was late afternoon and the sun was sinking low. As the afternoon had worn on she'd gradually realised, with a certainty that grew deeper by the hour, that this month there'd be no escape. Despair gripped her and she knew that it would soon be time. She felt jittery and jumpy as usual, but over-riding it was her terror of what would happen to her tonight. Miranda had made her bathe and change into the silver dress, which she now loathed. Her bare arms and legs felt cold and she pulled a cover from her bed to wrap around herself. She trembled with fear, hoping, wishing and praying that Yul would somehow manage to stop this from happening, with or without Mother Heggy's help. She knew that if it were humanly possible he'd save her. She knew how he loved her.

She heard them coming through the sitting room, the men's voices seeming loud after the silence. Her heart thumped in her chest and her stomach clenched with dread. They came into her bedroom without knocking. Sylvie caught a glimpse of her mother's face in the doorway smiling anxiously. Magus was brusque and business-like, glancing peremptorily at her. He took her arm and led her towards the arched door, tossing the bedcover onto the floor. Clip picked it up.

'She'll need this, won't she? It'll be cold up there.'

They both wore warm clothing, she noticed.

'Yes, alright, but let's get on with it. I've got the key.'

'Goodbye!' called Miranda. 'Have a nice time!'

When they reached the cliff path Sylvie started to climb but Magus stopped her. Neither he nor Clip had spoken to her; it was as if she didn't exist as herself, only as a means for providing them with what they wanted. Magus picked her up, shifting her in his arms. She had to lie passively, despite her terror and rising moongaziness, pretending to be docile and still under the spell. She felt his hands gripping her and she laid her head against his chest, breathing in his scent. She forced herself to relax; her body screamed to escape.

'Good,' said Magus, 'she's put on some weight. She feels heavier than last time thanks to Miranda feeding her up. Does that make you feel better, Clip? She'll be stronger now and it won't matter so much if she doesn't eat for a few days afterwards.'

'Yes, I suppose so. She became so thin last time it worried me.'

'Well don't be worried. And remember what I said before – I think there's a certain amount of attention-seeking and malingering going on, and she'll just have to learn to cope with it. She'll be doing this every twenty-nine days for the foreseeable future and she'd better get used to it.'

Magus shifted her in his arms and she felt like a sack of grain, especially when he cursed and then slung her over his shoulders in a fire-fighter's lift. Her arms and long hair dangled down his back, while his shoulder pressed into her stomach. Sylvie started to cry silently at this added indignity. Seagulls wheeled and cried overhead as they reached the cliff-top, and she saw that the sun was close to setting in the watery sky. There was some broken cloud and a light breeze blew up from the sea, making it feel chilly. The strange glittering rock, placed so unnaturally on the grass, was like a massive round table standing empty, waiting. Sylvie knew, with a clutch of fear, that she was the feast.

Magus put her down, righting her as she nearly overbalanced. She started to tremble, partly from the cold but also with fear. She had a strong feeling of unreality, not helped by her natural tension and jumpiness this close to moonrise. Could this really be happening to her? Would it be as bad as Yul had made out? Clip came over and looked into her face, smiling hesitantly.

'I love to dance at Mooncliffe,' she said, for good measure.

'And so you shall, Sylvie,' he said, patting her arm kindly. 'Here, let's wrap you up whilst we wait for the moon.'

He carefully draped the cover around her, although her bare legs and feet were still cold. Magus was over at the wooden chest fiddling around with a padlock. Next to it lay a new chest, also padlocked.

'Come and give me a hand, Clip,' he called. 'I want to shift all these eggs up to the rock so they're ready to load on her. Then we can put them straight back into the chest as soon as she's charged them.'

'But there are more here, Sol, a whole new crate of them! What have you done? She barely managed the first lot and she'll never cope with all these extra stones as well.'

'We'll see how it goes – we've got nothing to lose. And look, the new ones are much smaller so they won't take as long. Did I tell you I've got some people interested in buying them? The smaller ones are to sell and I'll keep the larger ones for our own use. I thought that when she can't stand upright any more, we'll lay a load of these smaller ones on top of her rather than having her hold just two at a time. I don't know if it'll work, but we can try. Remember I said we're going to stay up for a bit longer tonight.'

'No, Sol! I didn't agree to that! You promised you wouldn't be cruel tonight. You promised! I only agreed to come on that basis.'

'Oh for Goddess' sake, stop whinging. Look what I brought up here earlier, to keep us going. A couple of bottles of the strong brew mead and a tin of your favourite cakes with their special new ingredient. We'll celebrate the Moon Fullness in style tonight.'

Sylvie stood in the slight breeze with her hair blowing around her whilst they shifted all the stone eggs to form a circle around the edge of the rock. It seemed to take forever as they shuttled backwards and forwards, Clip muttering objections half-heartedly but without the will to protest further. She shook with cold and fear, not sure how she should be behaving if under hypnosis, but feeling that familiar rising within her as darkness began to fall. Finally the two men stood ready, and all three of them stared out to sea, waiting.

I can't dance the magic into Stonewylde in this terrible place of suffering! The snake awaits, greedy and sparkling, and I can't do it!

Yul, hidden in the bracken, was also shaking although not from cold. He couldn't bear to see her shivering in the thin dress and barely covered by the blanket, silently waiting for her ordeal to begin. He knew that this time she was aware of what was happening to her. Several times, when they'd had their backs to her, she'd looked around desperately as if for a means of escape. He hadn't dared make himself visible to her in case they gave themselves away. The worse thing was that he didn't even have a plan of action. Despite Mother Heggy's warning he was still hoping some opportunity would present itself so he could rescue her. But time was running out and it didn't seem there was any chance now.

He noticed the little signs in Sylvie that the moonrise was imminent. She fidgeted, going up on her tiptoes, and then her arms started to rise. On the horizon he saw the rim of the moon, half buried in the cloud. The covers slipped off as her arms rose into wings. Magus noticed and grasped hold of her.

'Here we go, Clip! Take the other side – we'll lift her up like this.'

They manhandled her towards the stone but she began to struggle, thrashing around and screaming.

'What the hell's happening?' bellowed Magus. 'I thought she was still under hypnosis? Quick, grab her and get her up there!'

'Sylvie, Sylvie, you're at Mooncliffe!' said Clip. 'You love to dance here.'

'No!' she screamed, kicking and struggling. 'I hate it! You've no right to do this to me! Let me go!'

Unsure what to do, Yul stood up in the dead bracken with his fists clenched, and took a step towards them. Sylvie flailed and almost broke free, until Magus grabbed her roughly with one hand and slapped her around the face with the other. Her head snapped sharply to the side and Yul jumped out of the bracken with a roar of rage and raced up onto the cliff top.

'What the hell is *he* doing here?' yelled Magus, still trying to get a good grip on Sylvie. She fought and kicked as he struggled to lift her up onto the rock. 'For Goddess' sake, keep still you stupid bloody girl or I'll *really* hurt you!'

'*Don't you dare touch her, you bastard!*' Yul screamed, leaping onto them and trying to wrench Sylvie away. Magus shoved him back and then in one quick, violent motion swung Sylvie off her feet and threw her sprawling onto the rock. She landed with a sharp cry, her body convulsing. In the near darkness she began to glow with silver threads of light. Yul was up on his feet again trying to scramble onto the rock to reach her. Magus punched him hard, catching him in the shoulder, and yelled at Clip who stood there uncertainly.

'Clip, get up on the rock now and stand her up in the centre! Quick! The power isn't flowing properly while she's lying there like that.'

Clip leapt onto it and took hold of her, but dropped her again instantly.

'Sacred Mother!' he screeched. 'I can't touch her! It's like an electric shock!'

'Come and hold him, then. Don't let him go!'

Magus jumped onto the rock and grabbed Sylvie, his face contorting with pain as he touched her. He yanked her upright and pushed her into the centre so she faced the rising moon, every bone in her body jolting and jerking. Her face was twisted in agony and her curtain of hair rippled violently.

'Let her go!' roared Yul, wrenching himself free of Clip's hold. He dodged to one side trying to get round Clip and onto the stone, but Magus dived at him and knocked him hard to the ground. For all he'd grown, Yul was still young and slim while Magus was a tall, powerfully-built man. There was no competition and within seconds Yul was lying face down in the grass, one arm twisted viciously up behind him, while Magus' knee pressed hard into the small of his back. Yul choked and gasped where he'd been winded.

'Keep still, you bloody peasant, or I'll break your arm!' hissed Magus, giving it a wrench for good measure. Yul cried out in agony and tried not to move. He felt Magus relax, the weight increasing on his back.

'Everything's alright now, Clip,' he called. 'She'll be up there for a good hour or more until we start to load her with stones. All we have to do now is deal with this damn nuisance and then we can crack open the mead. Didn't I say that he was trouble? Can you see now why I have to put an end to his rebellious behaviour?'

'What's he doing up here anyway?' asked Clip, wandering over to stare down at Yul.

'Come to rescue her no doubt,' Magus sneered. 'I've warned you before, Yul, to stay away from this girl but you just won't be told, will you? This time you really will pay for it.'

'Please!' gasped Yul, his face squashed into the grass and his lungs compressed by Magus' weight. 'Please just let her go. It hurts her up on that rock.'

Magus only laughed.

'Clip, there's a piece of rope in the new chest, I believe, from when it was dragged up here. Bring it over, will you?'

He proceeded to bind Yul's wrists tightly together behind his back, and then hauled him upright into a sitting position facing the rock. He looped the end of the rope through one of the iron rings set into the ground and fastened it securely.

'There!' he said. 'You're not going anywhere in a hurry and neither's she, not for a long, long time. Feast your eyes on my moongazy girl, Yul, if you're so keen. Look at her – she's even dancing for you.'

Yul let out a cry of rage at this.

'I *hate* you, you bastard! I'm going to kill you!'

Magus turned and with a vicious side swipe that Yul remembered well from his days in the byre, knocked him sideways to the ground. The side of his face was now agony, his lip bleeding freely. Magus yanked him upright to face Sylvie again.

'Not if I kill you first!' he spat.

An hour later, Magus and Clip had drunk much of the strong mead and Clip had eaten a few cakes. He lay on the grass on his back with his feet against the rock, humming softly to himself. Magus had climbed onto the rock and lay there soaking up the moon energy. Sylvie's terrible convulsions had quietened into tremors, and the silver light still crawled all over her arms and legs. Yul had been silent since Magus' brutal blow, fully appreciating his vulnerable position. It wasn't in his or Sylvie's interests to goad Magus into a rage, but Yul imagined how cold she must be now and couldn't let her freeze.

'Would you put the blanket around her please?' he asked quietly, hoping Magus would take pity on her. Magus raised his head from the rock and glared at him, his face clearly visible in the silver light.

'Aah, how touching, such sweet concern. Shut up, Yul!'

But Clip must have heard for he staggered to his feet and found the cover lying on the ground. He managed, after a few clumsy attempts, to climb up onto the rock and drape it around her shoulders. He could barely stand and almost fell against Sylvie.

'That'd better not interfere with the energy,' muttered Magus.

'No, look, it's still going into the rock,' mumbled Clip. 'Think I'll join you now it's calmer up here. What've you put in those cakes, Sol? They're so powerful! Sacred Mother, that's a good combination – cakes and moon energy. I can feel myself going . . .'

Magus sat up and reaching across, picked up two of the larger stone eggs. He placed them in Sylvie's unresponsive hands and lay back down again with a groan. Yul sat silently, anger seething through his body but mingled with sharp sadness. He'd let her down. She'd trusted him to rescue her and had stood there waiting, not trying to escape because she'd had faith in him. He'd failed her and he welcomed the pain in the side of his face where Magus had hit him; he deserved it. He hung his head and cried silently.

Magus continued to change the eggs at intervals once they were glowing, putting the charged ones back into the chests. Later, on his way across the grass with a pair of them he stumbled, kicking the forgotten tin of cakes still lying there. He came back to where Yul sat mutely in his own private hell and crouched down, grasping Yul's chin roughly and forcing the boy to look up into his eyes. They glittered coldly in the harsh, silver light. The strong mead had done nothing to mellow him; if anything he seemed possessed by a strange wildness, markedly different to his usual tight control. Yul sensed the icy quicksilver slithering inside him, not sparkling and magical like Sylvie's, but cruel and sharp as venom. Yul quaked with fear, for he knew only too well where this man's sadism could lead. But he met his gaze squarely, trying not to show any weakness.

'How are we doing, my lad? Still angry? Upset?' He chuckled. 'You really should've learnt not to defy me by now, Yul. You just don't seem to learn the lesson, do you? When we've finished up here tonight, I shall have to start all over again teaching you how to behave, just like I did before. This time I won't have your dear father to help show you the error of your ways which is a shame, because he took such pleasure in it. But never mind, I've someone else almost as good. In fact, better in many respects. You remember our friend Jackdaw?'

'Yes, sir.'

'Of course you do! How could anyone forget our Jackdaw? He'll enjoy correcting your behaviour, especially if I give him free rein. He has a much wider and more sophisticated repertoire than your father and maybe the two of us together will succeed in bringing you to heel. Or we might finish you off altogether.'

Yul's heart sank. It was two months until the Winter Solstice. Would he survive long enough to overcome this man? He closed his eyes, blotting out Magus' cruel face, and heard him chuckle again. This time there was a manic edge to the sound that made Yul's skin crawl with terror.

'You won't get rid of me like that. In fact you won't get rid of me at all, you bloody upstart! Who the hell are *you* to stop me taking what I need? I've just had such a good idea, in view of your attempts tonight to interfere with my moon magic and once again set yourself against me.'

He reached across and pulled over the tin, holding up one of the small cakes. It looked like an innocent fairy cake speckled with herbs and spices but Yul had seen what the cakes had done to Clip. Magus' face gleamed like white stone, the shadows deep in the hollows of his cheekbones and eye-sockets. He smiled and the moonlight transformed it to a snarl, glinting off his teeth. Suddenly he seemed demonic in his gleeful excitement.

'A little treat for you, Master Yul! You're probably feeling hungry, aren't you? I don't expect you ate tonight before coming to rescue your maiden in distress, and you don't know when you'll eat again, once I get you back into the byre. Remember last time? Five days of starvation, wasn't it? Well, wasn't it, boy?'

'Yes,' croaked Yul, his heart lurching with dread. Magus settled down more comfortably on the grass opposite him, the tin of cakes in his lap. He took a long swig of mead and corked the bottle carefully.

'We can't have you going hungry, not yet anyway. So I shall feed you, Yul, with Old Violet's very special cakes. You can join my brother on his spiritual journey. But let's hope you manage to return, for they say that when the soul wanders too far it can't always find the way back again. And that wouldn't be my fault – I'm only feeding you after all. Open wide, Yul.'

Yul shook his head and kept his lips clamped shut. Magus scowled at him, cake in hand.

'Open up *now*!'

He grasped Yul's jaw in his free hand and squeezed his cheeks to open his mouth. Yul tried to struggle as Magus jammed the cake hard into his mouth, banging his teeth.

'Swallow it! I SAID SWALLOW IT!'

Yul spat the cake into Magus' face and was rewarded with another violent back-handed blow, knocking him to the ground again. Magus reached over and hauled him upright, breathing heavily and wiping the crumbs from his face in disgust. He grabbed a handful of Yul's curls and wrenched his head backwards, leaning in close and snarling into his face. In the silver moonlight, Yul saw the writhing fury and hatred behind those black eyes.

'That was a stupid thing to do. Now I'll have to feed you even more. So let's start again. I'll put this delicious little cake in your mouth, you'll chew and then swallow it. Then I'll give you another one, and so on, and we'll continue until I decide you've had enough. If you don't obey me, I'll take that blanket off Sylvie. If you still won't obey me, I'll take her dress off too, and she'll get very cold indeed standing up there naked. So, will you co-operate now?'

Yul nodded, a sob of frustration and fury escaping his lips.

'Good!' chuckled Magus. 'I thought you might. Now open wide.'

Yul swallowed the first cake, and then another, and another in quick succession. He started to choke on the dry crumbs. Magus held the bottle of mead to his lips and forced him to drink deeply of the strong brew. His eyes were merciless and Yul saw that strange vicious light again. As he poured the mead down Yul's throat, watching him struggle to swallow it, Magus threw back his head and laughed. Then he fed him more cakes, far too many, cramming them relentlessly into his mouth one after the other and washing them down with mead with an unpleasant solicitousness.

'Swallow!' he cried encouragingly. 'Well done! And one more! You can take one more, I know you can.'

His breathing was heavy with excitement, and Yul whimpered at the sensations in his stomach. Everything started to tilt as the burning pain spread inside him. Magus knelt over him, another cake ready in his hand. Yul groaned pitifully and tried to pull away.

'Please!' he gasped. 'Please ... no more.'

Magus sat back on his haunches. As Yul raised his agonised eyes he sensed a shadow standing beyond. The shadow was unnaturally black; much blacker than the night around it. Magus seemed to sense something too for he glanced around and then flung the final cake away.

'No more cakes, then!' he gabbled. 'I've fed you well so no more, you greedy boy. I don't want to make you sick. How many did you eat?'

Yul had lost count and was beyond caring anyway. The dark shadow had faded as quickly as it had appeared and only Magus remained, silver and black. The night became very strange. Yul was aware of laughter, loud and harsh, which came and went in his head. It smashed over him in pounding waves, drenching him with mirth and madness.

Magus, the man with silver hair and black eyes, stood up like a great monolith. He moved back and forth, back and forth so many times, carrying glowing eggs in his hands. Yul knew they came from a magical creature who cried, who begged to be allowed to stop. He could hear her calling and crying, her bird-song so sad, and he wished he could help her. She was a strange creature with silver feathers covered in moons and stars. She continued to call and cry into the empty night while the Magus cat just laughed and purred.

He saw the coiled, glittering snake glowing with pleasure inside the massive moon stone. The snake had been well fed by the magical bird-girl and was now fat and satiated. It lay in sparkling ecstasy, pulsating with pleasure at feeling so full and satisfied. The beautiful creature still cried, sobbing piteously now, begging to be released. But nobody listened or cared. The snake wriggled with contentment and settled its slack coils for a long sleep. The eggs were still being filled; there were so many of them and the cat was tireless. He prowled about looking very pleased with himself. The cat with black eyes and silver hair, the cat who hated him, the cat loved to play with his prey first, before the killing, just to prolong the pleasure.

He sighed and saw the moon hanging like a bright silver disc up in the sky. On one side was the mistletoe and on the other the Green Man. But that image faded as he heard the flapping of great wings and then another bird landed on the cliff top. It was a raven, a big black raven which strutted across the grass and stared at him. He watched the raven's sharp eyes and beak slowly transform into a beautiful girl's face, with delicate features and such exquisite grey eyes, the irises pale with darker rings around them. Her long silver hair was wild and full of tangles and knots, but still lovely in the moonlight. She reminded him of someone he loved. She leant over and stroked his face gently with a small, rough hand and he saw such kindness in her eyes. She smiled and her pearly teeth were tiny and pointed, then she bent and kissed him on the forehead, whispering in his ear. He wished he understood what she was saying.

But then another cat appeared. It was much uglier than the beautiful, sleek Magus cat; fat and bloated, with thin silver hair and a blotchy face. Its teeth were discoloured and its eyes bloodshot. It pounced greedily on the raven, grunting with pleasure. Holding the bird between its huge paws, it lowered its head and began to feed voraciously. Before his eyes the Elm cat ripped into the raven girl, tearing her apart and devouring her, then spitting out the feathers when all the flesh was gone. Yul started to scream at this, scream and scream at the horror of it. The sleek Magus cat came over and laughed, then kicked him hard, until the screaming stopped and the groaning began.

A little while later, the magical creature on the rock fell down. The cat knelt and spread her out flat on her back, and then he began to cover her with stones. He piled them all over her in a heavy, crushing blanket and she lay very still, buried alive beneath the stones. Inside each stone was a tiny, hungry snake wanting to be fed by the silver bird; every little snake wriggled and clamoured for her special nurture. After a long time they too began to glow as the bird satisfied them as well. The cat was very pleased and replaced them with yet more stones, insatiable in their need. The poor bird was nearly empty now and had little more to give them.

A shadowy, wispy creature with silver hair rose up from the snake rock, moaning and shaking his head. He covered the bird-girl and the little snake-stones with a blanket from her nest, and then he lay down again in a heap and went on a long journey to a faraway place where wolves howled and eagles soared.

Much, much later, everything had turned into solid cold stone that wouldn't bend or move. The Green Man inside was dying slowly and he hung his head as his halo of leaves changed into stone carvings about his face. The black shadow had returned and waited in the corner of his vision. A heavy darkness danced all around the shadowy figure, black like the raven's feathers only thicker and deeper. It was cold – so very cold.

Then the wispy man with silver hair rose up again, angry and frightened. He spoke to the cat and the blanket was pulled off the magical bird-girl. The stones were glowing quite well and were put in big boxes. When all the eggs were stored away safely in their wooden nests, the Magus cat came over and stared. His eyes were black in a silver face. The face kept changing, melting and reforming into a different face, each one more horrific than the last. But the eyes always stayed the same – black and cold like death itself. His mouth was moving and he seemed to be shouting but no words came out, only a stream of black wasps that buzzed angrily in the air. They swarmed towards the dark, deathly shadow and merged into its depths, making the blackness even deeper.

Then the Magus cat lifted the magical creature from the round white moon where she lay and threw her over his shoulder. She was limp and hung there, floppy and lifeless, her poor feathers quite bedraggled. Her magic was completely gone, drained away. They left with the wispy man, and then it was lonely up on the cliff top, lonely and cold. Only the dark shadow remained, hovering nearby, waiting so patiently. He felt a feeble beating in his chest. The beating became slower and slower and the shadow edged in closer.

Magus kicked open the arched door and strode into the bedroom. He was slightly out of breath from carrying Sylvie all the way home and then up the stairs, but so fired up on moon magic that he barely noticed. He laid her on her bed and looked down at her. She was pale and completely still. A wild surge of power throbbed within him at the sight of her, exhausted and defenceless and entirely at his mercy. She was the magical one and yet he was the one getting all the special energy. He'd learnt how to tap the source and he'd never be without moon magic again.

He laughed softly at the prospect and pulled the blanket from beneath her body to cover her up. She felt very cold and he stroked her alabaster cheek with one finger. She was such a beautiful girl, so perfectly, exquisitely beautiful. And not a girl for very much longer. He held his breath for a moment, staring down at her with different eyes. That boy Yul, left out in the cold night up on the cliff, loved this quicksilver girl, and despite all the warnings and threats, he'd carried on loving her. But no more – they'd never see each other again. Magus had a very different future in mind for this moongazy girl.

He left the room by the stairs, not wanting to deal with Miranda tonight. He considered going back to Yul on the cliff top; he ought to bring the boy down to the byre now, whilst it was dark. But he didn't relish the prospect of visiting that shadowy cliff top again, knowing what was lurking there. He'd leave the boy up there alone – or maybe not alone. It was out of his hands and nothing to do with him anyway. He'd done nothing but feed a hungry boy, after all. Besides, it was the night of the Moon Fullness and he brightened at the prospect, determined to put all thoughts of Yul and his fate aside.

As Magus skirted the enormous, silent building he slipped through the porch into the entrance hall and picked up a phone. Time to call in reinforcements. If Jackdaw drove through the night he'd be at Stonewylde before morning and he could have the tedious task of bringing the boy down from the cliff. Alive or dead. Magus smiled as he made his way in the brilliant moonlight down to the Village. His earlier cruel frenzy had passed, vented on the boy who sat tethered to the ground stuffed full of cakes. Now all he felt was the moonlust, strong and tingling as ever in his veins. The night wasn't over yet and he throbbed with anticipation, feeling omnipotent. So much moon magic this time – the best yet. He thought again of the pale girl he'd just left, lying silent and unmoving in her bed, and the gift she'd given him.

'Bright blessings, Sylvie,' he said softly to himself. 'You've served me very well tonight.'

In the tumbledown cottage the black cat leapt off the table and huddled by the fire. Mother Heggy gazed into the meagre flames, moaning softly. She knew the boy was in danger. She'd warned him not to force a battle tonight; it was not yet time and he couldn't win. As she looked into the flickering firelight, she saw the awful truth. Despite her binding spell, despite the cloak of protection she'd wrapped about the boy since birth at such great cost to herself, he was now in mortal danger. Somehow the evil one had stepped around the spell she'd cast so long ago; the spell that had been the only thing between the boy and death all these years.

Magus was clever – too clever. What had he done to Yul tonight? How had he managed to put the boy's life in danger without consequence to himself? She sensed dark magic afoot and knew it must be that other one, the one who fancied herself a Wise Woman. She'd played a part in this and Magus had surely used her dark powers tonight. Why hadn't the boy listened? The prophecy was foretold but it was only one path of many and nothing was fixed. Must the bright one walk alone and face the evil times ahead without him by her side?

Mother Heggy shook her wizened head and muttered. She made the sign of the pentangle and called upon the Moon Goddess as Mother to protect the boy tonight, to banish the black shadow that hovered so close and threatened to summon him. She called upon the powers that were left to her, old and withered as she was, with her magic all but used up since that Solstice so long ago. She rocked in her chair and tried to keep hope alive in her heart. The cat by the hearth turned and stared up at her, blinking its yellow eyes and purring hoarsely.

The raven swooped down to the cliff top again and looked sadly at the figure huddled on the cold grass. This boy was the future, the only one who could make everything right again. He alone could stop the events that would unfold, the cruel times ahead for the folk of Stonewylde. He was the guardian of the Earth Magic, favoured by the Goddess; on his young shoulders rested the future and all bright hope. But he was fading. His hands were bound tightly behind his back and the rope held him fast to the iron ring. His deep grey eyes gazed up at the moon but saw nothing, for his head was an inchoate mass of images, completely out of control. The raven pecked at him gently but there was no response. His heart beat slower and slower in his chest. The powerful hallucinogens from the cakes he'd been forced to swallow crept relentlessly through his body, poisoning his system.

Yul sat near the bright disc of snake-stone as if made of stone himself, slowly petrifying as the night grew colder. Above him the Moon Goddess blazed in silver glory, her magic spent. Beneath him lay the Earth Goddess, her spirals weak at this place of suffering. Nearby stood the Dark Angel, watching and waiting to summon his soul. His heartbeat grew ever more feeble as the stars danced through the night. Slowly Yul's head dropped to his chest and his eyes fluttered shut. All around him, Stonewylde shivered silently in the silver moonlight . . .

Acknowledgements

My acknowledgements written for the original, self-published edition of this book still stand. So continued and deepest thanks to:

Clare Pearson, my first agent, for your vision and encouragement.

My three sons George, Oliver and William for your love and support.

All my family and friends, many in Dorset, for your constant enthusiasm.

Sue Andrew and the team at the Three Hares Project for your source material – further information about their research can be found at www.chrischapmanphotography.com.

Rob Walster of Big Blu Design for the original covers.

Mr B – for your unfailing support and passion for Stonewylde.

Now that Stonewylde has been taken on by Gollancz and this new edition published, I must add some more sincere thanks to:

My readers – the thousands of you who bought and loved the original books. Deepest, most heartfelt thanks to each of you for your loyalty to me and enthusiasm for Stonewylde.

My family and friends again – for such boundless love and support from you all. I'm so very lucky.

Piers Russell-Cobb, my literary agent, for being totally brilliant.

Gillian Redfearn, my editor, for your excellence.

My sister Claire of Helixtree and Rob Walster of Big Blu Design for the beautiful Stonewylde logo.

Gillian Nott of The Guild of Straw Craftsmen for your advice and knowledge about corn dollies and harvest customs – more information on this ancient craft on www.strawcraftsmen.co.uk.

Mr B for continuing to 'do the business' with such expertise.